Dee Williams was born and brought up in Rotherhithe in East London where her father worked as a stevedore in Surrey Docks. Dee left school at fourteen, met her husband at sixteen and was married at twenty. After living abroad for some years, Dee and her husband moved to Hampshire, close to the rest of her family. KATIE'S KITCHEN is her eighth novel set in Rotherhithe, following the 'brilliant' (*Woman's Realm*) MAGGIE'S MARKET.

Katie's Kitchen

Dee Williams

HEADLINE

First published in 1998
by HEADLINE BOOK PUBLISHING

First published in paperback in 1999
by HEADLINE BOOK PUBLISHING

20 19 18 17 16 15 14 13 12 11

ISBN 0 7472 5537 7

Typeset by Avon Dataset Ltd, Bidford-on-Avon, Warks

Printed and bound in Great Britain by
Clays Ltd, St Ives plc

HEADLINE BOOK PUBLISHING
A division of Hodder Headline PLC
338 Euston Road
London NW1 3BH

Thank you, Emma and Samantha, for this title.
Love you lots.

Chapter 1

Katherine stared at the man sitting opposite her, her green eyes wide and blazing. 'What do you mean there's nothing for me?' she said, fighting back tears. She was angry with Gerald for humiliating her like this.

Mr Cannon, a tall middle-aged man, looked the perfect solicitor, but he appeared uncomfortable as with his finger he eased the stiff white shirt collar away from his flabby neck. His morning suit did nothing for his pale complexion.

'I'm sorry, Mrs Brown, but as the late Mr Edwin Brown didn't leave a will, and unless you can prove you were married to the late Mr Edwin Brown, produce a marriage certificate, there is nothing I can do to help you.'

Katherine's mind was racing. What was she going to do? She was thirty-eight, with a twelve-year-old son to bring up. 'Are you sure there was no will?'

Mr Cannon cleared his throat. He was sitting behind a very neat and tidy wide desk. 'As the late Mr Edwin Brown's solicitor I can assure you he never made one in my presence.'

'Could there be one in the house?'

'I shouldn't think so. He always conducted his business affairs through me.'

Katherine felt stifled. The windows were tightly shut and heavily draped even though it was a warm bright spring morning.

Mr Cannon looked over his rimless glasses. His mouth twitched and he appeared embarrassed. His black hair was sleek and flat against his head and when he glanced down at the papers

1

in front of him the glow from the gaslight above his head made his hair shine.

Katherine sat bewildered. 'How long can I stay at the house?' she asked quietly.

A slight smile lifted Mr Cannon's thin mouth. 'Mr Gerald Brown, the deceased's younger brother, has kindly offered to let you stay in his employment. As you know he has taken over the business and the house. Unfortunately you will have to leave the house if you do not wish to work with him.'

Katherine didn't need to be told who Gerald was. She didn't want to work with him or for him. As soon as she received the solicitor's letter telling her she would have to leave her home she knew it was Gerald who had told Mr Cannon about her and Edwin's 'arrangement'. When she'd confronted Gerald about it he had told her to see Mr Cannon.

Much to Edwin's dismay she could never see eye to eye with his brother. Gerald couldn't wait to get his hands on Edwin's estate. He was a waster and a womaniser. What could she do? She had Joseph to think of.

Mr Cannon continued. 'I'm sorry, but I'm afraid I do have to ask rather . . .' he hesitated, 'shall we say rather difficult questions. You do understand I am only acting on Mr Gerald Brown's behalf. Were you married to the late Mr Edwin Brown?'

Katherine shook her head. 'No.'

'But your name is Brown?'

She crumpled the black lace gloves nestling in her lap, then painstakingly smoothed them out again. She looked up. 'No. I was only known as Mrs Brown when we opened the restaurant. We met on the ship when we both came back to England from Australia in 1900.'

'Twelve years ago. You've done extremely well in that time.'

'We both worked very hard. When we opened the restaurant it seemed easier at the time to answer anyone, staff and customers, who called me Mrs Brown. But I didn't expect him to die and not leave a will. He was only fifty-eight. I've worked hard helping him, now I've got nothing to . . .' Tears tumbled from her eyes and plopped down on to her hands. She took a spotless white handkerchief from her small black brocade drawstring bag and dabbed at her eyes. 'What's going to happen to me and my son?'

Mr Cannon sat back and put his fingertips together. 'I'm sorry, Mrs . . . er, er, Brown, but I must ask, is the boy Mr Brown's?'

Katherine shook her head. 'No, he's my husband's. You see as far as I know Mr Carter is still alive, and I'm still married to him.' Did he need to know all this? And did all solicitors ask such impertinent questions?

Mr Cannon was visibly shocked. 'Don't you know?'

Again she shook her head. 'He stayed in Australia.'

'I see. Does your son know about this?'

Katherine nodded. 'Yes.'

'Did he call the late Mr Brown Papa?'

'No. He always addressed him as Grandpa. Edwin was very good to Joseph, making sure he had a good education. They were very fond of each other, and Edwin was like a father to me.'

'Is your son's name Carter?'

'Yes.'

'Didn't that cause complications?'

'No. I never explained it to anyone, we didn't see that it was anyone else's business.'

'I see,' Mr Cannon repeated. He wrote something on a piece of paper in front of him.

Katherine's mind was in turmoil. What if there was a will, where would Edwin have hidden it? She must begin looking before Gerald moved in. Gerald – his name made her cringe. Edwin was always so good to him and told her many times that if she had been free he would have liked to see her wed to his

3

brother. Katherine knew Gerald was devious. She had to get home, get to Edwin's room before Gerald.

'Is that all?' she asked eventually.

'I'm afraid so.'

She stood up. She had to go, get out of here. She was filled with panic. What was she going to do for money? How would they survive? 'Excuse me, Mr Cannon. Will Gerald Brown pay for Edwin's funeral?'

'Of course, it will come out of the estate.'

'Thank you.'

'I will see you in church on Friday,' he sighed. 'It will be a very sad and painful occasion for you and your son. Mr Brown will be sadly missed.' He held open the door and she swept past him, her long expensive black mourning gown rustling as she moved.

Katherine stood at the front door of their house, which overlooked Green Park. She loved this part of London. This was the home she and Edwin had shared for ten of the twelve years she had known him. Their house, with furnishings she had chosen. It wasn't overlarge, but it had a garden and a stable. It had been a happy place with plenty of laughter. Now she was about to lose it. Edwin had been a good man and she had been very fond of him, but even he never thought he would go so soon or so quick. As she opened the front door, Joseph came out of the drawing room.

'Uncle Gerald's been here.' Joseph was a tall slim lad who looked older than his twelve years. He seemed upset, and Katherine's heart was full of love for him.

'Did he say what he wanted?'

'He went into Grandpa's study.'

Panic again surged in Katherine, but she knew she had to act calmly to hide her fear from her son. She moved across the hall and stood in front of the large ornate mirror, the dust dancing where it was caught in the beams of bright sunlight. She removed the hatpins that secured her large-brimmed black hat and, carefully taking it off, placed it on the small green brocade chair that stood next to the hall stand. She gently ran her fingers up the back of her chignon. Her deep red hair blowing in the wind while she was being seasick was what Edwin said he had first noticed about her.

'What did Gerald have to say?' she asked, looking at her son in the mirror. She smoothed down the folds of her gown over her small waist; she was still very shapely.

'Uncle Gerald wanted to know if we were going to stay here. What did he mean? Are we leaving here, Mama?' Joseph, fairer than his mother, looked at her, his pale blue-green eyes full of sadness and bewilderment.

Katherine turned to face him. 'I'm afraid so.' She hadn't wanted to upset her son, so when she received the letter she went to see Edwin's solicitor to make sure she hadn't been told a lie.

'But this is our house.' Joseph's voice was full of pain.

'It was.'

'But where will we go? This has always been our home.' Frustration began to fill his flushed face.

'Yes I know, but it belongs to Gerald now.'

'But why? He didn't live here with us.' His voice had a slight tremor.

'I know. It's a long story, I'll tell you all about it one day.'

Joseph looked upset. 'I don't understand. Why can't we stay here and live with Uncle Gerald?'

'I'm afraid that isn't possible.' Katherine bent down and hugged him to her.

'Where will we go?' he asked again, freeing himself from her.

'I don't know,' she said out loud. Then to herself added: 'I only wish I did.'

Katherine closed the door and looked round Edwin's study. It was warm and manly. The smell of his expensive cigar smoke hung in the air. She opened the drawers in the desk and sorted through the papers. There was nothing she didn't know about. She sat in his armchair and studied the room. Where would he hide a document like a will? And would he have any reason to hide anything from her or any member of the household?

Perhaps Gerald had got here first . . .

Katherine put her head in her hands and wept. She wept for Edwin, Joseph and herself. What would happen to them now? She brushed the tears from her cheek and let a smile lift her sad face as her thoughts drifted to when she first met Edwin.

She had been leaning over the side of the ship being very seasick. She felt terrible. Every wave sent her hanging over the rail, her red hair blowing wild in the wind, and her body rejecting everything. They had only left Darwin a day ago; there were six months of this ahead of her. She let out a long groan and slumped to the deck.

'Can I help you?'

Katherine looked up at the friendly face. 'Only if you can make the ship keep still.'

The man smiled and sat beside her. He was tall and well-built with a shock of uncontrollable light brown hair. White lines caused through screwing up his blue eyes against the Australian sun appeared whenever he looked serious. 'I'm sorry I can't do that. Would you like me to help you back to your cabin?'

She shook her head. 'No thank you, that only makes me feel worse.'

'Would you like me to get you a drink of water or something?'

'Please.'

'The name's Edwin, Edwin Brown,' he said when he returned and handed her a glass of water.

'Pleased to meet you. I'm Katherine Carter.' She held out her hand.

'You're English.'

She nodded. 'So are you.'

During the long months that followed Katherine learnt that it wasn't only the sea that was making her sick, she was also expecting a baby.

She and Edwin became close friends. He told her he was going back home to England to start a business. He had made a little money in Australia but felt a longing to return home.

'It's a young man's country, new and exciting,' he had said. 'Full of opportunities for the young.'

'But you're not old.'

'I'm forty-six.'

She didn't have an answer to that as in another twenty years, when she reached his age, she too would be considered old.

'Also,' continued Edwin, 'I recently heard my mother has passed away and I have a young brother that I feel needs looking after.'

'I'm sorry. How old is your brother?'

'Gerald's twenty-five,' Edwin laughed. 'I know that's not young, but Gerald has always been Mother's baby, and in her eyes he could do no wrong, and I'm afraid now, well, who knows . . .?'

He was a year younger than Katherine. She remembered thinking to herself that he sounded a bit of a weed.

'What line of business are you considering going into?' she had asked, changing the subject.

'I rather fancy opening a restaurant. In a classy place somewhere.'

'Did your family have a restaurant?'

'Good heavens no. My father worked on the railway. He died when I was on my way to Australia ten years ago. I would have liked to come back right away, but Mother insisted I stay. My wife, whom I met in Australia, died in childbirth two years ago. The baby died too.'

'I'm so very sorry,' said Katherine. 'Do you have any other children?'

'No.' He smiled as if trying to blot out a painful memory. 'So you see now, well, I feel I should go back. What about you? Are you going back to your family?'

'No.' Katherine was definite about that. If her parents did take her back, which she very much doubted, she would be the laughing stock of the village they lived in. Those women would never leave their husbands. That part of her life was a closed book.

Katherine sighed and, leaving Edwin's armchair, moved over to the window. 'You were my family, dear, dear Edwin. What will I do without you?'

All the while they stood at the graveside Katherine could feel Gerald's dark smouldering eyes on her, boring into her. She put a protective arm round her son's shoulders. Joseph had taken Edwin's death very hard, and now that they had to move, it was all proving too much for him.

Gerald thanked the vicar and the assembled guests began to slowly move away. They were going to the restaurant. The restaurant she and Edwin had built up. Katherine had told Gerald she didn't want to go, but he had insisted. He came towards her and took hold of her arm forcefully.

Bending his head towards her he said in a hushed tone, 'I've arranged for the carriage to be at your disposal until the end of the month.' He stopped and gave a fellow mourner a nod and a brief smile, then added, 'He will take you and the boy to wherever you wish.'

She looked at him. He was thirty-seven, tall and slim, always well-dressed and very good-looking. Edwin had found him a good position in one of their suppliers' offices. He had never married but there were plenty of young women who would gladly grant him any favours, and he wasn't above boasting about his latest conquest.

'You are being a very silly woman, you know. You could always come and work for me, and you and Joseph could stay on at the house. He doesn't want to move.'

She quickly looked up. 'What have you said to Joseph?'

'Nothing.' He bent his head closer. 'We could be partners in more ways than one.'

Katherine didn't answer. He was still holding her arm tightly; as they moved across the uneven ground, she stumbled and trod on his foot. 'I'm so sorry,' she said smiling and without sounding remorseful. Under his fixed smile she saw him grimace.

'You know we could be very good together.'

Brushing his arm away she stopped. She knew the time had come to make a stand. She turned and faced him, and said rather loudly, 'Gerald, I don't know what sort of woman you take me for. I was very fond of your brother. Although we lived in the same house we never married. We never shared the same bed or even the same room. He was like a father to me, we were never lovers.'

Gerald looked about him, clearly agitated. 'Katherine, for God's sake keep your voice down,' he hissed.

'So you see I would never work or live with you, as I haven't the same respect for you as I did for Edwin.'

The people within earshot had stopped to listen. There were many raised eyebrows as well as intrigue and amusement on some of the men's faces, but the women looked shocked and were shaking their heads in disgust.

'Come along, Joseph, we have to go.' She began to move away.

Joseph looked at Gerald with blind hate as his mother ushered him to the waiting carriage. In so many ways Katherine could see herself in him – she couldn't hide her feelings either.

When they arrived home Katherine was still angry. She told Joseph to go to his room to make a start collecting all he wanted to take with him. He was not happy about leaving.

'I always thought Uncle Gerald liked you.'

'He probably does in his own way, but he still wants the house.'

Joseph stomped up the stairs. Katherine was beginning to worry – was he going to be difficult?

She sat in the drawing room looking out over the garden. The daffodils were still tight buds waiting to burst open. Soon they would be producing their annual display, then everything would look fresh and green. The garden would be a blaze of colour but she wouldn't be here to see it.

Tears ran down her cheeks. She loved this house and the thought of leaving it filled her with dismay. How would she manage? Where would they go? Edwin had been a wonderful person and partner. If only he'd made a will. *Had* he made a will? Katherine knew he would have made sure she'd have been well provided for if he'd had the chance, but his death had been very sudden. Surely she was entitled to something after all she'd put into the business. But not if Gerald could see a way of getting his greedy hands on all they'd worked for. Her thoughts went to Edwin and when after all those months at sea they'd finally arrived back in England.

By the time the ship had docked at Tilbury, Edwin Brown knew a lot about Katherine. How she had come from a well-to-do family in the north and was engaged to a Mr Thomas Carter. She was very young when she married, and soon after, her husband had been offered a good post in Australia. He took the job but Katherine had hated the heat and the flies and she had never felt well. She never told Edwin till much later in their relationship that most of her illness was the result of many miscarriages brought about by her husband's violence. It was after one particularly bad time, when she feared for her life, that she knew she had to return to England. Mr Carter refused to let her take their son, Robert, with her. Katherine spent many months torn between her sanity, health and her beloved boy.

When Robert was eight years old Mr Carter sent him to a boarding school many miles away, and Katherine knew she wouldn't see much of him from then, so after a great deal of soul-searching, she left. Although she had two sisters she could never go back home, the family would never accept her. She had married well and no woman left her husband for something so trivial. After all, she had promised to love, honour and obey, and like all good women, that had to be until death parted them.

It was when they arrived in England that Edwin offered her a home. By this time she had become very fond of him. Two months later her second son, Joseph, was born.

Soon after Edwin opened a small teashop, Katherine found she had a gift for cooking. The business had grown, and they moved into larger premises near to Green Park and opened the restaurant. Afternoon tea was always accompanied by a small trio playing in the background, and the beautiful chandeliers and tall potted palms all added to the grandeur.

Katherine sighed. What was she going to do now? Gerald hadn't mentioned money. Where would she go? If the worst came to the worst at least she had fine clothes and jewellery to sell. She stood up. Once again she was in charge of her destiny, and if she could travel halfway across the world on her own, she would get

11

through this. But although Edwin had helped mould her into an astute businesswoman, she was twelve years older now, and with a son to bring up alone.

Chapter 2

Katherine walked into the large kitchen. 'Dolly,' she called out.

A short, grey-haired, plump and jolly-looking woman came bustling out of the larder. Katherine could see she'd been crying. She sniffed. 'I'm sorry Miss Katherine.' She took a handkerchief from her white apron pocket and dabbed at her eyes.

'I understand how you feel. Losing Edwin has been very painful.'

'It ain't only that,' sniffed Dolly. 'It's the thought of you and the lad going.'

'I know. I feel very upset about it.'

Katherine and Edwin hadn't believed in their staff at home being formal, and had encouraged them to call them by their first names, much to the dismay of Gerald and some of their friends and acquaintances.

When they first came to the house Dolly Webb and her husband told Katherine they thought it odd. But after a short while they found that they had never been happier in all their years in service. Dolly was their cook and general cleaner, her husband, Tom, a quiet, tall, thin man, their gardener and handyman, who also looked after the horse and carriage. They didn't have any children and lived over the stable. They were almost part of the family, joining in at Christmas and birthday parties. Katherine had always looked on Dolly as a lovely elderly aunt who showed her many short cuts in the art of preparing food and cooking.

'Where're you gonner live?' asked Dolly.

'I don't know. I have a little money, but it won't last for ever.'

'What about the lad's school?'

Katherine shrugged her shoulders. 'I don't know. I can't afford to send him any more.' She pulled a chair out from under the large deal table which dominated the warm friendly kitchen and sat down.

Dolly began to get angry. 'Watched him grow up, I have, he's a lovely boy.'

'Yes, I'm very lucky.'

'I reckon it's a disgrace that young Mr Gerald turning you out like this.' Dolly pulled out another chair and sat opposite Katherine.

'He isn't exactly turning me out, it's my decision to go. Besides, Mr Edwin didn't leave him any option.'

Dolly shook her head. 'He went so quick. I'm sure he would have provided for you if he'd known. Treated you like a daughter, he did.'

'I know.' Katherine sighed.

'You won't consider staying on at the restaurant then?'

'No, Gerald and I could never see eye to eye.'

'I'm gonner miss our little chats and laughs. We've had a few in here when we've been trying out new dishes.'

Katherine smiled. 'And we've had a few disasters.'

Dolly laughed. 'Yer, but it's been good fun. It won't be the . . .' There was a sob in her voice. She quickly rose and walked out of the kitchen, dabbing her eyes on the bottom of her apron as she went.

Katherine followed her and put her arm round her shoulders. 'Come on now, Dolly, promise me no more tears.' Katherine hugged her close. She too felt tears stinging her eyes.

'I'm sorry,' said Dolly. 'But we've got on so well together, always felt like one big family.'

'Yes I know, but that's all over now. I'm going to have to

look for somewhere suitable to rent.'

'Any idea where to start?'

'No. It can't be too expensive. I might even have to go over the water.' She smiled. 'Mr Edwin and I lived south of the river for a short while when we came back from Australia.'

'My young sister lives over there by the docks. Rovverhithe. Do you know it?'

'No, I can't say I do, we lived at Kennington.'

Dolly pushed past Katherine's boxes lining the hall ready for her move. She suddenly took hold of her arm. 'I know I shouldn't say this, but if you ever get settled and wants someone to, you know, do for you, you know where to find me.'

'I would love that, but at the moment I couldn't afford you, even if I did manage to find somewhere large enough.'

'Would work for you for nothing.'

'Well, I wouldn't let you.'

'Well, just you wait and see. You've got a good head on your shoulders, I can't see you down for long.'

Joseph descended the stairs, his face set in anger.

'Joseph, what's bothering you?'

'This.' He waved his hands at the boxes. 'I don't want to move away from here.'

'You're not the only one, but we don't have a lot of choice, do we?'

'You could go and work for Uncle Gerald. He said we could stay here then.'

'He's been here to see you?' Alarm bells rang in Katherine's head. Was Gerald trying to get round him?

'Yes. D'you know he's thinking of getting one of these new motor cars. He's going to take me round the show rooms to see them.'

Dolly took a sharp breath.

Katherine quickly looked at her.

15

'He said I could sit in it. Mama, it's going to be such fun. Please let us stay.'

'Joseph, I don't want to work for Gerald, and I certainly don't want to live in this house with him.' Gerald had been getting at her son. He knew his weakness and was playing on it to get at her.

'Why not?' Joseph began to kick his toe against the bottom stair.

'Please stop that.' Katherine tried to keep her voice under control. She could see Joseph wasn't to be reasoned with. 'Come along, you'd better come with me.'

'I'll tell Tom to get the carriage ready,' said Dolly, quickly moving away.

Katherine called at a few houses she knew might be available, but at the moment the rents were way out of her price range. Was that because she was well-dressed and arriving in a carriage? People got a false idea of her wealth and quoted prices accordingly? She knew what little money she did have wouldn't last very long if she had to pay a high rent. Should she bury her pride and go and work for Gerald? That at least would keep Joseph and Dolly happy.

The carriage was halted when they turned into Whitehall, police everywhere. A column of women came down the road singing and waving banners. They were wearing green, purple and white sashes.

'Who are they, Mama?' asked Joseph.

'Suffragettes.'

'What are they doing?'

'They are women who are fighting for their rights.'

Joseph wasn't listening as he excitedly gathered leaflets that were thrown through the open window. Katherine picked one up. It told of future meetings. In many ways she would have liked to join them. She too had rights that were worth fighting for.

It was a lovely day, and after Tom had battled with the traffic and abuse from drivers of the motors and omnibuses, he suggested they take a turn along the river.

As they approached, Joseph eagerly rose to his feet and put his head out of the window. 'Tom, please stop,' he called.

He jumped out. 'This is a wonderful sight. I wish I'd brought my sketchbook with me.' Joseph loved drawing.

Katherine too left the carriage and watched the boats on the busy Thames that glistened in the afternoon sunlight. Large and small ships used the waterway to ply their trade. Long lines of barges tied together were strung out like a necklace, those very low in the water probably loaded with coal and pig iron. They all appeared to move effortlessly, up and down, back and forth. It was very calming and peaceful. The suffragettes were still on Katherine's mind. She shuddered. She admired these women: you had to be very dedicated to risk imprisonment and go on hunger strike.

'Look at those sails,' said Joseph, breaking into his mother's thoughts. 'Could we go over there?' He was pointing to the other side of the river at a ship with its tall majestic sails gently moving in the slight breeze.

'I don't know, I don't know my way around that part.'

'Oh please. They look so lovely.'

'No I'm sorry, Joseph, I have far more important things to do. Besides, Dolly will be waiting to get our tea.' Katherine smiled up at Tom. 'And Tom will be wanting to get back as well.'

Tom nodded and although he too had a general air of sadness, managed to smile back. 'Only when you're ready, Miss Katherine.'

As they made their way home Joseph said, 'When I sit in the kitchen Dolly often tells me about her sister who lives over by the docks.'

Katherine looked surprised. 'You never told me that.'

'Didn't see any point. I would love to see the docks. Her brother-in-law's name's Charlie and he's a docker. He loads and unloads the ships. It sounds very exciting, and I bet he's a nice man.'

Katherine grinned. From what she'd seen and heard of dockers she wasn't so sure 'nice' was quite the right word to use.

For days she searched for suitable rooms, having lowered her sights from a house, but all the while getting more and more frustrated and worried. Everything she found in her price range was either a dark and dismal basement, or rooms in a house with many other people that was noisy and didn't look very clean.

Gerald continually returned to the house enquiring how long would it be before she left.

'You have another week before I move in,' he told her on his most recent visit. 'I hope you have found somewhere by then – that's if you really wish to leave.'

After he went Katherine sat and stared out of the window. What was going to happen to them? Where could she go?

'Do you and young Joseph want tea in the drawing room for a change?' asked Dolly interrupting her thoughts.

Katherine nodded.

'Not had any luck then, with the rooms, that is?'

'No. I don't know what I'm going to do.'

'Tom said you've started looking a bit further afield.'

'Yes, I can't afford any of the fancy rents some of these people are asking.'

'Can't say we're looking forward to Mr Gerald moving in. He's already talking about changing things.'

Katherine didn't reply. She didn't want to know. It was all too painful.

Dolly plonked herself on the window seat next to Katherine.

'Look, I know it ain't none of my business, and you can tell me to shut it if you like.' She took Katherine's hand. 'I was telling me sister all about this 'ere carrying on with Mr Gerald when we went over to see her last Sunday – she rents out a room, you know. Her place ain't as posh as this but she's clean.' Dolly straightened her shoulders. 'Which is more than can be said for a lot of 'em round there. Well, to cut a long story short she said you could stay there till you got yourself sorted.'

'That's very kind of her, but I don't know.'

'Her last lodger's just left. Nice young man. Gorn to work abroad somewhere, so she said.'

'But what about her husband and children?'

'Charlie don't mind. It helps out with the rent when there ain't a ship in, 'cos he only gets paid when he works. He's a stevedore.'

'I thought Joseph said he was a docker.'

Dolly took a quick intake of breath. 'Don't let Charlie hear you say that. You see, stevedores are the skilled ones. They load and unload the boats, making sure it's right. Wouldn't do to have the boat lopsided now, would it?'

Katherine shook her head.

Dolly continued, 'Milly's only got the boy at home now, young Ted – he's apprenticed to the barrel-makers – named after our dad he was. Her girl, Olive's, married. Her and Ernie, that's her husband, don't live all that far away. She's just found out she's expecting,' whispered Dolly. 'Nice kids the pair of 'em. It'll seem funny our Milly being a granny.'

Katherine didn't want to offend Dolly, but she hadn't envisaged living near the docks. The other side of the water didn't hold any enthusiasm for her. 'Won't I look a bit overdressed round that way?'

Dolly looked her up and down. 'Yer I suppose you would. But once Milly's told everybody your hard-luck story they won't worry what you look like. 'Sides, you could even send young

Joseph to school over there. They only charge a penny a week.'

It seemed as if Katherine's plight had been well and truly discussed.

'Anyway give it some thought. If you like, Tom'll take you both over in the morning.' Dolly looked down at her hands. 'If Mr Gerald gets one of these newfangled motor things what's gonner happen to Tom?'

'Tom?' repeated Katherine.

'Yer. If he gets rid of the horse, what will Tom do? He can't drive one of those things.'

Katherine couldn't answer. She had been so worried about her plight she hadn't thought anyone else might be affected by these changes.

'Miss Katherine, I hope you don't mind, but I did tell our Milly you might be over.'

'But I—'

'Don't worry about it now. I'll bring in the tea.'

Dolly left Katherine bewildered. Should she go and stay with Dolly's sister? It would only be temporarily till she found something more suitable. But Rotherhithe . . . Perhaps tomorrow she would ask Tom to take her there, just to have a chat to Milly. After all, it wouldn't do any harm, and besides, she didn't have a lot of choice. She only had a week to come to a decision. Either she stayed here and lived with Gerald – she shuddered at the thought – or tried to make a new life for herself and Joseph. But what about Dolly and Tom? What was their future?

The next morning Katherine was toying with the idea about going to Rotherhithe when she heard Gerald downstairs.

'Katherine my dear,' he said as she walked down the wide staircase. 'I was just coming up to see you. Could we go into the drawing room? I have a proposition to put to you.'

'I'll ask Dolly to bring in some tea.'

'No, leave that till later. Wait till you've heard what I have to say first.'

Katherine followed him into the drawing room and sat in an armchair.

'I know you don't like me – you've always made that perfectly clear – though I can't think why.'

Katherine quickly glanced at him.

'Oh yes,' he smiled. 'There was that Christmas when I tried to, as you called it, seduce you. It was only a Christmas kiss.'

Katherine drew herself up with indignation. 'A Christmas kiss? You tried to get your hand down the bodice of my gown.'

'Well I'd had a few drinks. Besides, no one noticed.'

'*I* noticed.'

'I always thought you were wasted on Edwin. You could have a far more exciting life with me.'

'Don't you dare take dear Edwin's name in vain. He was a good man.'

'Good yes, but boring with it.'

'I'm not going to stay here and listen to you insult Edwin.' She stood up.

'Please, Katherine, sit down. You see I know how much you will hate leaving this house, so what I suggest is that you stay.'

'Why? What do you want in return?' she asked sharply.

'I need a hostess. I've found that now I am in charge of the restaurant I have many invitations, and a lovely woman at my side would be such an advantage.'

'I would have thought you could have any woman you want.'

'Yes, but I need an intelligent one, one who can hold a conversation.'

'I will not stay here just to be your, your . . .'

Gerald threw his head back and laughed very loudly. 'Good God, woman, I am not asking you to come to some of the places I frequent, just the odd Masonic do and parties I have to attend, and of course you will be here to entertain my guests. In return I will give you an allowance, buy you a new gown when you require one and you can stay and live in the custom you have become used to.'

'Sir, I will not be humiliated. I will not be treated like a child. Given an allowance indeed!'

Gerald stood up and walked to the window. He stared out and said in a low voice, 'Why not? I have felt humiliated ever since you and Edwin returned from Australia. I have always been given an allowance.'

'Yes, because you couldn't look after yourself.'

'That's all changed now. I'm in charge of a very good business.'

'Yes, but for how long will it be a good business?'

'You will see. I intend to turn over a new leaf, for my late brother's sake, and I would like you to be at my side to enjoy some of the fruits of his and your labour.' He came and knelt in front of Katherine and took hold of her hand. 'Joseph can stay on at school. Please, Katherine, stay, for young Joseph's sake as well as your own.'

'Please, Gerald, get up.' She sat for a while in silence. She had to think about Joseph. 'At this moment I don't know. Will you require me at the restaurant?'

He stood up. 'No, the chef seems to be managing without you, or me for that matter.'

'Where will you live?'

'I shall be moving into this house.'

Katherine flinched.

'Don't worry I'll be over the other side, well away from your room.'

Katherine's mind was churning over. What choice did she have? 'I don't know. I am still in mourning.'

'Yes, yes, I know all about that but it won't last for ever.'

'I will have to think about it.'

'Very well, you have till the end of the week.' He gently kissed her cheek. 'Remember, till the end of the week.'

As he closed the door behind him Katherine sat thinking. Had she misjudged him? He was younger than Edwin and Edwin had given him everything he wanted, he had also paid off a lot of Gerald's gambling and drinking debts. Katherine had never told Gerald she knew about that. That was another thing that had turned her against him. They worked hard while Gerald spent hard. Could he have changed? Perhaps he had, now he was in charge of the business.

As she climbed back upstairs, Joseph, who had had a change of heart, becoming very excited at the thought of going to see Ted and Charlie whom he had heard so much about, followed her into her bedroom.

'I'm taking my sketchbook. Dolly said to ask Charlie to take me to the docks.' He sat on his mother's bed.

'Don't expect him to take you right away, he has to go to work.' Katherine began searching her wardrobe for something suitable to wear. It had to be black, of course, but most of her clothes seemed much too grand for Rotherhithe. 'Besides we're only going over to see Milly and the room, and if I don't like it – well, we won't stay.' She wouldn't mention Gerald had asked her to remain there.

'Will I have to sleep in your room?'

'I don't know, we will just have to wait and see.' Katherine finally chose a simple black cotton gown and removed the fancy collar.

'Well, I can tell Milly about what I want to do when we get there.' It seemed Joseph had already made up his mind. She smiled to herself. He changed his allegiance almost daily. Wait till he sees what it's like in the dock area, she thought. He might change his mind again.

'Dolly, are you sure your sister won't mind us turning up unannounced?' Katherine asked as they made their way outside.

'Course not. 'Sides, I told her you might be over if you can't find anything.'

Katherine wondered what else this family had planned for her as Tom helped her into the carriage.

'Young Milly loves it when we goes over to see her. This outfit always causes a stir when we ride up Croft Street,' he said, then added sadly, 'Mind you, I don't know for how much longer I'll be in charge of it.'

'Don't worry Miss Katherine with our troubles. She's got enough problems of her own,' said Dolly, handing Katherine a small brown paper parcel. 'Tell Milly we'll see her the end of the month. That's just a bit of knitting I've done for Olive's baby,' she said, gently patting the parcel.

Katherine smiled and sat back. She felt strange. All these people relied on her decision. What should she do? She had had this feeling when she went to Australia, and again when she returned to England. Was this to be the beginning of another new journey?

She took hold of Joseph's hand as the carriage began to move away.

'Don't, Mama,' he said sheepishly, pulling away.

Katherine knew he was trying to grow up. But she needed his warmth and comfort. He had a huge grin on his face. To him this was the start of a great new adventure.

Chapter 3

Tom was right, their carriage did cause a stir when they crossed the Thames and approached Rotherhithe. Much to Joseph's amusement children ran beside them shouting.

'Scram,' shouted Tom as he cracked his whip high above their heads.

They didn't take any notice and continued laughing and running.

'Look, Mama,' said Joseph excitedly, twisting back and forth. 'They've forgotten to put their shoes on.'

'This is a very poor area. I don't suppose they have any. Shoes come after food.'

Joseph looked shocked. 'They look very dirty and scruffy.' In his sheltered life he'd never come across poverty. This was a lesson he hadn't learnt at school. He sat back with a worried look on his face. 'Mama, are we going to have to live here because we're poor?'

'Not really, it's just that I have to watch my pennies now.'

'If we get ever so poor, will I have to go without shoes?' Joseph sat back, his brow puckered.

'Goodness me, I hope not.' Katherine began to wonder if it had been such a good idea bringing him here.

Tom turned into Croft Street with its row of back-to-back terraced houses. As soon as he stopped Milly came racing out of her house and stood at the side of the carriage as Tom jumped down and opened the door for Katherine.

'Been looking out the window then, gel?' Tom said to his

sister-in-law. 'Milly, this is Miss Katherine what we told you about.'

Katherine wondered how Milly knew they were coming on this particular day.

Milly curtsied. 'Pleased to meet you I'm sure.' She held out a thin bony red hand. 'I was dusting the front room when I saw you. Don't get many posh carriages down this street.'

Katherine grinned. 'And I'm pleased to meet you. I'm sorry we couldn't let you know we were coming, but Dolly said it would be all right. I hope we're not putting you out.'

Milly blushed. 'No, course not. I've been hoping you'd come. And this must be young Master Joseph. How do you do?'

Milly, a thin, wiry woman, wore her naturally curly brown hair twisted into a bun at the nape of her neck, though many strands had escaped the pins. Her pale blue eyes darted nervously about. She was a lot younger than Dolly, but it was hard to guess her age. Katherine thought she could be about thirty-eight, the same as herself. Milly ran her hands down the front of her spotless white overall.

Tom burst out laughing. 'Good Gawd, Milly, they ain't royalty. They're just Miss Katherine and— Oh never mind. Got the kettle on?'

Milly gave him a filthy look. 'Yes, course. This way.'

Tom adjusted the nosebag he'd put on the horse and stepped aside to let Milly lead them into the house.

Katherine noted that in a few windows the lace curtains were quickly pulled into place.

Joseph was studying Milly's feet. He seemed almost relieved that she was wearing shoes.

They followed Milly down the passage with the faint smell of lavender polish filling their nostrils. Small hand-made scatter rugs at the foot of the stairs and at the door of what Katherine guessed was the front room, rested on the shiny brown lino.

When Milly pushed open the kitchen door the warm friendly aroma of baking filled the air.

'Please sit down.' Milly pulled a chair out from under the table.

'I hope we're not putting you out,' said Katherine.

'No, no, not at all.' Every word was carefully chosen, and said slowly. 'I'll see to the tea.' Milly took one of the kettles from off the hob and went off into the scullery.

Katherine sat and took in her surroundings. The kitchen was of modest size but very clean and tidy. The table where she sat dominated the centre of the room and was covered with a plum-coloured chenille cloth that almost reached the floor. An empty cut-glass bowl stood in the middle. Two wooden armchairs either side of the fireplace had comfortable cushions and headrests, neat and very colourful, which Katherine assumed must have been embroidered by Milly. Above the well-black-leaded cooking range was a large mirror, and the mantelpiece was full of china and brass knick knacks. The hearth had been whitened and the brass fender shone. One side of the fireplace was taken up with a huge dresser with plates and dishes tastefully arranged.

Milly returned with a tray. Pretty cups and saucers and a plate of biscuits were neatly laid out.

'This is all very nice,' said Katherine, trying to hide the surprise in her voice.

'Milly always likes to do things right, don't yer, love?' said Tom.

Milly beamed as a slight flush crept up her face. 'Oh go on with you, Tom. Mind you, I do try. That's till Charlie gets in.'

Katherine was smiling from one to the other till her face hurt. What was wrong with Charlie? she wanted to ask. Did he beat Milly? She knew all about that. Was he a drunk? Did she want to be here?

'Charlie's all right,' said Milly quickly. 'It's just that when he's working on lampblack he gets in a bit of a state, but he can't help it.' She turned to Katherine. 'He's a stevedore, and if a ship comes in that's carrying lampblack he gets filfy, and we don't have a barfroom, so if the public barfs is shut the tin barf has to come in and sometimes he makes a bit of a mess – but I only let 'im do it in the scullery.' The words tumbled out.

Katherine quickly glanced at Joseph. His eyes were like saucers. She could almost see his mind turning over. This conversation was like nothing he had ever heard before. There would be a hundred and one questions to answer later.

'If you've finished your tea perhaps you would like to see your room?'

Katherine was stunned. They all assumed she would be moving here. She was being rushed into things. Was this where she wanted to live? 'Well, yes, that's if it isn't any trouble,' she replied politely.

Milly's face was filled with a smile. 'It ain't no trouble, and I'll be that pleased to have you here. Ain't had a real lady living here before.'

'But I'm not . . .'

'Take a look upstairs 'fore you makes up yer mind,' said Tom.

Katherine and Joseph duly mounted the stairs behind Milly. At the top Milly flung open a door. 'This could be your room.'

Katherine stepped in and held her breath. The lace curtain at the long sash window was gently swaying in the slight breeze. The room was bright and airy. She moved to the window. Below was a tiny yard like all the others in the row. Every house had a scullery attached to the back looking like a large carbuncle, and a smaller building that was back-to-back with next door, and which Katherine guessed was the lavatory. She turned. There was a large mahogany wardrobe whose full-length mirror reflected the room. The matching dressing table with pretty lace doilies set out on top had long spindly legs and a green velvet stool pushed under. The bed had a spotlessly white folkweave bedcover thrown over.

'This is a lovely room,' said Katherine, genuinely impressed.

Milly beamed with pride. 'Don't get all me nice bits out when I've got blokes in. Never take in any riffraff, mind. Wouldn't let to dockers or the like, let Mrs Harris across the road 'ave them. Most of me good stuff was our mum's. Dolly only wanted a few small bits as her and Tom's always been in service, so I was lucky enough to get it. Lovely ain't it?' Milly gently ran her hand over the dressing table. 'Won't let any of the blokes smoke up 'ere just in case they leave burn holes on it.'

'It is very nice. Do you and Charlie have . . .?'

Milly laughed. 'Na. Wouldn't let him near anything good. He's a bit like our Ted, clumsy.'

Katherine was getting a little worried about Charlie; now there was Ted as well.

'The lad can sleep in with Ted,' said Milly, gaining confidence. 'This is his room.' She moved out and pushed open another door.

The difference was dramatic, and Katherine could feel Joseph reel back. It smelt of stale tobacco, clothes were strewn over a chair, and odd pieces of woodwork were on the table, but despite that, Katherine could see it was clean.

'My Ted might be clumsy with his feet but he's good with his hands and he enjoys making things, and drawing.'

Katherine noted Joseph suddenly take an interest.

'Takes after his granddad. Ted's apprenticed to a barrel-maker round in the Old Kent Road,' said Milly proudly.

'You only have the two children?'

Milly smiled. 'Yes. Me daughter,' she shuffled Joseph down the stairs and whispered over her shoulder, 'she's expecting.'

'When's the baby due?'

'End of September. It'll be lovely being a grandma.'

Katherine was beginning to warm to this family. In many

ways it would be good to live with a woman who, like Dolly, made her main pleasure in life looking after people.

'Shall we go down? That's me and Charlie's room,' said Milly, walking past the last door upstairs.

'Well, Miss Katherine,' said Tom when they returned to the kitchen. 'What d'yer think? I know it ain't like the place you live in, but our Milly's a good 'en. She's clean, and she'll look after you.'

Katherine didn't know what to say. The thought of no bathroom was one of the drawbacks. 'What kind of rent did you have in mind?' she asked tentatively.

Milly looked embarrassed. 'Well, I usually charge me other lodgers five bob a week, that's if that's all right with you. That'll be for the both of you,' she added quickly.

Katherine looked across at Joseph. He was unusually quiet. She tried to read his mind but his face was blank.

'That will of course include all your food,' said Milly. 'I do charge a bit more for washing, but if you're here you might want to do your own.'

Katherine was amazed. She could manage that for many weeks to come. 'Well, Joseph, what do you think?'

He looked downcast. 'Don't know.'

'We've got to live somewhere, and perhaps Charlie could take you to the docks.'

'Don't know if I want to sleep in Ted's room.'

'Well, you can't sleep in with your mother,' said Milly sounding more confident.

'What about schools?' asked Katherine.

'There's one not too far away,' came the quick reply. 'My Ted went there.'

'I don't want to go to school round here,' Joseph mumbled while playing with his fingers.

'Joseph, that's not nice,' said Katherine.

He looked from one to the other then lowered his gaze, his face full of pain.

'What about another cup of tea?' asked Tom, trying to ease the situation.

Milly jumped up. 'I'll put a drop of water on these leaves.'

'Milly, I'm afraid I will have to look for work,' Katherine said quickly.

Joseph's head shot up.

'We can't live for ever on what I've got,' she added before there were too many questions.

'Let's see. We've got the biscuit factory. My Charlie will know more about that.' She took the kettle, whose lid was bobbing up and down, from off the top of the range and filled the teapot.

There were many things Katherine wanted to know, but at the moment she didn't want to show too much enthusiasm just in case somewhere better to live came up. But would it in just a week? Then there was still Gerald's offer to consider.

'If I decided to move in, would it be convenient say, Friday?'

'Could come tomorrow if yer like,' said Milly.

'I do have rather a lot of boxes.'

'Not to worry, we can stack 'em in the front room for now.'

Milly appeared to have all the answers.

'I know you'll be happy here,' said Tom.

Katherine finished her tea and stood up. 'Well, we had better get going.' She held out her hand. 'Thank you, Milly.'

Milly smiled a broad smile that filled her face. 'Wait till the neighbours round here find out I've got a lady living in. Old Ma Harris will go green with envy.'

Katherine also smiled, but it was false. She didn't fancy being the subject of local gossip.

Although Katherine tried hard to make conversation with Joseph on the way home, he remained quiet.

'Well,' said Dolly, as they walked in, 'you gonner move in with our Milly?'

'I really don't have a lot of choice, do I?' Katherine stood and watched Joseph run up the stairs.

Dolly looked a little put out at that remark. 'I know it ain't like this place, but at least she'll look after you.'

'Sorry, Dolly. Yes, I know she will, but after having my own home, I'm not sure I want to share someone else's.'

Dolly straightened her shoulders. 'Well, as you said, you don't have a lot of choice at the moment.'

'No, I know.' Katherine removed her hat. 'I'd love a cup of tea.'

'I'll bring it into the drawing room,' Dolly said coldly.

Katherine sat staring out of the window. She should go and talk to Joseph, but at the moment she just wanted to be alone and wallow in self-pity. She wanted to cry, but knew that wouldn't help the situation. She had to be positive. Why is it when you think your life is all mapped out, something happens to turn it all about again?

There was a slight tap on the door and Dolly walked in carrying a tray. 'I'm sorry, Miss Katherine, if I got a bit . . . well, you know. It's just that I don't like to see you down, and I know our Milly will make you very welcome.'

'I know. If I do go I'll have to leave some boxes here. Perhaps when you come to see Milly you could bring them with you.'

'Course we will. That's if Mr Gerald will still let us have some time off, and lets us use the carriage. I always feel ever so grand when we go over in it.' Dolly fiddled with her fingers. 'I only hope he lets Tom stay on if he does get a motor thingy.'

'But he'll still have the garden and the odd jobs.'

'Can't do a lot in the winter though, can he?'

Katherine was suddenly made to realise it wasn't only to be her that was having a change of lifestyle. Her departure could affect Dolly and Tom as well.

'I'm sure Gerald will look after you.'

'I'm not so sure. If he can chuck you and the boy out, he ain't gonner have a lot of time for us.'

Dolly left the room leaving Katherine to her thoughts.

After a while she knew she had to talk to Joseph.

'I am not going to live over there,' said Joseph as Katherine opened his bedroom door.

'You will do as I say, young man.'

'If you make me go I'll run away.'

Katherine sat on his bed. 'Please, Joseph. We must give it a try. I thought you were looking forward to going there.'

'Did you see the state of that boy's room? How could you expect me to live in a pigsty like that?'

'I'm sure Ted's very nice.'

'Well, I don't intend to find out. I'm going to ask Uncle Gerald if I can live here even if you go.'

'Joseph, you will not. I forbid it.'

'I'll work for Uncle Gerald.'

'Don't talk ridiculous. Besides, Gerald isn't your uncle.'

'I know that. And Grandpa wasn't my real grandpa. Why haven't I got any real relations?'

'You know why.'

'What about your mother and father, my true grandparents? Have I got any real aunts and uncles? You told me you once lived here in England.'

'That was a long while ago and, over the years, we lost touch. I expect they have all passed away by now.'

'See, you never cared about them, you're only interested in yourself.'

'Joseph,' Katherine's voice was full of anger, 'don't you speak to me like that. When you are old enough to understand I shall tell you the full story.'

Joseph hung his head. 'So why can't you stay here and make

me happy?' His voice trembled. 'You're selfish and I hate you. You left my father and my brother in Australia, now you're going to leave me.'

Katherine was taken aback at that statement. This was the first time Joseph had mentioned Robert. She had told him about his brother and his father, she had never kept them a secret, but not about the violence she had suffered. To throw this in her face now and tell her he hated her was more than she could bear.

'I would never leave you, but we have to be—'

'If you make me go, as soon as I'm old enough I'll run away. I don't want to live there, I want to stay here in my own bedroom.'

Katherine couldn't speak. With tears welling deep inside her she quickly left the room.

That night as Katherine lay tossing in bed her thoughts flew round and round between Milly, Joseph, Gerald and Robert. What did her son look like now? Did his father ever talk about her? Would she ever see him again? What Joseph had said still had her reeling with guilt. True she hadn't thought about her family here but she had left many years ago and knew she wouldn't be welcome. That's if they were still alive. Her parents had thought Mr Carter was wonderful, so full of ambition, and they had been very pleased at getting the last of their three daughters off their hands. They always said Katherine was wayward because she preferred books to sewing. And what about her sisters? They never did see eye to eye; was that because she didn't conform and behave like them? Well, now it had all backfired on her and she was alone.

Katherine hadn't been looking forward to moving to Rotherhithe, and this outburst with Joseph had finally made up her mind. She had been selfish. She had lost one son and she wasn't prepared to lose Joseph.

'Well,' she said out loud, 'tomorrow Gerald will have my answer.'

Chapter 4

After telling Joseph they were not moving and getting Tom to take the boxes that had been lining the hall back to her room, Katherine sat waiting for Gerald. The atmosphere between Katherine and her son was very hostile. Even Dolly greeted the new arrangement with mixed feelings.

'Only hope you're doing the right thing in staying,' she said.

'Only time will tell.' Katherine hadn't told Dolly the real reason for her change of mind.

'Well, till Milly lets that room the offer will still be there, that's if you fancy it.'

'Thanks, and tell Milly I would have been very happy to move in with her.' Katherine turned away. She didn't want to go into detail of why she'd had a change of heart.

When Gerald arrived he appeared to be genuinely pleased Katherine had decided to stay.

'I'll get Tom to collect my belongings from the hovel I live in.' He strutted round the hall. 'I must say I am really looking forward to moving into this house. Always admired your taste, my dear. I'm so glad you saw the sense in staying. So, perhaps this could be the beginning of a very happy liaison.'

Katherine flashed him a look which she hoped said 'Keep away from me.' 'I'll get Dolly to bring tea into the drawing room.'

'Katherine, wait. I am very fond of you, and I know it was Edwin's dearest wish that we got on. He always said that if you had been free he would have liked us to marry.'

'But I'm not free.'

He laughed, moving away. 'I promise not to get under your feet too much.'

'I'll fetch the tea.'

She stood in the hall for a few moments. Was she being too hard on him? After all, he had lost his only brother.

For the next two weeks Gerald was as good as his word. They saw very little of each other. He seemed to be busy with the restaurant and only joined Katherine and Joseph on Sunday for dinner. Joseph was happy but said very little to his mother, for there was still a big gulf between them that Katherine was determined to heal.

Katherine was also beginning to get bored. Needlepoint was not one of her strong points, and now she wasn't needed in the kitchen she wandered aimlessly about. Even her beloved garden didn't hold her interest for long. She needed to be busy, but what at? So far Gerald had not required her to exercise her social skills on his behalf.

'Katherine,' called Gerald, as he walked into the drawing room late one Saturday evening. He was handsome and looked immaculate in his evening dress. His dark hair shone as it caught the light when he moved across the room. 'I have some exciting news. A few of my friends have persuaded me to hold an Easter party here. A good idea, don't you think?'

'I don't know. We should still be in mourning.'

'Oh, I'm sure old Edwin wouldn't mind us having a bit of fun. After all, we can't bring him back, can we?'

Katherine would have liked to smack his face at the remark. 'This is your house now, and it's up to you. Of course you will have to hire extra staff.'

'I will leave all that up to you. It will give you something to look forward to. I must say you have been looking a bit down lately. Now I must dash. Just came back for a change of clothes. I'm off to the theatre after we close tonight.'

In many ways Katherine too would have loved to have gone to the theatre. That was one of the many things she missed, but would never have dared to tell Gerald.

Dolly looked angry when Katherine told her the news about the forthcoming party.

'So how many's coming to this 'ere do, then?'

'I don't know.'

'Will they be stopping overnight?'

'I don't know that either. When I find out more I'll let you know.'

'Can't say I'll enjoy having someone else mucking about in my kitchen.'

'It's only for one night.'

Dolly straightened her shoulders. 'Well, I never thought I'd hear you approve of this sorta goings-on.'

'I didn't say I approved. It's just that this is Gerald's house now and we have to make the best of it.'

'Suppose so.'

'I'll try and see Gerald and ask him to give me more details.'

'That's a laugh.'

'Why? What do you mean?'

'Walks in at all hours of the night and morning and then 'as the cheek to wake me and ask for food. Mind you, nine times out of ten he's three sheets to the wind.'

Katherine smiled. 'I expect he has to meet a lot of people.'

'You and Mr Edwin met a lot of people, but you didn't carry on like he does.'

'I don't hear him.'

'Well, he's crafty. Creeps in after you're in bed, and he don't get up till about noon, then it's straight down to the kitchen and out the back way.'

Katherine wanted to laugh at the thought of Gerald creeping about. 'I don't know why he does that. After all, it is his house.'

'Don't want you disapproving, so he said.'

'Then I only hope he's looking after the business side of things. I would hate to think that all our hard work . . .' Katherine stopped. It wasn't her business now.

'Well, that's up to him,' said Dolly disapprovingly.

It was early Sunday evening. Gerald hadn't been home for dinner. Katherine was taking a leisurely stroll round the garden when she heard his voice.

'Katherine my dear. I must say this is a pleasant surprise. Dolly said you wanted to see me.' Walking towards her he took hold of her shoulders and kissed her mouth hard.

She pushed him away. 'How dare you!'

He laughed. A strand of his dark hair fell over his face. 'I couldn't help it, you look so lovely and I thought—'

'Well, sir, you thought wrong. All I want to do is go over the arrangements with you for this party.'

'I told you, I'll leave all the details up to you.' He waved his hand dismissively. 'By the way, buy yourself a new gown.' He threw a small purse of money on to the garden table. 'And get any colour but black.'

Katherine looked at the purse. She felt like a kept woman. 'I don't need a new gown.'

'I'm sure you do. I don't know of any woman that turns down the offer of a new gown.'

'But—'

'Oh for God's sake, woman, don't make such a fuss,' he said angrily.

He followed her when she went in the house. She wanted to tell him there wasn't time to have one made, but gave up, he wasn't interested, and besides there were many gowns upstairs that he had never seen, so he wouldn't be any the wiser at what she wore.

In Edwin's study she picked up a pencil and paper from the desk and sat very upright in the armchair. 'We must sit down and discuss the guest list, and what time you wish the event to commence.'

He went to the drinks table and poured himself a very large whisky. 'Can I pour you a drink? Sherry perhaps?'

'No thank you.'

'Oh dear, I've ruffled your feathers. We are Miss Efficient, aren't we? You, madam, are a cold fish. I'm surprised Edwin let you stay in this house if you didn't share his bed.'

Katherine was blazing inside but tried hard to keep her feelings under control. She wanted to kill him, but she needed a home. 'Gerald, you are being very rude and offensive, and if Edwin had left a will I wouldn't be in this situation. Now can we get on with this list?'

Gerald stood behind her and lightly touched her hair. 'This is a beautiful colour. Edwin always admired your hair.' He bent forward as if to kiss her neck.

'Please, don't touch me.' She could feel his breath on the back of her neck and quickly stood up.

'Can't you show any warmth towards me? After all, you could be out on the streets if it wasn't for my generosity.'

'I am aware of that.' She sat down again. 'Now can we continue with the guest list?'

Gradually the list was completed. There were so many names Katherine didn't know, and the few she did were people she would never have had in her house.

The date was settled and Katherine in many ways was looking forward to being busy.

Joseph came down the stairs.

'Off to school then?' asked Katherine as she stood back to

admire the vase of flowers she had placed on the hall table.

'Uncle Gerald said I can stay up for this party.'

'Did he now?'

'Well, will you let me?'

'I shouldn't think so for one minute.'

'That's what I told him.'

'He's not your father.'

'I know that, don't I?' He pushed past her and slammed the front door.

Katherine walked into the kitchen. She felt like stamping her feet in temper.

'You look annoyed. What's got your goat?' asked Dolly.

'Gerald. D'you know he's told Joseph he can attend the party.'

'Don't say I approve of that, not with all the wine and drink that's been delivered.'

'I didn't order that much.'

'You didn't, but he did.' Dolly inclined her head towards the door. 'Take a look in the outhouse.'

'No, I can't be bothered. Dolly, what am I going to do?'

'Don't ask me. I only work here.'

The friendly atmosphere that had always prevailed in this kitchen somehow seemed to have been lost. Katherine felt an outsider.

'Have there been any other changes?'

'Not as far as I know.'

As the weekend of the party got closer so the food and flowers arrived and preparations began in earnest. Dolly and Katherine were kept very busy.

At eight o'clock on Saturday evening Gerald banged on Katherine's bedroom door. 'Come along, Katherine, let's go and meet our guests.'

'I'll be down in a moment.'

The guests began arriving by horse and carriage as well as motor cars. Joseph was hanging out of his mother's window.

'Why can't I go down?'

'Because I say so.'

'You don't let me do anything I want. I want to go and see those motors. Uncle Gerald is going to buy one and he said he would take me with—'

'Joseph, be quiet!' shouted Katherine. 'I'm sick of hearing what Gerald says and promises. Now, you can stay here and look out of this window if you wish. When Dolly has a spare moment I'll get her to bring you up a tray. I must go.'

Katherine left the room. Her heart wasn't in this, but she knew she had to put on a show, it was part of their agreement. She smoothed down her dark navy gown, the darkest she had that wasn't actually black.

A trio began to play. Gerald smiled and took her hand ready to introduce her to various people – there were very few she already knew.

'You look lovely,' he whispered.

As the evening wore on and Katherine moved about, she caught snatches of conversation and was surprised to hear her name linked with Gerald's. What had he been saying?

'Katherine my dear.'

Katherine turned to see Mrs Emily Hawthorn walking towards her.

She came and kissed Katherine's cheek. 'I was so sorry we missed dear Edwin's funeral. And now what's this we hear about you and Gerald? You do make a very handsome couple, and this house is very nice for you both.' While she was talking to Katherine her sharp beady eyes were darting round the room. 'Never been invited here before, but then you and Edwin didn't entertain that much, did you? Oh look, there's the actress Pamela

Courtney Jones, must have a word with her.' With that she turned and hurried away.

What was Gerald telling them? She must try to get him on his own, ask him to quash these rumours.

All evening he was busy with his guests. The wine was flowing and conversations were getting louder. The room was hot and stuffy and thick with cigar smoke. Katherine felt tired and miserable, she didn't enjoy the company of these people, they were noisy and showy.

She decided to take a walk in the garden to clear her head before going to bed. Her thoughts were full of Edwin. Young men were behaving foolishly, picking the flowers and tramping on the borders. Edwin would never have allowed this. Was this how her life would be from now on?

She tried to talk to Gerald but she could see he was in no mood for a serious conversation.

Before she retired to her room she looked in at Joseph. He was fast asleep. She smiled. The tray on his table had just a few crumbs left. Please let us be friends. I need a friend, she thought.

As she lay in bed the laughing and shouting drifted up. Motor car doors were being slammed and engines bursting into life. Every now and again a horse would neigh – how much nicer these sounds were. But this was progress, and she must accept it. Her life was changing now whether she liked it or not.

Chapter 5

Katherine woke and for a while lay listening to the birds singing. What did the future hold for her? For the second time in her life she felt trapped and miserable. How she envied the birds their freedom, they could fly away. After dressing she went downstairs.

''Ave you seen the mess in there?' asked Dolly, as soon as Katherine opened the kitchen door. 'Broken glass and all sorts.'

'No, I came straight in here.'

'It's a bloody disgrace. I hope we ain't gonner have too many of these dos.'

Katherine sat at the table as a cup of tea was put in front of her. She couldn't tell Dolly that she'd overheard people eagerly talking about the next one. 'That will be up to Gerald,' was the only answer she could give.

Dolly was busy bustling about. 'Tom's in there now clearing up. There's some burn holes in Mr Edwin's favourite chair. And someone's squashed their cigar out in the carpet. You wait till you see it.'

Katherine wanted to cry. This had been her house, now it was being taken over. She should have been strong and stood her ground. She should have gone to Milly's. 'Is Gerald up yet?' she asked.

'Shouldn't think we'll see him till dinner time.' Dolly clearly wasn't in the mood for any kind of polite conversation.

'What about Joseph?'

'He's out in the garden.'

All day Katherine had to listen to Dolly complaining about

the mess and the behaviour of some of the guests, while Joseph moped about grumbling that he never got to look over the motor cars properly.

'I wanted the chance to draw one up close, that's all, but you wouldn't let me.'

Katherine didn't reply. There was no point.

Gerald wasn't seen until afternoon tea was over. Katherine was sitting in the garden surveying the damage. Tomorrow she would ask Tom to help her make a start to clear it, she wasn't in the mood today.

'Last night was a huge success,' said Gerald, sitting next to her. 'And I have you to thank, my dear, for that.' He condescendingly patted her hand.

'I can't take the credit, it was the staff who made it go as smoothly as possible. Dolly isn't very happy about it, or the mess.'

'She works for me now, so she'll have to get used to it, won't she? You don't approve of my friends, do you?'

'No, and I don't know what you told them about me, and us. What did they mean?'

'I just happened to mention to one or two of my very close friends that, in the very near future, we may well be married.'

'Gerald, how could you? You know that to be a lie. You know I am already married. Can't you see I don't like you, or your friends, and I only stay here because, as you so rightly say, I have nowhere else to go.'

He smiled. 'I'm glad you see things my way.'

Katherine walked away in temper. Why did this man always make her so angry? Tears of frustration stung her eyes. Was it because he never listened to her? Or because he thought he could own her?

That night Katherine was tossing and turning in bed. Sleep

wouldn't come. Her mind was going over and over what Gerald had said when she heard the creaking of her bedroom door being slowly opened.

'Joseph? Joseph, is that you?' Katherine sat up.

He didn't answer.

She pushed back the bedclothes and slid out of bed. 'What's wrong?'

The door was clicked shut. Katherine froze when in the gloom she recognised Gerald's shape. Quickly grabbing her dressing gown and regaining her composure, she asked, 'What do you think you are doing coming into my room?'

'I've come to talk to you.'

'I'm sure we have nothing to talk about that can't wait till morning.' She wanted to move round the bed to get near the door, but he was blocking the way.

'Katherine, I'm in love with you. I have been for years. Since the first time I saw you. You are the reason I have never married.'

'Please, Gerald, this is ridiculous. Have you been drinking?' Katherine was shaking with temper and fear.

'Ridiculous, is that what you think?' He slowly moved towards her. 'Let me tell you, madam, that at this moment ridiculous is the last thing I feel. And yes, I have been drinking. I've been sitting downstairs trying to think of a way to make you like me.'

'Well, this certainly isn't the way, now kindly leave my room.' Katherine stepped back and fell against the dressing stool, stumbling to the floor.

Gerald quickly came towards her. She tried to scramble to her feet but her nightclothes hampered her.

He was on his knees, and with his arms round her he pulled her close. The smell of whisky almost took her breath away. She tried to pull away but he held her face tightly in his hands and passionately kissed her lips, face, and hair. She rocked her head from side to side in an effort to break free. She pummelled his chest and tried to push him away but he was strong. She wanted to scream out, but who would hear her? Her room was the other side of the house from Joseph's. His hands tore at her nightgown revealing her bare breasts. Like a wild animal he bit into her soft white flesh; she cried out in pain.

'You like it, don't you? You want me. You have been without a man for years,' he hissed.

'Let me go.' Her long hair caught on the buttons of his waistcoat and pulled her head back.

She screamed out hysterically and dug her nails into his cheek.

He put his hand over her mouth and she bit his hand.

'You bitch.' He pulled at her nightgown and it came away in his hands. She was naked.

She tried to get to her feet but he was holding on to her, his fingers digging deep into her flesh. They rolled on the floor with their legs entangled. He put his forearm across her neck; she couldn't breathe. With his free hand he pushed her legs far apart. She thought he was trying to suffocate her and somehow she managed to bring her hand up and hit his face hard. He sat back on his haunches and laughed. Then with the back of his hand he struck her hard across her face. Her teeth rattled and warm sticky blood filled her mouth. Her head was swimming.

Between her sobs she heard him say, 'I've waited a long while for this, and I'm going to have you one way or another.'

For Katherine everything went black and she didn't feel anything any more.

Slowly Katherine opened her eyes. She was still lying on the floor. Through the open window she could hear the birds singing their hearts out. Outside dawn was just beginning to break. Red streaks painted the sky. It took her a moment or two to get everything in focus. Every part of her body hurt. Gradually, after a great deal of effort, she got to her feet and sat on the bed. She looked down at her naked body. It was covered with red weals and bite marks. Long scratches ran from her breasts down to her waist. The bruises on her legs took on many colours. Ashamed, she hastily pulled a sheet over her nakedness. Her head throbbed and her body ached. When she caught sight of her face in the mirror she cried out and put her hand to her cheek. A yellow and black bruise filled one side of her face. She lay back and let her tears flow. 'How could you do this to me, Gerald?' she groaned.

When Katherine opened her eyes again the sun was up. She carefully got to her feet when she heard Joseph slam the bathroom door and clatter down the stairs. 'I'll wait till he's gone before I make a move,' she said to herself. Every movement was an effort.

Gradually, after she knew Joseph had left for school, she bathed, and when she felt a little stronger made her way downstairs.

'You're late,' said Dolly with her back to her. 'Tom's taken young Joseph off to— Oh my God!' Dolly quickly put her hand to her mouth and rushed to Katherine's side. 'What happened to you?'

Katherine tried to give her a reassuring smile, but it hurt.

'Did he do that?'

Katherine nodded and tears slowly rolled down her cheeks.

'Bloody animal, wants locking up. I knew you should have gorn to Milly's. You can't stay here, not now.'

'When Tom comes back perhaps we could have a word.'

'You go on up to your room, I'll bring you something nourishing. 'Sides, you don't want to come face to face with that cowson.' Dolly took hold of Katherine's hand. 'I don't like to ask,' she gave her a knowing look, 'but did he – you know . . .?'

Again Katherine only nodded.

'Wants bloody castrating. You wait till my Tom hears about this, he'll go mad. Why didn't you scream out?'

'I couldn't.' Katherine stood up. 'I will go on up.'

'I'll bring up a cuppa.'

As Katherine climbed the stairs every bone in her body seemed as if it were complaining. She just wanted to lie down and weep.

Dolly followed her up. She sat on the bed. 'Here, lay back and let me take your shoes off.'

Katherine did as she was told and closed her eyes.

'Tea's on the side,' said Dolly.

'If Gerald asks about me, tell him I've gone out.'

Dolly quietly closed the door and left Katherine to her thoughts.

She would have to leave this house, she couldn't stay under the same roof as Gerald, not now. Despite what Joseph had said she would get Tom to take them to Milly's today. She had to get away. Slowly she sat up. Her mind began to get things in order. She had to pack. She would only take essentials. Money and jewellery, and as many clothes as she could. Then there were Joseph's things she would have to take. Suddenly she felt stronger as she began to put her plan into action.

Gradually and very painfully she managed to fill two boxes. That was all she could take at the moment. Perhaps later, when Dolly and Tom visited her sister, they could bring a few more.

'Miss Katherine, what you doing down here? I was just coming up with some broth.' Dolly was leaning over a large steaming pot.

'Has Gerald gone yet?'

'Yes. And he didn't ask about you. He's got some nasty scratches on his face. Felt like giving him a piece of me mind, I did, but then thought better of it.'

'I'm going to stay at Milly's.'

Dolly's face lit up. 'You are? Oh I'm ever so glad. She'll look after you. When you going?'

'This afternoon, when Tom picks Joseph up from school.'

'So soon?'

'I can't stay another night under this roof. Do you think Milly will mind me turning up like that?'

'Shouldn't think so. Mind you, that's if she ain't already let the room.'

Katherine was filled with fear. She hadn't thought about that. 'Well, I'll have to keep my fingers crossed. I've packed two boxes, so when Tom's ready perhaps he'll put them in the carriage.'

'What about the rest of your stuff?'

'Have a sort through and if there's anything you'd like please take it, then perhaps you could bring the rest over sometime.'

Tom made no comment when he saw Katherine's bruised face. She guessed Dolly had given him all the details.

Katherine didn't leave the comfort and the obscurity of the carriage and sat waiting for Joseph to come out of his expensive school. All the boys were wearing uniform and it was hard to pick him out, but when he caught sight of Tom he bounded up to him.

'Didn't expect to see you here,' he said eagerly. 'Can I ride on top with you?'

'No, son, get inside.'

He looked a little puzzled as he opened the door. 'Mama, what are you doing here?'

Katherine sat back in the shadow as they moved off.

'Where are we going?'

She took hold of his hand but he pulled it away.

'We are going to live with Milly.'

'What? I told you I wasn't going to live there. Tell Tom to take me home. I am not going to . . .' His voice trailed off when Katherine sat forward. 'Mama,' his voice softened. 'What's happened to your face?'

'This is why we have to leave Gerald. He attacked me last night, and I'm afraid I fear for my life.'

For a full minute Joseph sat and stared at his mother, then he threw his arms round her and, hugging her close, cried, 'Why Mama? Why did Uncle Gerald do that to you?'

'I told you, we had a disagreement. I can't live in that house any longer – we are going to Milly's.'

Joseph sat back. 'But I don't like it there.'

'Well, I'm sorry, but I have decided. It's time to go.'

Chapter 6

After Joseph got over the shock of seeing his mother he asked what had happened. Katherine explained that Gerald had drunk too much and wanted her to marry him.

'So why don't you?'

'Because I am still married to your father.'

'I forgot. Anyway he lives miles away, so who would know?'

'Even if I wanted to, which I don't, it's illegal, and I don't love Gerald.'

'Does that matter? If you did marry Uncle Gerald we could stay at the house.'

Katherine chose not to answer that. Is that all he was worrying about?

'Perhaps he didn't mean to hit you.'

'I'm sure he did. Men do silly things when they drink.'

Joseph sat back and looked sad. 'But I don't want to go to Milly's.'

'Well, I'm very sorry, but that is how it's going to be. Besides, you don't know, you may like it there.'

'Don't think I will,' mumbled Joseph.

'That's quite enough,' said Katherine sternly.

Joseph didn't pursue the conversation any further and the uneventful journey continued.

Katherine was cross and hurt that he didn't seem to be very concerned at what Gerald had done to her.

Once again Milly was on her doorstep as soon as the carriage came to halt outside number 12 Croft Street. Tom jumped down and helped Katherine to alight.

Milly gasped when she caught sight of Katherine's face. 'I'm so pleased you've made up your mind to come,' she said, not commenting on the bruising. Two bright pink spots of embarrassment and excitement coloured her pale cheeks. 'Put those boxes in the front room for now, Tom.' She turned to Katherine. 'You've certainly got a lot.'

'Can't stay long,' said Tom anxiously. 'His nibs might start yelling for me.'

'I'll give you a hand,' said Joseph sullenly.

'I'd like to move in today if it's convenient.'

'Course. Charlie and Ted will give you a hand to get this stuff upstairs if we can't manage it. Kettle's on. I expect you'd like a cuppa, Tom?'

'Only if it's quick,' came the reply as they moved into the kitchen. Tom looked nervous and drank his tea as soon as it was put in front of him, then left.

'Now,' said Milly to Katherine. 'When you've finished your tea I'll show you where everything is. I don't go out much, but if at anytime you fancy a cuppa it's best you know where to look.'

Katherine was shown the scullery and all the cooking implements. She was taken into the back yard for a look into the lavatory, then followed a lesson on how to raise and lower the washing line. Next the large wooden mangle was uncovered for her inspection.

'Charlie said that if you did come over here he'd take you and show you where the biscuit factory is, and where the boy can go to school.'

'Thank you, that will be very kind of him.' Katherine put a restraining hand out to stop Milly from entering the house. 'Milly, Gerald, Mr Edwin's brother, did this,' she pointed to her face, 'when I wouldn't let him share my bed.'

'Guessed as much, but don't worry about it, most of the wives round here get beaten regularly, 'specially poor Mrs Addams across the road. Not that my Charlie would ever lay a finger on a woman. Reckons those blokes are cowards, can't fight men, most of 'em.'

Although Katherine felt very apprehensive she was beginning to warm to Charlie. Suddenly everything in her life was going to be so different.

'Not got bad neighbours,' said Milly, not taking that conversation any further. She peered over the low wall and lowered her voice. 'Mr and Mrs Parsons lives next door. Got two boys – don't see a lot of 'em, they works away, that's when they're not in clink. Mr and Mrs Duke live there,' she pointed to the other side of the yard. 'Quiet couple. Kids married and moved away. She's a bit of a busybody, but not nasty. We're lucky we don't have hordes of kids banging and shouting. Feel sorry for that lot across the road, they've got the Addams family to put up with.'

Milly was in an excited chatty mood, and Katherine didn't ask questions.

Between them and with Joseph's help, they carried the boxes upstairs. They returned to the front room, which had a damp unused feel to it. A hard uncomfortable-looking brown Rexine three-piece had been carefully positioned around the fireplace. A shining brass firescreen hid the empty grate. In front of the lace-curtained bay window stood a long-legged rickety-looking table with a large pot on top. It held a huge aspidistra. The dark green shiny leaves overhung and looked like a giant spider ready to pounce.

Milly stood back and proudly pointed to the grandfather clock in the corner. 'That was me mother's. It don't work, but it's a nice piece of furniture. Lovely wood. Ted gets in first, about six, and now we have the lighter nights Charlie works on a bit – that's when there's a ship in, of course. It's timber mostly at the Surrey Docks.'

Katherine smiled. 'Dolly will be bringing some more of my clothes when they come over to see you, not that I'll have a lot of use for them now.'

'Don't chuck any away,' said Milly in alarm. 'What you can't pawn p'raps we can cut up.'

'Do you do alterations?' asked Katherine, noting the sewing machine in the corner.

Milly grinned. 'Can turn me hand at most things.'

'Do I have to sleep with your son?'

Katherine was suddenly aware they had almost ignored Joseph.

'Well it's that or down here in the front room on the floor. I ain't putting a bed up in here for you. It's gotter be the floor.'

'I'd rather sleep on the floor if you don't mind.'

'I don't mind, it's you that'll find it hard.'

Katherine wanted to sweep him up in her arms and hold him close, but she knew he would hate that.

'Will we live here for ever?' he asked his mother.

'I don't know. When I get a job perhaps we could look for a small house.'

'Jobs round here ain't that easy to get.'

Joseph was very quiet and at times Katherine caught him studying her face. He was obviously very shocked at what Gerald had done. Such violence was all quite alien to him. What a blessing no one would ever see her body.

Katherine sat in the kitchen while Milly busied herself with the dinner. She glanced at the clock on the mantelpiece. It was almost six, soon Charlie and Ted would be here. Joseph had sat all the while in her bedroom with his books. He had made it very clear he didn't like this situation. Katherine was worried. Would he ever accept living here?

The laughing and noise from the passage told her that Ted and Charlie had arrived home together.

''Allo there, love,' said Charlie, pushing open the kitchen door. He wasn't overtall, but stocky and well-built, with the healthy complexion of an outdoor worker.

Ted followed, a tall thin lad whose pale colouring was the same as his mother's, such a complete contrast to his father's weatherbeaten looks.

'All right then, gel?' Charlie asked Milly. 'Dinner smells good.' His thick brown hair sprung up when he removed his flat cap and threw it on to the armchair. That was followed by a well-patched jacket that had definitely seen better days. The thick heavy metal docker's hook that Katherine had seen men dig into large sacks and timber to give them a grip when they had arrived at various ports, had been hitched over his wide leather belt, but was now carefully placed on the dresser.

'And you must be Miss Katherine?' Charlie stopped when he caught sight of her face.

'That Gerald did that,' said Milly quickly.

'Did he now? Well anyway, pleased to meet you. Won't shake yer hand as I ain't all that clean.' He slipped his braces off his wide shoulders and, letting them dangle, took the large black kettle from off the hob and disappeared into the scullery.

Milly smiled as she hung his jacket and cap on a nail behind the door. 'You're having a good influence on him, he don't usually do that till he's had a cuppa.'

'Yer, but it won't last,' said Ted. 'By the way, I'm Ted.' He looked down shyly. 'Where's yer boy then, missis?'

'He's upstairs,' said Katherine, pleased they didn't ask any more questions about her bruises.

'I'll go on up and have a word with him.'

'Don't you sit on that bed in your work clothes. I'll just nip up and get Charlie a clean shirt,' said Milly, leaving Katherine on her own.

After a few minutes Ted came clattering back down the stairs and Milly passed through with a shirt and then returned to the kitchen with the kettle.

'He said he'd like to see my drawings,' said Ted beaming.

'Well, they are good,' said Milly.

'Joseph also likes to draw, perhaps you could help him.'

'That's what he said. He's ever so quiet.'

'I expect he's a bit shy,' said Milly, clearly enjoying having her family around her.

'That's better,' said Charlie, walking in and rolling up his sleeves. 'Right then lass, how's my Milly treating you?' He pulled up his braces and standing in front of the mirror ran both hands over his hair that had been slicked down with water.

'Very well, thank you.'

'Ted, you can go and have a wash as well,' said Milly, handing him another kettle.

'But, Mum, I ain't had a cuppa yet.'

'It'll be on the table by the time you're finished.'

'Do you want me to get Joseph?' asked Katherine.

'You could do.'

'Just yell up the stairs,' volunteered Charlie.

'Miss Katherine is a lady, remember, and she don't yell,' said Milly, giving her husband a filthy look.

Charlie laughed. 'Yer, I forgot.'

Katherine hastily left the room. She didn't want to keep being called a lady and Miss Katherine, she was living in their home now. She had to become one of them, but how?

She pushed open her bedroom door. 'Joseph, are you coming down to eat?'

'I'm not hungry.'

'Come on now, don't be silly.'

'Bet she can't cook as good as Dolly,' he mumbled.

'I expect Milly can. They both had the same mother to teach them, remember. Anyway, why don't you come down and find out.' She knew he must be hungry, and the smell of the dinner wafting up the stairs would soon change his mind.

He slid to the edge of the bed.

'What did Ted have to say to you?'

'He said he would show me how to draw properly.' For the first time that day he smiled. 'After tea he's going to show me his sketches, that's what he calls them.'

'Do you know what his favourite subject is?' she asked casually.

'No, but he said I mustn't tell his mum about his sketches.'

Katherine was taken aback. What if they weren't the kind of thing she wanted her son to see just yet? 'So, will you tell me?'

'I don't know,' he said, pushing open the kitchen door.

''Allo there, young 'en,' said Charlie. 'Glad to have you living here with us.'

'Thank you, sir.'

Charlie threw his head back and laughed. ''Ere, Mil, did you hear that, he called me sir.'

'Well I told you, they've got very good manners, and it wouldn't hurt you two to take a leaf out of young Joseph's book.'

The first meal was full of laughter and chatter, as Charlie told them about his day at the docks. He made everything sound as if he enjoyed the hard work. Katherine could see Joseph was intrigued.

'Bit worried about all these strikes though,' said Charlie, pushing his empty plate away. He sat back and began rolling a cigarette.

'D'you think it'll get to the docks?' asked Milly, jumping up to collect the plates.

'Don't rightly know, love. It don't take much to set 'em off.'

'Well, I hope it don't happen. Don't know how we'll manage with only Ted's bit coming in.'

'You've got Miss Katherine's money as well now,' said Charlie.

'Anyway, we'll worry about it if and when it happens.'

'That was delicious,' Katherine said to Milly as she handed her her empty plate. She noticed Joseph's plate was also empty.

'She ain't a bad cook, is she?' Charlie smacked his wife's bottom as she passed his chair.

She blushed and giggled. 'Oh, go on with you. There's seconds if you fancy any.'

'Not for me, thank you,' said Katherine.

'That's not what I fancy,' said Charlie, giving Katherine a wink.

'Charlie Stevens,' shouted Milly, 'I trust you to watch your mouth. We have a child as well as a lady present.'

'I'm not a child,' said Joseph.

'And I'm not a lady,' laughed Katherine.

'And I was talking about having a pint,' said Charlie.

Milly sat down and laughed with them.

'Come on, Joe. Can I call you Joe?' asked Ted.

Joe nodded.

'Right, let's show me what you can do.'

'Please, Mama, may I leave the table?'

'Of course.'

'Oh, he's got such lovely manners,' said Milly.

Katherine looked round at the happy faces. Even Joe, as she guessed he had now been christened, was grinning. At that moment she knew she had made the right decision in coming here. She only hoped the neighbours would prove as friendly. With the way she spoke and her clothes, she felt, and was, an outsider in Rotherhithe.

Katherine had decided to wait a few weeks before she looked for work. She wasn't in that much of a hurry, not all the while she had a few sovereigns left. She hadn't returned the money Gerald had given her for a new gown.

* * *

The following morning Milly took Katherine shopping. As Milly closed her front door Mrs Duke from next door came out.

'Good morning, Milly.'

Milly was beaming. 'Mrs Duke, this is Miss Katherine.'

Mrs Duke was a large woman with rosy cheeks and her grey hair piled up on top of her head. Her white wrapover overall was tied tightly round what should have been her waist, but she was the same size all the way down.

'Pleased to meet you,' said Katherine, giving her a slight nod.

'Christ. Miss Katherine, eh? That sounds a bit posh for round here.' Mrs Duke had a slight lisp.

'Miss Katherine is staying with me till she finds suitable accommodation.'

'Down on yer uppers then, girl? See yer old man's been knocking you about. Oh look out, here comes that poor cow Mrs Addams and her tribe.'

Katherine gasped when she saw the woman walking towards them. She wasn't old but looked very weary; she was heavily pregnant and holding on to two small boys, one in each hand. Their clothes were tatty and well patched, but they weren't wearing any boots. Another child, who was struggling to see over the top of a large battered bassinet, was desperately trying to keep it going in a straight line. Inside a child sat at each end; one was much too big to be sitting in a pram and both were sucking huge grubby gobstoppers made from rag. Katherine guessed they were full of sugar and they almost covered their faces.

Two older girls deep in conversation were trailing behind. They all had masses of dark hair like their mother, and as they got closer Katherine could see that apart from the styes and yellow matter in most of the children's eyes, they were all the same dark blue.

'Hello, Mrs Duke, Mrs Stevens,' said Mrs Addams politely, with a slight nod. Her lilting Irish brogue was a joy to hear. 'I trust this fine weather is helping to keep your rheumatics at bay, Mrs Duke?'

'Yes thanks. You all right?'

'Mustn't grumble. Won't be sorry when this one's here.' She patted her large stomach.

'You'll only get yourself up the duff again.'

She smiled, lightened up her blue eyes. 'I expect you're right, but 'tis the will of the Lord.'

The two in the bassinet began yelling and fighting when the older one pulled the other's dummy out. The child holding the handle started to rock it violently. Katherine looked on in horror, she thought they would fall out with the intense movement.

'The Lord, eh?' said Mrs Duke, smugly crossing her arms. 'That's all very well, but He don't have to feed 'em, does He?'

'That's true,' said Mrs Addams, putting out a calming hand to steady the bassinet and shoving the dummy back into the child's mouth. She smiled. 'I trust you and your family are keeping well, Mrs Stevens? When does your Olive have her baby?'

'Not for a while yet. September sometime.'

'Well, send her over if she wants some advice.'

'It ain't no good her coming to you to find out how to stop 'em coming though, is it?' laughed Mrs Duke.

'No, Billy, don't do that, it ain't nice.'

Billy had broken free from his mother's hand and was sitting on the kerb picking his nose, then running his only clean finger down his tatty coat.

'That's a nice frock, missis,' said one of the girls who had been hanging back. She began to run her dirty fingers over the fine material of Katherine's dress.

'Leave it be,' shouted Milly.

The girl put her tongue out.

'Briony, you mustn't be so rude,' said her mother. 'I'm sorry, but she ain't used to seeing such fine cloth.'

Briony looked thin and undernourished. Katherine guessed she must be about the same age as Joseph. She looked up at Katherine with adoration in her eyes.

'Miss Katherine is staying with us till she finds something more in keeping with her lifestyle,' said Milly in a very pompous way.

'Oh yer, and what sort of lifestyle's that then?' asked Mrs Duke.

'Miss Katherine once owned a lovely restaurant, and my sister – you know my Dolly – well, she used to do for her.'

Katherine stood dumbfounded. They were talking about her as if she wasn't there. Was all her history about to be discussed? She was used neither to gossiping in the street nor being treated as an object of curiosity.

'So what yer gonner do round here then, girl, open a posh restaurant?' Mrs Duke threw her head back and laughed very loud. Katherine was fascinated that her bright pink gums held one lone tooth, which accounted for her lisp. 'Christ, this lot round here don't know what it is to sit at a table, let alone sit in a restaurant and use a knife and fork. No, girl, I think you'll have to think of something else.'

Opening a restaurant, especially round here, was the last thing on Katherine's mind.

'Mum, what's a rest— What that lady said?' asked Briony.

'I'll try to explain later,' said her mother. 'Now come on, we must be off.'

'They live across the road,' said Milly, when the Addamses were well out of earshot.

'She's got another three boys, the eldest goes to work and the other two run errands for the blokes down the market. A bit like bookies' runners they are, do all the dirty work,' added Mrs Duke.

Katherine didn't like to ask what a bookie's runner did. 'Don't the boys go to school?' she enquired instead.

'Na, can't afford it, poor cow.'

'How many children has she got all together?' asked Katherine, staring after them.

'Let's see. It'll be eleven when she drops that one,' said Mrs Duke.

'Eleven,' repeated Katherine. 'She can't be that old. How does she manage?'

'Dunno. They ain't been here that long, just a couple of years or so. Her old man works on the new tunnel. They brought a lot of Irish over to dig out the tunnel. Stinks to high heaven, he does. Still, I s'pose you and her have got something in common,' said Mrs Duke to Katherine.

'Oh, and what's that?'

'After work her old man goes to the pub then gives her a bloody good hiding when he gets home.'

Katherine cringed.

'Then,' continued Mrs Duke, enjoying getting into her stride, 'when they gets into a lot of debt, like the rent, they moves on, or so I heard. Poor cow, what sorta life's that?'

It was obvious to Katherine Mrs Duke knew all about them, and one way and another it shouldn't take her long to find out everything about this newcomer to Croft Street.

Chapter 7

Following Milly's instructions Katherine soon found the school and Joseph started the next day. She was pleased to hear he was far ahead of all the other pupils of his age. She had been worried he might have been picked on because of his smart clothes, but with Milly's help she managed to dress him down.

All week Milly was also busy in the front room with her sewing machine altering the gowns Katherine had managed to bring with her. With much laughter they removed most of the trimmings and took out the many petticoats, trying to make them suitable for Rotherhithe. Any they decided were far too grand finished up in the pawn shop along with a few pairs of her dainty shoes.

'You sure you want to do this to all these frocks?' said Milly, wistfully. 'What if you find yourself a good job – you might need them?'

'I don't think that will ever happen, and if it did, I could start all over again,' said Katherine, lightheartedly. But she knew she would never be in a position to wear such fine clothes again.

'Milly, you've made a lovely job of this one,' she said, holding a gown against her.

'What shall I do with all this cloth that's over?'

'Can you or your daughter make use of it?'

'Miss Kath – sorry, Katherine –' Katherine had asked her to drop the 'Miss' as it sounded as Charlie would say, 'too hoity-toity for round here' – 'you've been so good to us already. I've got so many lovely pieces in my workbox,' continued Milly, gently fondling the fine silk. 'Olive's baby's gonner be wearing some lovely things, and so will she when she can get into them.'

'I've got an idea. Sort out any pieces you can't make use of and I'll take them over to Mrs Addams.'

'You are kind.'

Katherine felt embarrassed. 'You don't think she'll take offence, do you?'

'I should say not.' Milly straightened her shoulders. 'She should be grateful you're taking an interest in her.'

'I don't want her to be grateful, it's just that young Briony always gives me such a lovely smile when I see her, but she has such sad eyes. I wish I had a daughter.'

'She has a lot to put up with, poor mite.'

That afternoon Katherine picked her way across the road, carefully avoiding the piles of horse dung, and knocked on the Addamses' front door.

Briony opened the door. The smell of dried urine filled Katherine's nostrils and almost made her cough. Briony was wearing a dirty frock that was at least two sizes too big for her. She was balancing one of the babies on her hip. He only had on a short vest and Katherine blanched at the sight of his red bare bottom. It was scabby and looked very sore. Briony's dark hair hung matted and lank, and with her free hand she pushed some strands behind her ear.

''Allo, missis, what d'yer want?'

'I'm sorting out some of my clothes and I was wondering if you would like this material that's left over.' Katherine held out a bag.

Briony quickly looked over her shoulder. 'I'd ask you in, but it ain't conveni— It ain't very tidy.'

'That's all right. Here, take this, I'm sure your mother can find a use for it.' Katherine wasn't that keen to go into the house.

'Thanks.' Briony's smile lit up her very pretty face.

As she made her way back to Milly's, Katherine noted that in a few of the houses the lace curtains moved slightly.

Katherine was happy. She had found a friend in Milly and every morning they would go off shopping together. Joe appeared to have settled down at school and most evenings he and Ted would sit and discuss their drawing. At the weekend Ted took him to the docks and Joe excitedly told his mother about the ships, and proudly showed off his sketches. Katherine had been shown the biscuit factory, the docks and many other things. She didn't want to go to work, but knew her money wouldn't last for ever.

It was the slums that upset her the most, the dirt and the squalor. Women sat outside their front doors with babies and children squabbling round their feet or sucking at their breasts. Young girls dragged the younger ones round with them. Shoes seemed to be unheard of. Katherine always felt overdressed when she passed these people, and she could feel their eyes boring into her back. After a few days one or two gave her a slight nod.

'Why do these people have so many children?' she asked Milly.

'Most of 'em because the old man says so. They have a few drinks then take what they knows is their right. Then the wives have to put up with more babies. Some of 'em go to any old crone who'll help 'em out – that's those that ain't Cath'lics, of course. Mind you, some don't always come off all right, poor cows, then they finish up in a pauper's grave.'

Katherine was shocked. 'You mean they die?' she asked softly.

'Sometimes.'

'I'm surprised that some of these women don't become suffragettes.'

Milly laughed. 'They ain't interested in getting the vote. Their main worry is where the next meal's coming from. 'Sides, most of 'em can't read.'

Katherine was beginning to find out it was an even more unfair world than she had ever imagined. So many had everything while others had nothing.

'I like to keep me place neat and tidy,' said Milly, almost as if reading Katherine's mind. 'Me mum was always a stickler for keeping the place nice and clean, so I suppose it rubbed off on me and Dolly.'

On Sunday Olive and her husband came to tea. Olive looked so much like her father, with her dark hair, brown eyes and a big ready smile. Ernie, a slim man, was quiet and wore a very serious expression, but they were a happy couple, eagerly looking forward to the arrival of their baby.

One morning after shopping Milly and Katherine were walking back down Croft Street when they saw Briony coming towards them. Her hair was tied back with a piece of string, she looked clean and was wearing a frock made out of some of the material Katherine had given her. It wasn't particularly well made, and she looked very overdressed.

'You look very smart,' said Katherine kindly.

She beamed and her beautiful blue eyes twinkled. 'I've got to go and see Mr Wilks in the ironmongers. He said he might give me a job.'

'How old are you, Briony?' asked Katherine.

'Thirteen.'

'You're a little older than my son, Joseph.'

'I tried to talk to him once but he walked away. He's a right snob, ever so stuck-up.'

Katherine grinned. 'I'll have a word with him.'

Briony began to move away. 'Don't bother. I don't need him to talk to, got plenty enough of me family. By the way, d'yer like me frock?'

'It's very nice,' said Katherine. 'Did you make it?'

'Na, me mum did.'

As she walked away Milly laughed. 'Poor little cow. Did you see the size of those stitches?'

'It was all done by hand,' said Katherine. 'She's very young to be going to work.'

'It's a case of having to.'

'I suppose it's good of Mr Wilks to give her a job.'

'That's as may be. But I can't say I'd fancy her serving me. Did you see the colour of her neck?'

Katherine nodded. 'She does smell a bit, I'll grant you that.'

'Don't suppose she's ever had a bath. It's a good job it's an ironmongers and not the grocers. Wouldn't fancy her touching me bacon or butter.'

'It's such a shame. She seems to have a good head on her shoulders despite everything.'

'I only hope for her sake all what we hear about old Wilks ain't true.'

Katherine stopped. 'What do you mean?'

'Well,' Milly also stopped. She looked around and said quietly, 'Some kids don't stay long, and talk is that he, you know, interferes with 'em.'

'That's dreadful. Are you sure?'

'Well, he's always got new kids in there, and that's what the rumour is.'

'No,' said Katherine, deeply shocked.

'It's what they say.'

'Don't any of the parents report him?'

'Who to? 'Sides, with some parents they worry more about the kid losing the job and the extra few shillings coming in.'

'That's awful,' said Katherine.

'That's life,' said Milly casually.

Briony was on Katherine's mind all afternoon. She liked her and wanted to help her, but how? Briony didn't go to school and

67

the family obviously needed her wages so perhaps starting work could be something positive in her life. At least she would be away from the children for a few hours a day, and she would be meeting people. But what if Mr Wilks interfered with her? What was it with men? Did Briony have anyone to confide in if he did? Would she tell anyone if her job depended on it? Perhaps it was all rumours and he'd teach her to read and add up?

Katherine was still thinking of Briony when Joe came home from school. 'Why won't you talk to her?' she asked him.

'She smells.'

'That isn't a very nice thing to say.'

'Well, she does. 'Sides, I don't want to go near that family, they all smell. A lot of people round here smell.'

Katherine wanted to smile, but she managed to keep a straight face. 'She's going to work in the ironmongers.'

'Well, paraffin will be better than dried pee.' He ran from the kitchen into the front room which he now called his room.

Milly walked in from the scullery laughing. 'I heard that. He's got his head screwed on 'as that one.'

On Saturday Milly was busy making cakes for Sunday's tea. 'Dolly and Tom should be over tomorrow,' she said to Katherine, who was helping her.

'It will be interesting to find out how things are going at the restaurant and what changes Gerald has made to the house.'

'Do you still miss that way of life?'

Katherine brushed the flour from her hands. 'In some ways, but certainly not Gerald.'

'Not thought any more about going back then?'

'No. That part of my life is over.' It was true: if she did not yet feel entirely part of Milly's world, she certainly was not part of Gerald's.

'Do you worry about Joe?'

Katherine looked puzzled. 'I suppose I do, why do you ask?'

'He's always telling Ted he's going back there to live one day.'

Katherine sat at the table. 'He does?'

Milly laughed nervously. 'You know what boys are like, always telling each other things to make it sound good.'

'I hope that is all he's doing. I don't need any more worries at the moment. Milly, I must find something to do soon, my money won't last for ever.'

Milly looked embarrassed. 'I honestly don't think I could take any less, especially if the docks do come out on strike.'

Katherine flushed. 'Oh Milly, I'm sorry. I didn't mean that. Please forgive me. I'm so happy here.' She suddenly threw her arms round the startled Milly. 'You've made me feel I'm part of your family. And I wouldn't dream of asking you to . . . I'm sorry.'

''S all right,' said Milly, straightening up. 'It's nice having you here.' She ran her hands down the front of her overall. 'You ain't given the biscuit factory any more thought then?'

'I don't think I'd like that. I'm not used to taking orders. I'm sure I'll think of something,' she said breezily – but to herself silently added, But it will have to be soon, very soon.

Chapter 8

Sunday afternoon found Milly backwards and forwards looking out of the front-room window.

'I wonder what's happened to Dolly?' she asked, clearly agitated.

'Could be Gerald had visitors and couldn't let them come over,' said Katherine, trying to ease the situation, but deep down wondering if he'd taken it out on Dolly and Tom for helping her to move.

'But she always lets me know if that's gonner happen.'

'P'raps she didn't have a chance,' said Charlie, looking up from his newspaper. 'There's pictures in 'ere about the *Titanic*. That must'a been bloody awful, all them lives lost, and after they said it wouldn't sink, an' all.'

Katherine shuddered. All week the newspaper placards and the paper boys had been shouting the tragic news about the sinking of the *Titanic*.

'Terrible thing, ships going down. They're sorta like living things, seem to have souls somehow. I remember me dad telling me about the *Princess Alice* sinking in the Thames,' said Charlie reflectively.

'I didn't know about that,' said Milly. 'You ain't said about it before.'

'Never thought about it before. Not many bought a paper in them days, not many could read. Me dad knew all about it though as he worked at Woolwich creek – that's where it sank, run down be the *Bywell Castle*. Seven hundred lives lost, so he said.'

Ted let out a long low whistle. 'Seven hundred, that's a lot of people.'

'Yer. Poor buggers. They was coming back from a day trip to Sheerness.'

'But it ain't as many as the *Titanic*,' said Ted.

'Well, that was an ocean-going ship, son. You was on a big ship when you come back from Australia,' said Charlie to Katherine as he folded his paper.

'Yes, but it wasn't as big as the *Titanic*.'

'Must'a been exciting though,' said Ted.

'Not when you keep being seasick,' laughed Katherine. She knew Dolly had told them about her background and how she came to be living with Edwin.

'Mama said I've got a brother who lives in Australia. I might go and see him one day.'

'You have?' asked Ted.

Katherine was taken aback at Joe's statement. 'Yes, Ted, he has. Robert was twenty last month.'

'That must'a been awful for you, leaving your son,' said Milly sadly.

'Yes, yes it was.' This was the first time Milly had mentioned this.

'What was Australia like?' asked Ted eagerly.

'Hot, with a lot of flies.'

'I'd like to travel,' said Ted.

'That's a laugh. Who'd wash yer socks?' asked Charlie. 'Mind you, I admire you. That was quite a journey for you to tackle on your own.'

'Yes, it was.' Even after all these years it was still very painful for Katherine to talk about. 'I wish there was some way I could get in touch with Robert. To find out if he's well.'

'Did you ever write to him?' asked Milly.

'I did when I first arrived back in England, but I never received a reply.'

'Perhaps he didn't get it?'

'That's possible.' But Katherine suspected his father had probably destroyed it.

'Don't know what I'd do if I ever lost one of mine,' said Milly softly.

'We get some ships in from Australia, but most of 'em come from Canada or Norway. Wood's the main stuff we handle at the Surrey,' said Charlie, quickly changing the subject.

Katherine liked Charlie. He was always ready to talk, even to women, which some men still regarded as beneath them.

'Tell you what, I'll take young Joe over a ship one day,' said Charlie.

'Would you?' His eyes lit up. 'I'd really like that.'

Katherine was pleased that he was beginning to settle down, but that was due mainly to Ted, who somehow enjoyed taking him under his wing. Most evenings you could hear them laughing together.

At the end of the evening Milly was upset Dolly hadn't been to see them.

'You might get a letter tomorrow telling you why,' said Katherine. But she too was apprehensive. What if Gerald was making Dolly and Tom unhappy? She was very fond of them. Was this her fault? She could have avoided it if she had stayed. That night she slept with a heavy heart.

The following morning Milly and Katherine were wandering round the shops when Katherine noticed a sign in the window of a place called Trent's: 'Help Wanted.'

Katherine stood looking at it for a few moments. 'I'm going in to ask what kind of help they want.'

Milly looked aghast. 'You can't go and work in there.'

'Why not?'

'Well, it ain't nice. It ain't proper for a woman of your—'

'I've got to do something.'

'I know, but that? You get all sorts in those places, real rough 'ens. Mind you, I ain't got nothing against a nice bit a saveloys and pease pudding, but you working in a pie and mash shop.'

'I'm going in.' With that Katherine swept inside.

After a few moments she came out with a huge grin on her face. 'I've got a job.'

'I don't think you should be working in a place like this. When you supposed to be starting?'

'Tomorrow. Look, why don't we go in and have a cup of tea?'

'Dunno.' Milly looked about her. 'Is anybody inside?'

'A few people.'

'Well, all right then.'

Katherine pushed open the door and ushered Milly inside.

'Two teas, please,' she said to the large red-faced man behind the counter. He lifted the heavy brown enamel teapot, poured out the tea, then wiped his hands down the front of his dirty white apron. 'That'll be tuppence. Just 'cos you're gonner work here you've still gotter pay.'

Katherine smiled, putting her money on the counter. 'Of course.'

'Sugar's there.' He pushed a tin bowl towards her. The spoon was caked with sugar that had turned brown.

After putting two heaped teaspoons of sugar in each mug she replaced the wet spoon in the sugar bowl and carried the two thick mugs of steaming dark brown liquid to the table where Milly was sitting.

'Oh my Gawd, what does he call this?' asked Milly, peering into the mug.

Katherine smiled. 'Tea.'

'How long's it been stewing?'

'I dread to think.'

Milly took a sip. 'Well it's warm. I'll grant you that. You sure you want to work here?' she asked, looking round.

'Yes.' Katherine sounded confident.

'It don't look very clean.'

'Perhaps he needs a woman round the place.'

'Bet he don't pay much.'

'Well, not at first and after all he did only want a young lad.'

'So how come you got the job?'

Katherine smiled. 'It's my winning way.'

'You'll be nothing but a skivvy.'

'Watcher, Josh, me old mate,' said an old woman walking in and plonking her basket on the floor. 'I'll have a nice cup of rosy.'

Katherine was taking all this in. She leant forward and asked Milly in a whisper, 'What's rosy?'

'Rosy Lee, tea. You've certainly got a lot to learn,' laughed Milly.

Katherine laughed with her. Milly was right.

Later that day Katherine was excitedly telling Joseph about her new job.

'The pie and mash shop? I pass that place on my way to school. It doesn't look very nice.'

'Well, I'll just have to wait and see. Who knows, I may be running the place soon.'

'Why? Is the old man going to die?'

'I shouldn't think so.'

The following morning Katherine felt a little apprehensive as she made her way to start work in Trent's shop.

'Good morning,' she said breezily.

'Oh yer. Christ, you look a bit dressed up for round here.'

Katherine knew the gown she was wearing really didn't look right, but she didn't have much choice.

'Right, now get this apron on and cut up those eels.'

The apron he handed her was dirty and Katherine turned up

her nose. It smelt of fish. She squirmed when she saw the live shiny black eels wriggling about in a large tray.

He handed her a large thick knife. 'What's a matter, woman, ain't you got no stomach for it?'

She half smiled. 'Not really used to doing things like this.'

'Well, you'd better learn quick. I did tell yer I just wanted a lad, but you said you'd done a bit of cooking, and well, that persuaded me to give you a trial.'

'Yes, I know, and I'm grateful, Mr Trent.'

He threw back his head and laughed. ''Ere, you'd better call me Josh like everyone else does.'

'Thank you.'

He was a tall, big man with a beer gut. He had a large nose and a florid face. His grey hair was sparse, his small watery blue eyes looked Katherine up and down. 'So, how comes you're round this way looking for work?'

'I've had a bit of trouble.'

'Not with the law I hope?' he said quickly.

'No, family.'

'I see.'

Katherine was pleased most of the bruising on her face had faded. Milly had warned her not to tell him too much otherwise it would be all round Rotherhithe before she got home. In any case Katherine didn't have any intention of getting too friendly; she was there to work, and that was all.

All morning she was kept busy pouring out tea, dishing out faggots, saveloys, pease pudding, jellied eels, meat pies and grey lumpy mashed potatoes. She filled jugs with parsley liquor, and in between did the washing up. After the shock of seeing her behind the counter the customers were polite and quiet. Gradually they began to ignore her and she quite enjoyed listening to the banter that came from the in-depth discussions they had. The subjects ranged from the *Titanic* to the suffragettes, the latter bringing a lot of noise from the men. It was obvious to Katherine that they didn't want women to get the vote, and thought the Pankhursts were a bunch of troublemakers. But it was the talk about strikes that brought the most reaction. Nearly all the men were really worried.

Josh Trent was a gruff man, who made sure she didn't stand around. 'Go over and wipe that table down,' he growled.

She picked up a cloth, it stunk and the feel of it made her heave. It felt greasy and slimy and was full of holes.

'Cor, we don't normally see the likes of you round here,' said a man sitting in the corner next to the marble-top table she was busy trying to clean. ' 'Ere, Josh, she ain't a bad looker – what's yer missis gonner say when she claps eyes on her?'

'Nothing, she's here to work.'

Josh had told Katherine he lived above the shop, but he hadn't mentioned a wife, and why didn't he have her down here helping him out?

'Don't hang about, woman,' he yelled. 'I said wipe it, not polish the bloody pattern off it.'

A couple of the men laughed and she felt cross as she made her way back behind the counter. She couldn't see how she could polish the pattern off of a marble-top table. 'Shall I make a fresh pot of tea?' she asked Josh.

'Na, that one will do till after lunchtime. Just leave it on the stove, that'll soon get it stewing.'

Katherine shuddered as she poured out the thick dark liquid, but the customers didn't seem to mind and drank it without question.

After the lunchtime rush the customers began to drop off. Katherine picked up the cloth and started to wipe the tables again.

'I like that,' said Josh.

Katherine looked up surprised.

'You didn't wait to be told. I like that. Some of the silly cows

I've had here have to be told to do every single thing.'

Katherine only smiled. She wasn't going to tell him about the restaurant, and that she knew all about staff.

When the last customer left Katherine was wondering if she should go. 'How long shall I stay?' she asked.

'Till I say you can go.'

She felt uneasy. 'You and your wife live upstairs?' she asked casually.

'Yer. She ain't too good these days.'

'Oh I'm sorry.'

'Why should you be, you don't know her.'

Katherine didn't have an answer, so she busied herself wiping the rest of the tables.

'Look, I'm gonner go out back and start cooking the meat for tomorrow's pies. You can manage out here.'

Katherine went back behind the counter and looked round. 'I'd like to give this place a good clean,' she said to herself.

The door opened and a young girl wearing a large black hat with a pink feather draped across the brim came in. She kept her head bent and slouched up to the counter. 'Cuppa,' was all she said.

Katherine quickly pushed a mug of tea towards her. The girl's two bright pink rouged cheeks looked clownlike on her pale face. 'Are you feeling all right?' Katherine asked.

'What's it to you?'

'I just thought—'

'Well, don't think, and mind yer own bloody business.' She took her tea and sat at the far end, the smell of her cheap scent following her.

A few moments later a man walked in. He was reasonably dressed, which was very unusual for round this way. He looked around but didn't come to the counter, just went and sat with the girl.

Katherine couldn't hear what was being said, but the girl looked very unhappy as she stood up and walked outside with the man.

Well, this place certainly has some strange customers, thought Katherine. But it looks as if it could be far more interesting than the biscuit factory.

Chapter 9

Josh let Katherine go about six. She was happy as she made her way back to Milly's.

'Well,' asked Milly, pouncing on her as soon as she walked in. 'How did you get on?'

'Very well. You're certainly kept on the go during lunchtime, then when it dies down Josh goes outside to make the pies and leaves me in charge.' She laughed. 'Mind you, he takes the money with him.'

'Cheeky sod,' said Charlie. 'So it's Josh, eh?'

Katherine grinned. 'It seems he likes everybody to call him that.'

'Been worried about you all day,' said Milly, plonking a cup of tea in front of Katherine.

'You smell a bit,' said Joe.

'It's the eels. Can I take the kettle into the scullery before dinner?' she asked Milly.

'Course.'

Katherine felt better after she'd washed and changed, and all through dinner she told them about her customers.

Katherine was a little worried that Milly still hadn't heard from Dolly. 'Would you like me to write to her?' she asked as they washed up.

'No, thanks all the same, but I can drop her a line.'

Katherine enjoyed working in the pie shop, and as the week progressed she found Josh was a fair man. The customers, who on the first day regarded her with suspicion when they heard her speak, began to accept her. She also noticed that now and again Josh disappeared upstairs. She guessed it was to see to his invalid wife, but he never mentioned her. Katherine wondered if she had ever worked down here. After that very first comment none of the men spoke about her, and Katherine didn't ask.

On Friday she was curious about the young girl who often came in and sat facing the door. Today she was wearing a very tight skirt that made it difficult for her to walk, and that large black hat with the feather again. It was much too old for such a young face. She had rouge on her lips and cheeks.

'What yer staring at?' she asked when she looked up.

'Nothing,' said Katherine quickly.

The man wearing a suit came to the doorway and the girl walked out.

Katherine was full of it when she got home. 'Such a pretty girl, and her friend was a lot older than her, and better dressed than most round here. He didn't come in.'

'Don't reckon he was a friend,' said Charlie. 'Sounds like more of a customer.'

'And how would you know about that, Charlie Stevens?' asked Milly.

Charlie winked at Katherine. 'Only what I've been told, old girl.'

'That's all right then,' said Milly.

Katherine smiled at Charlie. She guessed he had seen many of her sort hanging around the docks. What drove those girls to that sort of life?

Josh was very surprised when she took in some material for cloths the next day, and on Saturday she asked to take her apron home to wash.

'You ain't getting any extra money for it.'

'I don't expect extra, I just like things to be clean.'

'Please yourself, but I don't want yer making the blokes feel uncomfortable.'

'Why should they?'

He grinned. 'Most of 'em here are used to more than a bit of dirt.'

On Saturday Katherine received her first wage of five shillings. That was just enough to pay Milly and, for the moment, she could still manage Joe's school money – but how long would that last? She would make sure she was useful and then in a few weeks' time, she would ask Josh for a rise. That evening Milly read out the letter she'd had that morning from Dolly.

'She said she couldn't get over 'cos Mr Gerald's got rid of the horse and bought one of these 'ere motor cars.'

'I was going to go with him to get that,' said Joe glumly.

'Don't worry about it,' said Ted. 'We can have a ride in it when Tom comes over.'

'They don't know when they're coming over as Gerald keeps 'em busy with a lot of wild parties, so Dolly says,' said Milly, still holding the letter.

'I bet that doesn't please Dolly. Does she mention what he said about me leaving?' asked Katherine.

'No, only that he was very cross. She wishes you all the best, by the way.'

Katherine gave Milly a weak smile. 'Give her my regards when you write.'

'I will. I shall miss 'em not coming over here,' said Milly, sniffing and stuffing the letter back in her overall pocket.

'Perhaps one day you could meet her halfway,' suggested Katherine.

Milly smiled. 'Perhaps we could.'

At the end of the second week at Trent's Katherine knew she had made the right decision. She was really enjoying her work even if it was hard on her feet all day. It was when she had a name change she knew she had been accepted and was very happy about it.

'I ain't gonner keep calling you Katherine or Mrs Carter, it's too much of a bloody mouthful. What about if I call yer Kate?'

'I don't mind.'

'You look more like a Kate.'

Kate was pleased about that.

Very soon all the men followed suit. Some of the older ones enjoyed a laugh when she had to ask them to explain cockney slang, and she wasn't sure they were always telling her the truth. After a while many told her to call them by their first names, so it was that she began to talk about Percy, Bert, Bill and many more. Sometimes during their heated conversations she was asked her opinion, but she was careful how she answered. She didn't want to upset anyone, least of all Josh. She still hadn't seen Mrs Trent and nobody ever mentioned her.

Milly came in one morning when she was out shopping.

Katherine gave her a beaming smile. 'Sit down, I'll bring you over a cuppa.'

Milly laughed as she looked round. 'I must say it looks a bit cleaner in here. What yer done to the place?'

'Nothing really,' she said, putting the mug on the table. 'Just washed the lace curtain and cleaned the window and underneath the tables.'

'Well, it certainly looks brighter and better without all those dead flies lining the windowsill.'

'And these cloths smell better. Yes, Josh, before you say anything I'll put the money in the box. He thinks you might be trying to get away without paying.'

Milly fumbled in her purse. 'I wouldn't dream of it.'

'This one's on me,' said Katherine.

'Just been in the ironmongers. Young Briony don't look very happy.'

Katherine looked at Josh, who was deep in conversation with a well-dressed man Katherine hadn't seen before. 'You don't think,' she came round the counter and wiped down a table next to Milly's so she could lower her voice, 'you know, that Mr Wilks . . . you don't think he's . . .?'

'Dunno.'

'I wish I could talk to her.'

'Her mother's baby's due any day now, p'raps you could pop over then.'

'I could do, I could take her a little gift.'

A small boy wearing such a large cap that it almost covered his eyes, came in. He was very short and could hardly reach the counter. Standing on tiptoes he put a bowl and money on the counter. 'Faggots and pease pudding, please, miss.'

Katherine filled the bowl. 'Thank you, young Walter. How's your granny today?' She looked at Josh, he wasn't facing her direction so she quickly spooned another dollop of pease pudding in the bowl.

'She ain't too bad. This warm weather's doing her feet in, though. Swelled up like big balloons, they have. They look really rotten. 'Bye.' He picked up his bowl and left.

Katherine smiled. 'He's a nice little lad, told me his granny looks after him.'

Milly laughed. 'Good job this place don't belong to you otherwise they'd all be round here for a handout.'

'Shh.'

'Well, I must go. See you later.'

Josh was still in conversation and Katherine carried on with her chores. When she went out to the back yard to get some more potatoes ready to peel for the next day she heard someone calling.

She hurried back into the shop. 'Josh, I'm sorry to interrupt but I think your wife's calling.'

He looked annoyed. 'You can see I'm busy. Go up and find out what she wants.'

Katherine smoothed down her apron and made her way up the stairs.

'Yoo-hoo,' she called out. 'Which room are you in?'

'I'm in the bloody bedroom. Who are you and what d'yer want?'

Katherine pushed open the door from behind which the voice had come. The smell almost took her breath away. The room was stuffy and stank of urine and an unwashed body. It took a moment or two for her eyes to get accustomed to the gloom as the curtains were drawn.

'Who the bloody hell are you? And what yer doing up here? Where's Josh?' The woman who was sitting up in bed was small and wizened. She became very agitated. Her thin mouth was turned down and from her pale lined face faded blue eyes set in deep dark sockets stared out. They looked Katherine up and down. Her grey frizzy hair stuck up like a witch's and it didn't look as if it had been brushed or washed in years. Her gnarled hands and bent fingers twitched and pulled at the bedclothes.

'I heard you call out and as Josh is—'

'Josh? What you calling him Josh for?'

'He ask me to.'

'Did he now? So are you his fancy bit?'

'No. I work for him,' said Katherine haughtily.

'Oh you do, do yer? And how long 'as this cosy little setup been going on?'

'I've been employed by Mr Trent for three weeks now.'

'Oh, so it's Mr Trent now, is it?'

'Can I get you anything?'

'No you can't Miss High-and-Mighty. And where did he find you?'

'I answered his notice.'

'I bet you did. I told him to get a boy, not another tart. Mind you, you're a bit old for him, he normally likes 'em young.'

Katherine was finding it hard to keep her temper. Who did this woman think she was talking to? She wasn't a child. But she knew she had to hold her tongue, her job could depend on it.

'Your husband is busy at the moment, so if I can't be of any help I'll leave you in peace.' Katherine turned to go.

'No, hang on a minute. You say you work for Josh? What's yer name?'

'Kather— Kate.'

'Well, Kate, you can bring me up a cuppa, and I don't want any of that stewed stuff he dishes up to the customers. Make me a nice fresh pot. And if there is any hanky-panky going on down there, I'll soon find out about it. Got lots of friends who comes and sees me and tells me all what goes on. So make sure you keep yer nose clean.'

Katherine closed the door and took a breath. How could he let his wife stay in a room like that? And how long had she been there? What was wrong with her? And who looked after her? And who came to see her? It wasn't in the day, unless they came in the back way. All these questions were going over and over in her mind as she slowly made her way down the bare wooden stairs.

'Oh, there you are. Go on out front. What did old Nellie want?'

'A cup of tea.'

'Pour her one out and I'll pop it up.'

'But she wanted a fresh one.'

'She'll have what she's given. Well, go on then, move yourself. By the way, that was the landlord, Mr Sharman, I was talking to.

Make sure he talks to me when he comes for the rent. Now get Nellie's tea.'

Katherine hurried to the shop and poured out a mug of dark liquid. As she passed it to Josh she felt sorry for his wife. Fancy just lying there. She would wait till the right moment, then ask him if she could do something.

That evening she was full of it when she got home as she now called it.

'I'm going to ask him if I go in an hour earlier perhaps I could try to make her comfortable.'

Milly waved at her the wooden spoon she was using to stir something on the range. 'First it's Briony, then the kid in the shop, now it's his wife. Nobody worried about you when you was down and finished up with a pasting.'

'That was different.'

'Why?'

'I don't know. Perhaps it's because I like to think I can look after myself, and others aren't so strong.'

Milly turned and continued her stirring.

'Besides, I had you and Dolly looking after me.'

Milly laughed.

Charlie looked very worried when he came in. 'Looks like we might be on strike,' he said, throwing his cap on the chair.

'Oh no,' said Milly, hanging his clothes up as usual.

'Been dreading this for weeks. You'll have to manage somehow, love, if the worst comes to the worst.'

Katherine sat quietly listening to the distress in Charlie's voice.

'Don't worry, we'll get by,' said Milly, dishing up the dinner. 'There's plenty worse off than us.'

'I was hoping to give Olive's new baby something nice,' said Charlie.

'Don't worry, Dad. We'll manage,' said Ted. 'With me at work and Joe's mum, we'll all get by.'

Katherine smiled at Ted. He was a shy, sensible lad who didn't quite know what to call Katherine.

'And Olive will understand,' added Milly. ''Sides, it might not be for long.'

'Dunno about that. The miners and dockers up north have been out for weeks – that was till they got the minimum wage bill passed for miners.'

'Now stop all this talk about strikes and get on with your dinner.'

The rest of the meal was finished in silence.

As the week went on Katherine was getting more and more concerned about Briony.

'Do you ever see her now?' she asked Joe.

'Sometimes.'

'Do you ever speak to her?'

'No.'

'Joseph, next time you see her could you ask her how she is?'

'No I won't. She thinks I'm posh and stuck-up.'

'Perhaps you could try?'

'She'll probably spit in me eye.'

'She wouldn't do a thing like that, and it's *my* eye.'

He giggled. 'No it ain't, it's mine.' He ran away laughing.

Katherine could see she didn't stand a chance trying to keep him speaking well now he went to school here, but did she really mind? She smiled, not as long as he was happy, and next Sunday, 12 May, was his thirteenth birthday. Despite the fear of the forthcoming strike Milly and Katherine planned a little tea on that day. Olive and her husband were also coming. Katherine was sorry Dolly and Ted wouldn't be there, but in the letters Milly had from her, Dolly said they were all right. Katherine would have liked to have asked Briony over, but knew Joseph wouldn't approve of that.

Chapter 10

On Sunday the birthday tea was a great success. Joseph was thrilled with his drawing book from Ted. Olive gave him a book about boats, and Milly and Charlie gave him some socks. Katherine bought him a model of a motor car.

'Perhaps you'll have a real one, one day,' she said laughing.

'I'm sure I will,' he said with a serious look on his face. 'You see, I intend to get a job that teaches me to drive.'

'You've got another year at school yet,' said Ted.

'I know. I wish I could leave now. That Briony goes to work and she's only thirteen.'

'Don't think she's ever been to school,' said Milly. 'So you see how lucky you are.'

Joseph didn't have an answer.

He was pleased to receive a birthday card from Dolly and Tom.

'I'd like to go and see them one day. P'raps Uncle Gerald would give me a ride in his new motor, and he might teach me to drive.'

'I don't think that would be such a good idea,' said Katherine.

'See, you always stop me from doing what I want.'

Katherine left that statement unanswered.

'I will, you know.'

That too was left unanswered.

It wasn't till the following week that Katherine had the opportunity to talk to Josh about Nellie. She was pouring out a mug of tea he said he wanted.

'If you like I could take this up. Perhaps she would like me to comb her hair and try to make her feel a bit comfortable.'

'I pay you to help me, not act as nursemaid to her,' was the answer she received as he took the mug from her.

But it worried Katherine that his wife could lie upstairs day after day without a visitor or nurse.

When Katherine told Milly how she felt, Milly reminded her that he was the boss.

'That's as may be, but I still think it's heartless to leave her alone like that.'

Katherine knew she had to mind her Ps and Qs as jobs were going to get harder to come by, as at that moment, for most people, their biggest worry was the looming dock strike.

All week the men had been in and out of the shop, going to meetings and reporting back to those who had managed to get work that day. They had stood on the docks waiting to be called for work, then, disheartened, had come to sit in groups with their heads bent deep in conversation and worried expressions on their faces. Many times raised voices sent Josh over to quieten them down. But he was more concerned that they wouldn't have enough money for a cuppa.

'Feel sorry for some of 'em,' said Charlie after he'd been to another meeting. 'Worried sick about their little 'ens. They was saying they'll have to get the Salvation Army to open up soup kitchens or something if the worst comes to the worst.'

'Well, that's not a bad idea,' said Milly. 'After all, most of 'em spend a lot of time in the pub when they've got a few bob, and when they've had a few they all end up buying the *War Cry*.'

Katherine listened to these conversations with great sadness. These people had nothing but were willing to stand by their fellow workers and their convictions.

* * *

She was walking home one evening when Briony caught up with her.

''Allo, missis,' she said cheerfully. 'Heard you was working in the pie shop.'

Katherine smiled. 'Yes I am. I'm so pleased to see you, Briony.'

'Why?'

'Well, it's been quite a while since we bumped into each other, and I'd like to get to know you.'

'Why're you so interested in me, missis?'

Katherine was a little taken aback at her directness. 'I think you're a nice intelligent young woman, and I'd like to talk to you, that's all.'

'Your son don't think I'm nice. He's a right stuck-up little sod just 'cos he goes to school and wears posh clothes.'

'You mustn't take any notice of Joseph. Would you like to go to school?'

'Yer. Mr Wilks is teaching me to add up, he says I'm a quick learner.'

'Does Mrs Wilks ever come in the shop?' asked Katherine tentatively.

'Oh yer. She's nice. D'yer know, I can read a bit. Me mum taught me. She went to a Catholic school in Ireland for a little while before she met me dad.'

'I could always help you with your reading,' said Katherine.

Briony's eyes shone. 'Would you? I'd like that. Mind you, I don't get a lot of time. P'raps one Sunday afternoon when Dad's sleeping it off I could come over.'

'Of course. Whenever you can.'

'You must really be down on yer luck to come and live round here and have to go to work.'

'Yes, I think you could say that. How's your mother?'

'Not too bad. I wish she'd chuck me old man out though, and not keep having babies.'

'But your father does work to feed you.'

Briony laughed. 'He only goes to work to get money for booze and the horses. If we're lucky we might get any that's left – that's if he's won a few bob on the gee-gees. I could kill him sometimes. Mind you, me mum's clever. She always goes down his pockets when he's sleeping it off. Where's your old man? Did he do a runner?'

'No, it was me that left him.'

Briony's big blue eyes opened wide in amazement 'No! You mean you walked off and left him?'

Katherine nodded. She wouldn't say from the other side of the world – well, not yet.

'Did he beat yer?'

'Once.' Katherine thought that would be enough of an answer.

'And you walked off and left him just for that?' Briony laughed again, lighting up her pretty face, making her blue eyes twinkle. 'Christ, me dad beats me mum nearly every week. He reckons it keeps her under control, 'specially when he finds she's taken his last few bob.'

Katherine stopped and took Briony's arm. 'But your mother's having a baby.'

'That don't matter. If she lost this one she'd soon be having another.'

Katherine was shocked. 'Does your father hit you and your brothers and sisters?'

'Course. And with his belt.'

Katherine was amazed that this child took this way of life for granted. 'What about Mr Wilks?'

Briony smiled. 'He don't hit me. He's not a bad old man. In fact he can be quite kind at times. Lets me bring a broken candle home sometimes for free.'

Katherine wanted to ask if he did anything to her, but thought better of it. She would wait till she'd gained her trust. If his wife was around perhaps all the talk was rumours. They turned into Croft Street.

'When's your mother's baby due?'

'Couple of weeks, I think. I ain't never gonner get married.'

'You're young yet, you may change your mind one day.'

'Na, don't think so.' Briony stopped. 'There's that bloody priest again and that old Mrs Duke nosing.'

Katherine had been avoiding Mrs Duke since she started work. She didn't want her asking too many questions.

Katherine stood with Briony a short distance away and watched the bent figure dressed in long black flowing robes come out of the Addamses' house. He stopped and, looking back, shook his head. He took a handkerchief from a pocket, dabbed at his forehead then, holding the handkerchief to his nose, hurried away.

'I bet me mum's given him her last couple of pence. He tells her she'll rot in hell if she don't pay her way to heaven.'

'That's terrible,' said Katherine. 'He can't be a true man of the Church.'

'Dunno about that. All I know is that he puts the fear of God up me mum. He gets her on her knees chanting and patting her head and waving his smelly incense about. Do you go to church?'

'No, I'm afraid I don't.'

'I bunk off when I should be there. Can't stand all that stuff. Better go and help me mum. 'Bye, it's bin nice talking to yer.' Briony crossed the road.

'See you're still here then?' Mrs Duke folded her arms as Katherine walked past. 'Thought you might have moved on before now.'

'I'm very happy staying with Milly.'

'I bet she is as well.'

Katherine felt through the letter box for the key and quickly opened the front door. 'Been nice talking to you,' she said, closing the door behind her.

Katherine told Milly about the conversation she'd just had with Briony. 'She said the priest took money from her mother. I think that's dreadful.'

'It's a way of life with some of 'em round here,' said Milly.

'How can they take from people like that?'

'Fear,' came the reply.

'Of what?' asked Katherine.

'Not finishing up in heaven.'

All evening Katherine couldn't get Briony off her mind. She was trying to think of an excuse for going over and talking to her mother, but Milly advised her not to interfere.

'They won't thank you, and more often than not she'll get a bigger hiding from her old man for telling you what goes on in there. 'Sides, she might be over for a reading lesson.'

'I'd like that,' said Katherine, beginning to feel at ease living here. She had no regrets. At first Joseph had been troublesome, but he appeared to be settling down now he'd found he and Ted had a lot in common, and their laughter was a joy to hear.

Weeks went past and Briony didn't take up Katherine's offer to teach her to read.

'P'raps she'll have more time in the summer,' Milly said.

One fine warm evening, as Katherine made her way home from work, she couldn't believe her eyes when she turned into Croft Street. It seemed all the women were out of their houses and huddled in small groups on their doorsteps, talking in low whispers. Some were sitting knitting or sewing while children played in the gutter; others were drinking tea. An ambulance was outside the Addamses' house.

She hurried across the road, hoping to see Briony.

'Katherine, psst! Katherine!' called Milly in a loud whisper, beckoning to her frantically.

Katherine picked her way back over the cobblestones. 'What's happened?' she asked.

'It's Mrs Addams, been taken bad be all accounts.'

'Who called the ambulance?'

'It seems old Ida Fairfield. She was delivering the baby when complications set in. She sent one of the boys round for the doctor and he sent for the ambulance. It's been there a long while,' said Mrs Duke, who was sitting on her windowsill.

'Is Mrs Fairfield a nurse?' asked Katherine.

'Dunno,' said Mrs Duke. 'She might have been. She does most things round here. Helps out with a few potions when somebody's ill. She births 'em, lays 'em out, and she—'

One of the Addams boys came out and ran up the road, stopping Mrs Duke as she was in full flow.

She stood up. 'Reckon he's gorn for the priest,' she said excitedly.

'Oh no,' said Katherine. 'You don't think . . .?'

'Not surprised at what goes on over there. Be happy release if you ask me for the poor little cow.'

'You mean it could be Mrs Addams?'

'They wouldn't make all this fuss if it was just the baby. Na, it's got to be her. They'd just wrap the baby up and take it away.'

'What about the children?' Katherine was shocked at the way she was writing Mrs Addams off.

'They'll be better off in a home if you ask me. Was surprised to see you in Trent's. Guessed you was working as I see you go out the same time every day, but I thought that place was a bit below you. I nearly came in and had a cuppa when I saw you, but thought better of it. Can't go lining Trent's pockets.'

Katherine gave her a wan smile. To have Mrs Duke come in while she was working was the last thing she wanted.

'Katherine's only doing him a favour, just helping him out,' said Milly defensively.

Mrs Duke gave Milly a funny look. Katherine knew she didn't believe her.

When the priest walked down Croft Street Mrs Duke's face took on a smug expression. 'See, I knew I was right.'

'Is her husband in there?' asked Katherine.

'Na, he ain't home from the pub yet.'

'What about Briony?'

'She ain't home from work yet.' Mrs Duke certainly knew all that was going on.

'Shouldn't someone go and get Briony?'

'Not till we're sure the poor cow's gorn,' said Mrs Duke.

Katherine felt guilty at standing around waiting. She wanted to go inside, but like the rest of them she felt she had to wait and see what was going to happen. This was a major event. Normally they would all be hiding behind their lace curtains but today they were outside filled with anticipation and curiosity.

After a while the ambulance went away empty. Then the doctor and priest came out and stood for a while deep in conversation.

'She's gorn,' whispered Mrs Duke.

'It might be just the baby,' said Katherine.

'Na. It's got to be her.'

The priest and doctor moved away.

'What should we do?' asked Katherine. 'Those children will be in the house alone with Mrs Addams, and if she's—'

'Don't worry about it. When Ida Fairfield comes out she'll give us all the details,' said Mrs Duke knowingly. 'Think I'll just pop inside and bring a chair out. This bloody windowsill's a bit cold on me bum, and all this standing about makes me feet ache and don't do me piles much good either.'

'Ida Fairfield's probably laying her out now,' said Milly.

'She makes a very nice job of it as well,' said Mrs Duke. 'But Gawd help yer if you hang on to the pennies she puts on their eyes, she nearly goes mad.' Mrs Duke came up close. She looked around before adding the next sentence in a low voice. 'And if yer ever gets in trouble – you know what I mean – well, Ida's yer girl.'

Katherine laughed. 'I don't think I'll need Ida for that,' but she was intrigued with this conversation.

Once more a young boy came out the house and ran down the road.

'She lends money as well, you know,' said Mrs Duke, straightening up.

Katherine smiled. Ida Fairfield sounded like a very enterprising woman.

Charlie walked up to them. 'What's going on?' he asked.

Milly went into great detail of what they thought had happened.

'Well I want me dinner, so you'd better come in.'

'You don't sound very happy, mate,' said Mrs Duke. 'Who's crawled up your arse?'

'Out on bleeding strike, ain't we? I tell yer, missis, this is gonner be a bloody long hard struggle.'

'Well, we'll just have to make the best of it, won't we,' said Milly.

'Mrs Duke, will you knock and let me know when Briony gets home? I'd like to have a word with her,' said Katherine.

'Course, girl.'

Charlie, Milly and Katherine went inside the house.

'What d'you want to see Briony about then?' asked Milly.

'If it is her mother she may not have a black frock for her funeral.'

'I don't suppose she has.'

'Perhaps we can alter one of mine. Poor Briony, what sort of life will she have now?'

'Dunno. Was it all that good before?'

'Who will look after the rest of them?'

'Dunno. We'll have to wait and find out after the funeral,' said Milly.

'Don't reckon it'll be much of one,' said Charlie.

'But surely the Church . . .'

'Dunno about that,' said Milly. 'Mind you, we ain't had an Irish funeral round here before.'

'I believe they have a wake,' said Katherine.

'What's a wake, Mama?' asked Joseph.

'Well, they celebrate, have singing and drinking.'

'Now that don't sound a bad idea to me,' said Charlie grinning.

'And who will pay for all this then?' asked Milly.

'Don't know,' replied Katherine.

They had almost finished their meal when Mrs Duke banged on the door.

Katherine hurried down the passage.

'She's just come in, but mind, the old man's over there now. Can I come in?'

Katherine looked over her shoulder. 'Well I don't . . .' But Mrs Duke had pushed past her.

'Got a cuppa, Milly? I'm fair parched.'

Katherine looked at Charlie and shrugged her shoulders as Mrs Duke plonked herself at the table.

When Milly put a cup of tea in front of her, Mrs Duke poured some in the saucer. Joseph sat looking on silently as she slurped this noisily.

'Look, if you and Ted's finished,' said Milly, noting Joseph's face, 'why don't you go upstairs?'

They scurried away from the table like a pair of startled rabbits, laughing all the way.

'Now, Mrs Duke, I didn't want the boys to hear. So is she dead?'

'Yer, and it seems, so Ida said, that her body was covered with bruises, a right mess, great weeping sores, and she was so thin that her bones were almost sticking through her skin.'

Katherine was shocked, and relieved they'd finished their meal.

Mrs Duke continued to hold the conversation. 'Well, the old man wasn't very pleased when he found that Ida had laid her out.'

'That's so very sad. So what's going to happen now?' asked Katherine.

'Dunno. Ida said the old man fell to his knees and, grabbing her in his arms, began rocking back and forth and wailing, bloody hypocrite. When Briony came in she took one look at her father and walked away. She's a good kid. Mind you, Ida said it's like a madhouse over there. There's the old man crying, the kids shouting and poor Briony trying to get 'em a bit of tea.'

'What happened to the baby?' asked Milly.

'Dead,' said Mrs Duke, very matter-of-factly. 'Ida wrapped it up in a piece of dirty cloth and laid it beside her, another girl be all accounts. They're gonner be buried together, so Ida said.'

Katherine shuddered. 'That poor woman.'

'Well, in some ways it's a happy release for her and the kid.' Mrs Duke was certainly enjoying her moment of glory.

'What will happen to the children?' asked Katherine.

'Probably finish up in a home,' sniffed Mrs Duke.

'Will the neighbours get up a collection for a wreath?' Katherine wondered.

Charlie laughed. 'You'll be lucky. With most of 'em on strike they've got to think of their bellies before they think of flowers.'

'Yes, but not all of them work at the docks,' said Katherine.

'No, but a lot like the shops and the pub rely on the dockers for their money,' said Milly.

'Well, I'd go and knock on the doors,' said Mrs Duke, 'but me feet play me up something rotten in this weather.' She looked pointedly at Katherine. 'I reckon someone should try. At least it shows we care.'

'Do we?' asked Charlie.

'I care about the children,' said Katherine.

''Sides, what good's flowers? That won't help 'em,' said Charlie.

'It shows a sign of respect.'

'I reckon any money you did manage to get should be given to them and not buy flowers,' said Milly.

'Any money you give 'em he'll use to buy booze,' said Charlie.

'Not if I give it to Briony,' said Katherine, warming to the idea of helping.

So it was settled that on Friday night Katherine and Milly would start a collection for the late Mrs Addams's family.

'Good luck, and I only hope you know what you're doing,' said Charlie offhandedly.

Chapter 11

At seven thirty on Friday evening Katherine and Milly set out to start collecting along both sides of Croft Street for the Addams children. Although Katherine wasn't expecting to be showered with money, she didn't expect to meet with such aggression. Many times they had doors slammed in their faces.

When front doors were opened wide enough for her to see inside, it was a shock. The noise, shouting and cursing made her want to run. Men waved their fists at her, and the babies sitting on women's wide hips were dirty and unclothed. Passages were full of rubbish and dirt, and some of the smells indescribable. There were a few like Milly who kept their homes neat and clean but these were rare. There were women with fear in their eyes who hardly opened their front doors, and those that did talked in whispers, telling her they were sorry but they hadn't received any money from the breadwinner yet. Others told her in no uncertain words to push off. Family came first round here. Some were sympathetic and managed to give her the odd halfpenny and farthing. All in all they managed to collect one shilling and thrupence ha'penny.

'It's not a lot,' said Katherine, as they sat at the table counting out farthings, halfpennies and pennies.

'Didn't expect a lot,' said Milly. 'Still, it's a nice thought.'

'I'll find out when the funeral is and I'll get three penno'th of flowers from us and give this money to Briony,' said Katherine.

'You don't have to get flowers, you know,' said Milly.

'I know, but I want to, and I said I'll pay for them.'

Milly looked put out. 'Just 'cos Charlie's on strike—'

Katherine put her hand on Milly's. 'You've helped me out, now it's my turn.'

'I'd try and get her on her own if I was you.'

Katherine nodded. 'Yes, I don't fancy going over there when Mr Addams is around.'

The following day when Katherine finished work she made her way to the ironmongers, pleased to see Briony was still there. She was busy filling a customer's can with paraffin. Katherine noted her pale face and dark circles under her lovely eyes. Her face lit up when she caught sight of Katherine.

''Allo, missis. What d'you want?'

'What time do you finish?'

'Not long now.'

'I'll wait outside and we can walk home together.'

Katherine gave Mr Wilks a smile and went out.

'So, how are you managing?' asked Katherine as they began to walk home.

'Not too bad. Young Bridget helps a bit. The boys can be a bit of a handful, but we'll manage.'

'Mr Wilks treating you all right?'

'Yer, he said I can have an hour off for me mum's funeral.'

'That's kind of him. How's the rest of the family?'

'All right. They don't like seeing Mum and that baby in the front room, though. Young Billy keeps having nightmares and Dad's threatened to lock him in the coffin and bury him with Mum if he don't behave.'

Katherine gasped. 'I'm sure your father doesn't mean it.'

'You don't know me dad. D'you know, he picked up our Kenny – he's our youngest – shoved the dead baby out the way and put Kenny in with Mum. He didn't half scream when Dad made him cuddle the cold stiff baby.'

Katherine couldn't believe it. This man sounded wicked or mad or both. 'When's the funeral?'

'Friday.'

'Have you got a black frock?'

Briony shook her head.

'I'm sure I can find you one. Why don't you come over to Milly's later on and we will sort something out for you?'

'Dad won't be having me accept charity.'

'It's not charity. I've got far too many gowns and I'd like you to have one.'

'That's ever so kind of you. I'll try and get over later.'

Milly was very angry when Katherine told her what the father did to the children.

'If you ask me, he wants locking up,' was Charlie's comment. 'He'd better watch out when those boys get a bit older. The old man might be found lying face down in some dark alley with his throat cut.'

'Don't talk like that, Charlie,' said Milly. 'It ain't nice. And don't you go saying anything in front of that young girl when she comes over.'

He grinned. 'As if I would.'

When Briony called, Milly and Katherine took her up to Katherine's bedroom.

'Cor, what a smashing room,' she said, standing in the doorway.

'Yes, I'm very lucky, Milly really does look after me,' said Katherine. 'Now, let me see. I think we can do something with this.' She held out a plain black cotton dress.

'I can't take that.'

'I don't see why not,' said Katherine.

'Let me hold it against you. I'll be able to take it in and shorten it a bit,' said Milly, promptly taking charge. 'Mind you, it won't want a lot off the bottom. You're quite tall, young Briony.'

Briony giggled as she held the dress against her. 'It is ever so nice, and I would feel ever so grand. But I don't think I should. Dad might not like it.'

'Don't be silly, of course you must,' said Katherine.

'Well, could I have it a bit shorter? Seen some pictures in a book about the ladies wearing frocks that don't come down to the ground.'

Milly smiled. 'I'll take a lot of this fullness out as well.'

'Could you make our Bridget one out of the scraps? That's if you don't mind.'

'Which one is Bridget?' asked Katherine.

'The next one down to me. She's gonner go to work soon.'

'How old is she?' asked Milly.

'She's a year younger than me. She'll be thirteen next month, and I'll be fourteen then, so Mum said.'

Milly looked at Katherine. 'I'll just pop down and get me pins.' She left the room.

'Briony, Milly and I have got a little money from the neighbours.'

'What you telling me for?'

'We want you to have it to help out.'

'What? I can't take it.'

'Why?'

'Me dad'll go mad if he thought everybody was feeling sorry for us.'

'Does he have to know?'

'He'll find it. He can sniff out money.'

'Well, it's not a lot. One and thrupence ha'penny to be exact. But it might help.' Katherine went to her dressing table and put the money into Briony's hand.

'I don't know what to say. I shouldn't be taking—'

Katherine patted her hand. 'Don't say anything, just make sure your father doesn't get his hands on it.'

On Friday evening Milly told Katherine the funeral was a very noisy affair with Mr Addams hanging on to the coffin weeping and wailing. The children were crying and looking terrified as they followed the handcart and the priest, who was chanting loudly and waving the incense about as they went slowly down the road.

'Yours was the only flowers. Briony and Bridget looked nice in their frocks. D'you know, young Briony wasn't crying.'

'She was probably storing it up for later. Grief's a funny thing,' said Katherine.

'I expect she's a bit worried about what will happen to her and the kids,' said Milly.

'She might have to give up her little job, which would be a pity as she does like it there.'

'Can't see that. Her and the boy that goes to work are the only ones bringing in any money, that's not counting the two boys that run a few errands. Don't think the old man gives 'em much, not to feed 'em and pay the rent.'

'Who'll look after the little ones when Bridget goes to work?'

'Dunno. Like Mrs Duke said, I reckon they'll put 'em in a home. That kind don't have any hope, do they?' said Milly with a sigh.

'No, they don't,' said Katherine.

On Sunday morning Katherine sat up ready to get out of bed. She sat on the edge to gather her senses. She didn't feel right, and when she stood up she felt giddy and nauseous. She quickly sat down as hot flushes swept over her. Was this confirming her worst fears? Since she moved in with Milly she hadn't had the curse, but she put it down to all the upset she'd had, and her age, even though she thought she was a bit young to be starting the change. Now she was sure what was wrong with her. She was pregnant, and Gerald was the father. She burst into tears. This was the worst thing that could happen to her just as she was getting her life together.

After a while, when her tears subsided, she slowly dressed and made her way downstairs.

'Good morning, Milly.' She tried to sound cheerful.

Milly looked up from the frying pan. 'You all right?'

Katherine sat at the table. The smell of cooking was turning her stomach and her legs felt like jelly. She was barely able to stand. 'Yes, I feel a bit funny, think I might be getting a cold.'

Milly gave her curious look. 'At this time of year?'

Katherine smiled and nodded.

'I must admit you do look a bit off colour.'

'Well, we do get all sorts in the pie shop, coughing and sneezing all over the place.'

'Suppose you do, fancy a bit of bacon?'

She swallowed hard. 'No thanks. As it's a nice day I think I'll go for a walk.'

'Please yourself.'

Katherine took her coat from off the nail behind the door and hurried up the passage. Outside she stood taking in great gulps of fresh air. She prayed Mrs Duke wasn't looking out of her window waiting to pounce on anyone to talk to.

Katherine's mind was churning over and over as she walked along. Questions were coming thick and fast. What was she going to do? What would Joseph say? What would they do for money if she had to give up her job? Or be given the sack if the strike continued for very long and Josh's business went down? With Charlie not working Milly couldn't keep her for nothing. The disgrace. She hated Gerald so much she wanted to kill him. He had taken everything from her, and now this. She didn't want his baby, she wanted to die.

As Katherine slowly made her way towards the docks she was confronted by the scene she had witnessed every day since moving to this area. Screaming children playing, fighting and racing round the street. Women sitting outside their front doors knitting or with babies at their breasts, young ones clambering over them, while others were yelling and shouting at their offspring. Could she finish up living like this? With all the noise and confusion she couldn't think straight. The smell of dinners cooking wafted out of the open doors and made her vomit. She stopped and held on to the lamppost.

'Go on, move on, yer dirty cow,' said a woman tutting and tucking a baby into a pram.

'Looks like a right old tart ter me. Bet yer bin on the beer all night,' said a woman, coming up to her and pushing her along the road.

'Bin on somethink or someone,' yelled another. 'Go on, shove orf, you old tom.'

Katherine wiped her mouth and after taking a deep breath hurried past them, afraid they would harm her. She didn't know where she was going. Should she go and see Gerald? But what good would that do? She couldn't marry him. She didn't want to marry him. Tears ran down her face. She felt so miserable and alone as she wandered on. This was the dock area and she didn't know it at all. Katherine thought about the swirling water. Could that be the answer to her problem? No, only cowards took their own lives. Besides, what about Joseph? There must be another way out.

When she turned the corner some girls had one end of a rope tied to the lamppost. At the other end a young girl wearing a dirty torn overall over a brown frock was busy turning the rope. A girl in the middle was skipping, and they both were chanting: 'Touch collar never holler. Touch lip never catch dip, never catch the fever.'

Katherine stopped and brushed her tears from her cheeks with her hand.

'What yer staring at, missis?' asked the young girl who was turning the rope.

'Sorry, was I staring?'

'Yes you was. What yer crying for?'

'Nothing. I seem to be lost.'

She stopped turning the rope. 'Well, yer don't wanner go down there.' She pointed along the road.

'Why?'

'Oh come on, Rose, don't stop and talk to 'er,' said the girl who was standing with the rope at her feet.

'No, she's upset, and we can't let her go down there.'

'Well, if she don't know, well then that's up to her.'

'Excuse me,' said Katherine. 'But what is down there?'

The first girl pointed to the name plate on the red-brick wall. It said 'Redfiff Road'.

'Down there's the smallpox receiving station. And if you go down there you could finish up with the pox.'

Katherine shuddered. 'Smallpox? Thank you,' she said, turning away.

The girls began laughing and chanting again. Were they laughing at her? At this moment she didn't care, she had to get back to Milly, her only friend.

Soon Katherine was back on familiar ground. She had made up her mind. As much as she hated the thought, she would ask Milly about Ida Fairfield.

Chapter 12

Katherine sat at the table and picked at her dinner.

'You sure you're all right?' asked Milly.

'Yes, of course.'

'Well, you look a bit peaky to me,' said Charlie.

Katherine smiled. 'I'm all right, really.'

'If you don't want that potato can I have it?' asked Joseph.

'Of course.'

'Here, don't you go telling your mates at school I don't feed you,' said Milly.

'I ain't got any mates,' he said, stabbing at the potato and putting it on his plate.

'Don't give me that,' said Charlie.

'They all think I'm too posh. Can't wait to start work.'

'And what are you going to do?' asked Katherine.

'I told you before, learn to drive a motor car. That's why I need feeding. I'm a growing boy,' he said, grinning.

Ted laughed. 'He's always hanging round that new place looking at the motor cars. You should see his sketches of 'em.'

Katherine knew she should be taking more interest in this conversation and be pleased that Ted and Joseph were getting on so well, but she couldn't concentrate.

All afternoon and evening Katherine was hoping to get Milly on her own but the situation never arose.

The following morning when she left the house, the thought of working with food was just about as much as she could bear.

' 'Allo there, Kate,' said Josh when she walked in. 'Christ, you look bloody awful. You all right?'

'Yes, thanks.'

'You don't look it.'

She smiled. 'That's not very complimentary.'

'Ain't known for me compliments.'

'Well, don't worry about me.'

Katherine knew she had to keep her food down and herself busy.

As usual they had the dockers filling the shop. It had become a meeting place for the strikers. At times the arguments became very heated and everybody appeared to be shouting at once. Josh wasn't happy that only a few mugs of tea were being consumed. Ron, the bookies' runner, wasn't happy either: nobody was putting a bet on. Josh had pointed him out to Katherine weeks ago. He'd told her what he did was illegal.

'So, just remember to say nothing to the coppers if they ask. You don't know nothing. It pays to keep yer nose clean and yer mouth shut, and out of other people's affairs round here.'

After the dockers left Josh looked worried. 'I hope this strike ain't gonner go on for too long. Still got me overheads, and you, to pay. Had the landlord in, he's worried about his rent.'

Katherine didn't need reminding that ultimately she could lose her job because of the strike.

Josh went out the back. Katherine was busy wiping the tables down when the young girl who had come in on her very first day appeared. She had been in before and after a short while men came and sat with her – most times people Katherine had never seen before. Then the girl would leave with them. Some were scruffy and dirty. Katherine shuddered at the thought of what she did with these strangers.

Katherine poured out her tea, the girl took it and sat in the far corner like before.

'What yer staring at?' the girl suddenly shouted out.

'Sorry, I was miles away.'

'Yer you was. What's a posh cow like you doing in a place like this?'

'Earning my living,' said Katherine aggressively.

The girl laughed. 'Bet yer don't get much.'

Katherine decided not to answer.

'Kate,' yelled Josh from the back. 'Pour the missis out a cuppa.'

'Would you like me to take it up to her?' Katherine asked eagerly, smoothing down her apron. She had been waiting for an opportunity to go up and see Nellie Trent again.

'You could do while we're quiet. But don't stand around chatting, and don't go putting any fancy ideas in her head. And don't go telling her too much about the strike. I don't want her worrying.'

Katherine smiled as she poured out the tea. The bell over the door rang and she looked up to see a well-dressed man, possibly an office type, which was unusual round here. Katherine thought she'd seen him in here before. He stood in the doorway and beckoned to the young girl.

She stood up and walked across the room, giving Katherine a grin. 'I bet I'll make more in half an hour than you'll make in a week,' she said as she sauntered past.

Yes, thought Katherine, but what about in a few years' time? Will you have someone to love you? And what if you have a— She was suddenly plunged into despair when she remembered her own plight.

As she climbed the stairs Katherine's thoughts were still on her own problem. She must have a word with Milly tonight.

She gently tapped on the bedroom door.

'Who is it?' called Nellie Trent.

'It's me – Kate. I've got your tea.'

'Well, come in yer silly cow, don't stand out there. Me tea'll get cold.'

Katherine pushed open the door and stood for a moment to get her eyes accustomed to the gloom.

'Put it down here.' The old woman flapped her gnarled bent fingers towards the table by her bed.

'Mrs Trent.'

'Nellie. Call me Nellie. Where yer been? Ain't seen yer for weeks.'

'Josh keeps me busy in the shop.'

'Yer, well he would. He said what a good worker you was. Reckon he'll be sorry to lose yer if this dock strike carries on for long.'

Katherine was taken aback that Josh and his wife talked about what went on. He had told her not to mention the strike, but she seemed to know all about it.

'He likes you, yer know. But don't get any fancy ideas about moving in.'

Katherine wanted to laugh. She couldn't think of anything worse than moving in with these two, but she was pleased he'd said he liked her.

'Nellie,' said Katherine, looking nervously over her shoulder, 'I know Josh said I mustn't stay up here too long, but would you like me to come up and comb your hair one day?'

'Why? What's wrong with it?'

'Nothing, but I thought—'

'Well, you thought wrong. Josh looks after me now.' She grinned. 'And if he says it's all right then that's all I worry about.'

Katherine was surprised at that answer. 'I'd better go.'

Nellie, ignoring Katherine, took hold of the mug with both hands and took a mouthful of tea.

'I said I didn't want this dish water. Next time bring me a proper brew.'

Katherine left the room. Why was Josh so against Nellie having visitors and a nurse, Katherine wondered as she made her way downstairs.

As the day dragged Katherine was again deep in her thoughts. What if the strike continued for a long while? What would happen to her? Would she lose her job? Would Josh lose the shop?

At six o'clock Katherine began to make her way home. She had to talk to Milly soon but with Charlie being home it was getting very difficult. He didn't go out for a drink now as money was very tight.

After dinner Katherine asked Milly if she would come to her room to sort out something.

'You ain't gonner give Briony any more frocks, are you?'

'No.'

'Well, can you wait till we've done the washing up?'

'Of course.'

They were halfway through it when Olive and her husband walked in.

Olive kissed her mother's cheek. 'Mum, me and Ernie are going over the West End on Saturday.' She smiled at Katherine. 'It's our wedding anniversary and we're gonner go and see a show, only in the gods mind.'

'That's lovely,' said Katherine.

'We thought as we were over the water we might go and see Auntie Dolly first, so if you've got a letter, we can take it.'

Milly's face lit up. 'That'll be really nice. You must tell us all about how she's getting on. Look, why don't you and Ernie come to tea on Sunday?'

'We could do. But you sure you can manage – you know with Dad being out of work and all that?'

'Course we can. Don't worry about it.'

'Well, I'll bring a cake.'

All evening Olive and Ernie sat with them. Katherine was

desperate to get Milly on her own, but it wasn't to be.

It wasn't till Friday that Katherine finally managed to get Milly alone in her room.

Milly sat on the bed next to Katherine as she told her her story.

Milly's mouth fell open. 'How long you known?'

'I've been sure for a week.'

'And you ain't told no one?'

Katherine shook her head. 'Milly, what am I going to do? The disgrace. What will Joseph say?' Great tears fell from her eyes. All her pent-up emotions bubbled up and she put her head in her hands and cried bitter tears.

Milly put her arm round Katherine's heaving shoulders and held her close. 'That Gerald's a wicked sod. He wants castrating.'

'Milly, what am I going to do?' she sobbed.

'Do you want to have it?'

Katherine shook her head.

'Well, the only answer's got to be Ida Fairfield.'

Katherine dabbed at her eyes. 'I don't want anyone else to know, and if she tells Mrs Duke . . .'

'Ida ain't that bad, or daft. She charges, though.'

'I can always sell something.'

'You ain't got much left, have you? And I don't think what frocks you've got left will cover it. What about jewellery?'

'All that I brought with me has gone. I didn't get a lot for it.'

'Well, you don't when those blokes know you're down on your uppers.'

'In fact all I've got left is my wedding ring.' She twisted the ring round her finger.

'Is it that sentimental?'

'No. But as I'm known as Joseph's mother I like everybody to know I was married.'

'Well, you can always get a brass one. Most of the women round here have hocked their wedding rings, that's them that had one in the first place.'

'Do you think that would be enough?'

'Should think so.'

'Look, tomorrow morning I'll get some senna pods and make you some strong tea.'

'Will that help?'

'Dunno, but anything must be worth trying. Can't afford gin. The senna pods might give you the runs and if that don't work then I'll go round and see Ida.'

'You won't tell Charlie, will you?'

'Not if you don't want me to.'

'No, I only want you to know.'

'He's going off early anyway. There's going to be a big rally in Trafalgar Square on Sunday and him and a lot of the dockers are going, so he'll be out most of the day planning it.'

'How are they going to get there?'

'It seems the union's putting on buses. It'll be like a day out for 'em.'

On Saturday as Katherine walked home she felt a little happier. She had got two shillings for her wedding ring and bought a thrupenny brass one from the jeweller. But would one and ninepence be enough? Fear grabbed her. What if it wasn't? Would Ida let her borrow the rest? She hated this living from hand to mouth every week. If the dockers hadn't been on strike perhaps she could have asked Josh for a small rise, but now it seemed her job could also be at stake. Well, with luck by this time next week her biggest problem would be behind her.

'Did you manage to see Ida?' whispered Katherine as they washed up.

'No, I didn't, she was out, but I'll pop round in the morning.'

Milly looked at the closed kitchen door. 'Here, I've made you this senna tea.'

Katherine screwed up her nose. 'Can't say I fancy the look of that.'

'Go on, get it down yer, and if it don't work then tomorrow I'll go and see Ida. She should be in on a Sunday.'

Although Katherine was disappointed at Milly not seeing Ida, she braced herself and drank the tea.

Sunday morning Charlie went off with his sandwiches. He kissed Milly's cheek. 'Don't know how long we'll be up there. Some real big nobs coming – let's hope they listen and give us all a living wage.'

Milly waited for Katherine to come out of the lavatory before she put her coat on. 'Anything happened?'

Katherine shook her head.

'Well, I'll pop out now,' she said over her shoulder as she walked up the passage and opened the front door.

'Olive. What you doing here? Did you have a nice time yesterday? How's Dolly?'

'Can we come in, Mum?'

'Course, silly me,' said Milly, stepping to one side.

'Was you just going out, Mrs Stevens?' asked Ernie.

'It can wait.' Milly quickly took off her coat. She suddenly looked worried. 'You was coming round later for a bit of tea. So why you here now?'

'Mum, it's Auntie Dolly.'

Milly put her hand to her mouth. 'Oh my God. What's happened to her?'

'She ain't well, and that Mr Gerald's got someone else living in and doing her work. Auntie Dolly and Uncle Tom've finished up in the basement.' The words tumbled out.

'What's wrong with her?' asked Katherine.

'Don't know. She's ever so thin and she can hardly speak.'

'Thin?' shouted Milly. 'Our Dolly's always been plump. What's wrong with her?'

'I don't know.'

'What did Tom have to say?' asked Katherine.

'Not a lot. He's still doing the garden, that's why that Mr Gerald lets them stay in the basement. If not, he said they'd have to get out. Oh Mum, he looks ever so old and weary. They was just sitting there.' A tear ran down her face.

'Dolly hasn't said anything in her letters, has she?' Katherine was very concerned about them.

Milly shook her head.

Olive gave a sob. 'They look like they're waiting to die.'

'Olive, don't say such a wicked thing,' said Milly. 'I've got to go over and see her. They'll have to come and move in here.' Milly was getting agitated.

'But you ain't got the room,' said Olive. 'And me and Ernie's only got the two rooms, so we can't help out, not with the baby as well.'

'We'll manage somehow.'

Katherine suddenly felt like a stranger. These people were going to look after their own, and she felt in the way.

'Joe will have to move in with Ted, and Dolly and Tom can have the front room. It won't be so bad.'

Katherine knew Joseph wouldn't be happy about that, as much as he admired Ted.

'I must go and see Dolly,' said Milly, quickly tipping the contents of her purse out on to the table. 'What will it cost to get there and back?'

'About sixpence or even a bit more. You have to get a couple of buses,' said Ernie.

'I've only got fourpence ha'penny,' said Milly, sitting at the table.

'I can't help you,' said Olive. 'We spent a lot yesterday. What about Ted?'

'He give me all he could on Friday.' Tears filled her eyes. 'Why did the bloody docks have to be on strike now.' She ran the back of her hand under her nose.

Katherine looked from one to the other. 'Milly, I've got a few pence you can have. It's enough to get you over to see Dolly.'

'But you wanted that money for . . .' She sniffed. 'I can't take that.'

'Yes you can. I'll go up and get it.' Katherine left the room. Upstairs she took the money she got from the jeweller out of her purse and sat on the bed. Tears filled her eyes. She was crying for Dolly, Tom and herself. If she gave Milly this money she had nothing left to sell to pay Ida Fairfield, and if she lost her job she wouldn't have anything at all, and would still have to have Gerald's baby.

Chapter 13

After Milly left, Katherine wandered about unable to concentrate on anything. Even preparing the dinner, which she normally enjoyed doing, didn't hold her attention for long.

'Where's Mum?' asked Ted when he finally left his bed.

Joseph was sitting at the table. He listened very quietly while Katherine explained all that had happened.

'Thought I heard Olive's voice,' said Ted.

'So Dolly and Tom could be moving here?' Joseph's voice was full of alarm.

'It looks like it.'

'Well, as much as I like Ted I don't want to sleep in his room.'

'Can't say I'd fancy it, but it's family, ain't it, and we've gotter help out.' There was a touch of anger in Ted's voice which was unusual. He was normally a quiet lad not given to voicing his opinions, or expressing his feelings.

Katherine was very angry with Joseph. He was just thinking of himself. 'Well I'm sorry, but we don't have any choice. It's either that or . . .' She didn't finish. How could she tell him all her other troubles? 'We'll have to wait till Milly gets home before we make any rash decisions.'

Ted said softly, 'I hope Auntie Dolly's gonner be all right.'

'I'm sure she will be,' said Katherine, glaring at Joseph.

All afternoon she sat in the front room looking out of the window. This was a cold room but Joseph was happy in here. He had a mattress on the floor and a small cupboard for his books. The few other belongings he possessed were in Katherine's room.

She sat and mulled over what he had. Was anything worth selling? Not really. Besides, that would be the last straw, especially if he had to move in with Ted.

'You're quiet,' said Ted to Joe as they sat on a narrow bridge over part of the docks waterway.

'Well, you're always telling me to shut up when we're fishing.'

'I know but we don't ever catch nothing. But it ain't that, is it?'

'No.' Joe let the piece of wood he was holding that had string tied to it, go limp. The other end of the string was dangling in the water below them; it had a safety pin bent open and a piece of a worm they'd managed to find stuck through it.

'It's this business with Dolly and Tom,' said Joe, shifting his legs, which were sticking through the iron railings, to a more comfortable position.

'Thought as much.'

'I like you, Ted, but I don't want to share your bedroom.'

'Well, go on, tell me what else we can do?'

'Don't know.'

'They've got to live somewhere. Mind you, I dunno how Mum's gonner manage to feed 'em with Dad being on strike. She's only got me and your mum's money coming in.'

Joe wedged his back against a post. 'I wish I was going out to work.'

'Your mum won't hear of it, not till you're fourteen.'

'I don't know why. I can never do what I want.'

Ted looked at him. 'D'you know, you are a selfish bugger. I don't know why I put up with you hanging round me.'

Joe was horrified. 'But I thought you liked me. You're the only friend I've got.'

'So whose fault's that? You want to listen to your mother. You're bloody lucky with the kind of schooling you've had.'

Joe wiggled his fishing line. 'I don't know why she worries about me going to school. I'm better than all of 'em there.'

'See what I mean? You're also a puffed-up little sod at times.'

'I'm not, am I?'

'Sometimes, especially when you put on all yer airs and graces.'

'Like when?'

'Well you won't talk to that Briony, for one thing, and I think she's got a soft spot for you.' Ted laughed.

'Briony? I don't like her, she smells.'

'She's always looking at you, and giving you the eye.'

'How can you say that? Here, you don't . . . you know, not with her.'

'No,' said Ted quickly, and looked away. 'I feel sorry for her, that's all. She's good to her family. It's a pity you don't start thinking of other people and not just yourself for a change.'

Joe was taken aback at Ted's comments. He began to reflect on the people round him. Since Edwin's death his mother had had to lower her standards, but she didn't complain. The Addams family had had a great tragedy but they still carried on. Charlie was on strike but he didn't keep on about it. Now Dolly and Tom were in trouble.

'I'm going to try and get a job after school,' said Joe suddenly.

'What's brought this on?'

'You, you've just made me realise what a selfish bugger I am.'

'You've just grown up, so welcome to the real world, and don't let your mother hear you swear or I'll get the blame.'

Joe laughed. 'And if I've got to share your room, just you make sure you don't leave those sweaty socks about.'

Ted put his arm round Joe's shoulders. 'You ain't a bad kid.'

'So, do you want me to have a word with Briony about you?'

Joe ducked as Ted went to give him a clout.

* * *

As the evening approached Katherine went into the kitchen. It would have been a waste of gas to light the lamp in the front room now every penny had to be accounted for. The boys were still out, and this morning Olive had told her mother they wouldn't be coming round for tea.

Sitting in Charlie's armchair in front of the fire was comforting and gradually she began to drift off.

She sat up when somebody banging on the front door made her jump. Who would knock like that? All the family used the key that hung on a string behind the letter box.

She hurried along the passage and pulled open the front door.

'You Mrs Stevens?' asked the man standing there.

'No, no, she's out. What did you want her . . .?' Katherine's voice trailed off when she realised he looked agitated.

'It's Charlie. Charlie Stevens.'

'Oh my God,' said Katherine, her voice breaking with emotion. 'Not more trouble. What's happened to him?'

''Fraid he's been nicked.'

'What, arrested?'

The man nodded.

'You'd better come in.' She was sure Mrs Duke must have heard their knocker, and any minute she would be poking her nose round the door.

The man stepped just inside the door and snatching off his cloth cap, stood in the passage pushing the door to behind him.

'What's he done?' asked Katherine.

'There was quite a skirmish at Trafalgar Square this morning and the police was called in to try to contain it. I must admit it did get a bit out of hand. Well, to cut a long story short the last I saw of Charlie Stevens and some others was 'em being thrown in the back of a Black Maria. He yelled out for me to tell his missis, so here I am.'

'Thank you,' said Katherine. 'Do you happen to know which

124

police station they would have gone to?'

'Na, can't help yer there.'

'I'll tell his wife as soon as she gets home. Thank you, Mr . . .?'

'Davis. Frank Davis.'

'Mr Davis.' She opened the front door just as Ted and Joe came along.

'Who was that?' asked Ted, watching the back of Mr Davis as he walked up the road.

'I'll tell you when you're inside.'

'You're making it sound very interesting,' said Joe. 'You haven't got yourself a man friend have—'

Katherine turned on him, her green eyes blazing. 'No I haven't.' She pushed open the kitchen door with such force that it banged against the wall.

'I'm sorry, it was just a joke.'

'Well, I don't need those kind of jokes, and for your information it was a man from the docks telling me that Charlie has been arrested.'

Ted's face went ashen. 'Why? What's he done?'

'It seems a lot of men were arrested just for being in the wrong place at the wrong time.'

'My dad ain't a troublemaker.'

'I know, and I'm sure they won't keep him for long.'

'What's Mum gonner say?'

'I don't know. Your poor mother has got more than enough to worry about without this.'

Tea was a quiet affair with just a sandwich, and as the evening wore on they all became fidgety and apprehensive.

'I wish there was something we could do,' said Ted.

'I know. Let's hope they're only going to keep them in prison overnight to teach them a lesson,' said Katherine.

'Prison,' said Joe. 'Will they really put him in prison?'

'I don't know.'

'I don't reckon it'll be that bad,' said Joe.

'How would you know?' asked Ted.

'Well, I don't think those suffragettes would keep being arrested if it was that bad.'

'S'pose so,' said Ted soulfully. 'See they've been at it again.'

'Doing what?' asked Katherine.

'It said on the placards outside the newsagents this morning that they've been smashing windows again.'

'Silly women,' said Katherine. 'Look, why don't you both go to bed? I'll wait up for your mother.'

'She's very late,' said Ted, a worried expression filling his face. 'She's not used to being out on her own. I hope nothing's—'

'She's all right,' said Katherine, gently tapping his arm. 'She's probably helping them to pack.'

'Just as long as she's not been smashing windows,' said Joe with a grin.

'If that was meant as a joke, young man, then I for one don't think it was funny.' Katherine looked very stern.

'Sorry. Where shall I sleep tonight?' he asked quietly.

'In the front room, and we'll see what happens tomorrow.' Katherine was dreading the tantrums and sulks if he had to go in with Ted.

Once again Katherine was alone with her thoughts. What else could go wrong? If only Milly would come home. She shouldn't be as late as this. Had she got lost, or in some kind of trouble? She didn't know her way about. Please God, don't let anything happen to her, Katherine prayed.

Her thoughts went to the suffragettes. She could never do things like that. They appeared to be very well organised. They must have a lot of help. She was sitting in the armchair, quietly thinking, when Milly finally walked in.

'Milly, you're late. Where have you been all this time?' Katherine jumped to her feet. 'Thank goodness you're home. I've been so worried about you. Sit down and I'll make you a cup of tea. Didn't Dolly and Tom come with you?'

Milly shook her head and, after removing her hat and coat, sat at the table and began picking at the tablecloth. 'She looks ever so ill.'

'Do you know what's wrong with her?'

'No. She said it started with a cold. She's got a terrible cough, and she's so thin. Was she thin when you left?'

'No. She was losing a bit of weight, but we put it down to all the extra work she was doing. How's Tom?'

'He ain't much better.' Tears filled Milly's eyes. 'I wish they'd let me help 'em. They're living in that bloody cold basement.'

Katherine filled the teapot and sat at the table next to her. 'Why won't they come over here?'

'Tom's still working, he's doing a bit of gardening for that Gerald, and you know Dolly – she likes to keep her independence.'

Katherine nodded and smiled.

'I think Dolly's worried she's got something that might be catching, and that's why she's not said anything. Where's Charlie, he in the bog?'

Katherine took hold of Milly's hand. 'It seems there was a bit of trouble this morning and—'

Milly jumped to her feet. 'You've let me sit here and all the time my Charlie's in hospital?'

'No, Milly, he's not in hospital.'

'Oh my God, it's worse.' Her tears fell.

'No, it isn't. What I mean is, he's in prison.'

'What?'

'A Mr Davis came and told me Charlie and a lot of others were taken to prison, but he doesn't know which one.'

Milly sat down. 'Why? What's he done?'

'It was to do with the strike.'

'My Charlie in prison? He's never been in trouble in his life. What we gonner do?'

Katherine choked back her tears. 'We'll have to wait till morning. Then we'll go to the local police station and see if they can find out what we have to do.'

'Will it cost money to get him out?'

'I don't know.'

'We ain't got none now, have we?'

Katherine toyed with the spoon in her saucer. 'Only a few pence.'

'My poor Charlie. Will they feed him?'

'I don't know.'

'Does Ted know about this?'

'Yes.'

'What did he say?'

'What can any of us say?'

'I can't believe this is all happening.'

'Well, they say trouble comes in threes, so we've had our share.'

Milly looked down at her hands. 'We ain't.'

'Why? What do you mean? There's my problem, Dolly and now Charlie. What else can happen?'

'That's a terrible journey, took me ages.'

'Milly, what else has happened?'

'I'm sorry.'

'Sorry, what for? I didn't mind giving you that money. Perhaps when we see Mrs Fairfield we can explain . . .' Katherine's voice trailed off. She felt uneasy. Somehow she knew this wasn't what Milly was talking about.

'You see when I saw the place Dolly was living in I very nearly went mad. They're couped up in that dark damp basement. That Gerald's got a lot to answer for.'

Katherine quickly took a breath; she'd almost forgotten about Gerald and what part he had to play in Dolly's illness.

'Well, I went and gave him a piece of me mind. D'you know, he just told me to shut up and go away. Said he wasn't interested in my affairs, and I was making it harder for Dolly, said he could throw them out on the street if he felt like it, and I should be grateful he was still letting them stay there.'

'That sounds like Gerald.'

'Then I saw red, didn't I, and I told him in no uncertain words what I thought of him. I told him he was a selfish bugger that didn't deserve all he'd got from your hard work. I knew I wasn't making it any easier for Dolly, but then . . .' Milly blew her nose. 'I'm ever so sorry, Katherine.'

Katherine sat with her eyes wide open. 'Why?'

'I told him about you going to have his baby.'

Katherine gasped. 'What? Why did you tell him that?'

'I dunno. It just all came blurting out.'

'But I'm not going to have his baby, I'm going to see Mrs—'

'He wants to see you.'

'What? Well, I don't want to see him.' Katherine began to feel threatened.

'He was very interested, and seemed very pleased.'

'I bet he was.' She stood up. 'How could you do that, Milly? I trusted you.'

'I'm sorry, Katherine, really sorry. As soon as I said it I felt like biting me tongue off, but he was standing there smirking at me like Lord High-and-Mighty, thinking he knew everything, so I told him something he didn't know about.'

Katherine was in shock; she couldn't cry. 'I'll have to move, find somewhere else to live.'

'Why?'

'I don't want him to come here looking for me.'

'But he don't know where you live.'

'Dolly still lives there, remember, and Gerald has a funny way of finding out things, and the last thing I want is for him to come here making a scene and forcing me to go back.'

'D'you think that's what he'll do?'

'He'll try. He's had everything else of mine, so I suppose he thinks this baby will be his right.'

'Oh Katherine, what we gonner do?'

'I don't know. I don't want him here. I don't want Joseph to find out about this.' She gently touched her stomach. 'And if I know Gerald, he'll take great delight in telling Joseph.'

'Oh Katherine . . .' Milly's eyes were full of sorrow.

Katherine put her arm round Milly's shoulders. 'We can't do much tonight, and you look very tired.'

'It's been a long day, and so much has happened.'

'Well, I suggest we go to bed, then tomorrow we'll see about finding out what's become of Charlie.'

'What a bloody mess,' said Milly.

'Yes, life is a bloody mess,' said Katherine sadly.

Katherine knew as soon as she closed her bedroom door that sleep wouldn't come. She lay on the bed staring up at the ceiling. What was going to happen to them? If she lost her job because of the strike where would they live? What could they afford? She could understand the suffragettes. She almost felt like joining them, anything to get back at men. When she closed her eyes she could see Gerald laughing at her. Should she bury her pride and go back to him? It would make a lot of people happy. She would insist Tom and Dolly were employed again. Joseph could have his old room, that would make him very happy. Tears ran down her face.

'Looks like you've got everything on your side again, Gerald,' she said out loud.

Chapter 14

Everybody was up and about very early on Monday morning.

'I couldn't sleep,' said Milly as Katherine wandered into the kitchen.

'I know how you feel,' replied Katherine.

'Mum, I'm coming to the nick with you,' said Ted.

'No, you go to work, son, we need the money.' Milly knew if he didn't go into work, like anybody else, he would not be paid.

'I'll go with you,' said Katherine. 'As it's on the way I'll go in to Josh and explain.'

'What if he sacks you?' said Milly in alarm.

'Well, we'll have to cross that bridge if and when it happens.'

'What about Olive?' asked Ted. 'She's gotter know before some busybody tells her.'

'Would you like me to do that?' asked Joe. 'I could go before I go to school.'

Katherine looked at him. This was the first time she'd heard him volunteer to do anything to help anyone.

'Thanks. I'd really appreciate that,' said Milly, going out of the door.

Milly and Katherine were very quiet as they walked to the shop.

When they turned the corner they were taken aback at the amount of men crowding round Trent's doorway and spilling into the road.

'Oh my God,' said Katherine. 'What's happened now?' She started to push her way through.

' 'Allo, Kate. I bet old Josh'll be glad to see you,' said a white-haired man.

'Why? What's happened?'

'It's so bloody crowded in there, we can't get in.' He leant against the wall and proceeded to push more tobacco into his pipe. When he was satisfied he put it in his mouth and puffed hard. Katherine was not going to get any more information out of him.

She got to the door and after elbowing a lot of men out of the way, managed to get through. She hurried behind the counter. 'Josh, what's happened?' she asked, straightening her hat. 'What's everybody doing here?'

'Thank Christ you're here. I'm running out of mugs. Ain't you heard?' He had to shout above the din. 'A lot of 'em finished up in the nick yesterday and all these are in here trying to sort something out. Hurry up and get your hat and coat off and start pouring out some tea. And make sure they pay.'

'But . . .' She was going to tell him where she was going but it was too late, he was round the other side of the counter and lost in the throng as he tried to collect the dirty mugs that were strewn about.

Milly pushed her way through the crowd and was being squashed against the counter. 'Looks like I'd better go on me own.'

'No, hang on a minute,' shouted Katherine as she ran the full teapot over the mugs, filling them to overflowing. 'Look, come round here and give me a hand.'

It went deathly quiet after a lot of spoon banging and shouting for order. A man stood on a table.

'Now we all know what happened yesterday, and if our mates is gonner get bail I think we should see the union blokes about it.'

A great chorus of 'Hear, hear!' went up.

'Right, I need to know who was carted off.'

'Milly, hang around,' said Katherine. 'We can find out where Charlie is from this lot.'

Names were being called out and written down, including Charlie's. Gradually the men drifted outside and along to the docks for a meeting with the union.

Frank Davis came up to Katherine and Milly and told them all the men had been taken to a police station near Trafalgar Square. 'They're going in front of the beak this morning. He'll probably let 'em off with a fine and a caution. Can't do a lot else, otherwise it could cause riots.'

'A fine?' asked Milly in alarm. 'Any idea how much?'

'Na, but don't worry about that, the union will have ter pay.'

'Are you sure?'

'They'd better, that's what we pay our dues for, for them to look after us.'

Both Milly and Katherine looked relieved.

'Right, Kate,' said Josh as the place began to empty. 'Better get some clearing up done ready for the lunchtime rush.' He laughed. 'I only wish.'

Katherine knew they hadn't been very busy since the strike started, but was afraid to ask too much in case he said he didn't want her any more.

'I best be off,' said Milly.

'Oh yes,' said Katherine. 'Thanks for your help.'

'Well, at least we should soon have one of our problems over,' she said smiling.

'You think you've got problems, missis,' said Josh. 'You don't know the half of it.' He went out the back.

'He don't know what we've got to worry about,' Milly whispered.

'And he's not going to find out,' said Katherine as she began clearing the tables and wiping them down.

* * *

As she walked home Katherine was almost afraid to turn into Croft Street. What if Gerald had found out where she lived? She sighed. Thankfully there was no motor car in the road.

The atmosphere was a lot happier when Katherine went in and found Charlie sitting in his chair.

He jumped up and gave her a big hug. 'Thanks, gel.'

'For what?' she asked, taking off her hat, which he had knocked sideways.

'Standing by Milly and helping her out with the fare to get over to Dolly.'

'It was nothing. How was prison?'

'Don't ask. Bloody awful. Don't think I'm gonner make a habit of it. What with one thing and another it's been a bloody awful weekend all round.'

'I agree with you there,' said Katherine, giving Milly a quick glance.

'Anyway,' continued Charlie. 'Thanks for giving Milly that money. I'm really grateful. She told me you sold your wedding ring. I'm sorry about that, she shouldn't have let you do it.'

'I didn't mind.'

'I know, but yer wedding ring . . . I wouldn't like it if Milly—'

'Charlie, I said it doesn't matter,' said Katherine forcefully.

'But it must'a meant something.'

Joseph was sitting at the table, drawing. He looked up.

Katherine felt her face flush with anger. 'Milly, I told you not to say—'

'I couldn't help it. I had to tell Charlie where I got the money from.'

'You're as bad as Mrs Duke. Your mouth will get you and me in a lot of trouble very soon.' She stormed out of the kitchen.

'Why is Mama so angry?' asked Joe.

'You and your big mouth,' said Milly, turning on Charlie. 'I shouldn't have told you.'

'Why? What did I say that was wrong?'

'Milly, why is Mama so angry?' asked Joe again.

'It doesn't matter,' said Milly dismissively.

But it mattered to Joe. What difference did a wedding ring make? Why was his mother so angry? He moved away from the table and went upstairs.

The gentle tapping on Katherine's door made her quickly wipe her eyes. 'Who is it?' she called.

'It's me,' said Joe. 'Can I come in?'

Katherine knew she couldn't refuse and opened the door.

'Why are you crying? Was your wedding ring so important?'

She shook her head. 'No, not really.'

'But you're still wearing it.'

She half smiled. 'No, this is brass.'

'Does it matter then?'

'Only if my finger goes green and drops off.'

Joe looked horrified. 'It won't, will it?'

'No.'

'Are we ever so hard up now?'

'Yes, I'm afraid we are.'

'So why did you give that money to Milly?'

'I had to. Come and sit down.' She patted the bed on which she was sitting. 'You see, I feel that in many ways it was my fault that Dolly is ill and Tom has lost his job.'

'Why?'

She put her arm round her son's shoulders; he didn't pull away. 'When I left Gerald I think he used Dolly and Tom as a kind of revenge.'

'But, Mama, what he did to you was wrong.'

'I know.' Katherine was pleased he now thought that way.

'Will Dolly and Tom come here to live?'

135

'I don't know. Things will be very hard if they do.'

'Is that why you sold your ring?'

'Yes.'

'What're we going to do?'

'Let's hope this strike doesn't last for too long.'

'I know you don't want me to leave school so I'm going to try and get a job after school, that'll help out.'

Katherine pulled him close and kissed his cheek. 'I'm pleased about that.'

'Don't you mind?'

'No, but you are a bit young. Where are you going to start looking?'

'I thought of going to that place that sells motor cars.'

'It's a long way away.'

'Don't matter. It's what I want to do more than anything else.'

'And why not?' she smiled.

He jumped up and threw his arms round her neck. 'I don't like to see you unhappy, and I promise I'll try to help and I don't mind if I have to sleep in Ted's room.' He laughed. 'He said he'd keep his smelly socks outside.'

Katherine wanted to hold him and kiss him. He had changed. He had had to grow up, and she loved him dearly. He knew jobs were hard to get but he was willing to try.

Milly knocked on her door, telling her the meal was on the table.

'Just coming. Go on down,' said Katherine to Joe. 'I just want to tidy myself up.'

When Joseph left she sat back down on the bed. How could she tell him her real problem? And would it be solved? And what would he say if Gerald came here looking for her?

'I'm sorry, girl,' said Charlie when Katherine walked into the kitchen. 'Didn't mean to upset you.'

'That's all right. What with one thing and another, I was just being a bit silly, that's all.'

Later that evening when Milly and Katherine were in the kitchen, Milly closed the door.

'I'm gonner go and see Ida tomorrow. I'm gonner tell her we'll pay as soon as everything gets back to normal.'

'Thanks.' But what was normal? thought Katherine.

Trent's wasn't very busy at all the following day, and Katherine grew more concerned for her job. She cleaned and swept and tried to make herself as useful as she could, and she kept out of Josh's way. She would have liked to go up to Nellie, but dare not ask.

As she left the shop she knew this couldn't last. He would have to sack her soon. What if she was ill after seeing Ida? That would be the last straw. More and more the option to go and live with Gerald seemed to be crowding in on her.

Milly gave Katherine a knowing look when she walked in, and Katherine followed her into the kitchen and closed the door behind her.

'She's busy tonight,' said Milly. 'But she said she'll see you tomorrow.'

'Did she say how much?'

'Three and six and no questions asked.'

'Three and six,' repeated Katherine in alarm. 'But that's over half my week's wages.'

Milly shrugged her shoulders. 'Don't look like you've got a lot of choice.'

'No. But it will take me for ever to save that.'

Milly smiled. 'When Charlie gets back to work we'll think of something.'

'But how long will this strike go on for?'

'Dunno.'

'And how long is Ida willing to wait for her money?'

'Dunno,' repeated Milly. 'But you can go over that with her.'

'Milly, do you think she would wait till Saturday to do . . . you know? Then I'll have Sunday to get over it.'

'Look, I'll take you round tomorrow night, then you can sort it all out with her.'

Katherine kissed Milly's cheek. 'Thanks. I don't know what I should have done without you.'

'Don't thank me till it's all over.'

'You sound as if you don't approve.'

Milly turned away. 'In some ways I don't, but then again it wasn't your fault you got in this mess.'

Katherine was taken aback. 'No, it wasn't. Do you think I should go back to Gerald?'

'No. But you leaving him has caused a lot of grief all round.'

Katherine was beginning to get angry. Everybody seemed to be blaming her for everything. 'I'm sorry for what happened to Dolly.'

'Well, when I can afford it I'll go over and see her again.'

Katherine didn't volunteer to go with her.

'Now come on, take these plates in the other room and sit down and have your dinner.'

Katherine did as she was told but she was upset at what Milly had said.

After dinner the following evening Milly and Katherine told the family they were going round to see Olive.

'What if Olive tells them we didn't go there?' said Katherine when they left the house.

'Charlie won't bother to ask questions when I tell him it was woman's talk.'

As Milly knocked on Ida's door Katherine felt her stomach churn and her knees go weak. The memory of all the miscarriages she had had in Australia came flooding back to her. All those lovely babies lost, and now she was deliberately going to get rid of one. She felt sick and wanted to run away. But what future would the child have? No, deep down she knew this was for the best.

'Come in,' said Ida, opening the door. Her face glowed with good health, her grey hair was in a neat bun and she was wearing a spotless white overall. There was nothing dirty or shoddy about Ida Fairfield.

They followed her down the passage and into the kitchen.

'Sit yourself down.' Ida pointed to chairs at the table.

Milly and Katherine quickly did as they were told. 'Right. How many months?'

'Two.'

'You sure?'

'Yes.' Katherine could have told her the exact day and time if she'd asked. It was stamped on her mind. So much had happened since Edwin's death. Ida's voice broke into her thoughts.

'Only had some silly cows in here three and four months, that can lead to all sorts of complications.'

Katherine played with her gloves. 'Mrs Fair—'

'Call me Ida, everybody else does.'

'Ida. I think Milly has explained our financial situation to you.'

'Yes, she did.'

'You see, all the while this strike's on we have to be very careful with our money.'

'I understand that. I hear you come from somewhere very posh, so did a bloke from the gentry get you up the spout?'

Katherine nodded.

'Married, is he?'

Katherine didn't answer.

'Want bloody shooting, they do. Mind you, it takes two, you know?'

Katherine wasn't prepared to go into details of what had happened.

'Ain't he prepared to pay then?'

'I haven't asked him.'

'More fool you. I shouldn't think he wants his wife to know all about it.'

Katherine wasn't going to pursue this conversation any further. 'So, Ida, are you prepared to wait for your money?'

'Yer, but I'm gonner get you to sign an IOU. Can't have you trying to get away with it when things get better.'

Katherine almost wanted to laugh. How many women sign bits of paper in order to pay later for an abortion? 'Would it be too inconvenient if I came straight from work on Saturday, then that will give me Sunday to get over it?'

'No, that should be all right. Ain't got no husband round watching what I'm doing, so me life's me own. Mind you, it was sad when I had to lay him out. Been gone over ten years now, but I still miss the old bugger.'

'Did you have any children?' asked Katherine.

'No, more's the pity. But then again I might have felt different about helping the likes of you if I had. Might even have tried to talk you into keeping it.'

Katherine shuddered. The last thing she wanted was a baby.

When they got outside Katherine sighed. 'Well, that's the first hurdle over.'

'Yes,' said Milly. 'Let's hope everything will be all right.'

'Why? What do you mean?'

'Well, it ain't natural, is it?'

'No. But do I have any choice?'

'No, don't suppose you do, and the last thing you want is a little 'en.'

'I'm very worried about it,' said Katherine as they walked along.

'If you like I'll meet you at Ida's on Sat'day.'

'Would you? I'd like that.'

'Well, that's settled. Now come on,' said Milly, tucking her arm through Katherine's. 'We've still got time to go and see Olive.'

In a few days' time another problem will be out of the way, thought Katherine. But how many more were waiting to crop up?

Chapter 15

On Saturday morning Katherine woke with fear in her heart. This evening she would be going to see Ida. She was dreading it. Was she doing the right thing?

The day seemed to drag and at last it was time for her to leave.

Josh handed her her wages. 'Look, Kate, I don't know how long I can keep you on. You've seen what business is like.'

She nodded.

'Come in on Monday and we'll talk it over.'

Katherine was upset as she left. Would this be her last week? She didn't want to have to leave. What other job was around? With the strike they needed the money. She was happy here, but other things were crowding in on her mind as she made her way to Ida's house.

'Oi, you!' A man was shouting after her.

She stopped and turned. 'Mr Addams,' she said, surprised that he would want to talk to her.

He reeled towards her. 'You're the tart what's been putting ideas into my Briony's head, ain't yer? Seen yer walking up Croft Street with all yer airs and graces.'

'I'm sorry?'

'You will be when I've finished with you.'

Katherine stood back; the smell of beer and his unwashed body made her catch her breath.

'I said,' he poked his fat dirty finger into her shoulder, 'you're the one what keeps giving my Briony ideas.' He belched loudly in Katherine's face.

She screwed up her nose in disgust and turned her head. She looked up the road, desperately hoping someone would come along. Milly said she would be waiting for her at Ida's, but that was streets away. Katherine silently prayed that she would come round the corner. Although she was frightened – drunks were so unpredictable – she knew she had to remain calm. 'If giving your daughter a few clothes gives her thoughts of her own, then yes, I'm guilty,' she said haughtily.

'Don't start giving me all yer fancy talk.' He rocked back on his heels, putting his hand on the wall to steady himself. 'I don't want yer charity. I can look after me family well enough, so keep yer snotty nose out o' our business.'

'I like Briony, I think she's a very nice girl, and I don't think you should stop me from giving her a treat now again.'

'Saucy cow. Don't you answer me back. Ain't ever had a woman answer me back.'

'It's a pity somebody didn't. You wife might still be alive if she had.' She went to move on.

He grabbed the top of her arms. 'What did you say?'

She tried to shake him off but he was gripping her very tight. 'Let go of me.'

'Now you just listen to me.' He shook Katherine and put his face close to hers. 'I loved my wife very dearly.'

'I said, let me go.' Although she was beginning to get very nervous, Katherine tossed her head and said defiantly, 'You can't frighten me.'

'We'll see about that.' He raised his clenched fist to hit her. As he let go, she stepped back and he overbalanced. She wasn't quick enough to get out of his way and fell to the ground with him. He fell heavily, hitting his head against the wall with a sickening thud as he went down.

For a moment they lay very still. Then shaking with fear Katherine got to her feet. She stared down at Mr Addams in panic. Why didn't he get up? What if he had injured himself? She couldn't just walk away and leave him.

As she stood over him, brushing the dust from her coat she noticed blood very slowly beginning to seep from beneath his head. She put her hand to her mouth and let out an almost silent scream. Carefully she bent over him. To her great relief he was still breathing. He was a drunk, and drunks often fell and were left to sleep it off. Should she walk away?

She stood up and looked around. It was very quiet in this street. There weren't any houses, just warehouses, windowless buildings which were closed for the weekend. Dirt and rubbish filled the gutter; in the light breeze paper blew about Katherine's ankles. She knew there was a pub at the end of the street – she had just passed it. Should she run back and get help? What if they blamed her? Gradually Katherine began to inch away from him. Milly would be waiting for her at Ida's.

''Allo there, missis.'

Katherine groaned when she recognised the voice of the person who was shouting after her, and quickly spun round as Briony came hurrying towards her.

'Thought it was you. 'Ere, ain't that me dad?' Briony ran the last few yards. 'What's he doing on the floor? And what you done to him?' She was on her knees cradling his head in her lap. She looked at her hand. 'He's bleeding,' she screamed. 'What you done to him?'

'I haven't done anything.'

'So why's he on the floor and bleeding?'

'We were talking and he fell and hit his head on the wall.'

'What was he talking to you for?'

'He told me not to give you any more things.'

'Did he now.' Briony calmed down and looked at her father with contempt. 'I've got to get him back home.'

Katherine thought she knew Briony, and was amazed that she

now sounded far older than her years. 'Look, I'm sorry, but I must go.'

'You can't leave me here with him. Can't you help me get him home?'

'No I'm sorry. Perhaps someone in the pub will help you.'

Briony sat back on her heels. 'Shouldn't think so. They're probably all in the same state as him.'

Katherine began to walk away. 'Look, I really must go.'

'What's your hurry? And what you doing round this way? It ain't on your way home.' Briony stood up. ''Ere, you wasn't meeting me dad, was you?'

'No I wasn't.' The idea was absurd.

'So, you meeting a friend? A man friend?'

'Briony, what I do is my business, so I trust you to keep out of it.' Katherine was beginning to get cross with this young girl. How dare she pry into her affairs?

'Well, my business is getting me dad home. And if I go to the pub and tell 'em the lady what hit him has scarpered they might come looking for you.'

'I didn't hit him.'

'Only you and me dad know that, and he ain't talking, is he?'

'Briony, are you trying to blackmail me into helping you with your father?'

She looked at Katherine with defiance in her face. 'Yer, think you could say that.'

'I thought you hated him.'

'I do.'

'So why don't you leave him here to sleep it off?'

''Cos if the coppers come along and put him in the nick we'll have to find money to get him out. And we ain't got any to spare, and they might put the kids away.'

'What made you come this way home?'

'I was looking for him. Thought I'd get him before he boozed all his wages away, but it looks like I was too late.'

Mr Addams began to moan.

'It's all right, Dad. I'm here, Briony. Me and the missis here's gonner take you home. Can you stand?'

He groaned again and tried to get up. Briony bent down to help him.

'Come on, give us a hand.'

Katherine did as she was asked and helped him stagger to his feet.

He leant heavily on them as they pushed, weaved and struggled with him along the road. At first he tried to hit out at Briony, but she told him in no uncertain words to behave. Then he began singing at the top of his voice.

Katherine felt so embarrassed. A few people smiled as they passed them, others looked at this sorry trio with contempt. They probably thought Katherine was part of the family.

As they slowly made their way back to Croft Street Katherine could have screamed. Why was this happening tonight of all nights? How dare this man confront her and get her involved. Why did he use that pub? She wanted to run away, she felt trapped. She couldn't tell anyone where she was going. Milly would be wondering where she had got to. What if Ida were going out later? It had to be done tonight.

As soon as they got to the Addamses' front door Katherine left them. She could almost feel the eyes following her from behind the lace curtains as she hurried back along the street. Was Mrs Duke watching her? When she didn't go into Milly's she knew there would be some questions asked.

Breathlessly she ran. She hoped she wouldn't be too late.

She banged on Ida's knocker and almost collapsed with relief when Ida opened her door.

'You're late.'

'There was a bit of a problem,' she panted.

'Problem,' said Milly, who was right behind Ida. 'What sorta problem?'

'It's nothing to worry about. I'll tell you about it later.'

'I was getting a bit worried about you,' said Milly, frowning.

'And I thought you'd got cold feet,' said Ida over her shoulder as they trooped down the passage.

'No, I'm all right.'

When Ida opened the kitchen door the strong smell of disinfectant almost took Katherine's breath away. The table was covered with newspapers. She stood in the doorway for a moment or two, fear filling her mind.

'Well, get yer drawers off then. Pull your skirts up and get up on the table and open your legs.'

Reluctantly, Katherine did as she was told.

Chapter 16

Katherine lay in bed watching the sunbeams filter through the curtains, her head full of what had happened last night. She brought her knees up to help ease the stomach cramps. Although she knew what she had done was for the best, it still troubled her conscience. This was something she would keep to herself for ever, another burden she would have to carry. Well, if Gerald did find her, he wouldn't have anything to call his now. Her thoughts drifted to Dolly and Tom. Milly hadn't heard from them and was worried. As soon as money allowed they would go and see them. A tap on her bedroom door brought her back.

'You awake?' asked Milly.

'Yes, come in,' said Katherine sleepily.

'Brought you a nice cuppa. How you feeling?' Milly put the cup on the small table.

Katherine sat up. 'Other than guilty, not too bad.'

'You'll be all right. It's a good job you had Ida do it. At least she knows what she's doing, not like some of 'em who go to any old dear. But then again if you ain't got two ha'pennies to rub together you'll go anywhere if it helps.'

Katherine smiled at those words of wisdom. 'Did any of them ask why I went straight to bed when we got back?'

'I told them it was women's troubles, and that seemed to satisfy 'em.'

'Thanks. What would I do without you?'

Milly dismissed that statement with a smile. 'Now, d'you fancy a bit of breakfast? What about a bit of toast?'

'Thanks,' said Katherine again. 'I'll be down in a minute.'

'You don't have to get up till later. Just you take it easy this morning.'

'Milly, you shouldn't have given Ida that sixpence, you know.'

'I had to give her something, just to show we ain't gonner welsh on the deal.'

'But you'll be those few pennies short this week. And what if I get sacked? We might need that. Ted doesn't bring in that much.'

Milly shrugged. 'We'll let next week take care of itself.'

'Do you think she'll charge us interest?'

'Dunno. Why d'you ask?'

'Well, she is the money lender.'

'Yer I know, but for all that, I wouldn't like to say. Now come on, drink this tea 'fore it gets cold.'

This question had been at the back of Katherine's mind, but she wouldn't know the answer till all the money had been paid. 'I wouldn't be surprised if Mrs Duke doesn't come banging on the door soon,' said Katherine, grinning and sipping her tea.

'I bet she's bursting to find out what happened and why you brought old Addams home. And you, my girl, was very lucky he didn't clock you one.'

Katherine had told Milly the story as they made their way home.

'I must admit I was a bit worried. But he was so drunk he probably doesn't remember anything about it.'

'Let's hope so. Right then, I'll go down and see to the dinner.'

Katherine lay back when Milly left. She felt a bit sore, but quite well considering. The money she owed Ida worried her and kept returning to her thoughts. She had never been in debt before. This strike must end soon so that they could all get on with their lives.

Joe tapped on her door. 'Can I come in?' he called.

150

'Of course.' She sat up and twisted her long hair into a knot. 'Come and sit on the bed.' She patted the covers.

'Are you all right?'

'Yes I'm fine.'

Joe looked at her suspiciously. 'I wanted to tell you about me job. Mr Lacy let me stay there all day yesterday, and d'you know he showed me all sorts of things. He loves those motors, and he gave me a shilling. He said I was a help.'

'A shilling? You are a lucky boy.'

'I ain't a boy. And you can have this.' He held out a sixpence.

'I can't take this.'

'Why not?' He looked downcast. 'D'you want it all?'

'No, of course not. It's yours. You earned it.'

'All the money you earn you give to Milly, so.'

'I know, but that's because she feeds us.'

'Well, I want to help. It ain't easy for Milly and you know Charlie's out of work, and I'd like to help, so please take it.'

Katherine wanted to cry. 'Oh Joseph,' she said, hugging him, 'you are a good boy.'

He wriggled free and sat up. 'Now why are you in bed? You look all right to me.'

'I'm getting up soon, so don't worry about it.'

He moved towards the door. 'Mama. We seem to be happy here, don't we?'

'Are we?'

'Think so.' He grinned and left.

Katherine looked at the silver coin in her hand. She did feel happy. She would give this to Milly, so she wouldn't be short. As she carefully got out of bed she felt as if her inside was going to drop out. 'Please God, don't let this last for too long,' she prayed.

Katherine had sat around all day Sunday but on Monday she

knew she had to go to the shop, so she slowly made her way to work.

When she walked in Josh said, 'Christ, girl, you look awful.'

'Thanks,' she said, removing her hat and sitting at a table.

'D'you feel all right?'

'Yes, thanks. Josh, shall we talk about my job?'

'If yer want. I'll pour us out a cuppa.'

'Have I got a job?'

'Let's put it this way: I don't wanner lose you, but as you know things ain't that good.' He put two heaped spoonfuls of sugar into both mugs and slowly stirred them.

'I see.'

He took the tea and sat at her table. 'What if . . .' he paused. 'What if you work for less money?'

'I can't do that.'

'Well, it's that or nothing.'

'How long would it be for?'

'Just till the strike ends and things get back to normal, then I can pay you like before.'

'What sort of wage would it be now?' She held her breath while waiting for the answer.

'What about four shillings, and see how it goes after next week? I might have ter put it down every week.'

'I'll have to see if Milly can manage on less.' Katherine played with the spoon, her mind quickly turning over. Was there any other place round here she could find work? 'Do you own this shop?'

'Well yes, in a way. I rent it from the landlord. Why?'

'Nothing. I just wondered, that's all.'

''Ere, you ain't got a fortune stashed away, have you, and you wanner buy me out?'

She laughed. 'If only. But it must be a little gold mine when things go well.'

He looked at her quizzically. 'It ain't bad.'

She sat up. 'All right. I'll work for less money, but only until the end of the strike, then I want six shillings a week.'

'Six bob,' he grinned. 'You're a good one, Kate. You ain't afraid of hard work, or speaking your mind. Don't hear you moan like some of 'em I've had. And the blokes like you. You've got a good head on your shoulders. OK, it's a deal.'

For the first time in months Katherine felt in charge of her life, and she had plans for her future.

'Well,' said Milly, when Katherine arrived home and opened the kitchen door. 'Have you still got a job?'

'Yes. But I have to take less money.'

'How much less?'

'I'm only going to get four shillings a week. Will you be able to manage on that?'

'I'll have to.'

'That's not all the bad news. He's going to review the situation again. I might only finish up with three.'

'Christ, that will be bad news. Ted'll be earning more than you, and he's only an apprentice.'

Katherine shrugged. 'That's the way it is, but it's only until the strike ends, then I told Josh I want six.'

Milly laughed. 'Well, I've got to hand it to you, you know how to drive a bargain.'

'Let's hope the dockers have the same luck.'

Milly took her hand. 'I'm glad to see you're looking a lot better. Everything all right?' Milly gave her a knowing look.

'Yes, it is now.'

For two weeks they just about managed, but at times the atmosphere got a little fraught. Charlie was getting more and more upset at not being the provider. When Olive came round with a pot of stew, that really upset him.

'We can't take this.'

'Course you can, Dad. I made much too much. 'Sides, Ernie will get fed up with it if he has to have it day in and day out.' She gave a little giggle. 'It ain't that bad.'

Milly put her arm round her daughter's shoulders and glared at her husband. 'I'm sure it's very nice. Take no notice of yer dad, love. I'll get a few extra bits of veg and that'll do us all.'

'I wish we could help more,' said Olive.

'Never thought I'd have to rely on me kids feeding me,' said Charlie, slamming the door as he left the room. Katherine had noted the hurt look in his eyes.

'I'm sorry, Mum. Have I said the wrong thing?'

'No, not really. He's just fed up, that's all. I won't be sorry when this is all over. I'm as fed up as he is with him under me feet all day.'

Olive turned to Katherine. 'How's Joe getting on? He was telling Ernie all about these 'ere new motor cars.'

'He seems to be very happy. He spends all day Saturday there.'

'Who buys 'em? They seem ever so expensive.'

'I don't really know.'

'Wouldn't have thought anybody round this way had that sorta money,' said Milly.

'I think it's because the garage is a lot cheaper this side of the water.' Katherine was proud he was bringing in a shilling a week – half of which he gave to Milly – even though she wasn't that happy at the state he got into.

'Just about manage to get his things clean,' Milly said, folding her arms. 'Gawd only knows what he gets up to in that place.'

'Well, at least he's doing something he likes,' said Katherine.

'Bloody lucky, ain't he?' said Charlie, coming back in. 'I can't even afford a pint.'

'Do you think it will end soon?' asked Katherine.

'Wouldn't like to say.'

'I feel really sorry for some of 'em round here,' said Milly. 'You see the rent man, then the tally man banging on the doors. They know they're home but no one opens the door.'

'Can't really blame 'em if they ain't got it to give him,' said Charlie. 'I bet they're sorry they bought stuff on the never never.'

'Seen some of it took away. It's really sad to see a woman standing at her door after the means test man's been and she has to watch her home being taken away just so she can get some money from the relief office.'

'If this goes on much longer we might be in the same boat.'

'Don't say that! I don't want to go on relief, and I couldn't bear to see me home go.'

'If the worst comes to the worst I'll try and find another job,' said Katherine.

Milly smiled at her. 'You're a good 'en, Katherine.'

She grinned. 'That's only because I don't want my bed to be sold.'

'It's the kids I feel sorry for,' said Milly sadly. 'Look half starved, some of 'em do.'

'That's what'll end it,' said Charlie. 'Most blokes can't bear the thought of the kids having to go without.'

As there was no sign of the strike breaking, Katherine knew it wouldn't be long before her money went down to three shillings. Then they would really be in trouble. Even though she was thinking of looking elsewhere for a job, she knew deep down that would never come about. She liked it at Trent's. Over these past weeks she was even managing to see Nellie now and again, and hoped that in time she could get her to talk about herself.

It was the middle of June when the strike finally ended. At last the docks were full of ships and the men had plenty of overtime.

Katherine was pleased Trent's was busy once more. Gradually things were getting back to normal. Debts were being cleared,

people were beginning to smile again. So far she'd paid off two
shillings of Ida's loan since her rise.

Milly was worried about Dolly. Charlie had promised to take
her to see her as soon as he got a Saturday afternoon off.

'Can't turn down the overtime.'

Three weeks later, on a Monday evening, there was a lot of
laughter as they sat round the table discussing the day out Milly
and Charlie were planning to have on August Bank Holiday
Monday.

Katherine looked round the table at the happy faces.

'Fancy Southend?' asked Charlie.

'Cor, I'd like some of that,' said Ted. 'Reckon there's plenty of
girls down there. Reckon you could come with us, Joe.'

Charlie gave him a friendly clip round the ear. 'You ain't
going nowhere, me old son. Well, not with us, anyway.'

'I hope you two ain't going out with girls,' said Milly. 'I never
knows what you get up to when you're out.'

Ted grinned at Joe. 'Wouldn't tell you if we was.'

Katherine and Joe laughed together. She thought her heart
would burst with the love she had for this family, and to see Joe
happy again was more than she could have ever hoped for.

'We ain't had a day out on our own since Ted was born.'
Milly's cheeks were flushed with excitement. 'But I must get
over to see Dolly first.'

'Course, love. Think I might be able to manage next Sat'day
afternoon, how would that suit you?'

Milly smiled at Charlie, and Katherine could see the great
affection these two had for each other.

'That'll be lovely. You lot'll be all right, won't you?'

'No,' said Katherine gravely. 'I'm sure we'll starve and won't
know—' She stopped when a tea towel flew through the air.

'You,' said Milly, walking round the table and picking the tea
towel off the floor. 'Now, I'll leave something simmering so you

won't have to worry.' She was interrupted by someone banging on the front door. 'Who can that be at this time o' night?'

'I'll go,' said Ted.

They all sat listening to the voices that floated back down the passage.

'That's Tom,' shouted Milly, jumping up. 'It's Tom and Dolly.' She ran out of the room.

Katherine's heart missed a beat. Were they alone, or was Gerald with them?

The voices stopped and it became very quiet.

Chapter 17

Katherine sat perched on the edge of the chair, shaking. All the fear and anger towards Gerald was closing in on her again. It seemed like a lifetime before Milly walked into the kitchen. Her face was ashen. Tom followed her, then Ted, who shut the kitchen door behind him. Tom was alone.

''Allo, mate. This is a nice surprise. How are you, then?' Charlie jumped up and shook Tom's hand vigorously. 'Where's Dolly?' he asked, noting Tom's concerned look.

'Sit down, Tom,' croaked Milly as tears streamed from her eyes. 'Charlie, our Dolly's dead.'

Katherine heard herself shout out loud, 'No, not Dolly. She can't be.'

Tom, who appeared to have aged a great deal, stood beside the table with his cap in his hand and his head bowed.

'Not our Dolly? Tom, what can I say?' Charlie clasped Tom to him and patted his back. 'I'm so very sorry. How did it happen?'

Katherine glanced at Joseph. The colour was visibly draining from his face.

'I'll make some tea,' said Katherine.

'Leave it a minute,' sniffed Milly. 'Let's hear what Tom's got to say first.'

Katherine sat down again. She didn't want to hear that her beloved Dolly had gone. She knew she would blame herself. If only she'd . . .

Tom was speaking very low. 'It was last night. Doctor said it was her heart. Mind you, she ain't been that well for a while now.' He gave a weak smile. 'It's the way she always wanted to go.'

Milly sat at the table and dabbed at her eyes. 'I can't believe it,' she said softly. 'I ain't seen her for weeks. Sodding strike. I should have tried somehow to have got over there. I should have brought her back here.' With her anger Milly's voice rose with every sentence, and tears fell from her eyes. 'Never even said goodbye.'

'You can't blame yourself,' said Tom. 'It was meant to be. She was a stubborn old thing, and you wouldn't have got her here, not to live, anyway.'

Charlie put his arm round Milly's heaving shoulders.

Dolly, their round laughing Dolly, was no more. Katherine felt like an intruder. She wanted to share their grief, but felt it was wrong. She picked up the kettle that was always singing on the fire and took it into the scullery to make the tea.

Joseph was right behind her.

'Poor Dolly,' he whispered. 'I loved Dolly, Mama. She was like a lovely aunt and grandma all rolled into one.' A tear ran down his cheek and Katherine cradled him in her arms and, for a few moments, cried with him.

When he was in control he pulled away. 'I would have given up my room for her, you know.'

'I know you would.' Katherine wiped her eyes on the striped towel that hung on a nail behind the back door.

'What's Tom going to do now?' asked Joseph.

'I don't know. He may have to come here.'

'He can sleep on my mattress.'

'We will have to wait and see what he wants to do.'

Joseph went out the back door. Katherine let him be alone with his thoughts and grief. In his young life he had lost two people he had loved dearly, and who had helped shape his childhood.

As if in a dream, Katherine made the tea. The happy years she had spent with Dolly flooded back. The laughs and long conversations. But Katherine never really knew her. She didn't know her likes or dislikes, other than what was to do with running the house. She didn't know if she had ever wanted children. And Tom was always a quiet man who had kept his own counsel.

Katherine put the tea things on a tray and carried it back into the kitchen.

'Miss Katherine, you will come to her funeral, won't you?'

'Yes of course, Tom. When is it?'

'Thursday morning. That's what I've been doing all day – racing round trying to get things sorted out.'

She went and patted his hand. 'Don't worry, we will all be there. Now I expect you'll like a cup of tea?'

He nodded.

'What you gonner do now then, Tom?' asked Charlie.

'Dunno. Mr Gerald said I could stay on if I like, but I'm not sure.'

'Why don't you come over here when it's all over, just to give yourself breathing space?' said Milly softly.

'I might just do that. I need time to think. It'll be strange not having her around. Been together for over thirty-five years.'

'That's a bloody long time,' said Charlie. 'But as Milly said, there's always a bed here if you fancy it.'

'Thanks.'

'What did Gerald have to say about all this?' asked Katherine.

'Not a lot. Just that he was sorry, that's all.'

'Will he be at the funeral?'

'No, he said he's busy on that day and he'd rather leave it to the family.'

Katherine wanted to shout out, we don't want him sharing our grief, but was pleased she wouldn't be bumping into him.

'There won't be many there then, Tom?' asked Charlie.

'Na, just the family. Mind you, it's just as well if we've gotter fit in our couple of rooms after.'

Katherine thought about Edwin's funeral, and the large congregation that had filled the church, but there wasn't genuine love from that crowd, not like the love that would radiate from Dolly's true friends and relations.

'I'm sure Olive and Ernie will come, and what about you, Ted? Can you get the morning off?'

He nodded. Till now he had sat very quiet, just looking from one speaker to another.

'Someone had better go and tell Olive,' said Milly.

'Me and Joe will go,' said Ted. He seemed almost relieved to get away. 'I'll go an' get him.'

Ted found Joe sitting in the lavatory on the closed lid of the closet with the door wide open. 'What you doing in there?'

'Nothing. Just sitting thinking about the good times we had at that house. Dolly would always let me scrape the bowl when she made cakes. I loved Dolly, you know.'

Ted, his hands in his trouser pockets, gently kicked his foot against the door. 'We all did. But I wasn't lucky enough to know her really well.'

'She was a lovely lady.'

'Joe, wanner come round Olive's with me? Mum wants her to know.'

'Course.'

'You ain't gotter go home tonight, have you?' Milly asked Tom after the boys had left.

'No. Didn't get a lot of sleep last night. I don't have to go and sit with Dolly. The undertaker took her.' He blew his nose hard. 'Is it all right if I kip here just for tonight?'

'Course. Joe and Ted can go in together.'

'I don't want to put anybody out.'

Milly gave him a weak smile. 'This is the least I can do. I only

162

wish I'd got the chance to see her 'fore she went.'

'I'm sure the undertaker will let you,' said Tom.

'Tom, what about money? Can you afford—'

'Don't worry about it. Me and Dolly have always put a bit by for a rainy day. Funny thing, Milly, she was on about sending you some as she guessed things was getting a bit rough for you.' He stopped. 'Never thought she'd be the first to go. I loved her, yer know, really loved her.' He buried his head in his hands and sobbed.

Katherine took the teatray into the scullery. He needed the family at this moment.

It wasn't long before Olive and Ernie came and joined this sad little gathering, and they sat and talked well into the night.

Katherine was nervous about going to the house again. If Gerald came back, how would she react? She knew nothing would stop her going to Dolly's funeral, but Katherine still hesitated as she made her way up the path to the house. She was pleased that everything looked the same. The roses were in full bloom, their scent wafted on the air. This had once been her house and she had loved it dearly.

'All right?' asked Charlie, coming out of the house and taking Katherine's arm.

She smiled. 'Yes, thanks. You go and look after Milly.'

'She wants to say her goodbye alone.'

'I can understand that.'

When Milly and the rest of the family had finished paying their respects, they came out of the tiny basement room where Dolly was lying, then Katherine and Joseph went in.

Dolly looked so peaceful.

Joseph gently kissed her brow, letting his tears fall on her face.

Katherine thought her heart would break for him and Dolly.

To see her lying there so still was very sad. Her face was thinner but a hint of a smile played round her lips. Katherine kissed her wrinkled forehead. She wanted to scoop her up and hold her, to breathe life into her. It was wrong, so wrong that a lovely lady like Dolly should go. She had been like a mother to her.

'You all right, Mama?' asked Joseph, wiping his eyes.

'Yes. Are you ready to go?'

He nodded.

Hand in hand they left the darkened room and walked out into the bright sunlight together.

The church was within walking distance and a vicar whom Katherine had not met before greeted them. She was grateful she didn't have to answer any questions. After Dolly was reverently and quietly laid to rest, the small party made their way back toTom's.

They were sitting drinking tea when Gerald came in.

He stood in the doorway like the lord of the manor and gave them all a slight bow. He had a catlike smirk on his face. 'Hello, Katherine, Joseph.' He walked over and kissed her hand.

She wanted to pull it away but he was holding it very tight. 'Gerald, this is Dolly's sister and her husband, and their daughter and son-in-law.'

'We have met,' he said to Milly. 'And I am pleased to meet all of you, but I wish it were under better circumstances.'

The family only nodded in return.

'So, Joseph, you certainly have grown. Why don't you come and look at my motor car?'

Joseph looked at his mother. He didn't want to upset her.

'You may go if you want to.' Deep inside Katherine was seething. How dare he intrude on these kind people's grief? He hadn't even said a word about Dolly. And had Joseph forgotten why they had moved away from here? She wanted to tell Gerald to go and leave them alone, but she didn't want to make a fuss.

As they went through the door Gerald put his arm round Joseph's shoulders. 'So, my boy, how's life treating you?'

'Not too bad, sir.'

'If you don't mind me saying so, you don't look that prosperous, or well-dressed. Grown right out of your clothes, I see. Is that mother of yours looking after you?'

'Yes, sir. She works very hard.' Joseph tried hard to pull the sleeves of his jacket down.

Gerald stopped. 'She works?'

'Yes, sir. And so do I.'

Gerald looked shocked. 'You're working? What about school? Or can't your mother even afford that?'

'I only work on Saturdays, and that's at a garage. Mr Lacy, that's the owner, tells me all about the motors and shows me how they work.'

'Does he now? So what do you think of this one?'

As they rounded the corner Joseph stood and stared at the shiny black Humber. 'That is really beautiful,' he said wistfully.

'Have you ever been for a ride in one?'

'No, I've only sat in those we have, we don't have Humbers.'

'Well, come on, get in, we'll go for a little drive.'

Joseph desperately wanted to, but he knew his mother wouldn't approve and it would only cause friction. He looked at the house. 'I don't think . . .'

'Come on, don't worry about your mother. I'll explain to her that it was me who persuaded you. Now hop in.'

As they drove along Joseph thought he was in heaven. The smell of the leather as he sunk back into the seat was intoxicating. To own a motor car one day was what he wanted to do more than anything else in the world. To see the trees rushing past was, to him, pure magic. He wanted this moment to last for ever.

'So what do you think?' asked Gerald, as they turned back into the drive. 'She's lovely, isn't she?'

Joseph nodded and ran his hand along the walnut dashboard. 'She is wonderful.'

Gerald stopped. 'Is your Mr Lacy going to teach you to drive?'

'I hope so.'

'You know, Joseph, if you lived here I could teach you to drive this. Would you like that?'

'Yes, sir.' Joseph's eyes were sparkling.

'We'll have to have a word with your mother, won't we? And when you and your mother move back here, we could be a family. I'm looking forward to being a father.'

Joseph smiled. 'I don't think Mama would like that. I never called Edwin Father.'

Gerald laughed. 'I'm not talking about you, I'm talking about my child. Your mother will be back here for the birth of my child. I can't have it born in the slums.'

Joseph felt as if he had been kicked in the stomach. 'Child? What child?' he said softly.

'Didn't your mother tell you? She's having my baby. Well, she won't be able to keep her secret for long, not once she—'

Anger filled Joseph's face. 'You're lying,' he yelled. He raised his clenched fist to strike Gerald.

Gerald took hold of the boy's arm and held it tight. 'Don' t be so foolish,' he laughed. 'So, I assume by this little scene she hasn't told you?'

Tears welled up in Joseph's eyes. 'You're lying. My mother isn't having your baby.'

'Oh yes she is. Why don't you go and ask her?'

'She wouldn't, not with you. You attacked her. I saw her bruises.'

Gerald threw back his head and laughed. 'Is that what she told you? I guess you're old enough to know that sometimes, when two people are enjoying themselves, things can get out of hand. We were just having a little fun and games.'

Joseph felt physically sick. He ran from the car and threw himself against the door of Tom's flat.

'Good God,' said Milly, opening the door. 'Whatever's wrong with you?'

'Where's Mama?' he shouted.

Katherine came out of the kitchen and ushered him inside. 'Joseph,' she said angrily, 'please lower your voice.'

He threw himself at her and held her tight. 'Please say it isn't true,' he cried.

Katherine looked about her, embarrassed. 'What's not true?' Suddenly she realised what he was saying. 'Gerald,' she hissed. 'What has Gerald been telling you?'

Joseph stepped back. 'He said you were having his baby.'

There was a stunned silence from the room. Katherine felt all eyes on her. 'Milly, tell him it isn't true.'

Milly sobbed, 'I'm sorry, Katherine. It's all my fault.'

'It doesn't matter whose fault it was, just tell Joseph it isn't true.' Katherine's voice was loud and high-pitched.

'It ain't true now,' said Milly, dabbing at her eyes.

'Now?' said Joseph. 'What do you mean, "now"? So was it once?'

'Come on now, son. For a young boy you certainly ask a lot of questions.' Charlie looked uneasy.

'I ain't your son and I ain't a boy.'

'Joseph,' said Katherine, shocked at his outburst.

He was hurt and angry and, ignoring his mother, continued, 'And if you must know, since I've been living with you lot I've had to grow up, and that school I go to is a good place to learn about life.'

Mouths fell open.

It took all Katherine's strength for her to regain her dignity. 'You will apologise for talking to Charlie like that, young man.'

Joseph left the room in silence.

'I'll go and talk to him,' said Ted, hurrying behind him, eager to quell the situation.

'So,' said Charlie, 'what's this all about?'

'I'll tell you later,' said Milly. 'Wait till we get home.'

'You mean to say you was going to have a baby?' Olive's face was filled with disbelief.

'She's not now,' said Milly.

'And you knew all about it?' asked Charlie.

Milly's voice rose. 'For Christ's sake, Charlie, shut it. I told you I'll tell you later. I'm sorry, Tom. I shouldn't be shouting, not today . . .'

'This is all my fault. Tom, I'm so sorry about this. Please forgive me,' said Katherine.

'Don't worry about it.' He gave a little grin. 'At least it gave everybody something else to think about.'

Katherine put on her hat.

'Where you going?' asked Milly.

'I am going to find Gerald.'

'No, Katherine. No!' shouted Milly. 'You can't.'

Katherine swept past her, closing the door behind her.

Chapter 18

'Katherine, my dear, I always knew you would come looking for me.' Gerald came striding towards her where she stood on the doorstep. 'I'm so pleased to see that you are looking so very well and, I might add, as beautiful as ever, but if you don't mind me saying, not quite so smart.'

When he was close enough, she struck him hard round the face.

Putting his hand to his cheek he tried to laugh it off, but Katherine could see the anger in his eyes.

'So, to what do I owe this little outburst of temper? It can't be because I don't approve of your gown.'

Katherine could smell the drink on his breath and her thoughts quickly went to Mr Addams. What was it about drink? Did men need it to give them courage? Gerald angered her so much that she knew she couldn't talk rationally to him, so she turned and began to walk away. 'No. It wasn't just for your bad manners,' she said over her shoulder.

Gerald fell in step beside her. 'I'm sorry, that wasn't very gentlemanly of me. Please forgive me.'

'You know very well why I came to see you.'

'I know.' He jokingly put his hands up in a gesture of surrender. 'It's because I took Joseph out in my motor car. I didn't think you would disapprove so . . .'

Katherine suddenly stopped. 'You know full well I am not here to talk about that. How dare you say the things you did to Joseph?'

He took hold of her elbow, forcibly moving her along the path. 'Like what?'

She tried to shrug his arm away. 'Don't you think he has had enough to put up with without you upsetting him?'

'Oh, I know, you must be talking about our child. And he wouldn't "have to put up with" it, as you so charmingly put it – my, we are going downhill with our phrases, aren't we? – if you hadn't been foolish enough to move out.'

'There is no child.'

'Now you don't think for one moment I am going to believe that?'

'I can look you in the eye and tell you there is no child.'

'So why would Dolly's sister tell me otherwise?'

'You had better ask her.' Katherine tried to pull her arm away from his tight grip.

'I don't believe you.'

'You can think what you like. And if there had been a child I would never have told you.'

He pulled her round to face him, his eyes narrowed. 'I said I don't believe you. Now you just listen to me. When this child is born I will take it from you and have it brought up respectably in this house under my guidance. I can find out where you live and if need be, I'll bring you back here and keep you till after the birth, then you can go wherever you like. But you will go alone.'

She laughed in his face. 'You, sir, are unbalanced.'

'I've been trying to find out where you went, but Dolly and that tight-lipped husband of hers kept it very quiet. I even thought of telling them I'd found Edwin's will.'

Katherine looked up.

'I knew that would get your attention.'

'Did you?'

'No,' smirked Gerald, 'sadly for you, he really didn't leave one. No, I've been giving our situation a lot of thought. It was a bit of luck, Dolly dying. I knew you would be here for the funeral.'

'How dare you think Dolly's death was a "bit of luck"? I'm not going to listen to this.'

'You will listen.' He clasped the tops of her arms with both hands. Despite the protection of her coat she could feel his fingers digging into her flesh. 'You see, I want my name to carry on. I know I could have any woman I choose but I like your bloodstock.'

Katherine laughed again and broke free from his grip. 'My bloodstock. You know nothing about me.'

'I knew from Edwin that you were a determined woman who would face up to any challenge. And to come from Australia alone meant you were a fighter. But it was your beauty that made all the other women pale into insignificance. Men would envy me when they saw you on my arm. You know what they say about redheads – full of fire and passion.' He stood back and looked her up and down. 'I must admit I am a little disappointed by the way you have finished up, but we can change all that.'

'I'm not going to stand here and listen to your mad ravings!'

'Edwin wasn't man enough for you, but when that woman told me you were having my baby, I was overjoyed. You are certainly a woman I approve of to be the mother of my child.'

Katherine went to move away but he blocked her path.

'I've worked it out. So when I think you are almost due I'll come and get you. I don't intend keeping you till it's necessary.'

Katherine thought she was hearing things and laughed. It was a loud nervous laugh. 'Gerald. There is no child now. I lost it.'

He looked as if he'd been struck. His cheeks began to twitch and his face turned scarlet with temper. He clenched his fists. Katherine began to slowly back away, suddenly fearing for her life.

'How did that happen?'

'Mother nature.'

'I'll hang for you. Taking my child away.'

'You can't prove it.'

He raised his hand.

'Mama!'

'Joseph,' cried Katherine.

'I've overheard all you've said. Gerald, Mama is right, you are mad.'

Katherine picked up her skirts and ran to her son's side. He was right, he wasn't a boy any longer. He had grown up.

From the expression on Gerald's face, Katherine thought he would explode he was so angry.

'Get out. Get out. Don't you ever come to this house again. And take that . . . that gardener with you, do you hear?' He wagged a finger at them. 'Tell him you have just lost him his home and his job.'

Katherine took hold of her son's hand and hurried away.

'Don't worry about it, Miss Katherine. I ain't sorry to go.'

When Katherine and Joseph walked into Tom's she decided to tell them all what had happened. She told them she had lost the baby, but she could see in Olive's face that she knew, and that she disapproved, but then she was young and had a husband.

'I'm so sorry, Tom,' said Katherine.

'He is bloody mad, if you ask me,' said Charlie.

'Look, we had better start getting Tom's things together,' said Ernie, looking towards the door. He was very agitated. 'We don't want him here causing trouble.'

'It'll be over my dead body,' said Charlie.

'Don't underestimate him,' said Katherine.

'Right,' said Milly. 'All grab a bag and start filling 'em. Charlie, take the sheets off the bed and fill 'em with the bedding, then tie 'em up.'

'We ain't got that much,' said Tom.

'I know, but we ain't leaving nothing.' Milly was in her element, organising.

They were loaded with bags and bundles as they all made their way down the drive.

Katherine turned and looked back at the house. Tears filled her eyes at the happy memories of long ago. She knew she would never return.

'It's all over now,' said Milly, putting her bundles on the ground and putting her arm round Katherine's shoulders.

'Yes, yes it is.' Katherine turned away.

It was too late for her to go to Trent's, and although she would be a day's pay short she didn't care.

As they sat on the bus Katherine thought about Dolly. In many ways she would have enjoyed today. She always loved a bit of scandal, but she would never have approved of what Katherine had done.

'Thought you might have made a bit of effort to get back yesterday afternoon,' said Josh when Katherine walked in on the Friday morning.

'There was a bit of trouble so I had to stay and help them sort it out.'

'Look, Kate, I know I let you down when the strike was on, but I didn't have a lot of choice now, did I?'

'What's brought this on?'

'Nothing.'

Ron, the bookies' runner, who was sitting at a table reading his paper, peered at her from under his large cloth cap. He was a small thin man whose eyes quickly darted about. He was always on the lookout for the law. He was friendly and enjoyed a laugh. 'He's only just found out what an asset you are to this place.'

Katherine laughed. 'I'm always telling him that.'

'Rushing round yesterday dinnertime like a blue-arse fly, he was.' Ron stood up and threw the butt end of his hand-rolled cigarette on to the floor and ground it out. 'Gotter go. Got a few bets to put on. See yer tomorrow, Josh, Katie.'

Katherine began singing as she worked.

'What you so bloody happy about?'

'Lot of things.'

'Well, pour out a cuppa for Nellie.'

'Shall I take it up?'

'If yer like.'

Katherine smiled. 'My, we are an old grumpy head this morning.' She ducked when she saw the dishcloth come flying through the air. She knew she made him happy, and he didn't want to lose her, so that could strengthen her position in the future.

'Hello, Nellie,' said Katherine, confidently walking into the bedroom.

'You're bloody cheerful today. Who's died and left you a fortune?'

'Nobody. It's just that suddenly I feel in control of my life. How about you, don't you wish you were in control?'

'No I don't.'

Katherine laughed. 'I could make you a lot more comfortable, you know.'

Nellie's eyes twitched. 'Why should you bother with me?'

Katherine sat on the bed. 'Because I think it's such a waste, you stuck up here on a lovely day like today. Don't you miss seeing the blue sky?'

'Can see it from me bed if I move round a bit.'

'Please yourself. But I'm sure with a bit of pampering life could be a lot better for you. Shall I close the door?'

'No, leave it open.'

Katherine smiled as she went down the stairs. She knew she was gaining Nellie's confidence.

Katherine piled pies, mash, saveloys and pease pudding on to plates, and jellied eels into bowls to be devoured here or taken home. She wiped her brow, it was warm work. After the lunchtime rush Josh went to the wash house out at the back of the shop to peel the potatoes for tomorrow. Katherine began cleaning the counter when the girl who arranged to meet men here walked in.

'Tea?' asked Katherine.

'Yer.'

'If you sit down I'll bring it over.'

'Why?'

'No reason.'

The girl eyed Katherine with suspicion. 'How long you been working here?'

'Must be, what, nearly three months.' Katherine put the tea on the table. All this time she had been intrigued with this girl but never had the chance to speak to her at length.

The girl lit a cigarette. 'You got any kids?'

'I have a son.'

'He at work?'

'No, still at school.'

'How old is he?'

'Thirteen.'

'Thirteen, and still at school? Blimey! I was out earning me living at ten.'

Katherine sat at the table. 'And how long ago was that?'

'Mind yer own business.' The girl pushed strands of her dark fuzzy hair under her large black hat.

'Don't you have any family?'

The girl blew smoke into the air. 'Why?'

'Are they dead?' asked Katherine softly.

The girl threw her head back and laughed. 'Na, the bloke me mum lives with has just come out of prison.'

When the girl's customer walked in, Katherine left the table.

They went out, leaving the smell of cheap scent behind. Katherine wondered where the girl took the men, and why she didn't finish up in the family way.

Tom was finding it difficult to settle down without Dolly. He couldn't get used to the idea of not working, and felt ill at ease hanging around the house all day, despite Milly trying to keep him busy with the odd job or two.

Even when Charlie told him he was pleased to have a drinking partner that didn't bring a smile to his sad face.

'P'raps Alf could find you a job in the pub,' said Charlie.

'That might not be a bad idea. I'll sound him out. I'll have to find work soon. Me money ain't gonner last for ever, and I don't expect you two to keep me in shirt buttons.'

Milly had told him to take his time in whatever he wanted to do.

Katherine knew he had quite a bit of money, and Milly didn't take a lot from him, but he was an independent man, and would always want to pay his way. He would go off for hours, not telling anyone where he'd been. Milly said she thought he went to the cemetery.

The other members of the Stevens household appeared to be contented.

Joseph was happy at the garage and eagerly waiting for his mother to let him leave school so he could work there full time. Everyone was pleased that he didn't cause any fuss about giving up the front room to Tom.

Ted's sixteenth birthday had come and gone. He was a young man now, but he still seemed to enjoy Joe's company.

On August Bank Holiday Monday Charlie and Milly took Tom to Southend-on-Sea for the day, and they enjoyed every minute of it. For days afterwards Milly talked about it.

At the shop Katherine was gradually winning Nellie's

confidence and now they often had a little chat. She still hadn't found out what was wrong with her, and why she stayed in bed. Katherine was pleased that at last she was managing to save a little from her wages, so things were definitely looking up.

The one person who seemed to be avoiding her was Briony. Even if Katherine went along to the ironmongers Briony made an excuse to hurry home and not to talk to Katherine. Did she really think that she, Katherine, was meeting her father?

It was Saturday evening, and Ted stood in front of the mirror, putting grease on his hair.

'Out again then, son?' asked Charlie.

Ted had been going out looking smart for a few weeks now, so everyone guessed he was meeting a young lady. He always said he was meeting Joe, but when Katherine consulted her son, he said he didn't know what she was talking about. They were keeping close together on this issue.

'What you tarting yourself up for, son? Got yourself a girl then?'

'No I ain't. I'm just going out, that's all.'

'I can see that,' Charlie laughed. 'Just as long as you remember to polish yer courting tackle.'

'Charlie Stevens, don't be so rude. Just leave him be. Have you got yourself a young lady then, Ted?' Milly had been dying to know.

Ted's cheeks turned bright red. 'No I ain't. I'm gonner meet Joe from work.'

'Joe didn't say he was going out,' said Katherine, grinning.

'He might not want to come tonight.' Ted was beginning to get flustered.

'I see.' Katherine gave Milly a knowing look.

'So where you going then, Ted?'

'I dunno, Mum. Don't keep on.'

'Move over, son,' said Charlie, pushing Ted away from the mirror. 'Let the dog see the rabbit. Me and Tom are just going out for a quick one, we won't be long.'

Milly tutted. 'I've heard all that before. Go on, be off with you. Good job I've got Katherine to keep me company.'

Charlie kissed Milly's cheek. 'See yer later, love.'

When they'd gone, Milly sat back in the armchair. 'I'm worried about Tom. He can't settle down at all.'

'It's hard for him to lose his job as well as Dolly. I still feel I'm to blame for that.'

'I dunno. I reckon that Gerald would have made his life a misery if he'd stayed there.'

'I think I'm inclined to agree with you,' said Katherine.

Ted poked his head round the door. 'I'm off, see you later.'

'Don't make too much noise when you come in,' Milly grinned. 'They can be a pair of noisy buggers when they get together. I wonder what they're up to.'

'They have been very secretive lately.'

'They're always that. It's all this going out tidy that worries me.'

'I haven't noticed Joseph going out tidy.'

'No, that's what worries me. I reckon my Ted's paying him to keep quiet.'

'Now that I can understand.' Katherine laughed. 'It's good to see Joseph happy. Moving here was the best thing that happened to both of us,' she said.

All evening they sat and talked. Milly was busy knitting and getting excited about the new baby. 'I'm very lucky. I've got so much.'

Katherine glanced at the clock. 'Ten o' clock. Joseph must have gone out with Ted. I hope he had something to eat at work.'

'Just like a mother. More worried about her son's stomach than who he's with.'

'He's with Ted.'

'Yes I know, but is there two young ladies?'

They laughed.

'I shouldn't think so,' said Katherine. 'Not if he went out in those dirty overalls.'

'That's true. I wonder where they've gone.'

'I'm sure they'll tell us if they want to.'

Their peace was shattered by someone banging hard on the front door.

Milly's face turned deathly white. 'Who can that be at this time of night?'

'I don't know. Perhaps it's Ernie, perhaps Olive's started.'

Milly jumped up. 'Of course. It must be him, silly bugger. He wouldn't use the key.' She flew down the passage and opened the door.

'Oh my God!' screamed Milly, her raised voice full of alarm.

For a second or two Katherine sat riveted, then she also raced up the passage.

Chapter 19

Katherine stood next to Milly, whose eyes were wide open at the sight of Briony standing there. 'Briony,' she whispered. 'What's happened?'

The young girl had blood on her face, hands and down the front of her frock. 'Ted, Ted,' she cried.

'Ted. My Ted?' screamed Milly.

Briony nodded, her thin body racked with sobs.

Milly sprang at her like a caged animal. 'What you done with my Ted?'

Mrs Duke suddenly appeared on the doorstep. 'What's all this racket? What the bleeding hell's going—' She didn't finish the sentence as she helped Katherine to prise Milly away from Briony.

Tears mingled with the blood on Briony's cheeks, turning the bright red smears to a soft watery pink. 'I ain't done nothing to Ted. I was supposed to meet him. I need him to help . . .' She couldn't finish the sentence.

Milly lunged at Briony again and, grabbing her shoulders, shook her violently. 'My Ted! What was you doing with my Ted? I'll kill you if you've hurt him.'

'It ain't Ted,' said Briony, sobbing and shaking her head.

'What's she bin doing with young Ted?' asked Mrs Duke.

'I don't know,' said Katherine. 'You'd better come in.' Katherine was pulling Milly away. 'We don't want all the neighbours to hear.'

'I can't leave the kids. I've got to go back. Please help me. It ain't Ted, missis, it's me dad.' She ran the back of her hand under her wet nose.

Milly jumped back as if she'd been scalded. 'Your dad? What's he done to my Ted?'

'Briony, what's happened?' Katherine was trying to take control.

'He's dead. Me dad's dead.'

Katherine also took a step back.

Mrs Duke put her hand to her mouth and let out a long gasp. 'Oh my God. How?'

All three women were dreading the answer.

'I've killed him.'

The silence that followed seemed to go on for ever.

Suddenly Milly broke the silence. 'What did you say?'

Briony didn't speak.

'How? Dead?' blustered Mrs Duke.

'Are you sure he's dead?' asked Katherine softly.

Briony nodded.

'We'd better go over and see,' said Katherine.

'Where's my Ted?' screamed Milly.

'I don't know, I ain't seen him,' sobbed Briony. 'I was s'posed to, but I . . .' Tears drowned the rest of the sentence.

'You was meeting my Ted?'

'Milly, let's talk about this later. Look, why don't you make her a cup of tea? Mrs Duke, you'd better come with me.'

'I can't leave the kids in there, not with . . .' sniffed Briony, 'Oh missis, please help me.'

Katherine threw her arms round Briony and held her close, as sobs racked her thin frail body. Katherine could have cried for this poor child who suddenly appeared small and vulnerable. She had lost all her bravado and courage.

'We'd better all come back with you,' said Milly.

They hurried across the road. Mrs Duke was shuffling and panting behind them, having a job to keep up.

Briony pushed open the front door. 'It's all right, kids, it's me.'

The three women stood in the dark smelly passage. The kitchen door flew open and a tight bunch of youngsters raced up to Briony and flung themselves at her, all trying to get as close as possible. Slowly they moved into the kitchen.

'Have you told 'em?' Bridget was standing in the corner, her voice harsh. Even in the dim gaslight they could see the tears glistening on her ashen face. She too had blood on her frock, and a baby on her hip.

Briony shook her head. 'Only that Dad is dead.'

'What's been happening over here?' asked Mrs Duke.

'Did she tell yer she done it 'cos she was jealous of me?'

'Jealous of you?' asked Katherine.

Bridget came towards them. She poked Briony in the shoulder with a skinny finger. 'Yer, she didn't like Dad being nice to me.'

'Nice? You call that being nice?' yelled Briony, taking the baby from her.

'Well, I liked it,' said Bridget. 'She didn't like it 'cos he showed her he loved me the best.' Bridget stood with her arms folded defiantly.

'It ain't love, it's dirty. And it's wrong,' said Briony.

'What's she talking about?' asked Mrs Duke.

Briony lowered her head. 'Me dad said he loved us, and he used to . . . He used to do things to us.'

'You don't mean . . . ?' Katherine hesitated. 'You don't mean touch your private parts?' she whispered.

Briony nodded.

'Bloody hell,' said Mrs Duke. 'The dirty sod. You mean ter say he . . . you know, to both of you?'

Briony looked up. 'He done it to me for a long while, even when Mum was here, but I didn't tell anyone. I didn't like it and he said if I told anyone he'd beat me and say it wasn't true.'

'How long has this been going on?' asked Katherine.

'With me, years,' said Briony. The baby began crying and she tried to comfort it with soothing noises and kisses.

'She didn't like it, but I did,' Bridget told them. 'When Dad took hold of me and kissed me and put his hands all over me it was lovely.'

Milly took the fretful baby from Briony and gently rocked it back and forth.

'Don't say that. Stop it, stop it!' Briony put her hands over her ears. 'It wasn't lovely, it was rotten. He hurt me.' She buried her head in Katherine's bosom.

'Well, I liked it,' said Bridget.

'Where were your brothers when all this was going on?' asked Katherine.

'They left home. They went after Mum died,' said one of the younger boys.

'Thought I ain't seen 'em around,' said Mrs Duke.

'How old are you, Bridget?' asked Milly.

'Thirteen.'

'Thirteen,' repeated Milly. 'Still a baby.'

'I ain't a baby, missis.'

'No, you're not, not now.'

'Briony,' said Katherine, gently pushing her away, 'where's your dad?'

'He's dead,' shouted another little Addams. 'Our dad's dead. Briony done it. She said she done it.'

'Where is he?' asked Katherine.

'Upstairs. I'll show you.'

'I'll go and look, you lot stay down here. Bridget, make sure they don't come up.'

Bridget pouted. 'Why? They've seen him.'

'I said, stay down here.' Katherine's voice was forceful.

'I'll stay here with them,' said Milly, still rocking the baby.

Slowly Katherine and Briony mounted the bare wooden stairs, with Mrs Duke close behind.

'Be careful. We ain't got any banisters 'cos me dad broke them up for firewood last winter. And watch your step in the bedroom as some of the floorboards is missing as well.'

She stood in the doorway. There was no door – that too must have been used for firewood. Katherine gently moved Briony to one side.

Mrs Duke, who was breathing heavily down Katherine's neck, peered into the room. The curtains, which looked like bits of rag, were stretched across the window. They could see Mr Addams lying on the bed. An old coat had been thrown over him, but a bare leg was sticking out.

Mrs Duke spoke first. 'Oh my God. What have you done?' She moved carefully into the room.

Katherine put her arm round Briony's shoulders and eased her away. 'What happened?'

'I didn't mean to kill him.'

'I'm sure you didn't.'

'Will they hang me?'

'Briony,' Katherine tried to keep the tone of her voice level, 'how did it happen?'

The frightened girl leant against the wall, fear in her eyes. 'I caught him with Bridget. He shouldn't have done it, not to her,' she sobbed.

Mrs Duke came and stood with them. 'He's dead, all right. Stabbed in the back. The knife's still in him, and he's starkers, naked as a new-born babe. We'd better get a copper.'

Briony began to shake uncontrollably. Her teeth chattered and her whole body was convulsing.

Katherine held her tight. 'No, wait,' she said, over her shoulder.

'What? Why? They've got to come and bring a doctor.'

'Just a minute. Wait till she calms down and can tell us how it happened.'

'We can see how it happened, she's stabbed him.'

Milly met them at the bottom of the stairs. 'Is he dead?'

'Yes,' said Katherine. 'Look, why don't you take all of them over to your house and give Briony a cup of hot sweet tea? She needs something to help her get over the shock.'

Mrs Duke straightened up. 'Well, I wouldn't have her in my house. She's a murderer. She might do for you if you take her to your place.'

'Don't talk such a load of rot. She thought she was protecting her sister.' Katherine was angry. Angry with Mrs Duke. Angry with Mr Addams. Angry with Briony, and angry with Bridget for allowing this to happen.

'Load of rot, is it? Always said there was something funny with this family and now they've proved it. Bad seed, the lot of 'em. You wait till my Stanley and the rest of the fellas hears about this. They'll run 'em out of the street, they will – all of 'em, kids an' all.'

'If you've quite finished, Mrs Duke, we'll be off,' said Milly. 'Perhaps you would like to go to the police then?'

'You bet I will!' She stomped down the stairs.

'Will she run the kids out of the house?' asked Briony. She looked at Katherine, her beautiful blue eyes red and swollen.

'No, she's all talk,' said Milly. 'Now come on, come and have a cup of tea.' Milly ushered Briony and the little band out of the door and across the road.

Bridget stood at the bottom of the stairs. 'I ain't going over there. I'm gonner stay here with me dad.'

Katherine looked at her. She wasn't going to argue, as she realised that the girl could still be in shock. 'Please yourself. You know where to find us when you feel like it.'

'Will they put Briony away?'

'I would think so.'

'What about the kids?'

'They will probably have to go in a home.'

'What about me?'

'I expect you will have to go with them as well.'

'I ain't going to no home.'

'Well, we will have to wait and see what happens. Now if you're staying here, when the police arrive you can tell them where Briony is.'

Katherine didn't want to leave her, but she knew if she tried to force her it would end up with a screaming match.

As Katherine made her way across the road her mind was in turmoil. She tried to imagine what must have been happening in that house. Poor Briony. They had been worried about Mr Wilks from the ironmonger's interfering with her. They never dreamt her father was doing things like that. Tears filled Katherine's eyes. And how was Ted involved? Were they lovers? Poor Briony, she could be hanged for murder.

They were sitting drinking tea when the front door slammed and they heard Ted and Joe laughing and talking all the way down the passage. Their laughter stopped when they opened the kitchen door and saw so many sad faces.

Briony ran up to Ted and threw her arms around his neck. 'I'm sorry I didn't meet you. I was . . .' She broke into more tears.

Ted's face flushed. He looked from one to the other, confused and embarrassed. He untwined Briony's arms from around his neck and, pushing her away, stepped back. 'What's going on?'

'Sit down, son,' said Milly. 'Something terrible's happened.'

'Our Briony's killed our dad,' said one of the children.

'What?' said Ted.

'I'm afraid it's true,' said Milly.

Joseph quickly took a breath. He looked bewildered as he glanced round the room at all the faces staring at them.

'How? Why?' asked Ted.

Briony sat down. 'I didn't tell you what me dad did to me, and when I saw him doing it with Bridget – well, I just lost me temper and got a knife . . .' Once again the tears fell.

Ted also sat down. 'You mean you killed your dad?'

She nodded.

'Why? What did he do that made—'

'Ted! Don't be so innocent, you know?'

He looked at his mother. His face became angry. 'He did that to you? And to Bridget? Then he bloody well got what he deserved!'

'Yes, but what about Briony?' asked Katherine.

'We'll just tell everybody what happened. They'll all say good job.'

'Not in the eyes of the law they won't.'

'You don't think . . . She won't go to prison, will she?'

'We will just have to wait for the police,' said his mother.

'Billy, leave that alone. I'm sorry, missis. Now you listen, kids. Don't you dare touch anything.'

Always the little mother, thought Katherine as Briony sat screwing the handkerchief she had given her into a tight knot.

It wasn't long after that the rumpus in the passage told them that Charlie and Tom were home. They must have arrived at the front door at the same time as the police and the doctor.

'What the bleeding hell's going on? There's a couple of coppers here and a Black Maria outside. What's this lot doing here?' demanded Charlie as he pushed open the kitchen door and saw the room full.

'For Gawd's sake sit down and I'll tell you all about it,' said Milly.

Katherine took the doctor across the road. When the police had been told all that had happened, and they had seen the body, they took Briony into Milly's front room.

'Will she go to prison?' asked Ted again.

'I'm afraid so,' said Katherine.

'What you been doing with young Briony then?' asked Charlie.

'I ain't done nothing. We just went out a couple of times, that's all. She's a nice girl.'

'So, Joseph, what were you doing while Ted was out with Briony?' asked Katherine.

'I stayed on at work.'

'Why didn't you tell us you was meeting Briony?' asked Milly.

'I didn't say 'cos I knew you wouldn't approve.'

'Too bloody right we wouldn't!' said Charlie. 'Bloody lot of scum bags, they are.'

'No we ain't!' protested Billy.

'See? Briony's not!' shouted Ted. 'She's nice, and what her dad did to her was rotten, really rotten. She's tried to look after all of them, but her dad never give her much money, she had to pinch it out of his pockets when he came home drunk, and he used to beat her.' Ted was almost in tears. 'I liked her, she was nice.'

The silence that followed was almost unbearable.

'I'll make another cup of tea,' said Katherine.

The kitchen door opened and one of the policemen came in.

'The doctor's getting in touch with the Salvation Army to take the kids away. Can they stay here till then?'

'How long for?' asked Charlie.

'Shouldn't be too long.'

'What about Bridget?' asked Katherine.

'She'll have to go as well. The doctor will be making the arrangements about the body. Trouble is it's late, and it may be a while before he can get things moving.'

'What about Briony?' asked Milly.

'She's coming with us to the police station.'

'What will happen to her?'

'She'll be charged with murder.'

'But she's only a child,' said Katherine.

'That's as maybe, but it's still murder.'

'Will they hang her?' asked Charlie.

'That's up to the judge. We've got to be off now.'

The shout that came from the front door sent them all racing out of the kitchen. They became wedged in the passage but were in time to see Briony run out of the house with a burly policeman behind her.

The kids started shouting. 'Go on, Bri! Run for it!'

'You've let her get away!' yelled the senior policeman, pushing past them.

'Couldn't help it, Sarge,' the other one said when they reached the street. 'She slipped away before I got a chance to put her in the van.'

'She won't get far.'

Ted grinned as the sergeant straightened his jacket.

'Where will she go?' asked Milly.

'Dunno,' said Ted.

'She went that way,' said Mrs Duke, who was standing at her door and pointing up the street.

'Could see that, missis, couldn't I?' said the policeman.

'Well, come on then,' said the sergeant. 'Let's get moving. We'll soon catch her up.'

As they drove away Milly turned to Mrs Duke. 'Trust you to have your two penn'orth! You didn't have to be so bloody helpful, did you?'

'She can't get away with it. After all, murder's murder, ain't it?' she said pompously.

'That's as maybe,' said Katherine, 'but at least it's not on our conscience that we didn't try to help her.'

Mrs Duke tossed her head, tutted, and went indoors.

Chapter 20

For the few short hours that were left of the night, nobody got a lot of sleep. As soon as dawn broke everybody began milling about. Milly began to worry that the Salvation Army had forgotten they had to collect the children. The house was at bursting point with kids screaming and yelling everywhere, and a steady stream filing out to the lav.

'It seems as if they've multiplied overnight,' said Katherine.

'You two!' shouted Milly, pointing a spoon at a pair of them. 'Stop that fighting!'

'She started it,' said the boy, picking his nose.

'I don't care who started it, I said stop it.' Milly sighed and carried on dishing out plates of porridge. 'I dread to think what it looks like out there,' she said, nodding in the direction of the back door as another child slipped down from the table and made his way through the scullery and outside.

'It wasn't too bad when I went out,' said Katherine, taking the youngest from the battered old bassinet.

'Do you think the police told them where they are?'

'Of course. Maybe it's because it's Sunday and they're busy,' said Katherine, as she changed the rag that was the baby's nappy.

'Even so, they should be looking after this lot.' Milly dished up more porridge to fill eager mouths.

'I'm sure we can manage for a bit longer. Just look at the state of this poor little mite's bottom.'

Milly straightened up. 'It's a bloody shame all round. I don't know what Ted and Joe think they were doing, dashing off like that first thing. How do they reckon they're gonner find Briony? I told 'em I reckon she's in clink, but they wouldn't listen.'

'Well, it gives them something to do.'

'S'pose so.'

Katherine admired Milly. She had been so good, and was making these children as comfortable as possible. For a few hours they had slept huddled together on the kitchen floor, and now she was busy giving them breakfast.

'When will Briony come back?' asked one little girl as she stuffed spoonfuls of porridge into her mouth.

'I don't know,' said Katherine, who was busy buttering bread as fast as she could.

'Will Bridget come here?'

'I don't think so,' said Milly. She had been over the road earlier to collect what few clothes the Addams children had, and asked Bridget to come and have some breakfast, but she said she wouldn't leave her dad whose body was still in the house.

Two of the children giggled. 'She don't know what she's missing.'

'We don't get stuff like this at home.'

'Will we get nice food when we're in that home?' The little voices excitedly filled the kitchen.

'I expect so,' said Katherine. To them this was almost an outing.

It wasn't until after her father's body had been taken away that Bridget asked to come in.

'Would you like something to eat?' Milly asked her.

She nodded.

'Missis here said we'll get good food in the home.'

Bridget looked at the child who had spoken. 'We might all be separated.'

'Na, they wouldn't do that, would they, missis?'

Milly shrugged. 'I don't know.'

Charlie came into the kitchen. 'It's a good job I ain't still on strike. Couldn't afford to feed this lot if I was.'

'Well you ain't,' said Milly crossly. 'And a bit of bread and porridge don't cost the earth.'

He pulled a funny face. 'Pardon me. Sorry I spoke.'

One of the kids laughed. 'You ain't half funny, mister. Our dad wasn't funny.'

Charlie looked at his hands. 'Yes, well, enjoy your breakfast.' He went out to the lav.

Later that morning the Salvation Army came and took the children away. The youngest was bundled with what few bits they had into the large bassinet. There were no tears as they marched up the street. Katherine, Charlie, Tom and Milly stood at the door and watched them go. So, it appeared, did all of Croft Street.

'Bloody hell!' said Charlie. 'I reckon they'll be selling tickets soon.'

'Are those the kids of the murdered man?' asked a man whom they'd noticed asking questions of the women up the road. 'That woman said you've been looking after them, that right?' He was writing in a notebook.

Katherine noted Mrs Duke was among the gossips.

'Who wants to know?' asked Charlie.

'I'm Fred, a reporter.'

'Are you now? Well, I'm Charlie, a stevedore.'

Milly laughed nervously.

'No, come on. What's this all about? My boss told me to find out if it's true that his daughter killed him. Then it seems she was full of remorse and last night threw herself under a train. Poor little cow.'

Katherine felt her legs go from under her. 'Oh no!' she cried out. 'Not Briony.' She held on to Charlie's arm to steady herself.

Milly's face drained of colour. 'Ted.'

193

'You'd better come inside,' said Charlie.

Katherine and Milly sat at the kitchen table that was still full of breakfast things, in a state of shock.

'I'll make 'em a cuppa,' said Charlie.

'I'm sorry, ladies, I thought you knew. Everybody in Croft Street seems to.'

'Ted. Where's Ted?' asked Milly.

'Who's Ted, Mrs . . .?'

'My son.'

'What's he to do with all this?'

'Nothing,' said Charlie quickly. 'He's just popped out.'

'Poor Briony,' whispered Katherine. 'What happened?'

'As I said, she threw herself under a train late last night. Right old mess, be all accounts. The poor train driver's in a bit of a state. She was what, only thirteen?'

'Fourteen,' corrected Katherine, trying to keep her voice under control. She didn't want this man to see how much this news had upset her.

'Still, it's a good thing in a way. Saves her all that trouble of a trial and being hanged in the end.'

'Get out!' shouted Katherine. 'Get out!'

'Why? What have I done?'

'You'd better go,' said Charlie.

'Sorry I spoke,' said the young man.

Milly stood up. 'She was a lovely girl who looked after those kids when her mother died. So don't you dare say anything bad about her.'

'Go on, clear off,' said Charlie, holding the kitchen door open.

The reporter closed his notebook. 'Not to worry. Got all the details I need from your neighbours. Just wanted to make sure I got all the dirt. All right if I send a photographer round?'

'No it ain't! Now scram before I start to lose me temper,' said Charlie.

The young man stood up. 'OK. Keep yer hair on. Well, so long, all. Nice meeting yer.' He sauntered to the door just as Katherine threw a plate at him. It crashed against the jamb.

'Who crawled up her?'

'Get out!' shouted Katherine.

Charlie, who was taller and bigger built than the hack, grabbed his coat. 'You heard the lady.'

The young man left the room in a hurry and slammed the front door after him.

'Sorry about that,' said Katherine, fighting back the tears as she swept up the mess. 'I'll get a new one tomorrow.'

'Don't worry about it. I only wished I'd done it, and it had hit him.'

'Look, I'm going out to find Ted,' said Charlie.

'I'll come with you,' said Tom, who had been very quiet all through. 'Poor little mite. Bad business, this.' He shook his head. 'Bad business.'

After they left, Katherine and Milly sat for a while with their thoughts.

'I'll have to ask the police where they'll be burying her,' said Katherine as she let the tears trickle down her cheeks.

'I can't believe all this has happened.' Milly began absentmindedly to pile up the dirty plates that were strewn over the table.

'I can't believe she would commit suicide. Not with the family to worry about. She was such a bright girl, she should have had everything to live for.'

'You always liked her, didn't you?'

'Yes.'

'I wonder what would have happened if Ted had got really serious?'

'I think he would have had a lot of trouble from Charlie.'

'For a while. But I could have got him to see sense if Ted had been really fond of her.'

'I think he was. But he won't say, not now.'

'That's something we'll never know.'

'She'll have to be buried in a pauper's grave,' said Katherine.

'What about her father? We never did find out where her mother and that baby were buried, unfortunately, otherwise they could have all been together.'

Tears quickly fell from Katherine's eyes. She was angry. 'What a wicked waste of lives. What a wicked waste.'

'You never know what goes on behind closed doors,' said Milly.

'More's the pity,' said Katherine.

Katherine was in her bedroom when Joseph, along with Ted, Charlie and Tom, returned.

'Can I come in?' asked Joseph at her door.

' 'Course. Have you heard what happened to Briony?'

Joseph nodded.

'Sit down. How's Ted taking it?'

He sat on the bed. 'Very upset. He liked her, you know.'

'We didn't till last night.'

'We went to the police station when some old women said a girl had been hit by a train. Somehow we knew it was Briony. They told us it was her and showed Ted a bit of the frock she was wearing.'

'Oh my God! Poor Ted. Why did they do that?'

'They said they wanted some sort of identification, but wouldn't let him see her.'

Katherine felt faint.

'You all right, Mama? You've gone ever so white.'

She gave him a weak smile. 'I'm fine. What about Ted?'

'A policeman took him and . . .' He hesitated. 'This policeman told Ted that he didn't think she – you know. What the papers are saying. He thinks she was running along the track when she slipped.'

Katherine put her hand to her mouth to stifle a sob. 'I didn't think she would take her own life. Those poor children.'

'Who's gonner look after them now?'

'They'll have to go into a home.'

Joseph looked down at his fingers. 'I feel ever so bad about all this.'

'We all do.'

'But I wouldn't talk to her. Ted was right. She was nice, and she made us laugh. She used to tell us what some of the kids got up to. She was ever so good to those kids, you know.'

'I know.' Katherine gently tapped his hand. 'We all have some regrets in our lives. Unfortunately we can't turn back the clock and rectify them.'

Joseph suddenly threw his arms round his mother and held her close and wept. He was weeping for Edwin, Dolly, and now Briony, and the child he had once been.

On Monday when Katherine walked into the shop Josh was leaning on the counter busy reading the newspaper.

'Morning, Kate love. Seen these headlines? They say this family comes from Croft Street. Ain't that where you live?'

She nodded and continued to remove her hat.

'Who's this old dear?' He pointed at a picture.

'That's Mrs Duke.'

'Did you know the family? They sound a right old lot to me.'

'I was very fond of Briony.'

'That the girl who used to work for old Wilks?'

'Yes. She was a lovely girl.'

He folded the paper. 'Don't sound very nice to me. She murdered her old man, then threw herself under a train. Couldn't face the trial, I reckon.'

'Do they say why she murdered her father?'

'No.'

'She caught him molesting her younger sister.'

'No!' Josh's eyes opened wide. 'It don't say nothing about that.'

'Well it wouldn't, would it? As far as the papers are concerned she was a murderess. She was only fourteen,' added Katherine softly.

'No,' said Josh again. 'Well I never. This is gonner be all the talk round here for days.'

Katherine was very aware of that.

As the morning wore on, so more and more people came in. There were photographers and reporters all asking questions, and a lot of people whom Katherine had never set eyes on before sat and looked at her.

'They might be a lot of ghouls to you, Kate, me girl, but to me it's good business.' Josh was beaming.

The questions came from all corners.

'They say you took her in?'

'Wasn't your landlady's son involved?'

'No he wasn't.'

'Well, that's what it says here.'

Katherine chose to ignore most of the comments. She wanted to run out. She didn't want her name to be associated with all this fuss, and she didn't want her name or picture in the newspaper. If Gerald realised it was her, she could just see him having a good laugh.

'It'll only be a five-minute wonder,' said Ron when he got his tea.

'I hope so,' said Katherine. 'I only hope so.'

'Hark at that silly cow,' said Josh.

Nellie was shouting out and banging on the floor.

'For Christ's sake shut it, can't you?' He walked into the dark passage and shouted back up. 'We're run off our feet down here.' There was a pause. 'You'll get your tea when we've got a minute.'

He came back. 'Take her tea up, Kate. Anything for a quiet life.' He tutted and cast his eyes up to the ceiling.

'What the bleeding hell's going on down there?' asked Nellie as Kate pushed the door open. 'Bloody racket.'

'It's full up.'

'Why, what's he doing, giving it away?'

Katherine smiled. 'No. It's because of the murder.'

'Oh yes. I heard about that. Josh said you live in that street, that right?'

'Yes, and I knew young Briony.'

'She worked for Wilks, didn't she?'

Katherine was always surprised at how much Nellie knew. 'Yes. She was a nice girl.' She put the tea on the bedside table and left the room. She didn't want to get too deep in a conversation as Josh would soon be shouting for her. She would tell Nellie all about it another day.

As the week wore on it seemed everybody wanted to get into the newspapers. There were pictures of Mr Wilks standing in his shop doorway. He had his arms folded and a smug expression on his face. There was another one of Mrs Duke, this time sitting on her windowsill with one or two others who lived in Croft Street. As the week drew to a close Ron was proving to be right. And by Friday it was almost back to normal.

Chapter 21

All week the atmosphere in the Stevenses' house had been very subdued. On Sunday morning Ted came into the kitchen carrying something in a paper bag.

'What you got there?' asked Milly.

Ted looked uneasy and didn't answer his mother. He turned to Katherine. 'You still going to try to find Briony's grave?'

'Yes. Why?'

'Well, when you said you might go I decided to make this, just to show where she is.'

Milly sat in stunned silence when he took a small wooden cross from the bag and very briefly showed them.

'That's lovely,' said Katherine. 'Do you want me to take it?'

'No.' He hastily put it back into the bag. 'I'd like to come with you, if you don't mind.'

'No, I don't mind. We may have trouble finding it. The police couldn't help much.'

'We can always ask the man in charge.'

'We'll try.'

When Ted went outside Milly looked at Katherine. 'I didn't know he was making that. That accounts for all the bits of wood in his bedroom. Did you know, Joe?'

He just nodded.

Later that morning Joseph, Katherine and Ted walked into the cemetery. They found an old man in overalls slowly sweeping a path. Katherine asked him where the people who didn't have any money or relations were buried.

'Over there.' The man stopped sweeping, and with his broom resting against his shoulder took a tin of tobacco from his pocket and carefully and methodically began rolling a cigarette. 'All the paupers in this parish finish up over there.'

The sad little trio went to the far side, passing the tall ominous-looking monuments. There were large stone crosses to mark the passing of loved ones. Angels with serene faces and cherubs with heavenly expressions looked down on them as the visitors picked their way across the graves. Some statues were old and weather-beaten, arms and noses falling off. Lichen and grass covered the ancient tombstones whose names had been worn away with time, and one or two had great chunks of masonry missing.

'Which one d'you reckon it is?' Ted anxiously asked Katherine as he moved from one dirt-covered hillock to another.

'I don't know.'

'These two don't look very old,' said Joseph. 'There ain't any weeds on them.'

They stood in front of two fresh mounds.

'I wonder which one is Briony?' Ted crouched down. 'I hope it ain't her dad. Would he be here?'

Katherine couldn't answer. Could Mrs Addams and her baby be somewhere near? If only she had asked Briony.

Ted took the cross from the bag and tears stung Katherine's eyes as she read what he had painted on it: 'BRIONY ADDAMS. Age 14. A good friend'.

'I hope this is the right one and this is the top,' he said, pushing the cross into the soft ground. He stood up and took a step back.

Katherine took Joseph's arm and gently moved him away, leaving Ted alone.

When Ted was ready the three of them slowly and silently walked from the cemetery. Katherine knew that for Ted things would never be the same. Losing your first love must be a terrible blow when you are just sixteen.

Days passed and everything and everybody began to drift along as normal. Even Milly was back on nodding terms with Mrs Duke, although Katherine said she would never forgive her for trying to put Briony away. Ted appeared to be getting over losing Briony. Tom had managed to get a job as a part-time pot man in the local pub and, much to Milly's relief, seemed to be settling down. Katherine was happy at work and Joseph said he lived only for Saturdays and the school holidays so he could be with Mr Lacy.

It was a Wednesday morning and at Trent's they were waiting for the lunchtime crowd when Josh asked Katherine to take Nellie's tea up.

'You busy down there?' Nellie asked her.

'No, not really, just the usual. It's better now the strike's over and all the fuss about Briony has died down.'

'That was a nasty business. Sit yourself down.'

'But—' Katherine looked towards the door.

'Don't worry about him. How long you been here now?'

'Getting on for five months.'

'You seem to hit it off all right with my Josh, don't you?' She eased herself up.

'Yes, he's a fair man.'

'Well, I must admit you've been with him longer than most, and you don't flaunt yourself.' Nellie shifted her position. 'Don't hold with that.'

Katherine gave her a faint smile.

'He likes you, you know. Reckons you could have been in business yourself the way you get stuck into things and don't hang around waiting to be told what to do. I'm glad you don't try to take things over down there. Don't say much about yourself, do you?'

Katherine laughed, but was immediately on her guard. 'There's not a lot to tell.' She hadn't told Josh anything about her past. At times, when the shop was quiet and they were talking together, he would ask her about herself but somehow she always managed to evade the questions. Was this a ploy to find out all about her?

'Well, did you have a business 'fore you moved round this way?'

'Don't be silly. Would I be working for Josh if I had?'

Nellie eyed her suspiciously. 'Might be if you're down on your luck. You talk nice and always look clean, and those frocks don't come from any pawn shops round here. And what about a husband? Ain't ever heard you talk about one.'

'He passed away.' Katherine was thinking quickly.

'Oh, I see.'

'He did have a good job,' she added, to justify her appearance.

'But boozed it all away, I s'pose,' said Nellie.

Katherine didn't answer. 'I must go otherwise I'll have Josh shouting for me.' She left the bedroom and slowly made her way downstairs. So much for her trying to find out about Nellie; Nellie was now probing her past.

'Been having a quiet word with Nellie then?' asked Josh.

Katherine wondered if this was a put-up job. What did he want to know? 'Yes. Josh, why won't she get up?'

'She does, when she feels like it. Those cups want rinsing out.' He rolled down his sleeves. 'I'm just going along to the off-licence 'fore they close. Nellie likes a drink at night.'

All day Katherine wondered why Nellie had asked her those questions. She hadn't told her the truth about her past, but then that was her business.

Tom was in the scullery whistling when Katherine got home.

'You sound happy.'

He turned from the sink where he was busy washing up.

'Didn't hear you come in, Miss Katherine.' He still couldn't drop the 'Miss'.

'Where's Milly?' She pulled the pins from her hat.

'Round Olive's. She sent a note to say she'd started, so Milly threw her coat on and left.'

Katherine put her hand to her mouth to suppress her joy. She was full of emotion. 'When was that?'

'This morning.'

Katherine smiled. 'At last, something nice is going to happen.'

'Yer, it's about time,' said Tom, turning back to his chores.

It wasn't long after that Charlie and Ted came in. Tom had put the pie Milly had made in the oven.

'About what time did Milly go off then, Tom?' asked Charlie.

'About eleven.'

'I wonder how long she'll be,' said Ted.

'She's not going to leave till it's all over,' said Katherine.

Ted grinned. 'I'll be an uncle.'

'I bet the old midwife will wish Milly further,' said Charlie.

'Not if it's Ida. Besides, it's a mother's privilege to be with her daughter,' said Katherine.

'We'd better get on with this pie Milly made this morning,' said Tom, carefully dishing out the pie and veg.

'What time d'you start tonight, Tom?' asked Charlie.

'Not till eight. He only likes me in to clear up. Don't want me hanging about for too long, might have to pay me more.'

After they'd finished dinner and the washing up they sat and waited for Milly to return.

Charlie looked up at the clock. He was getting anxious. 'She's a bloody long while. I hope everything's all right.'

'Of course it is,' said Katherine, hoping to reassure herself as much as Charlie. 'You know Milly, she won't leave till it's all over.'

'I know but it's nearly eight o'clock. I can't sit here any

longer, I'm going round to Olive's. I don't like the idea of Milly walking home on her own at this time o' night.'

'She'll be all right, Dad. 'Sides, they won't want you round there.'

'Ernie might. I know how I felt when your mother was having you and Olive. It ain't easy being outside waiting. No, I'll go round and give him a bit of support.'

'Why don't you take that bottle of stout round with you, then you can wet the baby's head,' said Tom. 'I'll bring another one in tonight when I finish.'

'Now that's what I call a good idea.' Charlie took his coat from off the nail behind the door.

'It's time I went to work anyway,' said Tom. 'I'll walk along with you.'

After an hour or so Joseph said, 'I think I'll go up to bed.'

'Me too. Can't do much down here waiting for news,' said Ted.

Katherine smiled and wished them both good night. She sat in front of the fire and watched the kettle's lid gently and silently lifting. The new life coming to this family was the best thing that could happen for all of them.

Katherine was dozing, and jumped when the kitchen door clicked open. She sat up and opened her eyes.

'Ain't they back yet?' asked Tom, taking his cap off.

Katherine shook her head. 'No. I'm getting worried, it's been a long while.'

'Look, why don't you go on up to bed?'

'I'd rather wait a bit longer.'

'I'll make us both a nice cuppa.' Tom had just picked up the kettle when they heard the front door close.

Milly walked into the kitchen, her face glowing. 'I'm a granny,' she said excitedly. 'She's got a dear little girl.'

Katherine leapt up and held Milly close. 'I'm so thrilled for you. Is Olive all right?'

Milly nodded.

'She's a real little cracker,' said Charlie, who was right behind her.

Katherine thought the buttons would ping off his shirt he looked so proud. 'What are they going to call her?'

Milly looked at Tom. 'Dorothy, after Dolly.'

Katherine swallowed hard.

'That's nice,' said Tom softly.

'Thought she might be carrying a girl, could tell somehow,' said Milly, her eyes dancing with pride.

'Would you like a cup of tea?' asked Katherine. 'Tom was just about to make one.'

'No, thanks all the same. Been drinking tea all day,' said Milly.

'That was a good idea of yours, Tom, taking that bottle round. Ernie looked like he could do with a drink when I got there.'

'She's got a mass of dark hair, and long legs,' said Milly.

'Was Ida there?'

'Ida?' asked Milly.

'Did she deliver—'

'No. A right upstart of a woman. Wanted me to wait outside. Well, I gave her a bit of me mind. Afterwards she thanked me for my help.'

'Will it be all right if I pop round to see her tomorrow after I finish the lunchtime stint? I won't stay long and I won't get in the way,' said Tom.

''Course. I'll be there most of the day. Katherine, I'll leave you all a bit of dinner, and I'll be back after I've seen to Ernie.'

'We can go out before you start work,' said Charlie to Tom. 'We've got to wet the baby's head.'

'Just as long as you don't drown yourselves,' said Milly, laughing.

Katherine smiled. There would be some celebrations going on tomorrow evening.

Olive's baby was lovely. She had lots of dark hair, and her dark eyes constantly looked about her. When Olive asked Katherine to be Dorothy's godmother she was overwhelmed and very proud at being invited to be part of this family. But when Katherine held Dorothy she felt a twinge of conscience. She would never rid herself of her guilt.

After the christening the party was soon in full swing, everybody enjoying themselves.

'Drink up,' said Charlie to Katherine.

'If he drinks to this baby's health once more we'll have him on the floor,' said Milly.

'Good job I didn't have twins,' said Olive proudly.

Charlie put his arm round his daughter's shoulder. His twinkling eyes misted over. 'You've made me a very happy man, love.' He tenderly kissed her cheek.

'Couldn't have done it without Ernie.'

'Yer, but he had the best bit.'

'Charlie Stevens, you watch your tongue.'

Charlie did a low sweeping bow. 'Yes, marm.'

Everybody shrieked with laughter.

'Bit different to the dos you had at the big house when Mr Edwin was alive,' said Tom, bending his head towards Katherine.

'Yes. In many ways this is much better. This is all family,' she replied, choking back a tear.

'Just you wait till Christmas,' said Charlie, trying to hold his drink steady. 'We'll really push the boat out then.'

'Well, thank Gawd you're back at work,' said Milly. 'And with Tom's bit and Ted getting a rise it should be a good one.'

Joseph sat next to his mother. 'Ma, can I talk to you?' He had long since stopped calling her Mama.

'Of course. I've just got to go and make a few more sandwiches. You can talk to me in the kitchen.'

After looking across at Ted, Joseph followed his mother.

'You can put these on that plate,' said Katherine. 'And then take them in the front room. Tell them they're fish paste.'

'As I'll be fourteen next May do you think I could leave school at Christmas?' It was said with a rush.

Katherine turned to him. Somehow she knew this was coming, and he knew she wouldn't start a fuss with everybody here. 'I suppose you want to start work?'

His face lit up. 'Yes, yes, please. Mr Lacy said I could start after Christmas so if it's all right with you—'

'Hold on a minute, young man.'

Joseph stopped in his tracks.

'I know you're not happy at that school, but are you sure you want to leave?'

Joseph nodded. 'I'm far in advance of any of them there.'

'I know, and I feel partly to blame because I took you from your old school. Edwin wouldn't have been happy at me doing that. But I didn't have any choice.'

Joseph looked up from arranging the sandwiches on the plate. 'I didn't think I would be happy living here, but I am, honest, and I really would like to go to work.'

Katherine put down the knife she was using to butter the bread and hugged him. 'Thank you.'

He pulled away. 'What for?'

'For sticking it. It hasn't been easy for you.'

'Nor for you.'

She brushed a tear from the corner of her eye. 'We've certainly had a few ups and downs this year.'

'Well, let's hope things will only get better.'

'I'm sure they will. You sound so very grown up.'

'I have grown up. I think when Briony died that made me realise all that she'd done for her family. To kill your father because of what he was doing to your sister, you've got to be very fond of someone to do that.'

'She was a nice girl.'

'Yes, and Ted was very upset about it.'

'I'm sure as time goes on his grief will fade, though it will never go away, and one day he will meet another young lady who will steal his heart.'

'I ain't gonner get married.'

'That's what all the boys say, but just you wait and see.'

'What was Australia like?'

Katherine was suddenly snapped out of her thoughts. 'Why? Why did you ask that?'

'I just wondered, that's all. Wouldn't mind going there one day. So you see, I don't want any woman hanging round me.'

Katherine wanted to laugh, but the thought that he was talking about Australia stopped her.

'I'll take these into the front room.' Joseph picked up the plate of sandwiches and walked out, leaving Katherine feeling utterly bewildered. What was going through his mind?

Later that evening, over the washing-up, she asked Milly what she thought about it.

'You don't wanner worry too much at what kids say. P'raps he'd just thought about it. Might be something they've talked about at school.'

'Could be. You don't think he wants to leave home, do you?'

'Na, course not. Could be he was just dropping a hint to put the frighteners on you, in case you said no to him leaving school.'

'Yes, that sounds more like it,' said Katherine, feeling reassured by Milly's common sense reaction.

'Ted was on about leaving home a while back when he couldn't get his own way,' Milly went on, 'but when I pointed out to him that he'd have to do his own washing and ironing he soon changed his mind. Anyway, since your Joe's been around, he's gone off the idea.' She put the plate she'd been washing on the wooden draining board. 'Seems all boys like to get their mothers worried from time to time. 'Sides, with Christmas coming up, he'll have more on his mind, especially now you said he can start work.'

Katherine picked up the plate and began drying it. She hoped Milly was right. Had she made Australia sound too exciting to a young man full of hope and adventure?

Chapter 22

Katherine knew that Christmas was going to be far better than she could have ever hoped for when she first moved to Rotherhithe. At work, she was surprised and very touched when some of the customers gave her their odd penny or halfpenny change and wished her a Merry Christmas.

'Blimey, you must have made an impression,' said Josh, observing. 'I ain't ever had nothing off 'em.'

'Well, you ain't as pretty as Kate,' said Ron.

'You watch it or I'll tell yer missis what you've done.'

Ron laughed. 'It's 'cos I've had a couple of good days at the dog track and I like to spread a little bit of good will towards me fellow men. Wouldn't hurt you to show a bit more good will. A few paper chains wouldn't come amiss.'

Josh nearly choked on his tea. 'What? Waste me money on things like that?'

Katherine laughed. She too would have liked to see a few decorations up, but Josh wasn't like that. She loved her job and this good-humoured banter. She was also surprised that some of the more sensitive men took her into their confidence when they were worried about their children or wives.

''Sides, I've told Annie all about Katie,' said Ron.

'Well, that's all right then,' said Josh. 'But don't expect her to give you a free cuppa.'

'Mean old sod. Where's yer Christmas spirit?'

'It's in a bottle and locked away upstairs.'

Before she left on Christmas Eve, Katherine took Nellie up a bottle of lavender water.

'I ain't got nothing for you,' she said.

'It's a Christmas present. I don't expect one back.'

'Well, that's all right then.'

Katherine had noted that over the past months Nellie had combed her hair and the curtains were open. Was she having some effect on Josh's wife, enough to make her start to take an interest in herself? But every time Katherine had tried to broach the subject of why she was in bed, Nellie shut up like a clam.

'Just a minute,' called Nellie, as Katherine was leaving. 'I've told Josh to give you a bit extra this week.'

Katherine stood in the doorway. 'What? Thank you.'

'Well, I dare say you can do with the money.'

'Yes. Thank you very much.'

Katherine made her way down the stairs. Once again Nellie had surprised her. Did she have more to say about the running of this business than anyone knew?

Katherine was amazed when she found Josh was giving her another week's wages. It was only Tuesday.

'Well, don't want you telling all the blokes I don't look after you.'

She kissed his cheek. 'Thanks.'

He smiled and touched his cheek. 'Don't let Nellie see you do that, otherwise she'll have me guts for garters. And don't be late on Friday.'

Katherine laughed. 'Have a nice Christmas.'

'Won't be much of one with just me and Nellie. Much rather be down here working.'

Katherine felt sad at that remark. If she hadn't moved in with Milly there could have been just her and Joseph sitting alone in rooms somewhere.

Katherine wandered past the shops. Many people were doing

their last-minute shopping. The butcher had chickens hung all over the outside of his shop and he was busy selling them off with lots of laughter and cheeky comments as he took them down with his long pole.

''Ere, I ain't 'aving this one,' shouted one woman as she pushed her way through the crowd. 'It's only got one leg.'

Laughter erupted as the woman took the chicken from her shopping bag by its neck and shook it at the butcher.

'It had two when it left here. I reckon you sawed it off when you got it home.'

'I ain't been home. Been in the pub having a quick one, ain't I?'

'Well, it looks like someone's gonner have a nice juicy chicken leg fer dinner tomorrow. Go back and ask 'em who pinched it.'

'I want me money back.'

'You ain't having it so clear off, you crafty old mare, and don't try any of yer old tricks on me. I wasn't born yesterday.'

'I'll send me old man round to sort you out.'

'Look, I'm shaking in me shoes.' The butcher shook his knees. He was a big man and it would have to be a very brave adversary who took him on.

Katherine smiled as she walked on. She knew a lot of women would be busy plucking these chickens all evening, getting them ready for tomorrow's dinner while their menfolk were in the pub.

The smell of chestnuts from a brazier was warm and inviting. Despite the damp and cold the hissing from the stallholders' kerosene lamps, and the shouts from the men trying to sell their wares all brought a great feeling of joy to her, as did the sound of badly sung carols from the youngsters rattling their tins under everyone's noses.

Bill and Bert, the brothers who had the flower and fruit stall, gave her a quick wave. Katherine gave them a smile. They were nice men, always friendly. They were well muffled up against the cold.

She slid down deeper into her coat and pulled her collar up. This was so different from the Christmases she'd had in Australia. They had been hot, with flies buzzing around all the while. It was too hot to eat during the day, and Christmas dinner didn't taste the same over there. What suddenly made her think of Australia? What would Robert be doing? What did he look like now? Her heart felt a longing to know how he was.

Then there were those Christmases she had shared with dear Edwin. They had to work late into the night in the restaurant on Christmas Eve, but Christmas Day they relaxed and enjoyed the celebration with Dolly and Tom. Dolly . . . the thought of her brought a lump to Katherine's throat.

Somehow she felt that this Christmas was going to be the best of all. She was happy living with Milly and being part of this community. They had very little, but were content to share and make the best of what they did have, and most of the time it was with a ready smile. She pulled up her coat collar and moved on. If only Edwin, Dolly and Briony were here to share it with her, but she knew she shouldn't dwell on the past.

Christmas for Katherine was just as wonderful as she knew it would be. The meal was delicious and with Olive, Ernie and the new baby, the kitchen was full of laughter and chatter. Come the afternoon they moved into the front room to relax and roast chestnuts on the cheerful fire. In the evening they played cards and charades, and finally it was time for bed.

For a while Katherine sat in her room reflecting. Over these past months she had been able to save, and even after giving Milly another sixpence a week she had managed to put a little away. She'd long since paid her debt to Ida Fairfield. She tipped the money out of the purse and began counting it. She wanted to help Joseph if he needed tools, but she also knew deep down she wanted to do more with her life. She wanted her own business, but it would take a lot more than the few shillings she had.

The New Year, 1913, started cold and very wet. Dense fog made everywhere feel dirty and damp. Men who hadn't been lucky enough to get work that day came to Trent's mainly to get warm as they sat with their cold fingers wrapped around their one and only mug of tea. They complained about the weather stopping the ships from coming up the Thames, while Josh complained they only wanted somewhere warm to sit and talk.

'Well, it's better than going home to have yer ear bent be yer old woman,' shouted someone when Josh was having a moan.

'And told ter pick yer feet up while she swept round yer,' said another.

'My old girl only asked me to bring the coal in the other day. I ask yer. I soon put her in her place. I told her straight – I'm the breadwinner so I'll do my job and you do yours.'

Katherine half smiled to look as if she were agreeing with him, but guessed his wife had a brood of youngsters to look after. She could understand that attitude when he was working in the docks, as the work was long and hard, but to sit in here and not help his wife was something Katherine always resented. Her job depended on her keeping quiet, though.

The air quality in Trent's, with all the pipe and cigarette smoke, was almost as bad as it was outside.

Charlie was getting restless as day after day he'd come home wet and miserable when the ships didn't arrive. When the odd ship did dock, the wood and sugar sacks were frozen and slippery, and every man was terrified of having an accident as no work meant no pay.

Katherine offered Milly more money but she refused.

'Now Tom's working and Joe gives me a shilling out of his wages we can manage for a bit.'

Katherine smiled. Joseph was so happy. He was doing something he really enjoyed.

Milly's voice cut into her thoughts. 'Besides, when things go good I always puts a little by, just in case. Charlie's been in the docks too long for me not to know bad times always seem to follow good.'

At last the winter gave way to spring and everybody was happy to see the ships waiting to get into the docks. Charlie worked longer hours.

At work Nellie seemed content and when it was possible enjoyed a chat. Katherine still hadn't found out what made her take to her bed, but she did suspect she got out sometimes. The smile on Josh's face told everybody the takings were up. Katherine asked for another rise. Life was good and she was more determined than ever to save. She wanted her own business. She wasn't sure what she would do but often she would daydream about being in charge and was thrilled to see her savings grow.

In June the biggest event that filled the papers and was on everybody's lips was Emily Davison throwing herself under the King's horse at the Derby. The pictures of the suffragettes lining the streets as her coffin passed by brought many heated discussions in Trent's. Even Katherine, who admired these women, thought that was a bit extreme.

There followed a long, hot, sizzling summer, and by the time August Bank Holiday Monday was almost on them, all at number 12 Croft Street eagerly decided to have another outing. Along with Olive, baby Dolly and Ernie, they all went to Southend for the day.

'Was it hot like this in Australia, Ma?' asked Joseph as he sat on the pebbles finishing off his ice cream.

'Hotter than this, and dusty.'

'Not my cup of tea,' said Milly. 'Don't really like this warm weather that much.'

'It's 'cos you've got too many clothes on,' said Charlie, lying back with his coat off and his shirt neck open. He was wearing a knotted handkerchief on his head.

'Well, I certainly ain't showing me legs off like some of 'em. Look at those tarts over there, showing all their knees. They don't have to hold their skirts up that high just to have a paddle.'

'Well, they've got nice pairs to show off,' said Charlie, raising himself up on his elbow and shifting out of the way of Milly's sharp finger.

'The boys are enjoying themselves,' said Tom. 'Look, they've gone up to those girls paddling.'

'I'm glad Ted washed his feet last night,' said Milly. 'I would have been that ashamed if he'd taken his socks off and his feet was dirty.'

The day went quickly and soon they were home, tired and happy.

At work Katherine had been very discreetly asking Josh about the shop. And once or twice she had seen the landlord come and talk to him. She knew now that she wanted her own business, but what and where? And, more important, where would the money come from to start? She had learnt from Edwin that you needed capital, and that was something she didn't have. The business had to be in food – she didn't know anything else – and she didn't want to move away from this area, but Josh wouldn't want her opening up a café near here.

One warm sunny Friday, there was nobody in the shop. Josh was out in the back room getting food ready for Saturday, which was always their busiest day.

Katherine was dreamily putting the clean mugs on the shelf under the counter when the young girl with the big hat and rouged lips came in. Today the perfume from her cheap scent was overpowering, and almost blotted out the odour of unwashed bodies and tobacco that mixed with the cooking smells always filling the air in Trent's. Sometimes they didn't see her for a week. Then the next she would be in almost every day. She seemed so young and didn't flaunt herself like some of the prossies. She wasn't loud and brash, although she could hold her own when some of the younger men made comments. Normally she just sat quietly with a mug of tea. The older dockers didn't ever appear to be that interested. Most Fridays she came in for one customer. Today Katherine could see she'd been crying.

'Are you all right?' Katherine enquired.

'Just give me a cuppa.'

'I'll bring it over.'

The girl, hobbling because of her tight skirt, went over to a table as far from the door as she could, and which was unusual, sat with her back to the entrance.

Katherine wanted to talk to her, so she sat at a nearby table. 'Is anything wrong?'

'No.' She took a cigarette from her handbag and lit it.

'If there's—'

'Just go away and mind yer own business, will yer, yer nosy cow?'

Katherine quickly moved off. She was worried the girl's harsh raised voice would bring Josh in, and he was always telling Katherine to keep out of other people's affairs.

He had got cross with her when she'd put a box on the counter to help young Walter's mother pay for his gran's funeral. She missed that little chap with the large cap coming for his gran's dinner. He was a good boy. She had since heard he had been sent away to another relation. 'I only hope they treat him all right,' she had said to Milly at the time.

Katherine looked across at the girl when she took a

handkerchief from her handbag and began wiping her eyes. She blew her nose hard. Katherine casually walked over to her table.

'I can see you're in some sort of trouble . . .' Katherine didn't get the chance to finish the sentence because the girl burst into tears. She looked up at Katherine, her dark brown eyes full of worry.

Katherine quickly sat at her table. 'Can't I help?'

The girl shook her head.

She reminded Katherine of Briony. What was it about these young girls who were full of bravado on the outside yet small and vulnerable on the inside? 'Look, please let me try to help you.'

'You can't,' she sniffed.

'If you're having a baby—'

'It ain't that.' She quickly looked at the door behind the counter, took a long hard drag on her cigarette and ground the butt into the ashtray.

'Don't worry, Josh is busy,' said Katherine gently, easing herself into the chair next to her.

'I know you think I'm a trollop, but I only go with men to help me mum out.'

Katherine was shocked. 'You mean your mother sends you—'

'No, me mum ain't well, and me dad . . .' She stopped. Fear filled her face. 'I shouldn't be talking to you.'

Katherine was intrigued. 'Please, if you need someone to talk to, who knows, I may be able to help.'

'I don't think so.'

'Is it your father that sends you out?'

The girl laughed; it was a hollow sound. 'He ain't really me dad. He don't like me or me mum but she give him a roof over his head and since he come out . . . Well, he's always hitting her and don't give her any money.' She stirred the remaining tea in her mug round and round. 'I shouldn't be telling you this, but you're always kind and you and Josh don't chuck me out like some shops do while I wait for me customers.'

Katherine wanted to throw her arms round this child and hold her tight, for suddenly she looked so alone and lost. 'What's wrong with your mother?'

'When the doctor told her she ain't got long to live I promised her she'd have a nice funeral, and the only way I can earn money, a lot of money quick, was to go on the game. You see, me dad didn't know – he thought I worked in a shop. That was till yesterday, and when he found out he knocked me and Mum about.' She stopped again as tears ran down her face. 'I tried to stop him. He took all the money I've saved.'

Katherine could have cried with her. 'What can I say? Why doesn't your mother throw him out?'

She sniffed. 'She won't. She says she loves him and you know what they say about love being blind.'

'Is your mother all right?'

The girl shook her head. 'I've just come from the hospital. She's in a bad way. He told 'em she'd fallen down the stairs.' She wiped her eyes again. 'What if she dies? I ain't got no money to pay . . .' Sobs shook her sad body. 'And I promised.'

'Don't you have any brothers or sisters?'

She shook her head.

Katherine felt so helpless. 'I don't like to ask, but are you, you know, expecting a customer?'

She nodded. 'But I can't let him see me like this. Me Friday one's a nice bloke. A real gent.'

'Look, let me help you tidy yourself up. I'll get a clean cloth, then you can wash your face.'

'Why you doing this, missis? I ain't bin exactly nice to you.'

'I too have been in trouble, and we all need someone to give us a lift up the ladder of life.'

A slight smile lifted the girl's tear-stained face. 'That's a really lovely thing to say. My mum would like you.'

'I'm sure your mother is very proud of you.'

'Dunno about that.'

Katherine hurriedly rinsed out a cloth and gave it to the girl.

'Does your mother know what you do for a living?'

She shook her head.

'Won't your father . . . that man tell her?'

'No, he's crafty. He'll just take me money so that way he'll keep his mouth shut.'

Katherine was at a loss for words. 'What's your name?' she asked as the girl rubbed at her face.

'Grace. What's yours?'

'Here, I'm called Kate.'

Grace gave a little laugh. 'So this could be called Kate's kitchen then?'

'Kate's kitchen,' repeated Katherine. 'Don't let Josh hear you say that. But it's a good name.'

Grace powdered her nose and painted her lips. 'Do I look better?'

'Yes. Now please come back and tell me how your mother gets on, won't you?'

'OK. I'd better go and sit down. Me Friday man wouldn't like it if he thought I talked to you.'

Just a few moments later, Mr Friday came in. Grace walked to the door, and in the doorway she turned and gave Katherine a big smile.

Katherine was watching her leave when Josh came in.

'That all you gotter do, stand about grinning?'

'I was just going to clear that ashtray.' The words 'Kate's kitchen' were buzzing round her brain. Was this what she was looking for?

Her thoughts went to Grace. She'd called Josh by his name. He had never spoken to her – well, not in front of Katherine – and they had never even exchanged glances. She grinned. Why didn't he throw her out? After all, she only ever had one mug of tea, and sometimes she'd be there all afternoon waiting for customers. Was there something going on? She admonished herself for her naughty thoughts.

Chapter 23

'You're at it again, ain't yer?' said Milly, running her hands over the crisp white tablecloth, smoothing out invisible creases.

Katherine had been telling her about Grace. 'What d'you mean?' she asked, as she put the knives and forks out ready for dinner.

'Always worried about other people.'

'I can't help it. I hate to see these youngsters taking on the world.'

'What is it about you that seems to attract all the waifs and strays?'

'Must be me sympathetic ear,' Katherine said, laughing and putting on a cockney accent.

'So what's gonner happen to this poor cow then?'

'I don't know. If her mother dies before she gets enough money together for her funeral she'll be devastated.'

'Fancy having to go on the game to pay for your mum's funeral. Does her mum know?'

'She said not.'

'It's sad.'

'Then to have someone steal it from you.'

'It's a shame.'

'What if I told her about Ida Fairfield?'

'Ida? What could she do?'

'Perhaps she could lend her the money, if need be.'

'Maybe. But she ain't got a regular job, has she?'

'No. But I think what she does pays well. I could tell her about Ida when she next comes in.'

Milly laughed. 'You're a good 'en, Katherine, and no mistake.'

'Well, I only hope I've got enough for Joseph to bury me when the time comes.'

'Don't talk like that.'

'But it comes to us all in the end.'

'I know, but I expect to be around for a few more years yet.' Katherine kissed her cheek. 'So do I.'

'What was that for?' asked Milly, rubbing her cheek.

'I just felt like it.'

Throughout the week Katherine eagerly waited for Grace to come in, but even on Friday she still hadn't turned up. When her usual man appeared, he looked around, then walked out without saying a word.

'I hope her mother hasn't died,' Katherine said to Milly that evening.

On Saturday morning Mrs Duke was standing at her door. Katherine gave her a polite nod.

'See you're still living here then? Thought you might have been long gorn be now.'

Katherine didn't reply.

'You know what I did was right, so don't go giving me any of your holier-than-thou looks. Thought you might be starting a posh café be now.'

'I hope to one day.' As soon as Katherine said that she regretted it.

'Must be a bit crowded in there with all you lot.' She inclined her head towards Milly's door. 'Still, Milly must be coining it in now old Tom's odd-jobbing in the pub. And I see you've got your boy out working as well now.'

'I must go.' Katherine hurried away and let her thoughts turn to the business she wanted to start. She hadn't said anything to Milly in case she thought she was trying to get above her station, but if that slip of the tongue got back to Milly, she'd be very upset if she thought she was the last to know Katherine's plans. Fortunately Mrs Duke hadn't taken her up on it.

Katherine had been taking an interest in what Josh bought, and made notes. She discreetly asked Josh where he got his meat and potatoes from.

He laughed. 'Why's that? You wanner start buying in bulk?'

'No. I was just wondering if it was cheaper for me to buy them off you instead of Milly going to the market.'

'Shouldn't think so, not when I add on me bit of profit.'

'You old skinflint,' said Katherine, laughing, pleased he didn't make too much fuss about it.

All week Milly was talking about baby Dolly's first birthday.

'Can't believe she's a year old. Charlie's that proud of her.'

'And of course you're not,' said Katherine, smiling.

Milly beamed. 'Well, she is a little darling, ain't she?'

Katherine nodded.

'Olive's giving her a little tea party. I'm gonner make a small cake. I'll bring you all a bit back.'

Friday came round, and once again Katherine waited for Grace. She was delighted when she saw her walk in. 'How's your mother?' she asked, pushing a mug of tea towards her.

'Not good. I dunno how I'm gonner pay for the hospital, let alone anything else.' She lowered her voice. 'And I ain't been able to work much with going to see Mum every night.'

Katherine closed the door behind the counter. 'Josh is busy so I've got a moment or two. Grace, I don't want you to think I'm – well, you know – speaking out of turn, but if you need money, I know of a money lender.'

Grace's face turned pale with anger. 'I ain't going to no shark!' she yelled.

Katherine looked anxiously at the door. 'Shh! Keep your voice down. She's not a shark.'

'They're all sharks. 'Sides, what's in it for you? How much d'you get out of it?'

Katherine was taken aback. 'Nothing. I was just trying to—'

'Well, mind your own bloody business! I should have kept me mouth shut. I knew I couldn't trust you.' She snatched up her tea, spilling some in the process.

'But Grace,' Katherine called after her as she made her way to the far side of the café. 'You can trust me. I'm sorry.'

'What's going on?' asked Josh, pushing the door open. 'Who shut this door?'

'I did.'

'What for?'

'There was a draught round my legs.'

'Well, hard luck. Nellie wants a cuppa. You can take it up.'

Reluctantly Katherine poured out the tea. She wanted to talk to Grace. She wanted to help her, but Grace sat with her back to Katherine.

Nellie was sitting up in bed and looked happy. Over the months, the change in her was noticeable; even the windows had been open during the summer, making the place smell a little sweeter.

'Hallo, Kate. Guess what? It's me birthday.'

'Why didn't you tell me? I would have brought you a little gift or even got Milly to make you a small cake.'

A huge grin filled Nellie's pale face. 'Would yer? Would yer really?'

'Yes.'

'That's real kind of you. Ain't never had a cake – well, not for years.'

Katherine could see Nellie was in a good mood. 'Would you like me to help you get out of bed as it's your birthday?'

'Na. Might later on. Josh said he'd bring me a drop of whisky.' She lay back. 'He used to be a good husband.'

'He seems as though he takes care of you.'

'Yer, now.' The scowl returned and she slid down into the bed.

Katherine felt uncomfortable. This woman's moods changed so quickly. She stood for a moment in silence. 'Is there anything else I can get you?'

'No. And leave the door open.'

When Katherine went back into the shop Grace had gone. Had her Mr Friday come to collect her?

'Josh, why didn't you tell me it was Nellie's birthday?'

'Didn't see the point.'

'Have you bought her anything?'

'No. What does she need, lying up there day after day?'

Katherine felt like saying 'A little love and affection,' but he would have thought she was mad. 'Not a lot really, but a cake would have been nice.'

Josh laughed. 'A cake? And who the bloody hell would help her eat it?'

'Just a small one.'

'Na, she'll have a drop of whisky tonight, that'll keep her happy.'

'Why won't she get up?'

'Personal,' he said gruffly.

'Can she walk?'

''Course she can.' He turned away.

Katherine knew that the conversation was now closed.

Autumn turned to winter. Grace continued to come in to meet her clients but after getting her tea she kept well away from Katherine.

It was a cold dark November morning, and Milly was standing in front of the kitchen window as Katherine got ready for work. 'Just look at that rain,' she said. 'You're gonner get soaked.'

Katherine looked at the heavy rain falling straight from the sky like stair rods. It bounced noisily off Mrs Duke's roof, and the gutter overflowed. 'I'll take another pair of shoes with me. I don't like standing about all day in wet shoes. I'm glad Joseph keeps an old pair at work to change into.'

'What about your skirt? It'll get soaked.'

'I suppose I could take my other one, just in case.'

'Why don't you hang on a bit, just till it dies down? You can't go out in this!' said Milly in alarm.

'I must. I can't let Josh down.'

'Well, I shouldn't think there'll be many venture out in this.'

Katherine looked at the clock, then out of the window. 'I really must go. Saturday's our busiest day.'

Outside it was worse. She got to the end of Croft Street and her umbrella blew inside out. 'That's all I need,' she said angrily, throwing it to the ground. The rain stung her face. She trod in puddles, and rain from broken pipes splashed down on her. She was wet through in no time. The water squelched in her shoes, and her skirt, heavy with water, flapped and stuck to her legs. She felt cold and miserable.

'Good God, woman!' said Josh, when she pushed open the door. 'Fancy coming out in this.'

She stood and let the water drop from her. The brim on her black velour hat dipped and drooped.

'Look, get out back and use the towel. I didn't expect you to come out in this. You'd better get those wet things off.' He took her coat. 'Put your hat over the stove.'

'I hope it doesn't shrink, it's the only winter one I've got.' Katherine slipped her feet out of her shoes.

Josh laughed. 'Here, you're quite a little thing without shoes.'

'I've brought another pair with me, and a skirt to change into. Where can I go?'

'Well you can't go out to the lav, not in this weather. Stay here, I'll go out front. I'd better light the gas under the urn just in case we get some customers.'

Katherine shut the door that led to the shop and began to remove her skirt. It was heavy with water and she tried to wring it out. Her petticoats and blouse had stuck to her and she decided to take them off and wear just her overall. It wrapped around her generously, and with its long sleeves she knew she would be well covered, and not attract too many ribald remarks if she stayed behind the counter. She ran her hands over her white lawn chemise. It was wet but it would have to dry on her, as would her pretty lace-decorated cotton drawers. Before she put the overall on she took the towel from behind the back door and began drying her hair.

A terrific clap of thunder made her jump. She screamed out when the back door flew open and the chimney came crashing down into the yard, bringing many of the roof slates with it.

Katherine could hear Nellie screaming.

'Bloody hell, what was that?' Josh almost fell into the back room.

Katherine threw herself at Josh. 'It's the chimney.'

The wind and rain came in through the open door, blowing and saturating everything. Above the din they could hear Nellie screaming for Josh.

'Nellie! Nellie! It's all right, girl!' Josh pushed Katherine aside and raced up the stairs.

Katherine was fighting against the wind, trying to shut the door, when Nellie came in.

'What's going on down here?'

Katherine stood open-mouthed at Nellie standing there in her nightgown. She was a short woman who shuffled in leaning on a walking stick.

'See, I told you it was all right, love,' said Josh with his arm around her. 'The chimney's come off the roof.'

'I know that, don't I? I thought me bloody time was up. Frightened the life out of me it did.'

'Kate, get Nellie a chair from out front.'

Katherine went to move.

'What's she doing standing there in just her drawers and chemise?' screamed Nellie. 'Josh – you bin up to your old tricks again?'

Katherine could feel the flush of embarrassment creeping over her. She made a move towards her clothes that were scattered on the floor and, scrabbling them up, held them against her.

'No, Nellie. She got soaked coming here and she was changing her—'

Nellie's stick landed heavily on his shoulder.

'No, Nellie! It ain't what you think!'

'Don't give me that old fanny! I know what you get up to! Thought you'd know better be now!' Every word was said with force and a blow to Josh's body with her stick.

'Nellie, Nellie, stop it!' cried Katherine.

'And you can shut it an' all! I thought I could trust you, but no, you're like all the other trollops we've had here!'

Katherine thrust her wet clothes at Nellie. 'Look! See, I got wet through and I was just changing.'

'A likely story! You ain't the first, but if I have my way you'll be the last.' She turned to Josh. 'I told you to get a lad in, but no, it had to be another tart!'

'Nellie, it's not what you think.'

'You!' She turned to Katherine, who shrank back out of reach. 'Get out! Do you hear me? Get out!' She brandished her stick as Katherine tried to put on her wet clothes.

'Please, Nellie, you've got to believe me. Kate's a good worker.'

'I bet she is!'

'I don't pay her a lot, only what you said.'

'Might not be a lot for working here, but what about her other favours?'

Katherine gazed in amazement as Josh grovelled in front of this woman who appeared to be in control.

'How dare you!' Katherine couldn't stand by and let her name be ruined by this woman.

'Kate's a good woman,' said Josh, moving towards her.

'A good woman, is she?' The walking stick came down with a loud crack to the side of his head. He fell heavily to the floor. 'Good at what?'

Katherine looked at Josh lying on the floor.

'Come on, get up, you stupid sod!' Nellie prodded him with her stick.

He didn't move.

Katherine fell to her knees. 'What have you done?'

'Dunno, but I should have done it years ago.'

'I'll have to get a doctor. You could have killed him, you, you—'

'You'd better put some clothes on first,' laughed Nellie.

Katherine hurriedly pulled on her wet things and ran out, oblivious to the rain. She knew the doctor's was a few shops away. She banged hard on his door.

It was opened by a tall thin woman whose black hair was pulled back into a tight bun, giving her face a taut, pinched look. 'The doctor is busy. Call back on Monday.'

'I can't! Please, he must come to Josh.'

'Who is Josh?'

'Josh Trent who owns the pie and mash shop.'

'Oh yes, I know,' she said, looking down her long hooked nose. 'Why?'

Katherine brushed the rain that was running down her face away from her eyes with both hands. 'He's had an accident.'

'Wait there.' The woman closed the door.

Katherine began to shiver. What had Nellie done? And why did she think Josh and she had . . . ? That was unthinkable. The rain had seeped through everything she had on. She shivered. She was cold and uncomfortable. She stamped her feet to bring back life to them. She could have cried when she looked down. Now both pairs of shoes, which were all she had, were wet and probably ruined. She waited for what seemed to be for ever. Should she go back and try to help Josh?

Eventually the door opened. 'So you say Mr Trent has had an accident?' The doctor was a small dapper man. He pulled his trilby down over his eyes and put up his black umbrella. 'Well, come on, woman! Don't let's stand about in this weather or I'll catch my death!'

He was shorter than Katherine and took small running steps. She hurried beside him, dodging the spokes of his umbrella.

'The shop door's open,' shouted Katherine. 'He's in the back.' She pushed open the door. Josh was still on the floor where she had left him. Nellie was nowhere to be seen.

'How did this happen?' The doctor was on his knees. He took a stethoscope from his black bag. 'Help me to turn him over.'

Josh had a strange twisted expression on his face. A bruise was beginning to show on his forehead.

'Has he been attacked?'

Katherine didn't answer.

'I said did someone attack him?'

'What's going on down here?' Nellie's voice was feeble and faint. She staggered in, leaning heavily on a stick.

Katherine stared at her disbelievingly.

Nellie was wearing a tatty dressing gown and her hair was a mess. 'Doctor Ballard! What you doing . . . ?' She gasped and put her hand to her mouth. 'Josh! Josh! What's happened to my Josh?' She slowly and painfully made her way across the room.

'I'm sorry, Mrs Trent, but it looks as if your husband has

234

been attacked, and it's brought on a stroke.'

'A stroke!' She started to sway.

'Quick, get Mrs Trent a chair.'

Katherine continued to stare at Nellie in disbelief.

'Woman! Don't just stand there! I said get Mrs Trent a chair.'

Katherine felt this was a bad dream, a nightmare. Would she wake up soon? She put the chair in front of Nellie.

'I thought I heard a noise a bit earlier on. Then the chimney fell off and I called for Josh and he told me not to worry. He came down to get me a cup of tea. Who would attack him?' She looked across at Katherine.

'It wasn't me, it was you!' yelled Katherine.

Doctor Ballard looked up. 'My dear woman, that is a very stupid thing to say. You can see Mrs Trent can hardly walk. Now stop this silly nonsense and I'll go and see about getting him into hospital.'

'I'm going,' said Katherine.

'No. I want you to stay here and look after Mrs Trent.' He turned to Nellie. 'Is there anyone you can contact to look after you?' he asked in his best bedside manner.

Nellie wiped her eyes and slowly shook her head. 'No, I'm all alone.'

Chapter 24

As soon as the doctor had left, Katherine turned on Nellie. 'Why? Why did you say that to the doctor?'

Nellie laughed.

'You're mad!' screamed Katherine.

'Maybe. You see, I've had a lot to put up with from Josh these past years and I won't be sorry to see the back of him.'

'What? After all he does for you?'

Nellie didn't reply.

'I'm getting a pillow and a blanket for him,' said Katherine. She left Nellie sitting looking at her husband, but there wasn't any sorrow in her eyes.

Katherine quickly returned. She knelt down beside the sorry figure lying on the floor and put the pillow under his head and covered him with a blanket. 'How could you? He's your husband!'

'I know.'

'He's looked after you for years and this is all the thanks he gets.'

'You shouldn't judge people till you know what it's all about. I'm going back to bed.'

'Well, don't expect me to be around to answer your every beck and call. I'm going home as soon as I've made sure Josh is safe.'

'Why? You worried I might do him in?'

Katherine couldn't answer. That hadn't entered her mind.

'I wouldn't kill him if that's what you think.'

'I'm not so sure about that, and I don't want to be accused of anything.'

Nellie left the room.

Katherine went into the shop, turned off the urn and locked the shop door. The last thing she wanted was the place full of people.

She sat looking out of the window at the rain still beating down. What was going to happen now? With Josh ill, who would run the shop? She suddenly sat up. She wouldn't have a job. She had to talk to Nellie.

'Nellie?' She carefully pushed open the bedroom door.

Nellie was sitting in front of the window. 'Well, what d'yer want?'

'I want to talk to you.'

'Filthy day, ain't it?'

'Nellie, what's going to happen to you?'

'Dunno.' She didn't take her eyes away from the window.

'Why did you hit Josh?'

' 'Cos he's bin carrying on behind me back. He shouldn't have done that. He knows it makes me mad.'

Katherine sat on the bed. 'He wasn't, you know. I just worked for him.'

'Might not be with you, but he was having it away with someone.'

'Well, it wasn't me.'

Nellie turned to face her. 'Didn't think it was.'

'You must tell the doctor that I didn't hit him.'

'He won't believe me. He thinks I can't hardly get out of bed.'

'But you can.'

'Yer. I only took to me bed when he first started with this carrying on lark.' Nellie moved closer to Katherine. 'You see, Kate . . . Well, I might as well tell you all the story. But I tell yer what, why don't you make us a nice cuppa? I expect you could do with one.'

Katherine nodded. This could be a long morning, and she had

to know what this was all about, and where her future lay, and if she had one at Trent's.

As she waited for the kettle to boil Katherine was brought out of her daydream by banging on the front door. She glanced up; it was the doctor.

'I've got to get Mr Trent into hospital. Can't leave him here with no one to look after him. I've managed to get someone to take him. Now about Mrs Trent. Can you look after her?'

'Well, I don't know.'

He was bending over Josh, who hadn't moved. 'Remember it was your doing that probably brought his stroke on, so I think the least you can do is look after her.'

Katherine wanted to shout at him, make him listen, but she knew it was no use.

'Good.' He mistook her silence as yes.

Another banging on the door sent her hurrying into the shop.

The butcher was standing there. 'The doc wants me to take Josh to the hospital. Me delivery cart's outside. Hope me and the doc can lift 'im. Bloody shame, him having a stroke like that.' The butcher looked down at Josh. 'Don't look too good, does he?' The butcher was a large man, and the doctor small, but between them they lifted Josh and put him inside the cart. Katherine stood in the doorway and watched them move away. The rain had wetted Josh's pale face. His eyes were still closed and he looked a very sad, sorry man.

Katherine took the tea up to Nellie.

'He's gorn then?'

'Yes.'

Nellie took the mug of tea and held it to her lips. 'This looks a bloody sight better than the stuff he gives to them poor sods downstairs.'

'Nellie, are you going to tell me what brought all this about?'

'Might as well.' She wiped her mouth with the back of her

hand. 'Mind you, there ain't that much to tell really. You see, this used to be me dad's place.' She stopped and looked round the bedroom. She patted the bed. 'This was me mum and dad's. When Josh married me he knew he was on to a good thing – walked right into a good business. Well, first Mum went, then Dad died, and that's when Josh started straying. I put up with it for a bit, then one day I'd had enough. I was working in the shop doing all the cooking and serving while he was out enjoying himself, so I went to bed and stayed there. That way he had to wait on me and run the shop, so that kept him busy and he didn't have time to go astray – that was till we had young girls working here. Caught him at it a couple of times, I did. After that I insisted we had young lads. That was till you come along. I somehow knew I could trust you, Kate. You've got breeding.'

'So why did you make all that fuss downstairs?'

'Dunno really. But it was a good excuse to give him a walloping.'

Katherine sat with her eyes wide open in amazement. She couldn't believe this woman would go to such lengths to make him suffer.

'Who will look after him when he comes out of hospital?' asked Katherine.

'I can't.'

'Who will look after you?'

'Dunno. I might write to me sister.'

'You've got a sister? But you told the doctor—'

'Yer, I know. She lives in Kent. She don't come up here, don't like London. I wouldn't mind going to stay with her for a bit.'

Katherine wanted to ask whether her sister would want her, but decided against that. 'Will you be able to manage financially?'

'I've got a few bob of me own. Dad made sure I wouldn't go short. 'Sides, the shop's in my name.'

Katherine was dumbfounded at all these revelations. She sat drinking her tea. How things could change in such a short space of time. Where would she go now? 'Nellie, when do you think you'll be going to Kent?'

'Dunno. I've got to think about that, and I shall need time to sort out things.'

'Josh? Kate? You there?' Someone was shouting at the bottom of the stairs.

'That's Ron, the bookies' runner,' said Katherine.

'He still comes here?'

'Yes. I'd better go down and tell him we're not open.'

'You can open up. You can run the place today, then we'll sort out some help for you later.'

'But . . . I . . .'

'You work here, so just get down there and open up!' Nellie's voice was loud and authoritative.

The last thing Katherine wanted was to work for Nellie.

'What the bleeding hell's going on?' asked Ron as Katherine came down the stairs. He banged his wet cap against his knee. 'She giving Josh a hard time?' He inclined his head towards the top of the stairs.

'Come on, Ron.' She took his arm and led him through to the shop.

'What's going on, Kate?'

She closed the door at the back of the counter. 'What do you know about Nellie?'

'Not a lot really. Where's Josh?'

'Sit down and I'll get you a cup of tea.'

With a puzzled expression on his face Ron moved over to a table, sat down, took his tobacco tin from his pocket and began rolling a cigarette.

Katherine knew she had to talk to someone. Soon everybody would be asking about Josh. The butcher would probably take great delight in giving his version, so she thought it best they heard it from her, and not any rumours that might grow. After all, she wouldn't stay after today – there was no way she was going to work for Nellie, and wait on her hand and foot.

'Josh is in hospital,' said Katherine, putting a cup of tea in front of Ron.

'What?' He took some coins from his pocket and put them on the table but Katherine waved them away. 'What's wrong with him?'

'He's had a stroke.'

'Bloody hell! When did this happen?'

'Early this morning.'

'What's gonner happen to this lot?' He waved his arm round.

'Nellie is taking it over and she expects me to work for her.'

'What?'

Katherine then went into great detail of what Nellie had told her, although she didn't tell him about her hitting Josh with her stick. 'Did you know Nellie was the owner?'

'Guessed as much. You see, me dad remembers her old man. Always wondered why she took to her bed, though. Did she ever say what was wrong with her?'

Katherine shook her head. She hadn't gone into Josh's indiscretions.

'So what happens now?'

'I'm not going to work for Nellie.'

'Can't say I blame yer. Mind you, we'll all be sorry to see you go, Kate.'

'And I shall be very sorry to go.'

'She won't be able to do much, stuck up there in bed, and if she does get someone in to run the place they'll soon see her off.'

'Don't know about that. Nellie Trent is a very shrewd woman. She was talking about writing to her sister.'

'Didn't know she had one.'

'She lives in Kent.'

'She can't run this shop from Kent.'

Katherine looked thoughtful. 'No, she can't.'

'Are you going to open up?' asked Ron.

'I think I will.'

'D'you want a hand?'

'I shouldn't be very busy, not on a day like this. Not many will venture out.'

'I'll hang about till lunchtime if you like.'

'Thanks, Ron.'

Katherine was right, she wasn't very busy. Ron left about one o'clock and an hour later she took a cup of tea up to Nellie.

'I'm going to close up now and go,' said Katherine.

'You can't go yet.' Nellie was still sitting in the chair. 'Who's gonner get me my tea?'

'You'll have to do it yourself.'

'I can't.'

'I'm going now the weather has improved. I don't want to finish up with a cold. My things are still wet from this morning. I'll get the takings.'

When Katherine returned Nellie counted out the money.

'Ain't much here,' she said.

'I haven't been very busy.'

Nellie snorted. 'I hope you ain't bin giving it away.'

'I'm off,' said Katherine, refusing to be drawn into another argument.

'You can't go yet.' Nellie was beginning to sound panicky. 'Will you be in on Monday?'

'Do you want me in?'

''Course. I ain't going down there. I ain't standing about all day serving that riffraff.'

'In that case I want a rise, if I'm going to be in charge.'

'A rise. Well, yes, I 'spect you would, but you're jumping the gun a bit. What if I get someone else in?'

'Well, that's up to you.' Katherine knew not many would work for her.

'We'll talk about it on Monday, and it'll only be till Josh comes back.'

'Do you think he will?' asked Katherine.

'Dunno.'

All the way home Katherine's head was spinning with everything that had happened. She almost ran into the kitchen, as she couldn't wait to tell Milly.

'You're early,' said Milly when she walked in.

'I've got so much to tell you.'

'Have a cuppa first,' said Charlie.

'And look at those shoes! Are your things wet?' asked Milly.

'Not now.'

'Well, get them off anyway.'

Katherine began laughing.

'What's so funny?' asked Charlie.

'It was me taking my clothes off that started it all.'

'Taking your clothes off?' repeated Milly. 'You've been taking your clothes off? You'd better tell us what this is all about.'

Milly, Charlie and Tom sat open-mouthed as Katherine went into all that had happened.

'Poor old Josh,' said Charlie. 'A stroke.'

'The old dear must be bloody wicked to do a thing like that,' said Milly.

'Well, she thought she had every right to.'

'' 'Ere, Kate, she didn't really think you – you know, with Josh, did she?' asked Charlie.

Milly leapt up. 'Charlie Stevens! What a terrible thing to ask!'

Charlie was grinning like a Cheshire cat. 'Well, I only asked.'

Katherine too was grinning. 'No, she just felt she needed a good excuse to give Josh a hiding, only it turned out to be far worse than she thought it would.'

'And she can walk, an' all?' asked Milly.

'Yes. She's a bit wobbly, mind, but she can walk all right.'

'Fancy that place belonging to her,' said Charlie.

'You gonner work for her?' asked Milly.

'I don't want to. I reckon she'll have me up and down those stairs all day, but I haven't got a lot of choice.'

'You'll have to have help if you do decide to stay,' said Tom.

'I can't see her staying upstairs. She'll be down making sure I don't steal anything, or at the very least give someone a cup of tea and don't take the money.'

'What a turn-up for the book,' said Charlie.

'Well, let's hope by Monday she'll realise what an asset I am. I've already asked for a rise.'

Charlie laughed. 'Good on yer, girl. Don't you let her push you about.'

Katherine slowly stirred her tea. 'I wonder if she'll change her mind about keeping the shop?'

'Does she own it or rent it?' asked Tom.

'I don't know. Wait a minute. They rent it. I've seen Josh talking to the landlord. Why?'

'If she can't keep it open she's still got her rent to pay on the flat upstairs.'

'Yes, but what about Josh? She'll have to look after him when he comes home or pay someone to do it.'

'Well, you'll just have to wait till Monday,' said Milly.

'Yes,' said Katherine slowly. Her mind was already moving forward. 'Any idea what the rent on that place would be?' she asked.

'Dunno,' said Charlie.

'Why?' asked Milly. 'Here, you're not thinking of—'

Katherine laughed. 'Where have I got the money to start a bus—' Her voice trailed off. 'Ida!'

'Ida?' said Charlie and Milly together.

'Why not? I could borrow it from Ida and pay it back, it's a very good—'

'Just a minute. Hold on a tick, Miss Katherine,' said Tom, interrupting her. 'I don't like to put a damper on things, but what about Mrs Trent? Would she let you have it, and would you like her living upstairs?'

'He's right, you know,' said Milly.

Katherine felt deflated. She knew it wouldn't come to her that easily.

Chapter 25

All day Sunday Katherine felt low and moped about, her thoughts continually going to Josh. What was going to happen to him? What was going to happen to Nellie? And more important, what was going to happen to her and her job? She didn't want to work for Nellie.

'I think you'd better take some liver salts,' suggested Milly. 'I think you might be coming down with something.'

On Monday morning Katherine could hardly open her eyes. She tried to lift her head from the pillow. Her throat felt as if it had closed overnight, she was hot, then cold, and every bone in her body ached. 'Oh no!' she moaned out loud. 'I've got a chill.'

For days she was vaguely aware of Milly bringing her tea, propping her up and spoon feeding her hot broth, and slipping a stone hot-water bottle beneath her feet. Days drifted into nights. Time meant nothing.

'You know this is because you got soaking wet on Sat'day, don't you?' she heard Milly say, as cold flannels were placed on her hot, fevered brow.

Katherine tried to give her a hint of a smile; the last thing she wanted was to be lectured to.

She tossed and turned. She could hear herself shouting and calling from far away. She thought she saw Joseph sitting on the bed, but it was misty and she couldn't get him into focus. Then he smiled and held her hand. When she opened her eyes again he had gone. 'Joseph,' she croaked.

The door creaked open. But it wasn't Joseph standing there. It was Robert. He had grown so tall and handsome, but he looked very angry. 'Why did you desert me?' he shouted.

'Robert!' she cried out. 'You've come to see me!'

Her first-born came towards her.

'Robert, I didn't want to leave you. Please forgive me.'

'But you did leave me, and Father. We will never forgive you, never, never!' He turned and walked away.

'Robert!' she screamed. 'Wait!' She struggled to get out of bed. Hands were holding her down. 'Please let me go! I've got to catch him. I've got to tell him how handsome he is, and how much I still love him.' She tried to get away from the hands, but they wouldn't give way. She cried out and salty tears ran down her cheeks. Strands of hair brushed across her face. Someone was wiping her forehead. She couldn't move. Finally she gave up and lay back, worn out and exhausted. Her Robert had gone, and the blackness returned.

Katherine opened her eyes. Milly was standing over her.

'Welcome back.'

Katherine struggled to sit up. 'What time is it?'

'Ten.'

'What? I've got to get up! I'm late for work and I promised Nellie . . .'

Milly gently pushed her back against the pillows. 'You ain't going nowhere, not today.'

Katherine felt bewildered. 'Why? Milly, what day is it?'

'Saturday.'

'What? Where . . . ?'

'You, my girl, have been very ill. You have been delirious.'

Katherine frowned. She tried to remember. 'Have I been here almost a week?'

'Yes.'

'Was I that bad?'

'You had us very worried.'

Gradually things started to become clear. 'I thought Robert came to see me.'

'Only in your mind. It took all me and Charlie's strength to hold you down. You tried to run after him.'

'I'm sorry.'

Milly silently patted her hand.

'Have I been a lot of trouble?'

'No, course not.'

'I'd like to get up.'

'Well, wait till after dinner, then if you feel like it I'll help you into the chair. But only for a little while.'

'Yes, nurse.'

Later that afternoon Milly left her sitting in the chair. Katherine gazed out of the window, but not seeing the houses in her view. She let her thoughts go to Robert. What did he look like now? Would he be an older version of Joseph? Why in her mind was it him she most wanted to see?

She heard Joseph bounding up the stairs. He flung open the door and, falling to his knees, held her close. 'Oh, Ma! I've been so worried about you.'

She gently patted his head.

'I didn't like seeing you so ill. Are you feeling better now?'

'Yes thank you.'

He sat on the bed. 'You know you were shouting about Robert?'

'So Milly told me.'

'Do you miss him?'

'In a way. I shall always feel guilty at leaving him.'

'You never know, one of these days he might come to England.'

'He wouldn't know where to find me if he did.' She knew she had to steer the conversation away from Robert. 'Now, could you get me a cup of tea?'

He kissed her cheek. 'Course.'

Katherine sat back. Would she ever see her first-born son again?

Every day, thanks to Milly's care, Katherine got stronger. They sat and talked at length just like they did when Katherine first moved in, but now they were true friends. They talked about Dolly and Briony, and when Olive, now pregnant again, brought baby Dolly round, all work stopped.

'She's a little charmer,' said Milly, lifting her high in the air.

'Well, I hope you're gonner be as pleased with the next one,' said Olive.

'Reckon I'll have me work cut out then.'

'How you feeling, Olive?'

'Not too bad at all. Mind you, I won't be sorry when May's over.'

'At least you won't be carrying all through the summer.'

'That's true.'

'Your mother's going to let me go out at the end of the week.' Olive laughed. 'She's a good nurse, but a strict one.'

'Yes, I have found that out.'

'The pie and mash shop's closed,' said Milly, as they walked along. 'Charlie said someone told him the old girl's gone away.'

'What, for good?'

'Dunno.'

'What about Josh?'

'He didn't know what happened to him.'

Katherine felt sorry for the man she had looked on as a friend. 'Has she left her home and everything?'

'Dunno about that. Charlie didn't learn much about it. The butcher might know.'

Katherine hesitated when they reached Trent's. It looked sad and forlorn with its closed sign hanging lopsided on the door.

She thought about the laughter and the bawdy remarks, the arguing over politics, the sad time during the strike when the shop overflowed with angry men, and now about poor Josh. She gave up a silent prayer: please make him well again.

Milly took her arm. 'Come on.'

The butcher smiled and looked genuinely pleased to see her. 'Hallo there, Kate. Heard you was poorly. You feeling better now?'

'Yes, thank you. How did you know I've been ill?'

'Word gets around. Mind you, you don't look all that good, very pasty-faced.'

She smiled. She knew she wouldn't get too many compliments. 'Do you know how Josh is?'

'Na. When you didn't turn up on the Monday we all thought you'd jacked it in, but then one of the blokes from the docks said you was ill. Ron said he went in to see how Josh was and his missis was going mad that you hadn't turned up.'

'Had she got up?'

'She must have. She's bloody barmy. D'you know, she was gonner set about Ron with her stick.'

Katherine laughed.

'It wasn't funny. Poor bloke looked scared out of his wits. Think it must'a bin then that she decided to go away. Nobody will work for her.'

'Do you know where she went?'

'Na.'

'She said she had a sister in Kent. But what about Josh, is he still in hospital?'

'Dunno.'

'What hospital did you take him to?'

'The cottage hospital up the road.'

Katherine turned to Milly. 'Could we go there?'

'Not today. You've done enough for one day.'

'That's right, Kate. You mustn't overdo it.'

Milly fussed with her shopping bag. 'It's her first day out,' she said to the butcher. 'I'll have a pound of scrag end while I'm here.'

Katherine grinned. She felt like a naughty girl who'd just been allowed out.

The following day they went to the hospital, only to be told that Mr Trent had been sent to a home by the seaside to help him recover.

'Will he ever be well again?' Katherine asked the nurse.

'That's hard to say. Some people recover from a stroke while others remain like a cabbage for the rest of their lives.'

It upset Katherine to think of Josh as a cabbage.

As they walked home Katherine said to Milly, 'I'm going to take over the pie shop.'

'I ain't surprised. So, how do you go about that?'

'First, I've got to find out who the landlord is and what sort of rent he's asking. Then I'll have to buy stock.'

'And what yer gonner do for money, may I ask?'

'I'll go and see Ida.'

'Will you be able to pay her back?'

'It's a good business.'

'You've got it all worked out, ain't yer?'

'I must admit it's something I've been thinking about.'

'Have you now? Will you live over the shop?'

Katherine stopped. 'Oh Milly, I hadn't thought about that.'

'I can't stop you moving on.'

Katherine felt guilty. 'I shall really miss living with you and Charlie.'

Milly tucked her bag under her arm. 'Well, you ain't got it yet, and I for one don't believe in counting me chickens 'fore they're hatched.'

Katherine could see Milly wasn't going to be happy with the arrangements.

The following day Katherine went alone to the butcher's to

find out who the landlord was. He smiled when he heard what she had in mind.

'Mr Sharman. He comes every month for his rent. He ain't due till next week.'

'What day?'

'Mostly on a Monday.'

'What's he like?'

'Don't have a lot to do with him. I just pays me rent and he goes off. I think him and Josh got on.'

'Was he a tall smart man, with a paunch?'

'Sounds like him.'

'They used to chat. Do you mind if I ask how much rent you pay?'

'I pay twelve and six a week. That's for the flat an' all, mind. I don't reckon Josh paid as much as that as they've been there years, and her old man before that.'

'I know. If I happen to miss him could you get his address for me?'

'Sure. No, missis, I ain't got any liver left.' The butcher continued serving his customers.

'You look done in,' said Milly, when Katherine walked into the kitchen. 'Sit down, I'll pour you out a cuppa. Well, did you see him?' she asked sharply.

'No. The butcher said he comes on Monday. I have seen him talking to Josh at times.'

'What about, rent?'

'The butcher pays twelve and six a week, but I reckon I'll have to pay more.'

'Why's that?'

'It'll be a new tenancy agreement and all landlords look for a good excuse to charge more.'

'Well, you know all about that, don't yer?' Milly was definitely put out. 'But he may already have let it.'

'Yes, there is that possibility.' Katherine didn't want to think about that. She had made up her mind: this was what she wanted to do.

On Monday she went to the butcher's about the time she knew the landlord called. 'Has he been yet?' she asked.

'Not yet,' came the reply.

She took a slow walk down the road. She passed the stalls and shops, and looking into the ironmonger's, thoughts of Briony came flooding back. They never did find out if all the rumours about Mr Wilks were true. Now Briony had gone and the Addamses had moved away.

She felt sorry for Josh and hoped he'd be better one day. What would happen to Nellie? So many things had changed in the short time Katherine had lived in Rotherhithe. As she began to wander back she caught sight of the man she knew to be the landlord hurrying along, and quickened her step.

'Excuse me, sir! Excuse me.'

He stopped and, turning round, asked abruptly, 'Yes, what do you want?'

'Could I have a word?'

'What about?'

'It's rather private.'

'What's it about?'

Katherine looked anxiously around, feeling very uncomfortable. 'I would like to rent the shop.'

'You used to work for Josh Trent, didn't you?'

'Yes.'

'Yes, I remember now, used to see you in there.' He laughed. 'It was the hat that put me off.'

Katherine touched her hat.

'Josh used to speak very highly of you. Did you say you wanted to rent a shop?'

254

'Yes.'

'Now where would you get the money from to start a business?'

Katherine felt ill at ease and awkward at having to stand in the street to discuss her future. 'I have been in business before.'

'And you finished up working in Trent's? It wasn't that successful then, was it?'

Katherine didn't reply.

'Can't say I approve of women in business. But then again if your money's good . . . Now, which one did you have in mind?'

'The pie shop.'

'Sorry, that's gone.'

Katherine gasped. He had dismissed her plans in a flash.

He took her arm and bent his head closer. 'I do have another not too far from here, that's if you are interested.'

'Where is that?'

'Look, take my card and come and see me tomorrow. Perhaps we can talk about it in my office over a cup of tea.'

She looked at his card. 'Thank you, Mr Sharman. When will it be convenient?'

'About ten. I shall look forward to it.' He raised his trilby slightly and walked away.

Katherine stood and watched him go. There was something about the man she didn't like. But she had to go and find out about the other shop. Where was it? And who had taken the pie shop? If it was near, would there be trouble for her opening another so close? She would have her own shop and show him that this woman could run a business, she resolved. Besides, she had to do something soon as her money wouldn't last for ever, and Milly still had to be paid.

Chapter 26

Sharp at ten o'clock Katherine knocked on Mr Sharman's office door.

'Come in, my dear.' Without his trilby, his balding head emphasised his round florid face. 'Take a seat.' He sat back. 'Now, you said you would like to rent one of my shops?'

'Yes.'

'You said you were in business before?'

'Yes.' Katherine didn't want to reveal too much.

'That does sound rather unlikely seeing as where you finished up.'

'It was a while ago.'

'I see. Where was that? If I'm going to let you rent one of my shops I need to have references, you know.' He took up a pen and began writing.

She knew he didn't need references, so was this just a ploy to put her off? Women round this way didn't start their own businesses, only market stalls and the like. 'It was over the water.'

'I see. You're not one of these silly suffragette women who believe in women's rights, and all that, are you?'

Katherine had to hold her tongue. She wanted to be independent and tell him that she did believe in women's rights but didn't have the courage to be truthful about her feelings. 'No. I lost the business when my husband died.'

'So it wasn't really yours?' He sat back. 'What sort of collateral have you?' He bent his head forward. 'You do know what I mean by collateral, don't you?'

How dare he think she was an idiot? Katherine wanted to storm out. No man would have to answer these mundane questions. 'Mr Sharman, if you would be so kind as to tell me where this shop is I can let you know if it will be suitable for my requirements.'

He laughed. 'That's what I like to see, a woman with a bit of spirit.'

She felt herself flush with anger.

'The one I have in mind is in Perry Street.'

'Perry Street? What, under the arches?'

'Yes. Nice little shops.'

'They are horrible, and well away from everything.' She stood up. 'No thank you, Mr Sharman.'

'What sort of business did you have in mind, Kate? I may call you Kate?'

'No, you may not. My name is Mrs Carter, and I won't bother telling you what I need a shop for, as it won't be any of your concern. Good day, Mr Sharman.' She went to move towards the door.

'Please, Mrs Carter, sit down.'

'Why?'

He came round the desk. 'Please.' He pointed to the chair.

Reluctantly Katherine sat down.

'Why did you want Trent's?'

She toyed with her gloves. 'I know I could run it well. Who will be taking it over?'

He coughed. 'Well, at the moment we are still in the negotiating stage.'

'So, in other words, you haven't let it?' Katherine was feeling stronger. She knew she had this man cornered.

'I have been waiting for years for that property to become vacant.'

'Why? Just so that you could charge a lot more for the rent?

258

I'll give you the same as the butcher, twelve and six a week.'

'I can't—'

Katherine stood up. 'That's my offer, take it or leave it.' She turned and walked to the door. 'Good day, Mr Sharman.' She was shaking. Had she gone too far?

His laughter caused her to turn round.

'I like you. Come back and we will draw up an agreement. The rent is paid one month in advance, you know.'

She smiled.

'Mind you, if you don't make a go of it and miss a month's rent, you'll be out on your ear.'

'Don't worry. I intend to make a go of it and I won't miss paying the rent.' She sat, trying to look full of confidence, but deep down she was worried. What if Ida wouldn't lend her the money for her first month's rent?

'Will you be using the flat?'

'Yes. My son will be living with me.'

'You have a son? I don't know what state the place is in, but then that's not my problem. I sent builders round to repair the chimney Mrs Trent was complaining had fallen down.'

'What about the Trents' furniture?'

'She didn't leave any instructions.'

'But you said you've heard from Mrs Trent.'

'Not really. She just sent a note round about the chimney, said she was going away and she didn't know when she would be back.'

Katherine froze. 'So she could come back and take it all away from me?'

'No. Once you've signed the agreement the shop will be yours.'

'So what shall I do with the furniture?'

'Sell it.'

'I can't do that!'

'As I said, that, my dear woman, is your problem. Now do you want to sign this?'

She nodded and he pushed the agreement in front of her.

He walked to the door and held it open for her. 'It has been a pleasure doing business with you, Mrs Carter, and as soon as I get the rent you can have the keys.'

'Thank you.'

Katherine almost ran home. She couldn't wait to tell all of them her good news. But would they think it *was* good news?

'I don't think I fancy living above the pie shop. Will it stink of fish from those rotten eels?' Joseph was the first to air his views.

'I hope to be doing more than jellied eels.'

'What's the place like?'

'When I've paid the first month's rent I get the key.'

'Where're you getting that sort of money from?' asked Charlie.

'She reckons she's gonner borrow it from Ida,' said Milly sharply.

'D'you think that's wise?' asked Tom.

'Of course it is. If I want to start on my own.'

'Well, I don't reckon a woman should run that sorta business,' said Charlie.

'Why not?' Katherine was trying hard to keep her temper.

''Cos of the sorta blokes you get in there – I reckon they'll lead you a right merry dance.'

'Why should they? I've known them for quite a while now.'

'Yer, but that was when Josh was in charge.' Charlie began rolling a cigarette.

'You men are all the same. You don't like seeing women get on.'

'There's no need to get on your high horse. It's just that I reckon they'll try it on with a woman.'

'Doing what?' asked Milly.

'Not paying. Making out they ain't got any money and a woman's gotter be a soft touch.'

'Not this woman,' said Katherine with dignity.

'Have you thought about a nice little haberdashery?' asked Tom.

'No.'

'Well, I wish you luck then,' said Charlie.

Katherine wanted to scream. This is what she had wanted and all they could do was try to pour cold water on it. 'I may ask your help to get the place cleaned up, especially upstairs,' she said calmly to Milly. She wanted to involve her.

'So, when you seeing Ida?' asked Milly.

'Tomorrow.'

'I see.'

'For your sake let's hope she's in a good mood,' said Charlie.

'This is a business deal.'

'Yer, I know.'

At first Ida was a bit hesitant about lending her the money, but Katherine's enthusiasm quickly won her over. All in all, she borrowed five pounds, which she had to pay back at the princely rate of ten shillings a week, plus one pound interest.

As soon as she got the key Katherine hurried to the shop. Her shop. Mr Sharman had wanted to come with her but she preferred to be on her own.

She pushed open the shop door and took a deep breath. The smell of rotten meat nearly knocked her over. She hurried through the door to the back of the shop and rats quickly scurried away. She would have to get herself a cat.

Very carefully she made her way to the back door. The whole place seemed quiet and eerie. She almost expected Nellie to jump out on her or yell from upstairs.

She studied the yard with a fresh look. This was going to need a good cleanup. She couldn't bear a lot of unnecessary mess.

The place felt cold and damp. She made her way upstairs, not knowing what she'd find. Nellie's room was as she had left it. Even the chamber pot was still full and it stank. The bedclothes were in a heap on the floor. She opened the window and moved into the other bedroom that must have been Josh's. It wasn't very clean, but it was tidy. She sat on his bed. What could she do with all his and Nellie's clothes, and what about all this furniture? Should she use it till Nellie got in touch? At the moment she and Joseph had nothing but their clothes.

She shivered, and moved into the last room upstairs, the parlour. Ashes were still in the grate. She knew she could make this room warm and cosy. The thought of being in her own home after all this time brought a tear to her eyes. 'I am the mistress of all this,' she said out loud and, with her arms outstretched, turned a full circle. 'And nobody is going to take it away from me.'

Before she made her way back to Milly's she called in to the butcher. 'Tell everybody the pie shop will be open for business as usual on Monday.'

He grinned. 'That's great news, Kate. I wish you the best of luck.'

'Thanks. I'll be in for meat on Saturday, and I expect a good price.'

'For you, my dear, I'll do a good deal.'

As she walked home there was a spring in her step. She felt so happy. Christmas was only four weeks away – would all the Stevenses like to spend it with her and Joseph? She had to get the place into some kind of order first. Tomorrow she would start on the cleaning, and as far as she was concerned it would be a labour of love. Rotherhithe would be her home for ever.

At first Katherine worried Milly wouldn't go with her to clean up. She began putting many obstacles in her way, but eventually her curiosity must have got the better of her and she reluctantly decided to help. On Wednesday morning, armed with cloths and various other cleaning implements, they set off.

'What's that stink?' asked Milly when Katherine pushed the door open. 'Thought you said you'd emptied Nellie's po.'

'I did. Josh left the meat out. I did throw it all away but the smell still lingers.' Katherine hadn't told anyone about the rats.

'This kitchen could do with a good cleanup. What's it like outside?'

'Not that good.'

'Blimey! It is a bit of a mess,' said Milly, wandering out to see. 'Look at the state of this bog,' she added, gingerly pushing the door open.

'I know. I tried to keep it clean but Josh wouldn't buy any carbolic. I'll pop along to the ironmonger's later.'

All day they swept and scrubbed. They stripped the beds and bundled up Nellie's and Josh's clothes in the sheets.

'What you gonner do with 'em?' asked Milly, pointing to the bundles on the bed.

'I'll clean out a cupboard and put them in there for the time being.'

'At least the furniture ain't bad. That three-piece in the parlour could do with a bit of a clean, though. And those curtains look as if one wash and they'll fall to pieces. What you gonner do about sheets and stuff for you and Joe?'

'I don't know. I was thinking of going along to the draper's to see how much I can have on tick.'

Milly laughed.

'What's so funny?'

'You talking about having things on tick. When you first came over this way you didn't even know the meaning of the word.'

'A lot has changed.' She sat on the bed. 'Milly, I'm very fond of you and you've been very good to me and Joseph and I hope we remain friends for ever.'

'Course we will.' She sat next to Katherine. 'Sorry if I've bin a bit . . . well, you know. But it's just that I don't want you to go. It's been nice having a woman round the house. I can let you have some bedding. Don't forget I've got all Dolly's.'

'Will Tom mind?'

'No.' She began scratching her arm. 'I reckon you've got a few lodgers here. When you go along to the ironmonger's get a flit gun and I'll give these rooms up here a good going-over. When you reckon on moving in?'

'I'd like it to be Saturday.'

'So soon?'

'Well, I've got to get the shop open as soon as I can.'

'Yer, I s'pose you have. If you like I'll come and give you a hand till you're on your feet.'

'You are a real friend.'

'So when you opening?'

'Monday.'

'Christ! We'd better get a move on. You've only got a few days.'

'Yes, and I've got to do the cooking and clean up downstairs.'

'Well, let's get cracking then. But first I think we deserve a cuppa, don't you?'

'Be my guest.'

'Here, I hope we ain't gonner have to put the money in the box?'

Katherine laughed. 'No, no yet, we're not open.'

On Saturday when Joseph finished work he came to his new home.

'Joseph!' said Katherine, opening the shop door. She had been looking out of the window, waiting for him, and greeted him with a hug. 'Welcome to your new home.'

Silently he looked around.

'Go through that door.' She ushered him through the door behind the counter. A lovely smell of pies cooking filled the air. 'We will use this room down here as the kitchen. It stays nice and warm with the oven. I'll show you upstairs, and your very own room. You've waited a long while for this,' she said eagerly over her shoulder.

Upstairs he stood in the doorway. 'Is this mine?'

She nodded and put her arm round his shoulders. 'Yes, it's all yours. Come and see the parlour.'

It was warm and inviting, with a fire blazing in the grate. 'Well, what do you think? Do you like this room?'

'Where did the furniture come from?' he asked, looking around.

'It belongs to Josh and his wife.'

'What if they come back and want it?'

'I'll have to cross that bridge when I come to it.'

'But he isn't dead, and you've taken over his home, his belongings and his business. It's as if you've waited for him to go.'

'I didn't. If I didn't have this place the landlord would have let it to someone else and they might have thrown everything out. This way I can take care of it for them.'

'What if they don't come back?'

Katherine was surprised at his attitude. 'When I know for sure I'll send them the money for it.'

'But what if they want the shop back?'

'This is our home now.' She was getting a little tired of his questions. 'You used to be on about having your own room, but now it seems you've changed your tune.'

'I'll miss Ted,' he said.

'And I shall miss Milly, but we have to move on. We couldn't stay there for ever, and an opportunity like this only comes now and again. You always did hate changes.'

He smiled. 'It does look nice and cosy here. But we won't have to live on pies and saveloys, will we?'

'No, I think we can go to a roast on Sundays.'

Katherine was happy. This was what she wanted. She and Joseph were together in their own home, and nobody was going to take it away from her.

Chapter 27

On Monday Katherine was surprised at the number of people who popped their heads round the door to wish her good luck. At lunchtime she was rushed off her feet. She desperately needed help. Would Milly be prepared to come and give her a hand every day?

After lunch, when trade began to settle down, Ron, wearing a huge grin, came in. 'Hallo there, Katie love. It's good to see you back. We all thought you'd gone for good.' He rubbed his hands together. 'It's nice and warm in here. I tell yer, it's bloody cold out there.'

She looked at the steamed-up windows running with water, and brushed a stray damp strand of hair back from her forehead. 'This is hard work on your own.'

'Well, you could get a lad in like Josh used to.'

'That might not be a bad idea.' She pushed a mug of tea towards him. He reached into his pocket for the money. 'Have this one on me.'

'You're not gonner make a packet like that.'

'You've been a good friend, so the least I can do is give you a cuppa. Mind you, this is the first and the last.'

He laughed. 'D'you know, I reckon you'll make a go of this place. Good mind to open a book on it.'

'What's the odds?'

'You've certainly changed since working here.'

'I know, and it's for the better. Mind you, I'll miss Josh. He wasn't a bad old thing.'

'Yer, that was a bloody shame. He had a lot to put up with from her. I reckon she was a bit . . .' He put his finger to his forehead and twisted it. 'D'you think she'll ever come back?'

'I hope not. But you can never tell with someone like Nellie. She's just as likely to come swanning in here as if nothing has happened and expect to take over.'

He looked alarmed. 'You don't really think that, do you?'

'I don't know. After all, she just upped and left everything including her overflowing chamber pot.'

Ron was taking a mouthful of tea when Katherine said that. He laughed and the tea went everywhere. 'I've heard it all now!'

That evening, after she'd closed the shop, Katherine made her way upstairs to Joseph, who had come in earlier. He had quickly passed through, only stopping long enough to say hallo and glance around.

'You look tired,' he said, looking up when she entered the parlour. He was sitting warming himself in front of the fire.

'It's been a long day, but a very enjoyable one.' She plonked herself down on the sofa.

'But has it been profitable?'

'Yes. I've taken enough to pay the butcher and the ten shillings I owe Ida. Things are going to get better. The fruit pies I made went down a treat, but I will have to have help.'

'What about Milly?'

'She might do it for a little while. I was thinking of getting a young lad in.'

'Don't look at me. I'm not skivvying for anyone.'

Any idea she'd had of their running the business together was quickly quashed.

All week Katherine worked hard. She was disappointed Milly hadn't been in to see her, but knowing Milly, she guessed her absence was because she didn't want to get in the way.

Every evening, after she closed, she prepared the food for the next day and then early in the morning, long before she opened, she would be busy making pies.

Joseph sniffed the air when he came down for his breakfast. 'Those pies certainly smell good.'

'And it's nice and warm in here. Don't you get cold in the garage?'

'No, not really.'

She knew he wouldn't complain if he did.

The following Monday morning Mrs Duke appeared in the doorway.

'Heard you'd took this place over.' She waddled up to the counter. 'Had to come and black me nose, didn't I? Doing all right then?'

'Would you like tea?' asked Katherine, ignoring her last remark.

'How much yer gonner charge me?'

'You can have this one on me.'

'Yer, why not? Ta very much. Mind you, you ain't gonner make that much if you keep giving it away.'

'Don't worry, Mrs Duke. That's the first and last.'

Mrs Duke put her shopping bag on the floor and, taking her tea, went to sit at the table near the counter. 'Well, how you doing then?' She rested her elbows on the marble-topped table and clutched the thick china mug with both hands.

'Very well, thank you.'

'Must say I was a bit surprised when Milly told me. Thought you was gonner get something better. A bit more snobby.' Her eyes scanned every corner of the room.

Katherine smiled. 'This is just a start.' She turned and wiped down the counter.

'Well, it looks a bit cleaner in here. But you don't wanner make it too posh otherwise you'll send all the riff-raff away. They're used to spitting on the floor.'

'Not in my place they don't.'

Mrs Duke was looking round. 'What yer gonner call it then?'

'Call it?'

'Yer, it ain't Trent's now, is it?'

'Well, no.'

'It'll have to have a new name.'

'Yes, I suppose it will. But I can't afford a sign writer just yet, so that will give me time to think about a name.'

'I reckon Kate's Place.'

'Kate's Place,' repeated Katherine. 'That's got a nice ring to it. I could well call it that. Or what about Kate's Kitchen?'

'Yer.' Mrs Duke put her head on one side. 'That don't sound bad at all.'

'Right. Welcome to Kate's Kitchen.'

'In that case I'll have another free cuppa for a toast and me advice.'

Katherine laughed. 'I suppose I'll have to be Kate from now on.'

'Please yerself about that. Two sugars in it this time then, Kate. By the way, did you know Ron the bookies' runner's been caught?'

Kate sat down. 'No. I didn't.'

'Yer, he got run in last week.'

'I thought I hadn't seen him.'

'Goes up before the beak on Monday. Some of the blokes reckons he could end up getting a year.'

'No! Poor Ron. A year in prison.'

'Shouldn't worry too much about him, he's had a good run for his money. Well, I best be off.'

Kate watched her walk out of the door. Her thoughts were still on Ron. She would miss him. He had been a good friend.

* * *

Kate was a bit disappointed that it wasn't until Friday lunchtime that Milly called in, and she was very busy.

'Milly. Please come round here and pour out some tea.'

'Mrs Duke said you was rushed off yer feet.'

Kate smiled. She hadn't been busy when Mrs Duke was here, so had the older woman just been trying to make Milly feel jealous that she'd been here and Milly hadn't?

'You'll find the plates over there and there's plenty more mash out back,' said Kate quickly, as she put a pie and some mash in a dish a woman had brought in. 'Yes, these are apple.'

'Stick it on top. I can scrape the tater off when I gets home. Me old man won't know the difference.'

The pie was plonked on top and taken away.

After a short while Milly seemed at ease collecting dirty plates and mugs and emptying the overflowing ashtrays. In between Kate told her about Mrs Duke and the name they'd come to.

'So it's Kate from now on, is it?'

'Well, it's less of a mouthful than Katherine.'

'Our Kate's certainly made a difference to this place, ain't she?' said an old man who slapped Milly's bottom as she passed him.

'She works hard.'

'Yer, but it's the cooking what counts. Her pies are . . .' He kissed his fingers in a gesture of satisfaction.

Milly laughed. Kate could see she was enjoying herself.

Later, in a quiet moment, they were sitting having a mug of tea and Kate said, 'How would you like to work here with me?'

'Dunno. Charlie wouldn't like it if his tea wasn't on the table when he got home.'

'What if it was only during lunchtime?'

'Dunno. I'll have a word with Charlie. He can be a bit funny about wives working. Likes to think he's the breadwinner.'

'Please, I need someone. Besides, it will give you some money of your own.'

'Don't know about that.'

'Please, Milly.'

'I'll see. Now I must go.'

'Would you like to take some pies for Charlie and Ted and Tom's dinners?'

'Na, ta all the same, but I've got a rabbit pie ready to go in the oven.'

'Perhaps another day then. Would you all like to come here to tea on Sunday?'

'No, sorry. Olive and Ernie's coming round. You and Joe can come if you like.'

'Thanks all the same, but I expect I'll be busy.'

'Well, please yourself.' She kissed Kate's cheek and left.

Kate touched her cheek. Milly's kiss seemed to lack the warmth they had known. She almost felt as if Milly were trying to keep her distance. Was she trying to tell her something? Had Charlie put his foot down? He was normally so easy-going. Perhaps he was frightened of women getting too strong. Or was this awkwardness because Milly didn't want to work for her?

It was a quiet spell, and Kate was thinking things over while washing up, when the door opened and Grace walked in.

'See you've opened up again then?'

'Yes. Grace, it's so good to see you,' said Kate, wiping her wet hands on a cloth and pouring her out a mug of tea. 'Is everything all right?'

'Yes, ta.'

'And your mother?' asked Kate tentatively.

Grace sat down and took a cigarette from her handbag. 'She died.'

'I'm so sorry.' She put the tea in front of Grace and sat at her table.

Grace looked nervously about her.

Kate was at a loss for words. 'Are you expecting your Mr Friday?'

Grace nodded quickly. 'D'you mind me coming in here?'

'No, of course not. Did you manage to get enough for your mother's funeral?' Kate asked softly.

Grace shook her pretty head.

'I'm sorry.' Kate looked up when the door opened and a cold draught blew in. Mr Friday stood in the doorway and Grace quickly stood up and left, leaving her tea untouched.

'My God, it's cold out there!' The door opened again and an old man of about fifty, wearing a raincoat tied round the waist with string, staggered in. He moved close to the counter and Kate stood back. While he looked around he stroked his pepper-and-salt-coloured beard. His white hair was sticking out from under his dirty trilby. He swayed and held on to the counter.

'The name's Seamus.' He held out his hand to shake Kate's.

Fear gripped her. He was Irish and they had a reputation for being volatile around here. Why did he have to come in here? She wanted to throw him out. 'What do you want?' There was no warmth in her voice.

'Seamus O'Brien, and I'm pleased to make your acquaintance, my dear lady. Just heard the other feller's gone. Couldn't get on with him.'

Kate stood and stared. 'You're drunk!'

'Well, I do like a little tipple now and again. Just the odd one or two, you understand. It helps to keep out the cold.'

Thoughts filled her mind of the problem she'd had with Mr Addams. She was alone and had to remain calm. All the while she was behind the counter she was safe. 'A tipple?' She laughed half-heartedly and waved her hand in front of her face. 'You're knocking me over with the fumes.'

He laughed. It was a soft lilting laugh, causing his bright blue eyes to twinkle. 'I like you, like a woman with a sense of humour. Don't see many these days. Most of 'em are tight-lipped and tight-arsed.' He put his hand to his mouth. 'Begging your pardon, me dear! I'm sorry. That just slipped out. No offence meant.'

Although nervous, Kate wanted to smile, but knew she shouldn't encourage him. On the other hand he appeared to be a pleasant man. 'Did you want a mug of tea?'

'Now that's real civil of you. I don't mind if I do.'

'That will be tuppence.'

He held up his hands. 'Now there was me thinking you was giving it to me out of the goodness of your heart.'

'Tuppence,' said Kate, holding out her hand and desperately trying to suppress the smile that wanted to break through.

'My, you're a hard woman.' Seamus paid his money and sat at the table near the counter. 'What happened to the other feller?'

'He had a stroke.'

'Did he now? Is his missis still upstairs?'

Kate shook her head. 'No. How do you know about Nellie?'

He touched the side of his nose. 'Don't give to tell all me knowledge at once. That way you'll be pleased to see me again to find out what more I know about Nellie.'

Kate had to burst out laughing. 'You've certainly got a touch of the blarney.'

'Have you ever been to my fair isle?'

'No.'

'It's very beautiful.'

Kate thought about Briony and her mother. Would they both still be alive if the Addamses had never left? 'So what brings you over here, then?'

'Work. Not a lot doing over there.'

The brothers Bill and Bert from the market came in.

'Give us a mug of hot strong tea, Kate,' said Bill. 'It's bloody freezing out there. I'm glad I'm not a brass monkey.' He turned to sit down. 'Blimey! It's old Seamus. What you doing round this way again?'

Bert grinned and asked, 'When d'they let you out?'

'Yesterday.'

Bill laughed. 'You wanner watch him, Kate. Right old charmer, he is.'

'I've gathered that already.'

'She's lovely,' said Seamus. 'Listen to that pretty voice. Reminds me of back home. It sounds like a gentle stream trickling over stones.'

'Hark at him,' said Bill. 'His dad brought him over when he was a baby, and he's been in the nick most of his life.'

'What for?' asked Kate in alarm.

'I was just unlucky,' said Seamus.

'Unlucky be buggered,' said Bert. 'You was caught nicking, and more than once.'

'As I said, I was just unlucky. I kept getting caught.'

They all laughed.

'You know old Ron's finished up inside?' said Bill to Kate.

'Yes, I did hear.'

'He got six months.'

'My God, six months! What terrible deed did he do?' asked Seamus.

'Bookies' runner,' said Bert.

'Well, if you ask me he didn't run fast enough.'

'Bit like you then, Seamus,' said Bill.

'Yes, I think you could say that.' He grinned at Kate.

She could see he was another larger-than-life character that she hoped was harmless, and would add to the interesting people who had become part of her life.

Kate was more than pleased when Milly walked in the following day.

'I can only stay an hour,' she said, taking her coat off.

Kate threw her arms round her. 'Thank you.'

Tea, pies, mash, saveloys and pease pudding were all quickly distributed to the many waiting customers, and again with plenty of compliments for Kate's cooking. Kate could see Milly was enjoying herself, and the hour flew by.

'Sorry I can't stay any longer.'

'Thank you so much. It's been wonderful having your help. Will I see you tomorrow?'

Milly nodded. 'But not on Sat'day.'

'That's all right,' said Kate smiling, but she was worried. Saturday was Josh's busiest day, and now news was getting around about Kate's cooking, she was getting more and more new customers, and she knew they didn't like to be kept waiting.

'Give Charlie, Ted and Tom my love.'

'Right. I'll see you tomorrow.'

Kate looked at the pile of washing up. She had to have regular help, and soon.

Chapter 28

All week Kate was happy working with Milly, and although it was tiring, she knew Milly was enjoying herself. But the problem of how to manage on Saturday grew on Kate's mind.

'Do you know of anyone who could come in for a few hours?' she asked the butcher on Friday.

He shook his head.

'What about your wife?'

'Na, she's got more than enough to do looking after all the kids and giving me a hand.'

'That's the trouble. The women I can trust and know would be fine all have families, and Saturday's the day husbands want them around. And most young lads don't want to work for a woman.'

'Don't worry, something will turn up.'

But she was worried.

That afternoon Kate thought her prayers could be answered when Grace walked in. She quickly poured her a mug of tea. 'Grace, I'm so pleased to see you.'

Grace looked startled. 'Why?'

The two mugs of tea were put on the table and Kate sat beside her. 'I've got a proposition to make to you.'

Grace opened her brown eyes wide. 'What sorta proposition?'

'Do you work on Saturdays?'

'I don't need any more clients.'

Kate laughed. 'Not clients. How would you like to work for me on Saturdays?'

Grace looked thoughtful. 'Dunno. What would I have to do?'

'Serve, help me wash up, that sort of thing.'

'Dunno. How much?'

'Well it wouldn't be as much as you probably get, but if you don't work during the day, well, it's got to be better than nothing.'

'How much?'

Kate held her breath. She knew whatever she offered it wouldn't be anything like what Grace was getting. 'I'll give you two shillings.'

'Two shillings!' she exploded. 'For how long?'

'From about eleven to, say, three.'

'Four hours! Four hours for a lousy two bob?'

When Grace said it, it did sound very paltry, but Kate herself had only got six shillings working for Josh all week. 'That's all I can afford at the moment.'

The door opened and Mr Friday stood in the doorway and looked at Grace. She gave Kate a smile and walked out. Kate knew then that her ray of hope had gone.

'Joseph, I'm so worried. What am I going to do?' That evening she sat next to him on the sofa and poked at the fire with the poker.

He looked up from the book he was reading. 'I suppose you could always get Mrs Duke in to help you out. She'd like that.'

'Don't be so silly! Why haven't you got a nice girlfriend I could rely on?'

'You started this business.'

'I know, but I thought you might have shown some interest.'

'You knew where my interest lay.'

'Yes.' She twirled the poker round and round in her hands. 'I only wish Briony were still alive.'

Joseph put the book down. 'So does Ted.'

'Is he still grieving?'

'Think so. He's changed.'

'Death has that effect on those that are left,' she said sadly.

He put his arm round his mother's shoulder. 'I'll tell you what. Tomorrow I'll ask Mrs Lacy if she knows of anyone that will give you a hand till you get yourself sorted out.'

She patted his shoulder and smiled. 'Thanks.' She was pleased. At last he was beginning to show a little interest in her life.

Joseph had never raised the subject of going to Australia again, so perhaps Milly had been right, and he'd just been trying it on with his mother, though these days he was very quiet and self-possessed, and it was hard for her to know what he was thinking.

Saturday, Kate was feeling very harassed. First the urn wouldn't light, then while she was busy with that the potatoes burned dry. Then the saveloys burst. She screamed out in temper.

'What's that rotten smell?' asked Grace, when she walked through the door at the back of the counter and began to take her coat off. She wasn't wearing rouge on her cheeks.

'Grace!' Kate threw her arms round her, almost knocking off her large hat. She was so pleased to see her she thought she would cry. 'You've come to work here?'

Grace pushed her away and took off the hat. She tucked up the few loose strands of hair that had slipped from the bun that sat on top of her head. 'Only for today, just to see if I like it.'

Kate regained her composure. 'First you had better peel some more potatoes. What you can smell are those which I burnt. Make sure you take all the eyes out. Don't like to see black bits.'

'Fussy, ain't yer?'

'Yes, I am. I'll go out front and get the tea ready.'

All morning as they worked together, Grace was almost as interested in the different people that came in as they were in her. Her presence was a great source of amazement, and brought forth a few comments, for which she had a good-humoured, quick and ready answer.

The most frequent question was, 'Here! Ain't that the tart that comes in here looking for customers?'

Kate's answer was abrupt. 'What she does in her spare time is her affair.'

Grace was a good worker, and when the rush finally eased off she sat at a table with a cigarette and a mug of tea. A lot more of the fuzzy hair had escaped the confines of the pins and hung in attractive tendrils round her face. Her lipstick had disappeared and her nose was shiny.

'Look at the size of me ankles.' Grace began rubbing them.

'Well, those shoes don't help,' said Kate, joining her.

Grace laughed. 'I ain't used ter working upright on me feet.'

'I can't thank you enough. Will you be able to come next Saturday?'

'Yer, why not? Bloody hard work, though, but d'you know, I really enjoyed meself.'

'I'm so pleased.'

Christmas was almost on them, and the Sunday before, Joseph had helped his mother make paper chains, which they hung round the shop.

Kate had asked Grace if she would come in every lunchtime till Thursday, Christmas Day, as Milly was too busy. Much to Kate's relief, Grace had agreed.

On Monday morning when Grace walked in, she stopped in the doorway. 'I ain't ever been in a place with paper chains up before. It looks ever so pretty.'

'Thank you. My son Joseph helped me.'

She took off the hat. 'He sounds ever such a nice boy.'

'He is,' said Kate proudly. 'You'll have to meet him sometime.'

'I'd like that.'

Later that evening, when everybody was closing down for the night, Kate had been to the greengrocer's and was on her way back, dragging a heavy sack of potatoes.

'What are you doing there?'

Kate straightened up and put her hand on her chest. 'Seamus! You gave me the fright of my life. I was miles away then.'

'Sorry about that. Here, let me give you a hand.' He quickly and effortlessly hoisted the sack on to his shoulder. 'I would have thought the greengrocer would have delivered them, especially to a pretty lady like you.'

'Now then, don't let's have any of your old blarney. What are you doing round this way?'

'I'm off to the Salvation Army for a bed. I'm a bit early, and I ain't got the money to go in the pub so I just thought I'd walk around and soak up the Christmas atmosphere. I love Christmas.'

'Do you?' she asked as they strolled along. 'So do I.'

'Do you have a family?' he asked.

'Yes, I have a son, Joseph, although he likes to be called Joe, but I can't get used to that.' They reached the shop door. 'Would you like to come in for a mug of tea?' She couldn't believe her own ears. She was inviting a man, a drunken Irishman, into her home. What was wrong with her? Was she so desperate for company? She knew she shouldn't be inviting him in, but he had a certain charm, and he knew now she had a son, and although he wasn't upstairs, there was no harm Seamus thinking that he could be.

'Only if you're sure it's no trouble.'

'It's no trouble, the urn's still on. Besides, you saved me a lot of hard work. Mr Finch or his boy normally bring them down but they are both very busy and I want to get them peeled tonight.' She closed the door behind him. 'If you could take them through and put them on the table I'd be most obliged.' She pushed open the door behind the counter. 'I'll get the tea.'

'My, this is a warm cosy room. Is this where all the work goes on?'

'Yes.' She put two mugs on the table. 'Please take a seat.'

He quickly removed his trilby. 'This is most kind of you, my dear.'

She smiled. There was something about him she liked.

'Begging your pardon, but would you like me to stop and help you peel some of those?' He looked at the sack.

'I have got to get them all done tonight.'

'Well, that's all right then. So we'd better get started.'

She could have kissed him. It was late and the thought of sitting here until well past midnight filled her with dread. 'Only if you don't mind.'

He took his coat off. 'It'll be me pleasure, my dear. 'Sides, I ain't in no hurry to bed down with that lot of toe rags.'

'I suppose I shouldn't let you in here, not with your reputation.'

His eyes twinkled as his face crinkled into a smile. 'I'm hoping to give up me wicked ways, so you have no fear. I wouldn't want to upset you.'

Joseph looked startled when he walked in. 'Who's this?' he asked, looking pointedly at Seamus.

Kate smiled. With his shock of white hair standing up he did look a bit of a sight. 'Joseph, this is Mr O'Brien. He has offered to help me peel the potatoes.'

'Oh, I see.' A puzzled look flitted across his face. 'Why?'

'He's a customer and on his way to—' Kate stopped. She didn't want to tell him where, not at this moment.

'Pleased to meet you. I won't shake your hand, me boy, as mine're a bit dirty. I'm sorry I ain't Father Christmas, son.'

'It's not Christmas yet. I'm off up. Will you be all right?'

Kate smiled. 'Yes. I'll be up later.'

'Good night, son,' said Seamus. When Joseph closed the door he said, 'A nice-looking lad – he should go far.'

'I hope so. Did you have a wife?' asked Kate.

'No, was never out of prison long enough to get one. Lost your husband, did you?'

'Yes.' Kate thought that was better than a lot of explaining to this man who was almost a stranger.

'Thought so. You're a brave woman taking on a business on your own.'

'I worked for Josh and saw it was good. Could never understand Nellie, though. Did you know her?'

'Quite a while back. She was a pretty thing in those days.'

'What happened?'

'Well, she met Josh and married him.' He cut the conversation off quickly. Kate could see he didn't want to talk about it.

The sack of dirty potatoes gradually became bowls full of gleaming white potatoes.

Seamus sat back. 'Those should last you the rest of the week.'

She laughed. 'No, only a day. I shall be doing the same tomorrow night.'

'Would you like me to give you a hand?'

'Are you sure?'

'I ain't got nothing else to do.'

'Well, you must let me pay you.'

'I'll tell you what. How about tomorrow I come in and have one of your pies and a nice plate of mash for me trouble?'

'It's a deal.'

'Now I'd better be off. Don't want them locking me out.'

They wandered through the shop together. 'Thank you, Seamus. It's been very nice having you to help me.'

'It's been my pleasure, my pretty lady Kate.' He kissed her hand and went out.

As she closed the door she touched her hand and smiled. The potatoes were done and she'd enjoyed his company. He wasn't like other criminals who'd come into the shop; somehow he was different. What a pity he was Irish and a thief.

* * *

'Who was he?' asked Joseph aggressively, as soon as she opened the parlour door.

'A customer who offered to carry the sack from Mr Finch's, and he stayed and helped me.'

'Do you know him?'

'Not really.'

'Did Josh know him?'

'I think so. He didn't come in when Josh was here.'

'Why was that?'

'Joseph, what's with all these questions?'

'I don't trust him.'

'You've hardly met the man.'

'I know, but he's scruffy and Irish.'

'So, he's down on his luck.'

'I bet he is. P'raps he thinks he's found a nice rich widow and before you know it he'll be sitting at our table.'

'Joseph! How can you be so cruel? The man only offered to peel some potatoes.'

'Yes, I know. I'm sorry. It's just that you seem to be so happy now and I don't want anyone to spoil it for you.'

She held him close. 'Nobody is going to spoil anything for me, or you. But I can't refuse free labour.'

Joseph pulled away. 'I know that, but what did he want in return?'

'A free dinner.'

He sat on the sofa. 'Where does he live?'

Kate was quickly on her guard. 'He didn't say. But it must be round here somewhere.'

'Is he married?'

'Joseph!'

'Well, I only asked.'

'I *didn't* ask.' Katherine kept her fingers tightly crossed. She didn't like telling lies but if Joseph knew Seamus's background he wouldn't have him anywhere near the shop. 'Besides, it really isn't any of my business, or yours.'

On Christmas Eve the customers in Kate's were full of laughter and good humour. Some of the women, laden down with heavy shopping bags, moaned about all the extra work Christmas brought, but with Seamus around – he had taken on the job of washer-up as well as the potato peeler – he soon put a smile on their faces with his blarney.

'You're a right old charmer and no mistake,' said Grace, who was busy rushing back and forth, clearing plates and emptying ashtrays of those that bothered to use them.

All day some of the young men had been bringing in sprigs of mistletoe, and taking great delight in trying to catch hold of Grace, but she was slim and wiry and was only caught if she wanted to be.

'D'you know, Kate, I can't believe you've been here for – what? – must be well over a year by now,' said Bill, leaning on the counter and watching all the activity.

'Last year Josh gave me double wages.'

'No! And I always thought he was an old skinflint.'

'Well, it was Nellie really. I often wonder how they are getting on.'

'He might be dead for all we know.'

Kate looked wistful. 'Yes, he could be. I'll always be grateful to him for giving me this job.'

'Yer. Never thought you'd be in charge one day. You've certainly made a go of it. You and the boy staying here for Christmas?'

She nodded. 'This will be the first Christmas we've ever had on our own. I rather fancied doing the dinner myself.'

'What does the boy say about it?'

'Not a lot. He wanted to go and spend it with Milly.' Kate

leant forward. 'To be truthful, Bill, I haven't seen her all week, and she didn't really make any arrangements with me so I presume we will be on our own.'

'That's a bit daft, if you ask me. Milly thinks the world of you. I reckon she'll be expecting you.'

'Don't say that. We just can't turn up now, can we?'

'S'pose not. What you doing for Christmas, Grace?'

Grace stopped wiping a table down and straightened up. 'Nothink.'

'What about your family?' Bill had said it before Kate could stop him.

'Ain't got any.'

'Well, that makes two of us,' said Seamus. 'Say, how about you and me spending it together?'

'If you think I'm going to the Salvation Army hostel and sitting down to dinner with a lot of dirty old men then you've got another think coming.'

Seamus had told them earlier where he was going.

'Well, please yourself, me darling. But I'll be having a grand meal.'

Kate looked at Grace's sad face.

'Well, I'd better be going,' said Bill, 'otherwise I'll have Bert screaming at me. Got a busy day.'

Kate remained deep in thought. Joseph was going round to see Ted straight from work. Would Milly tell him what time she wanted them round for dinner tomorrow? Although she wanted to be on her own she would miss their company.

'What time you closing up?' asked Grace.

'A bit later, but you can go off if you like.'

'I'll only be going to the pub.'

'Will you be looking for customers then, girl?' asked Seamus.

'Yer. 'Specially one with a warm bed and a full larder.'

'Where are you spending Christmas then, Grace?' asked Kate.

'Dunno yet.'

Kate didn't like prying too much into Grace's affairs. After all, what she did out of the shop was her business. 'What about you, Seamus?'

'I'm not in any great hurry. Besides, it looks very dark and cold out there. Is it all right if I stay a while?'

'Of course.' Kate enjoyed his company. 'When I close up perhaps we can all go out to the back room and have a drink.'

Seamus gave her a beaming smile. 'Knew from the moment I stepped through that door that you was a civilised woman.'

'Is that all right with you, Grace?'

She nodded and turned away.

It was getting late when Kate finally closed the shop. The late-night shoppers came in for tea to keep out the cold, and the market men came in for the warm.

'Now what will you have to drink? I've got port and gin,' said Kate, as she walked into the back room.

'I'll have a nice drop of gin,' said Seamus.

'Port for me.'

Kate noticed Grace was very quiet, not her usual bubbly self.

After wishing each other a Merry Christmas they finished their drinks and Seamus took a small packet from his pocket and handed it to Kate.

'For you, my dear, and you mustn't open it till tomorrow.'

'Seamus, this is very kind of you, but you shouldn't have. You've only known me a short while.'

'I know, but you have shown me more kindness in these few short days than anybody has in the whole of my life.'

Kate could feel the tears sting the backs of her eyes.

'I ain't got you a present,' said Grace.

'I didn't expect one,' said Kate. 'But I do have a little something for you. I hope you like it.'

Grace's eyes lit up. 'Can I open it now?'

'If you like.'

Grace held the necklace Kate had chosen for her in the flat of her hand. 'It's lovely! I ain't ever had anything so lovely bought for me before.'

'It's only a cheap imitation,' said Kate quickly.

Grace quickly kissed Kate's cheek. 'Seamus is right, you are a kind lady. Now I must be orf, might miss a good punter.' She plonked her hat on her head and ran out.

'Grace!' called Kate, going after her. The door slammed. She was too late. 'I haven't given her her wages,' she said, walking back into the room.

'She'll be back on Saturday. She might need them be then. Well, I must be off.' Seamus picked up his trilby. 'I hope you have a nice Christmas, Kate. You deserve it.'

'Merry Christmas, Seamus.' She kissed his cheek and his whiskers tickled her lips. 'Will I see you on Saturday?'

'I would think so.'

'Here, take the rest of the gin. I'm sure you can find a use for it.' She handed him the almost full bottle. 'But don't get into any trouble.'

'Thank you. I'll finish off before I go to the Sally Army. They're funny about this demon drink.' He held up the bottle. 'Good night, Kate love.' He closed the door behind him and Kate was alone.

They were nice people who were down on their luck, and it made her feel happy to help them. She felt the small packet in her pocket. She looked at it and turned it over. She was very tempted to open it, but she had made a promise and she didn't want to spoil it. After all, Seamus was Irish and, who knew, it might have a magic spell on it.

Joseph came in just as she was filling her stone hot-water bottle.

'Milly said be round about one. I said we would. Is that all right with you?'

'Of course.' She couldn't disappoint him or Milly, but deep down, she would have liked to have spent the day at home – her home – and had Grace and Seamus share it with them, but then Joseph wouldn't have approved of that.

Chapter 29

Although Kate liked being waited on on Christmas Day, and being with Milly and the family, Grace and Seamus kept filling her thoughts. She wondered where they were, if they were alone and what they were doing. Kate hadn't told the family too much about them as Milly would tell her off for worrying about the waifs and strays she seemed to collect, and Charlie certainly wouldn't approve of a thief and a prostitute working for her. Their occupations were something she had kept from Joseph as well. She had just told all of them that she had a girl in to work on Saturdays – she didn't tell them her name – and that Seamus was more of an odd-job-man down on his luck, and that seemed to satisfy them.

Kate smiled at the present Seamus had given her – a pressed flower. He had written a little poem. He had told her he learnt to read and write in prison: 'Didn't want to waste me time.'

> Shamrock I have none, but nevertheless
> this small flower for a pretty lady must
> be second best.

She had put it away; she wasn't going to share this with anyone. No one else would see that, although he was a rogue, underneath, she was sure, he was a good man. He had told her he had been very fond of Nellie in his young days but that Nellie had preferred Josh.

'Could be because I was sent down a couple of times. Anyway, she wouldn't wait for me. Once when I came back I found out she'd married Josh and he wouldn't let me in this place.'

'I'm not surprised.'

'Never did find out why she took to her bed, though. I don't think he made her very happy.'

Kate smiled. She would never tell him the reason.

'Ma.' Joseph was tugging at her arm. 'It's your turn.' They were playing cards.

Everyone at Milly's was having such a good time. Olive looked happy and content at the thought of another baby on the way. Dolly was so good. When Kate held her goddaughter the burden of guilt about the baby she'd got rid of still hurt her. Had it been a girl or another boy? Kate sat and looked around her. Tom was beginning to look old and tired, while Ted was growing into a very handsome young man. Perhaps one day he would find love again. Charlie sat back with a contented look on his weather-beaten face. He was proud of his family, and he and Milly loved having them round.

All too soon Christmas was over and it was time for Kate and Joseph to leave.

'It'll be lovely to go straight to bed and not have to prepare pies.'

'Is the novelty wearing off then?' asked Charlie.

'No, of course not,' she replied quickly. 'Look at that moon,' she added, when he opened the front door. 'We shouldn't be having any snow tonight. See how bright the stars are.'

'It's very cold,' said Joseph, pulling his muffler up round his ears. 'Thanks for the mitts, Milly. They'll be good for work.'

'Just as long as you don't get 'em too greasy. 'Bye, love.' She held his face in her hands and kissed his cheek.

Kate felt a pang of jealousy. Milly's gift had been much better received than the shirt she had given him.

After all the goodbye hugs and kisses they made their way home.

'Did you enjoy yourself today?' Joseph asked as they moved along at a fast pace to keep warm.

'Yes I did. Milly is so good to us.'

'I know. Funny, isn't it? At first I didn't want to live with them. Now I like being with them.' He stopped. He couldn't tell his mother it was better than being stuck up in the flat above the shop most nights with no one to talk to while she was busy working.

'Would you like to move back then?' In many ways Kate knew her son wasn't happy.

'No, of course not, not now I've got my own bedroom. I miss Ted and Charlie though.'

'I expect you do.'

'By the way, Ted's invited me to a New Year's Eve party. D'you mind if I go?'

'No, but remember, no drinking. You are still only a child.'

'I'm not a child!' He sounded angry. 'I've been out to work a year now.'

'Yes, I know and I'm very proud of you.' She tucked his arm under hers. 'Now come on, let's get home.'

He wasn't sure if he would ever be able to call a flat above a shop home.

On New Year's Eve Kate thought she would ask Seamus and Grace to join her and see the new year in together.

'I'm sorry, Kate,' said Grace, 'but I'm meeting a customer. Would have been nice though.'

Kate was pleased she'd asked Grace first, as now she wouldn't ask Seamus. She didn't want to spend the evening with just him. But where was he? She hadn't seen him since the weekend and now it was Wednesday. She hoped he wasn't in any trouble.

'Now you're sure you'll be all right?' asked Joseph.

She had been deep in thought. 'Yes, yes, of course. I can always find something to do.'

'You could go to Milly's.'

'Yes I know, but I really must prepare this food.'

'Well, I'll be off.'

'Now you go and have a good time, and remember what I told you.' She waved the spoon at him.

Laughing he kissed her cheek and left.

How she envied him when he went out. Tonight she would be on her own, seeing 1914 in alone. She couldn't remember being alone on New Year's Eve before. She suddenly felt lonely. She missed Edwin and Dolly, even Briony. She could go and see Milly. They would probably go to the pub where Tom worked. It would be very lively, but was that what she wanted? She picked up the bottle of port. 'It looks like snow out there so I'll stay here and wish myself a happy new year.' She poured herself a generous glass of port. 'Good health, everybody,' she said out loud. 'I wonder what 1914 will bring.'

It was a cold start to the year. Milly now came in every lunchtime for an hour, and Kate was more than pleased to see her, and Grace continued to work every Saturday. Seamus came and went as the mood took him, or whenever he was sober enough to find his way to the shop. She was always pleased to see him and to listen to his tales, but was always careful not to pry. He would help with the washing-up as well as peeling the potatoes. Sometimes when Kate was in her back room that doubled as the kitchen, she thought of Dolly. How she would have enjoyed this life and the customers she had in.

At the beginning of March the weather improved slightly. Kate was waiting for Mr Sharman to collect the rent, quietly singing as she put the mugs on the counter ready for lunchtime.

'You sound happy, my dear,' said Mr Sharman, politely touching his hat.

'Mr Sharman, I have your rent ready.' She went to go into the back room.

He followed her. 'Mrs Carter, I'm afraid I have some bad news.'

Kate stood frozen to the spot. 'Nellie wants to move back,' she whispered.

'Not as far as I know. She told me Josh has died.'

'I'm so very sorry to hear that. She keeps in touch then?'

'Not really.'

'Do you have Nellie's address? I would like to send her a letter with my condolences.'

'Yes I do. But there was something else.'

Kate held her breath.

'She's coming here to see you.'

'Why? What does she want?'

'I don't know.'

'She can't take this away from me, can she? I've been building this business up and I don't . . .' Tears of anger were ready to spring from her eyes.

'Not really. You pay the rent. I don't think she will want to take over. It could be that she just wants her things.'

Kate sat down. 'I hope so. Did she say when?'

'Next week sometime.'

'Thank you, Mr Sharman.' She felt a little calmer when she gave him the rent book and money.

'You have done very well, Mrs Carter.' He looked round. 'It's all very nice.'

'Thank you. Have you got time for a cup of tea?'

'No, thanks all the same, but I must get on.'

She held open the door. He touched his hat and left.

Kate was worried. What if Nellie did want to come back? But

it wasn't hers now; Kate paid the rent. What did she want to come all this way to see Kate about? Perhaps it was just about her furniture, but why wait four months before getting in touch, and why didn't she write direct to her?

A week later Kate's eyes opened wide when Nellie came in. She looked so different. She had on a lovely black hat and her coat looked warm and expensive. She was still leaning on her stick but not as bent over as she had been.

'See you've tarted the place up a bit.' Her eyes darted round the room. She sat down and ran a gloved finger over the table.

'I've just given the place a good—' Kate decided to hold her tongue. 'I'll make you a special cup of tea. I was very sorry to hear about Josh.' She didn't want to say too much as all the memories of that dreadful morning came back.

'Yer. It was sad.'

Kate cringed. There wasn't any emotion in Nellie's voice. No sign of regret that she might have contributed to her husband's death.

'Did you want anything to eat?' Kate asked quietly.

'No, ta. I'm up here with me sister. Her daughter's getting wed, silly cow, and our Flossy's looking for something to wear.'

'Nellie! Well, if it ain't Nellie Trent.' Seamus came out of the back room wiping his hands on the bottom of his apron. 'I thought to myself, I know that voice. I may not have heard it for years but I would recognise those lilting tones anywhere.'

Kate smiled.

'Seamus O'Brien!' Nellie's face was a picture of disbelief.

He took her hand and kissed it.

She quickly pulled her hand back. 'What the bloody hell are you doing here? And you're still talking a load of crap.'

'Working for young Kate here.'

Kate grinned; she was far from young. 'Sit down, Seamus. I expect you two have plenty to talk about.'

'Sorry to hear about Josh.'

'It was for the best in the long run. He wasn't himself towards the end, you know. How long you been out?'

'A short while.'

'Hope you've got everything tied down out there,' she said to Kate. 'Can't trust him with nothing.'

'Now that's not a nice thing to say, Nellie love.'

'Well it's true, and I ain't your love.'

Kate carried on serving, but all the time she was watching Nellie and Seamus.

'Who's that talking to old Seamus?' asked Milly walking in, and, taking her hat off, she nodded towards Nellie.

Kate bobbed down and whispered, 'That's Nellie. Nellie Trent.' She had told Milly Josh was dead and that Nellie was coming to see her.

'How'd she get here?'

'Her sister brought her.'

'Where is she?'

'Who?'

'The sister.'

'Gone shopping.'

'What's Seamus doing talking to her, and getting on very well by the looks of it?'

'They knew each other years ago.'

Suddenly Seamus and Nellie's loud laughter burst forth.

'What does she want?' asked Milly with a worried look on her face.

'I don't know. We didn't get a chance to talk.'

A scruffy-looking woman banged hard on the counter with her money. 'You two! We gonner git any service round here terday? Standing there bloody yakking. I ain't got all day.'

'Coming up.' Kate moved away to fill a plate for the customer.

Kate watched the two old friends talking and laughing almost the whole of the dinnertime. She was getting agitated. What did Nellie want? And was she about to lose Seamus?

Finally Seamus stood up. 'Better get on,' he said to Nellie. 'Might not get any dinner if I don't get back to me chores.'

'Never thought I'd see you in a apron.'

'Well, Nellie me love, needs must when the devil drives.'

After he'd gone into the kitchen, Nellie beckoned Kate over. 'I expect you're wondering what I've come for?'

Kate sat down. 'Yes, I am.'

'When I told Mr Sharman I was coming up, he told me you'd taken the place over. Said you'd turned it into a little goldmine.'

'But I don't make—'

Nellie put up her hand to silence her. 'Anyway, seeing as how you've been hiring me furniture all this time, I thought I'd come and collect what's due.'

Kate sat with her mouth open. 'I've not been hiring your furniture! I didn't know what to do with it. Mr Sharman told me to throw it out.'

'Ah, but you didn't, did yer? And what about all this?' She waved her hand at all the tables and chairs. 'My dad bought these, so now I wants me money.'

'How much?'

'Let's see now. How long you been here?'

'Four months.'

'Well, I reckon a pound a month for all the lot's fair, so give me four pounds.'

'What if I throw it all out?'

'Now you wouldn't be that daft. Got some good pieces upstairs, I have, and you'd have to buy more. Tell yer what though, you could buy all the lot off of me.'

'How much?' Kate sat dreading the answer. Although she was now saving some money, would it be enough?

'Ten quid would be a fair price.'

'Ten pounds!'

'Yer. You can keep me and Josh's clothes and the bedding. I don't want that.'

'I don't think I've got ten pounds.'

'It'll be fourteen in all.'

'Fourteen!'

'Yer. Don't forget the back rent on 'em.'

Kate sat back. 'I haven't got that amount.'

'Well give me what you've got.'

'I can give you five pounds.'

'That all? Then that'll have to do for a start.'

Kate hurriedly left the shop and ran upstairs to get the money.

She sat on her bed and counted out five pounds. Should she give Nellie the two she had left? She pondered on that for a short while but decided against it. Should she have tried to beat her price down? No, Nellie was a shrewd woman and Kate knew she was getting a good deal. Besides, Nellie could be cruel, and who knew what she might have done? The last thing Kate wanted was a shop full of broken crocks and furniture.

'Ta,' said Nellie, looking at the money in her hand. 'You can send me a postal order for the rest, nine pounds in all. I don't think you'll welsh on the deal, you ain't like that. Always told Josh you was a good 'un. He should have made you a partner, then I would still be getting a bit. Ta-ta.' She stopped at the door. 'By the way, tell Seamus he ain't ever gonner share me bed. Might sound daft now, but I really loved my Josh for all his carrying on. And you take my word, girl, you can't trust that one' – she waved her stick at the door behind the counter – 'further than you can throw him. 'Bye, Seamus,' she called out.

He came hurrying out. He hugged Nellie close. Kate could see she didn't like it.

'Don't let us part again, Nellie love. It would break my heart if I lost you again.'

She laughed. 'Well, hard luck, mate. I'm going back to Kent. I've got a good sister, she looks after me, and I don't want for nothink.' She walked out.

'Well,' said Kate, 'that was certainly something.'

'What did she want? Begging your pardon, I didn't mean to pry.'

'No, that's all right. She wanted money for her furniture. I expected that. At least now I can say everything is mine, or it will be when I've paid for it. By the way, Seamus, there's some clothes of Josh's upstairs. I'll bring them down and if there's anything you'd like please take it.'

'You are kindness himself.'

'Oh, go on with you! I'm afraid Nellie told me to tell you that she doesn't care for you any more.'

'And I don't care for her. She's changed. She's a hard woman now, and she ain't pretty like she used to be.'

'We all change, Seamus.'

He laughed. 'Ah yes, but some of us do change for the better.'

'While we are quiet I'll go up and start sorting out those clothes. You can manage down here for a while?'

'Sure.'

As she mounted the stairs her thoughts were full of Nellie and Josh. Nellie had said she had loved him, but all those years she'd wasted, making him wait on her, not running the business together – she could have been a good businesswoman but now he had gone.

She pushed open the bedroom door. The room was full of light now and it smelt clean and fresh, so different from when Nellie had lived here. When everything was paid for it would be all hers. At last she would be able to save a little and give Joseph some kind of inheritance.

Chapter 30

Kate didn't say a lot to Grace when she came in on Friday to wait for her man. So it was Saturday when she told her about Nellie coming in and Josh dying.

She looked very sad. 'I liked him,' she said.

'I didn't think you knew him. Well, I know you saw him but . . .'

Grace gave Kate a slight smile. 'In fact you could say I knew him very well.'

'How?'

'Well, he didn't let me come in here and sit about waiting for me customers without something in return, so now and again, when he give me the nod and after he'd shut up shop, I'd pop round and keep him happy.'

Kate looked at her in amazement.

'We used to, you know, in the shop. Quite exciting it was, knowing Nellie was upstairs.' She laughed. 'She'd bang on the ceiling shouting. Nearly caught us once and I finished up in that corner under the table. Funny old dear. She came hobbling in, waving her stick at him. Thought she was gonner bash him. It was comical to see him trying to do his flies up and run away at the same time. Poor old Josh.'

Kate grinned at that. 'Nellie knew he was up to something.'

Grace smiled. 'As I said, it was fun while it lasted. Mind you, I never thought I'd end up working here.'

'Do you like working here?' asked Kate.

'Yer, I do. It's warm and you make a good cuppa. It's bloody perishing some nights standing in a shop doorway with yer skirt round yer waist. That wind can blow a gale.'

'Grace, are you trying to shock me?'

'No, not really.'

Over the months Grace had been working with Kate they had developed a good relationship. Grace had changed. Her hair was more under control and her clothes and language weren't so outrageous.

'When Olive has her baby I can't see Milly wanting to come in. Would you like to come in every lunchtime?'

'Dunno. I'd have ter think about that. And I'd have to go early on Friday. Can't let that man down, he's very special.'

'Well, think it over.'

They both looked up when the door opened. A tall man shuffled to the counter. His bright blue eyes darted about and he had a worried expression. His blond hair was dirty and matted and his clothes scruffy.

He pulled up his coat collar. 'Please could I have tea?' He spoke with a thick accent.

'That's tuppence. Where yer from?' asked Grace as she cheerfully handed him a mug of tea.

Silently he held out a few pence in the palm of his hand.

Grace took tuppence. 'You don't come from round this way, do yer?'

He shook his head.

'So, where yer from then?'

'Germany.'

'Germany? We get a lot of sailors round this way. Your ship in the docks then?'

He nodded.

Kate didn't give him much of a glance. She was used to all kinds of people and different nationalities coming in off the ships. Grace was always happy chatting to the men, but Kate had told her, no picking up clients while she was working. Kate could never be sure that she didn't, and if Grace attracted the wrong kind of clientele, it could be very bad for Kate's reputation.

As the morning wore on they became very busy, but the German didn't move or buy any more tea. He just sat in the far corner, staring out of the window.

'Funny bugger,' said Grace, when he left about four.

'Perhaps he misses his home.'

'Yer, could be. He don't look very old, but you would have thought he'd have cleaned himself up a bit.'

'He may have been out all night.'

'Yer, and he might have jumped ship and sat here waiting till it sailed.'

'Suppose so, poor lad. It must be awful to be that unhappy.'

'He didn't look too pleased with life, did he? Right, time for me to be off. Got to get meself tarted up for tonight's customers.' She plonked her hat on her head and left.

Every day for the next week the German came at the same time, sat at the same table and left about the same time, after only having the one mug of tea.

'I'd chuck him out,' said Milly. 'Taking up all the table. He looks a bit funny to me.'

'He looks very sad.'

'You're at it again, ain't yer? Worrying about other people.'

Kate laughed. 'I can't help it.'

On Saturday Grace was behind the counter and Seamus was out the back, busy peeling potatoes, when the German walked in. Kate was stacking up the plates.

''Allo there, mate,' said Grace. 'See you're still around then.'

As usual he asked for tea and held out the money for Grace to take.

'This is a penny,' she said, holding up a penny, 'and this one makes two. Savvy?'

He gave her a slight smile and nodded. 'Twopence.'

'Yer, but we say tuppence.'

'Tuppence,' he repeated.

'That's right. What's yer name?'

The scowl returned and, picking up his tea, he quickly went to sit at his favourite table.

Kate shrugged her shoulders at Grace.

'He ain't very friendly, is he?' Grace commented.

'Doesn't seem to be.'

'He's very good-looking though. Blond hair and blue eyes. Very nice.'

'You don't miss much, do you?'

'Kate love, have you got a moment?' Seamus poked his head round the door. 'Will this be enough taters for Monday?'

'I'll come and look.'

Kate moved to the back room. 'I think so. I'll put them in the bucket outside.'

Suddenly Grace screamed out, 'Leave me be! Don't you bloody well touch me!'

Kate and Seamus both rushed into the shop together. The German ran from the shop with Seamus following close behind.

'What happened?' asked Kate, helping Grace to a chair. She was holding her wrist.

'He grabbed me. Look, I've come up all red.' She held her arm up.

'Why did he do that?'

'Dunno. Bloody pervert!'

'Did he touch you, you know, anywhere else?'

'Na, didn't give him a chance, did I? He might o' done, though.'

'What's going on?' asked Bill, hurrying in. 'Just seen Seamus rushing down the road after that German bloke. Bert's joined in the chase. He been pinching?'

'Only me,' said Grace. 'Look.' Once again the arm was put on display.

'What'd he do that for?' asked Bill.

'Dunno.'

'You wasn't giving him the come-on, was you?' asked Bill.

Grace quickly looked at Kate. 'Na, course not.'

The scuffle at the door caused them all to look up.

Seamus was pushing the German in front of him. 'Right, me lad. Now say you're sorry 'fore the missis here calls the rozzers.'

Bill and Grace's heads shot up.

'Here, steady on, Seamus! We don't want 'em poking about round here,' said Bill.

A small crowd had gathered in the doorway.

There was fear in the German's eyes as he looked from one to the other. 'Please, I only want to talk.'

'Well, you've got a bloody funny way of showing it. Look at me arm,' said Grace.

'I am very sorry.'

Grace rubbed her wrist. 'Well, that's all right then, but you do it again and you'll get me fist in yer face.'

He looked puzzled.

'I said,' said Grace very slowly and loudly, 'don't do it again.'

'He won't get the chance,' said Seamus. 'Reckon you ought to ban him, Kate.'

Kate tried to keep a straight face. 'I'm sure he meant no real harm. Give him a mug of tea, Grace, and go and sit over there where I can keep my eye on you and find out what he wanted.'

Grace went to the table carrying the tea. 'Come on, mate. Sit yerself down.'

The German looked at Seamus and Bill then, carefully avoiding them, did as he was told.

'Come on now,' said Seamus. 'It's all over.' He gently pushed people away from the door.

Every time Kate looked up, Grace, with her elbow on the table, was concentrating, trying to understand the German's broken English. Now and again she would look across at Kate and give her a wink.

After a while he stood up. He shook Grace's hand, causing her to giggle, and left.

'Well?' asked Kate. 'What did he want?'

'Poor bugger. I think he's jumped ship. Says he's staying with a friend, and he's looking for work.'

'Well, he won't find it sitting in here every day,' said Seamus.

'Where's he living?' asked Kate.

'He didn't say, but I reckon he's in a dosshouse.'

'Sad places, those,' said Seamus.

'He said if you don't mind he would like to come here again on Monday. It's warm, and it's better than walking the streets.'

'You tell him this ain't no dosshouse. He can't come here and sit all day with just one mug of tea.'

'Seamus, who owns this place?'

'Sorry, Kate, I was a bit hasty there, but I don't like to see you taken advantage of.'

'No one will do that and on Monday I'll have a word with him.'

Seamus looked upset. 'Kate love, you wouldn't be thinking of giving him me little job now, would you?'

'No – all the time you keep out of trouble, that is.'

He grinned. 'You're a fine woman and no mistake.'

'Christ! Look at the time,' said Grace. 'I'd better be off.' She rushed to the door, narrowly avoiding running into someone. 'Oops, sorry!'

Kate looked up. 'Hallo, Joseph. What are you doing home so early? Are you all right? You don't look very well.'

Joseph stood looking at the back of Grace as she hurried down the road. 'I don't feel too good. Who was that?'

Kate hurried round the counter with a worried look on her face. 'What's wrong? Go on upstairs. Seamus, keep an eye on things down here.'

'Who was that?' asked Joseph again.

'That was Grace, the young woman who works on Saturdays. Now go on up.'

Joseph was sitting on the sofa with his eyes closed when his mother came in with a cup of tea. 'What's wrong?' She held her hand against his forehead.

'Think my cold's got worse. That Grace is pretty, isn't she?'

'Grace is all right.' Kate was worried because Joseph was looking so pale. 'Now I think you should go to bed,' she fretted.

'What? I'm not going to bed. I'll be all right.'

'Didn't I say this morning that you should have stayed at home?'

'Ma, it's only a cold.'

'So why did Mr Lacy let you off early then?'

'My nose was dripping and I was sneezing. And we aren't very busy. That's all.'

'As long as you're sure. I'd better go down and see what Seamus is up to.'

When his mother left Joseph sat back. He wasn't going to tell her he had a pain under his ribs. She would be rushing him off to some doctor or another. His thoughts went to Grace. She really was very pretty. 'I'll have to try and get to know her. That'll make Ted jealous,' he said out loud.

On Sunday morning when Kate went in to Joseph, she found him in bed, bathed in sweat.

'Oh my God, what's wrong?'

'I can't move. I've got this pain here.' He touched his ribs.

Kate began to panic. 'I'll get a doctor.' She rushed out of the room.

Joseph tried to sit up, but fell back exhausted.

After the doctor had examined him he said he had a touch of pleurisy. He had to be kept warm and in bed.

'Ma, what about Mr Lacy?'

'Don't worry, I'll go round and drop a note through his door.'

All Sunday Kate was up and down the stairs, bringing Joseph hot drinks and cool flannels for his head.

'I'm really worried about him,' Kate said to Milly on Monday.

'He'll be all right in no time. I'll tell Ted to come round this evening to cheer him up.'

'Would you? That'll be lovely. He needs someone interesting to talk to.'

'Thanks for coming round, Ted. I'm getting fed up, stuck up here on my own.'

Ted sat on the bed. 'You've only been in bed a couple of days.'

'I know.'

'Brought you round some paper and a sharp pencil. Thought you'd like to do a bit of drawing.'

'Thanks.' Joseph struggled to sit up. 'Guess what? My ma's got a smashing girl working for her on Saturdays.'

'Oh yer?'

'She's got dark hair and goes in and out in all the right places.'

'Yer? How old is she?'

'Dunno. About eighteen, I reckon.'

'So she's too old for you?'

'Maybe.'

'I'll have to come in Sat'day and have a look.'

They sat idly chatting for a while, then Ted had to go.

'That was nice of Ted to come and see you,' said Kate, plumping up Joseph's pillows.

'He's coming again next Saturday.'

'That'll be nice.'

'I hope I'm better by then.'

'You'll have to be patient.'

The look on his face told Kate that was the last thing he was going to be.

When his mother left, he picked up the pencil and began idly drawing. It didn't matter how painful it was, he had to keep the picture of Grace in his mind's eye.

Chapter 31

During the day when Kate was busy, Seamus and Milly popped upstairs to make sure that all Joseph's needs were seen to. Towards the end of the week he said he was feeling a little better.

Although Joseph didn't approve of Seamus and only spoke to him when it was necessary, he had to find out more about Grace. 'Seamus, that Grace seems to be a bit of all right.'

Seamus gave him a long look. 'Yes she is, and your mother thinks a lot of her.'

'My mother thinks a lot of most people.'

'Your mother is a fine woman. Not many would take in the likes of Grace.'

'Why? What's wrong with her?'

Seamus quickly tried to cover his last sentence. 'I think she's been in a bit of trouble in the past.'

Joseph's eyes widened. 'With the police?'

'I don't rightly know. You see, it ain't any of me business. I best be going.'

That conversation put Joseph on his guard. He wouldn't ask his mother as she might laugh at him for taking an interest.

On Saturday Kate was surprised to see Ted walk in during the afternoon. 'Hallo, Ted. Everything all right?'

'Yes, thanks.'

'Thought you would have been round this evening.'

'Mum's going on a bit, so it's best I stay out the way. So I thought I'd come and see Joe.' As he was talking he kept glancing at Grace.

'That's kind of you. Go on up, he's in the parlour.'

Ted raced up the stairs, two at a time, and pushed open the door. 'I see what you mean, mate. She's certainly a good-looker. Have you found out much about her?'

'Oh hallo, Ted. Yes, I am feeling better, thank you. Her name's Grace and she's been in some sort of trouble. Is she down there, then?'

Ted sat next to Joseph. 'Yer, she's sitting talking to a bloke. Big, got fair hair.'

'I'll find out if it's her boyfriend.'

'So what did she do to get in trouble?'

'Dunno, nobody will tell me.'

'Has she been up here?'

'Na. Ma only sends up your mum or that Seamus.'

'Won't he tell you?'

'No. I think Ma's told him not to.'

'Oh, why's that?'

'Dunno, but it must be something really bad.'

'Can't be, your ma wouldn't have someone like that working for her, not if it was that bad.'

'You know my ma, always looking out for lost souls. Look how she tried to help Briony.'

Ted's expression changed. 'Yer. That was really awful what happened to her.'

'Yes, and I shall always feel rotten at not talking to her. D'you know, I reckon Grace has just come out of prison,' said Joseph, quickly changing the subject. 'Here, what do you think of my sketch of her?'

'That's really good. What does your ma think of it?'

'I wouldn't show her. And don't you go saying anything to her, or your mum.'

Ted grinned. 'As if I would. D'you fancy a cuppa?'

'Why not?'

'Good. I'll go down and get one.'

'Thought you might.'

When Ted walked into the shop Grace was behind the counter. He swallowed hard. His Adam's apple felt as if it had stuck in his throat and he could feel his face colour. 'Could I have a mug of tea for Joe and me?' He just about managed to finish the sentence.

'Thanks Ted, for coming round to cheer him up,' said Kate. 'He should be able to go out next week if the weather holds.' She was watching him look at Grace.

'Here yer are then, young feller me lad,' she said cheerfully.

Ted quickly looked down and picked up the tea when Grace smiled at him, and hurried up the stairs.

'Well,' said Joseph eagerly, when he walked in, 'did you see her?'

Ted put the tea on the table and, grinning, nodded. 'She really is beautiful. I've got to find out more about her.'

'Was she sitting with her boyfriend?'

'No, she was serving. But he was at the corner table watching her all the time.'

'I'll have to ask Ma all about her.'

'You've really captured a good likeness.' Ted was studying the picture Joseph had drawn of Grace. 'I think her eyes are a bit wider apart than that. You say she only works on Sat'days?'

'Yes.'

'I expect I'll be round to see you next week then,' said Ted, finishing his tea.

'Me or her?' asked Joseph.

Ted moved towards the door. 'You'll just have to wait and see.' He ducked when a pillow came through the air towards him. He laughed. 'I can see you're getting better.'

Ted's heart sank when he walked back into the shop: Grace

wasn't there, but the boyfriend was still sitting in the corner. *Was* he her boyfriend or just a customer whom she was casually talking to? She looked like the kind of person who would be friendly with anyone.

'Bye,' he called to Kate as he went out. 'See you next week.'

'Thanks Ted,' she replied. She smiled when she heard him whistling as he left the shop.

'What d'you wanner know about her for?' asked Milly sharply, looking from Ted to Charlie.

'Nothing. Just asking, that's all.'

'Charlie, say something,' said Milly.

'This paper's full of troubles. There's Ireland just waiting to flare up, then those silly suffragettes are still at it, and now Europe – it don't look too good over there.'

'Charlie! Speak to Ted about that – that Grace who works for Kate on Sat'days.'

'Is that the tart you was telling me about, the one what works for Kate?' asked Charlie, folding his newspaper.

Milly tutted. 'Yes. I've just said that.' Milly's mouth was set in a hard straight line. 'Always said Kate should be more careful who she takes on. There's that Seamus, he's a drunk and a thief, and then there's Grace. She ain't nothing but a—' Milly couldn't say the word.

Charlie laughed. 'And what about you? What dark secret have you got?'

'It ain't funny, Charlie Stevens. Kate will find herself in trouble one of these days, you mark my words.'

'You'll never stop Kate from taking in lost souls.'

'Why do you say Grace is a tart?' asked Ted.

''Cos she is,' said Milly. 'She comes in the shop to collect her customers.'

'Who told you?'

'I just know.' Kate hadn't exactly told her in so many words, but Milly had put two and two together.

Ted stood staring at his mother with wide open eyes.

'Ted, you know what your mother's talking about, don't you, son?'

Ted nodded. 'But she looks nice.'

'She does at work, I'll give you that, but you should see her when she's all dolled up and out on the game. All paint and powder.'

'I don't want you going out with that sort,' said Charlie, winking at his son.

'Don't you start encouraging him. You find yourself a nice girl,' said Milly, calming down. 'There's plenty of 'em about.'

Ted looked from one to the other. He didn't want a nice girl. He wanted someone beautiful like Grace. He left the room. As he walked upstairs he overheard his mother talking, so he stopped to listen.

'What is it with our Ted? First it was Briony, now this little madam. I'll have a word with Kate about it on Monday.'

'What can she do?' asked Charlie.

'Keep her eye on him.'

'Give him time, love. Let him sow a few wild oats first.'

'Is that what you did, then?'

'I ain't saying. But let him grow up and live a little.'

'Over my dead body.'

'He ain't a kid any more, you know. He's – what? – going on eighteen now.'

'He is still my baby.'

Ted closed his bedroom door.

'Grace.' Kate took Grace to one side when she arrived the following Saturday.

'What's wrong? I ain't been—'

317

Kate shook her head. 'It's nothing you've done. It's just that . . . Well, Milly's worried. It seems you have an admirer. Her son, Ted, will be in later and it appears he's – well – fallen for you.'

Grace threw her head back and laughed. 'What, that young lad what come to see Joe?'

'Yes, and I think my son is also smitten by your charms.'

'Oh, don't! I think I've heard it all now.'

'So please, have a word or something, but let him down lightly. Ted's been hurt once before and I would hate to see him hurt again.'

'So, what d'you want me to do, then?'

'Tell him you have a boyfriend, and you are going to get married.'

'Yer, I could say that.' She smiled. 'I feel rather flattered that I've got two nice young men fancying me.'

'Well, you are a pretty young lady.'

She giggled. 'Nobody's ever said that to me before.' She kissed Kate's cheek.

Kate was startled. 'What was that for?'

'Because you are a very nice lady.'

Later that day when Ted came in he went straight up to Joseph, looking very worried.

'Well, did you see her?' asked Joseph.

'Yes. Joe, me mum reckons she's, you know . . . one of those women that goes with men.'

'Oh.'

'You don't sound surprised.'

'Well no. You see Seamus said me mother wouldn't like it if I got too friendly with her as she said she was a bit of a loose woman.' He laughed. 'Ma said she was going to send her up to have a little talk to us.'

'Oh no! I'm going.' Ted began pacing the floor. 'I couldn't face her. What if she tries—'

Joseph threw his head back and laughed so hard he hurt his ribs. 'Don't say you'd be frightened of her?'

'No.'

When Grace went upstairs to talk to the boys, Kate could hear lots of laughter and she knew Grace was letting them down lightly.

'So?' asked Kate, when Grace came back. 'What did you tell them?'

'I told 'em I was getting married soon and that they were lovely boys and I hoped I had two sons just like 'em. I said I was ever so old.'

'And did they believe you?'

'I don't think so.'

'Thanks, Grace.'

But although Joseph had accepted that Grace wasn't for him, Milly didn't think Ted had, as she told Kate on Monday.

'He looks so miserable. I wouldn't be surprised if he didn't come in on Sat'day again just to see her.'

'I'll let you know,' said Kate.

For the next two weeks Ted came to see Joseph but most times he sat and gazed at Grace. Milly was beginning to get very concerned and voiced her worries to Kate again.

'Don't worry about it too much,' said Kate. 'It won't last. Joseph's going back to work next week and he doesn't finish till late afternoon on Saturdays, after Grace has left here, so Ted won't have an excuse to come round.'

Tuesday 12 May was Joseph's fifteenth birthday. He was preparing for work. Yesterday was his first day back and he had come home tired but happy. Now Kate looked round the shop, her shop. She was happy, she had almost everything she could wish for.

As Kate watched Joseph her thoughts went to his brother.

What did he look like? Was he tall, like Joseph? Was he married? She might even be a grandmother. A slight smile flitted across her face at that thought. But would she ever know?

Chapter 32

Every Saturday afternoon throughout May, Ted came and sat in the corner of the pie shop with just a mug of tea. Even Kate was beginning to get cross with his mooning about. Grace was making a big thing about sitting with the German, Kurt, whenever the opportunity arose, and their laughter would make Ted angry. Grace, making sure Ted was watching, would hold on to Kurt's hand and as she passed him would touch his hair.

'Ted, your mother isn't all that pleased, you know, about you hanging around here all afternoon,' said Kate, sitting next to him.

'I don't care. I'm going to go out with her one day, you'll see.' He nodded towards Grace. 'She don't go out with that Kraut, you know.'

'How do you know?'

'She told me she was getting married but I don't believe her.'

Kate didn't reply.

'I know she ain't going out with him 'cos I waited till he left here, then I followed him.'

'My God! If she found out she'd kill you!'

'I was very careful; he didn't see me.'

'Ted, you are being very silly.'

'I don't care. D'you know, if there is a war with Germany he'll have to go back or be interned.' He sat relaxed in his chair and put his hands behind his head. 'So you see, I have everything on my side.'

'Who told you that?'

'Some of the blokes at work. So it might be a good thing if there was a war.'

'Ted! You mustn't say things like that.'

'Well, it'll be that one out of the way.' He nodded towards Kurt.

Kate would have laughed if she didn't know he was serious.

'I know what she does, but I don't care.'

'Ted, I still think you're being a very silly young man.'

'Yer, that's what Dad says, and he said if I ain't careful I could end up with a dose of the clap, but that don't frighten me. I don't think she's as bad as everyone tries to make out.'

'But she's not interested in you.'

'She will be one day, you wait and see.'

Kate moved away. There was nothing she could do about this.

On Monday Milly didn't arrive as usual at lunchtime.

'Seamus, you'll have to come out here and give me a hand,' called Kate. She hated it when her customers tapped their money impatiently on the counter. She didn't like to keep them waiting as most of them had to get themselves or their husbands back to work.

Seamus came out from the back room, wiping his hands on his apron. 'What d'you think's happened to Milly?'

'I reckon it's Olive. The baby must be on its way.'

'Is it due, then?'

'Not just yet, but babies aren't known to obey the rules, and nothing will keep Milly away from Olive if she has started.'

Kate rushed about, clearing tables and dishing up food. Seamus was good at helping but he did like to stop and have a little chat now and again.

By late afternoon, Seamus had left and Kate was just finishing sweeping the floor. The door was wide open so she didn't hear Charlie walk in. He coughed, Kate looked up, and saw he looked very sad. 'Charlie, what are you doing here?' Fear gripped her as she kissed his cheek.

He took off his cap and rolled it nervously in his hands.

Kate felt the colour drain from her face. 'Sit down, Charlie. What's happened?'

'It's Olive's baby. It was born dead.'

Kate put her hand to her mouth. 'I'm so sorry. Poor Olive, how is she?'

'They've took her to the hospital as there's complications.'

'Oh my God! Is there anything I can do?'

He shook his head. 'Milly's taking it very bad. She went back to the hospital.'

'Who's got little Dolly?'

'We have.'

'What about Ernie?'

'He's at the hospital with Milly. Poor bloke, he's in a bad way.'

'I'll get my hat and coat and come back with you. Have you had any dinner?'

'No.'

'I'll bring some pies and mash and fruit pies. I've got enough for all of you.'

'Dunno if we feel like eating.' He began fiddling with the salt and pepper pots. 'Oh Kate, if anything happens to my Olive I don't know what I'll do.' He fished in his jacket pocket for his handkerchief and blew his nose hard.

She went to him and held him close. 'Nothing will happen to her. You mustn't think like that.' Her thoughts went to Mrs Addams. But this would be different. Olive was in hospital, she was a healthy girl and she had a lot of love around her.

'Sorry about that, Kate.'

'Don't worry.'

'I shouldn't show me feelings like that.'

'Why not? She's your daughter and you love her.'

'Yer I know, but it ain't very manly, is it?'

'Is that so important?'

'No, s'pose not. It's funny but I can share me troubles with you.'

'That's what friends are for.'

He sniffed. 'Thanks. Milly said she's sorry she didn't come in today. She couldn't let you know.'

Kate patted his back. 'That's the least of our problems. Now, let me get everything in my basket and we can be off.'

'What about Joe?'

'I'll leave a note, then perhaps Ted could come round and tell him what's happened.'

'Yer, it'll give him something to do.'

Kate was always flattered and pleased when they included her in their family.

Tom was sitting in the chair with Dolly on his lap when they walked in.

'She woke up so I took her out of her pram.'

Kate held out her hands and Dolly eagerly went to her. 'You're a lovely little girl and no mistake.' She gently kissed her forehead.

'Kate's brought some dinner,' said Charlie.

'That's kind of you, Miss Katherine.'

Ted looked very surprised to see Kate laying the table when he came in from work.

'Hallo, Ted.'

He quickly followed her into the scullery. 'What's wrong? Is it Grace?'

'No. It's your sister. She's in hospital.'

'Olive? Is she gonner be all right?'

'We hope so, but she has lost the baby.'

'Poor Olive! She was so looking forward to having another one.'

324

'Ted, when you've had your dinner could you go round and tell Joe? I'll be staying here for a while – well, at least till your mother gets back.'

'Yer, yer, of course.'

'Tell him to heat up a pie.'

'OK.' He began washing his hands in the scullery sink. 'D'you know, it seems that in this family every time you think things are going along all right something happens to upset the apple cart.'

'That's life, I'm afraid.'

'Yer, I suppose so.' He dried his hands on the striped towel that hung on a nail behind the back door. 'That pie smells good.'

After Ted left, Charlie, Tom and Kate sat gazing at the fire, waiting for Milly to come home.

It was a quiet entrance she made, so different from when Dolly was born.

'How is she?' asked Charlie, jumping up and taking her coat.

'Not too bad now. They've given her something to help her sleep. Mind you, she looks like death herself.'

'Where's Ernie?' asked Kate, taking the kettle from the hob.

'Gone home to bed. Poor lad looks done in. I said I'd keep Dolly here for a day or two. Where is she?'

'In the front room in her pram, sparko,' said Charlie.

'She's a good 'un.' A faint smile lifted Milly's troubled face.

Kate made the tea, and as she walked back into the kitchen, placing the tray on the table, she said, 'Look, I'll be off now. I'll send Ted home.'

'You don't have to go, you know,' said Charlie.

'I know that. I'll call in tomorrow.' One by one she kissed their cheeks, then left.

As she walked home she thought about Olive. She was still young enough to have another baby, but as Kate knew from experience, she would never forget this one.

* * *

When on Friday Kate told Grace what had happened, she was pleased that the girl volunteered to come in every day for a few hours.

Ted hadn't been in the shop for a couple of weeks and everybody was hoping he had got over his love for Grace.

Milly told Kate, when Kate went to see how Olive was, that Charlie was keeping him busy. Kurt was also making fewer visits.

'He's got a job,' said Grace one day when Kate commented on his absence.

'Where's that?'

'Round the docks somewhere, cleaning up, something like that. It's just casual labour.'

'Where's he living?' asked Kate.

'With me. He's a nice bloke and we have a few laughs together. I like him, Kate.'

Kate was taken aback at that statement. 'But what about your father?'

'He wasn't me dad,' she said quickly.

'I know, but he did live with your mother.'

'He buggered off when Mum died. D'you know, he didn't pay the rent or the coal man and left me a load of mess. I've only got a room but Kurt's been ever so good. He's been helping me get it looking nice.'

Kate was surprised to hear all this. 'What about, you know, your other job?'

'I don't take 'em back to my place, never have done. Him, me and Seamus go out together some nights for a drink when I ain't working. You know, Kate, I ain't ever had someone like him before. He's ever so kind, and I'm really happy.'

Kate smiled, but deep down she prayed no one would take this away from Grace.

'Old Seamus goes on a bit about Ireland. You'd think he'd lived there the way he talks.'

'I think he read a lot of books about it when he was in prison.'

'Yer. Right lot together, ain't we?'

Kate smiled. She knew they were but they all seemed to have found something.

At the end of June Olive came home, and although still weak, thanks to Milly's loving care she was improving daily.

'Don't know when she'll be strong enough to look after herself and Dolly,' said Milly one afternoon, when she popped into the shop. She had been out for a walk with her grandchild.

Kate went outside and peered into the pram. 'She looks so lovely, even when she's fast asleep.'

'Kate, I dunno when I'll be able to work for you again.'

'Don't worry about it. Now that Grace comes in I'm managing – that is, all the time I can keep Seamus away from the bottle. How long do you think you'll be looking after Olive?'

'Dunno. A few more weeks yet.'

A customer came up to Kate. 'Got a nice cuppa for an old friend?'

'Ron! Ron, how are you?'

'Not too bad.'

'You've lost a bit of weight.'

'Prison food ain't all that good.' He laughed. 'Reckon you could make a fortune selling your pies to 'em.'

'Don't think they'd let me.'

'I'll be on me way,' said Milly. 'It's good to see you back, Ron.'

'Ta.' He raised his cap to Milly and followed Kate into the shop.

'Well, what's all the news?'

'We thought you'd be away for at least six months,' said Kate, handing him a mug of tea. He went to pay but she waved his money away.

'Been a good boy, ain't I? Learnt it don't do to buck the system, so I got time off for good behaviour. It's good to be back, though. Missed me freedom. So, what's been happening?'

'Nellie came back.'

'No! What'd she want?'

'Josh is dead and she's living with her sister in Kent. She wanted money for her furniture.'

'Poor old Josh. I'm sorry to hear that. He was a decent bloke.'

'I've got Milly working in the week, or she was till her daughter lost her baby.'

'That's a shame.'

'I've got Grace – you know, the one that always sat waiting for her men friends – well, she works every day, and I've got Seamus O'Brien who washes up and does the potatoes.'

He laughed. 'Not old Seamus? He back on the scene?'

'Yes, do you know him?'

'I should say so.' He took Kate's arm and lowered his voice. 'You know he's been inside?'

Kate nodded. 'And so have you.'

'True.'

'But he seems to have mended his ways.'

'And so have I. What about Grace? She still on the game?' He gave Kate a knowing look.

'I think so, but as long as it doesn't interfere with her work here I'm not too worried at what she gets up to.'

'Sounds like a right motley crew to me.'

'Yes, I suppose it does, but they are nice people.'

'See you ain't changed the name outside yet.'

'No, had to pay off Nellie first before I could think about things like that.'

'I know a bloke what's a sign writer. I reckon he'd do it for you on the cheap.'

'That could be interesting.'

'It'll have to be out of hours, after he's finished.'

'Perhaps when you see him again you could ask him to pop in.'

'I'll do that, Katie love.'

It was the middle of July when Ted returned to Kate's.

When he walked in Grace looked startled. 'He's not gonner start coming back here again, is he?' she asked Kate.

'I hope not.' Kate hadn't mentioned to Milly that Kurt was living with Grace. 'Hallo, Ted. Everything all right at home?' Kate asked casually. 'Joe's not home yet.'

He stood at the counter and looked around, a grin spread across his face. 'See you've got rid of the Kraut.'

Kate began to clear away and didn't reply.

When he sat at a table Grace went over to him. Kate couldn't hear what she was saying but the look on his face told her it was something he didn't want to hear.

He stood up and stormed out.

'What did you say to him?' asked Kate.

'Told him I was marrying Kurt and asked him if he'd like to be a bridesmaid.'

Kate laughed. 'You didn't! Poor Ted. That's why he's gone off with a flea in his ear.'

'Yer, could be.'

Kate suddenly realised she could be telling the truth. 'Grace, you're not really thinking of marrying Kurt, are you?'

'Could be.'

'But he's not here legally. They will want to see his papers.'

'Yer, we know.'

'You've talked about this?'

'Yer. Seamus said he might know of someone who'll be able to help.'

Kate sat down. 'This is a bit of a shock.'

'Well, don't worry about it.'

After Grace had left Ted came in. He must have been waiting for her to go.

'Ted, what's wrong?'

'I forgot to tell you. Mum said they're all going to Southend again this Bank Holiday Monday and she said you've got to go with 'em.'

She smiled. 'D'you know, I think I will. Thanks.'

'Is it true? Is she really gonner marry that bloke?'

'She says she is.'

''Bye.' He walked out.

Kate felt sad as this time he wasn't whistling.

Chapter 33

Kate thought her life had settled down comfortably.

On the Saturday before the Bank Holiday, Grace and Seamus had both looked very nervous and guilty all day. They kept out of Kate's way and tried to avoid eye contact, so Kate knew something was wrong. It was almost the end of the day when they dropped their bombshell.

'What do you mean, you're leaving me?' screamed Kate, plonking herself at the table Grace and Kurt were sitting at.

'I'm sorry, Kate, but I love Kurt, and well, we've just got to go.'

'But why you as well, Seamus?'

He sat at the table opposite her and held her hand. 'It's like this, my dear Kate. We think a war is on the horizon, and Kurt here will be interned.'

'And I couldn't bear that,' said Grace.

Kurt held Grace's hand and smiled at her.

'So,' said Kate angrily, pulling her hand away from Seamus, 'what's that to do with you?'

'We're all going to Ireland,' said Seamus. 'Always wanted to see the land of me birth.'

'And if I want to marry Kurt, this is the only way out.'

'So how are you going to get there? Where will you get that kind of money from?'

'Kurt has got to know when the ships come in and he reckons there's one leaving for Ireland tomorrow night. He's seen the stoker who's said he can get us aboard.'

Kate was trying to take all this in. 'That means I'll be left on my own.'

'You've got Joe and Milly,' said Seamus.

'Can't you wait a few more weeks? There may not be a war.'

'We have to go tomorrow, as we may not get another chance,' said Grace. 'I feel awful at letting you down. You've been the nicest person I have ever met, except Kurt and Seamus. You've made me very happy.' Tears were brimming.

Kate swallowed hard. 'I can't believe this.'

'You are a very kind lady,' said Seamus. 'You have given me and Grace a chance and a reason for living. Who knows, perhaps one of these days when I've made me fortune I'll come back and take you out to a posh restaurant in London?'

That didn't hold any interest for Kate; she hadn't told them she ran one once.

They stood up and Grace threw her arms round Kate's neck and hugged her hard. 'I'm really gonner miss you.'

Seamus took Kate's hand and kissed it.

Kurt was smiling so hard Kate thought his face would crack. 'Goodbye and thank you.' His English was very hard to understand.

Seamus put a small parcel on the table. 'Just a little something to remind you of us.'

'I've got nothing for you. I can't even get you a wedding present, Grace. Oh please say you'll stay for at least another day?'

'I'm sorry, but we must get that ship.'

Kate hugged them. Tears were stinging her eyes. 'I've grown very fond of you two. Promise you'll write?'

'We will.'

'Grace, what about your Mr Friday?'

Grace laughed. 'You can have him.'

'Thanks.'

They left the door open and walked away.

Kate wanted to cry. She really did love these people. They had brought laughter into her life.

She opened her present. It was a small china jug with one of Seamus's poems attached.

> This jug is filled with kindness.
> The kind you gave to us.
> We hope the future gives you
> Love, hope, faith and trust.

She brushed the tears away and was still sitting at the table fondling the jug when Joseph walked in.

'You all right?'

She nodded and, standing up, put the jug in her overall pocket. 'I'll get your tea.'

'You don't look very happy.'

'I've just had some bad news.'

Joseph eased himself into a chair. 'What kind of bad news?'

'Seamus and Grace have left.'

'What do you mean, left?'

'They've gone to Ireland.'

Joseph laughed. 'What, gone off together?'

'Yes, in a way. Grace is going to marry Kurt.'

'That German bloke that Ted threatens to do in?'

'Yes.'

'What have they gone over there for, then?'

'It's all this talk about war.'

'What's he afraid of?'

'Well, he's a German.'

'Oh yes, that would make him run.'

'He wouldn't have a lot of choice.'

'No, s'pose not. Well, that's put paid to Ted's dream of marrying Grace. So, what's for tea?'

* * *

On Sunday Kate wished she knew what time their ship was sailing. She would have liked to have gone to the docks to see it off, though of course she wouldn't have seen them, not if they were stowing away. Please don't let them get caught, she silently prayed. Then she panicked. Would she even know if they got caught? Who would tell her?

All these thoughts were milling around as she prepared dinner. She was also trying to think of ways to get help. Perhaps Milly would come back again now that Olive was getting better. But who would do all those potatoes? The evenings she and Seamus would sit preparing the food for the following day were always a joy to her, and many times the chore would be accompanied with one of his many tales. She would miss him so much. 'I only hope you find what you're looking for,' she whispered.

'What did you say?' asked Joe, bringing her out of her daydream.

'Nothing. I was thinking out loud.'

'Are you still going with Milly and the family to Southend tomorrow?'

'I expect so. Look, don't say anything to Ted about Grace.'

'Why not?'

'Let him enjoy his day out first.'

'OK.'

Early on Bank Holiday Monday Kate arrived at Milly's with her basket overflowing with food. She put the basket on the kitchen table.

'Hallo, Olive. How nice to see you looking so well. Your mother has been keeping me informed about your progress.'

Without speaking, Olive stood up and walked out of the kitchen, leaving Kate standing with her mouth open.

'What have I said?'

'It's nothing,' said Milly quickly. 'Just her funny little way.'

Kate didn't think it was funny. In fact she was cross at being ignored. She wasn't that happy as it was, but was determined to enjoy herself today and would tell them all about Seamus and Grace later.

Tom said he didn't want to join them as he was feeling the heat. Milly was worried.

'We can't leave you on your own all day.'

'Of course you can,' he grinned. ''Sides, it'll be a nice change to be on my own for a while.'

'Well, I don't think we should go,' said Ernie.

'Why not?' shouted Charlie.

'It's all this talk about a war.'

'Christ, mate! If it does happen, they ain't gonner get over here, not while we've got the Channel. We'll soon chase 'em back. And I still reckon you ought to come, Tom.'

He shook his head. 'No, I'll be all right.'

'Leave him be, Charlie,' said Milly, folding nappies and filling the bottom of the pram with them.

Kate saw Tom looked tired and old.

Despite failing to persuade Tom to change his mind they finally left and happily made their way to the station. Ernie pushed Dolly in her bassinet, which would finish up in the guard's van. Kate was pleased to see that Ted and Joe were larking about in front. However, she was concerned at how Ted would take the news about Grace.

'Charlie, what's wrong with Olive?' asked Kate as they made their way to the ticket office.

He looked embarrassed. 'I don't know.'

'Yes you do. Why won't she talk to me?'

'She's not really been herself since she came out of hospital.'

Kate knew there was more to it than that.

The train was crowded, but everyone was in a bank holiday

mood and they arrived at Southend hot but happy, determined to enjoy themselves.

It wasn't till the end of the day, when they were walking back home from the station, that Kate had the opportunity to speak to Ted on his own. She told him what had happened. He didn't lift his eyes from the ground.

'I'm sorry, Ted, but she wasn't for you.'

'No, s'pose not.'

'You told him then?' asked Joe, bounding up to them.

'Joseph, behave!'

'Don't know why he's getting in such a state about her, she's only a—'

'I ain't getting in a state, so, Joe Carter, mind your own business.'

Joe shrugged his shoulders and they continued home in silence.

The following day, on 4 August, the news vendors and placards screamed that Britain was at war with Germany. The news spread like wildfire. Kate sat at a table looking out of the window. The door was wide open but the shop was empty. Young men were cheering and shouting as they made their euphoric way to one of the many recruiting stations that had sprung up like mushrooms. Some lads that Kate knew came and planted loud kisses on her cheek. She felt sad and alone, but pleased Joe wasn't old enough to join up. Her thoughts went to Grace and Seamus. She hoped they, along with Kurt, who wasn't a bad lad, would be happy in their new life.

'Don't worry, Kate,' someone shouted. 'It'll all be over by Christmas.'

She smiled and waved. 'I hope so. Good luck, boys.'

Business was very slow all day and just as she was closing Ted came rushing in and, throwing his arms round her, twirled her round and round.

'Ted!' she laughed. 'Put me down!'

'I've just popped in to say goodbye to you and Joe.'

Kate sat at the table. 'Why? What have you done?' She was dreading the answer.

He was beaming. 'Joined the army, ain't I? I'll show those bloody Krauts they can't mess with us.'

'Does your mother know what you've done?' asked Kate, getting her breath back.

'No, not yet.'

'She's going to be very upset.'

'I expect so. But I can't just sit here and wait for it to end, I've gotter do me bit.' He paused, and taking a cigarette from a packet in his pocket, lit it. ''Sides,' he said, blowing the smoke into the air, 'since you told me about Grace and the German it's a way of getting back at him. Who knows, I might meet him on a battlefield.' He laughed

'Ted, this isn't a game!' Kate felt a flush of anger. 'And you can't use that as an excuse to go out and get yourself killed.'

'I ain't gonner get killed.'

Kate stood up and paced the floor. 'My God! Your mother will never forgive me if she thought Grace was the reason you've enlisted. It's bad enough having Olive look at me as if I've committed a crime.'

'Yer, well. Olive's a bit emotional.'

'And you're not?'

'I must admit I was a bit upset when you told me Grace had gone off with that bloke.'

'Is that why you joined up?'

He stubbed the cigarette butt into an ashtray. 'Yer, s'pose it is in a way. But I would go anyway.'

'I only hope your mother believes you.'

'Ted! Ted, what are you doing here?' asked Joe, rushing into the shop. 'Have you heard the news?'

'I should say so. Guess what? I've joined the army!'

Joe stood open-mouthed. 'You lucky beggar!' He gave Ted a playful punch on the arm. 'I only wish I was old enough. I'd be off like a shot.'

Kate gave him a glance that almost said, over my dead body.

'So, when d'you go?' asked Joe.

'Soon. Got to have a medical first.'

'Well, let's hope you aren't half dead, otherwise you'll have to stay here.'

'Na. I think just as long as you can walk in you're fit.' He laughed, but it was a strange nervous laugh.

Please God, keep him safe, said Kate silently to herself.

The following day Milly came bustling in. She plonked herself and her basket on the chair. Kate could see she had been crying.

'What d'you think of that silly bugger joining up?' she sniffed, fumbling in her bag for her handkerchief.

'I'm so sorry, Milly. I've seen nearly all the young lads round here sign up. I suppose it's something they feel they've got to do.'

'Bloody daft, if you ask me. He's still a kid. You ought to hear Charlie going on about it.'

'I can guess,' said Kate, remembering his feelings about Olive. She walked round the counter, and after putting two mugs of tea on the table, sat beside Milly. 'What made him do it?'

'Dunno, said it was his duty. I ask you, his duty! A young lad like that. Charlie said it was the ones that got us into this mess who should be going off fighting.'

Kate was relieved she didn't say it was because of his love for Grace.

'Thank Gawd young Joe ain't old enough to go.'

Kate nodded in agreement. The thought of that upset her and she quickly changed the subject. 'You're not round Olive's then?'

'Na, thought I'd give it a bit of a rest today. 'Sides, she's got to earn to start standing on her own two feet soon.'

'Yes,' said Kate. She never thought she'd hear Milly say that. 'Milly, why was Olive so off with me on Monday?'

Milly toyed with her spoon. 'It was 'cos she lost the baby.'

'But why get upset with . . .' Suddenly the penny dropped. 'Was it because . . . ?'

Milly nodded. 'She thought that what you did was a terrible thing, but you don't want to take too much notice of our Olive.'

'That was a long while ago, and I wasn't very proud of it myself. But surely she knew the reason why I did it?'

'Course, but she needed to take her anger out on someone, and that person was you.'

Kate was upset. 'Well, thanks for explaining. How did she think I felt?'

Milly shrugged. She looked around and Kate could see she was embarrassed. 'You ain't very busy.'

'No. I only hope trade picks up. I've still got the rent to pay.'

'I was surprised when Ted told me about Grace and Seamus going. You didn't say nothing on Monday. Mind you, I ain't sorry to see 'em go.'

'Why? I'm left without any help.'

'No, I didn't mean that. It's just that Ted knows it ain't no use him hanging round here now she's gone.'

Milly didn't know Grace had gone off to marry Kurt.

'Kate, will it be all right if I come back for the hour or so a day?'

Kate could have kissed her. 'Of course. But are you sure about leaving Olive?'

Milly nodded. 'As I said, she's got to learn to cope. 'Sides, I'll be Ted's money short.'

Kate hadn't thought about the many women who would be a wage earner missing. It would strike some families very hard.

Although still sad about Ted, Kate felt happy at the thought of seeing Milly every day. 'Do you want to start today?'

'Why not?'

'There's some washing-up outside.'

Milly grinned. 'Thought there might be.'

Kate also realised that Milly needed something to take her mind off Ted leaving. After all, he was still her baby.

Chapter 34

That afternoon after Milly had left, Ron came in.

'Bloody awful news, ain't it?'

Kate sat at the table with him. 'What's going to happen, Ron?'

'Dunno. Think we'll just have to wait and see.'

'Do you think it will be all over by Christmas, as everyone seems to think?'

'Wouldn't like to say. By the way, tell Seamus his horse didn't come up.'

'Seamus, Grace and Kurt have left.'

'What, all of 'em?'

Kate nodded.

'What they pinched?'

'They haven't pinched anything.'

'So where they gone?'

'To Ireland.'

Ron burst out laughing. 'When did this happen?'

'Sunday. Kurt's been working in the docks and a ship was leaving on Sunday and they were smuggled out on it.'

'No! As stowaways?'

Again Kate nodded. 'Grace is going to marry Kurt, and as he's German, and without papers, it would have been a bit difficult, more so now.'

'I should say so. Mind you, they got out just in time.'

'Yes. I only hope they've done the right thing.'

'Don't look so worried. He couldn't stay here, could he?'

'No, but it's not really him I'm worried about.'

'She'll be OK, she's got Seamus with her.'

'I hope so. I thought everything was going along fine, then all this happens. Why does life suddenly come up and hit you when things are going well?'

'Sod's law.'

'It is as far as my life has been.' Kate stared out of the window and they settled down into an agreeable silence.

Ron put out his cigarette. 'Been busy?'

'No.'

'Seems quiet all round today somehow.'

'Yes, after yesterday. I think it's just started to hit people Milly's boy's enlisted.'

'Glad mine ain't old enough.'

'So am I.'

'By the way, I ain't seen that bloke yet.'

'Who?'

'The sign writer.'

'Don't worry about that. That's the least of my troubles.'

Over the next two weeks business was slow.

'Can't see things getting much worse,' said Milly one lunchtime.

'I hope not. How's Olive these days?'

'Coping. Tom don't look that well, though.'

'I'll come round on Sunday to see him.

'Come to dinner. It'll be nice having young Joe at the table. Even Charlie's been off his food since Ted went. And we've only had the one card which didn't say much. Charlie's taking it hard.'

Charlie was poring over the newspaper when Kate and Joe arrived on Sunday.

'See most of the boys that signed up at the very beginning finished up in France,' he said, folding the paper and putting it under his chair. 'Don't know why we have to help them.'

'Is Ted out there?' asked Joe.

'Could be,' said Charlie.

'Lucky old Ted. Bet he's with all those French floosies.'

'Floosies?' repeated Kate in alarm. 'So much for a good education,' she said, looking at Joe.

'Ted can't speak French,' said Milly.

'You don't have to speak the language to be understood to get all you want.' Charlie winked at Kate. 'Signs is all you need; just as long as you can wave your arms about, you're in.'

Throughout dinner everyone was trying to be jovial, but Kate knew it was all a show. She was watching Tom. He had never been a great conversationalist, and today he was very quiet. 'How's work, Tom?' she asked.

'Not too bad, Miss Katherine. Don't do a lot.'

'Keeps him out of mischief, though,' said Milly.

He gave her a faint smile. Kate could see he wasn't well.

As the weeks progressed things gradually got back to normal. Kate's regular customers, those that were left, drifted back. The war wasn't going the way everybody thought it would, and at the end of the first month the terrible battle at Mons was on everybody's lips. As time went on Kate noticed many men and women wearing black armbands.

'D'you know, every time I see that telegraph boy come riding by on his bike me heart stands still.' Milly was drying the mugs. 'I dunno what I'd do if anything happened to my Ted.'

'You mustn't say things like that,' said Kate, but she too worried if Milly was a little late coming in, in case she'd had bad news.

'See they're asking women to go out to work.'

'My Olive gets very fed up. She'd like to get out more.'

'She can't go to work, not with Dolly to look after.' Kate was worried. What if Milly was thinking of having Dolly while Olive went to work?

'That's what I told her. We had a long talk about it. I suggested she comes in here for a few days a week. Would that be all right with you?'

Kate could have hugged Milly. 'I'd be more than pleased to have her, but—'

'I know she's been a bit of a cow towards you, but don't worry, she's a lot better now. I'll be having Dolly the days she works. If she likes it, she's even going to ask Ernie if she could do an hour or so on Sat'days.'

'That's wonderful news! Seems you've got all this sorted out.'

'D'you mind?'

'Mind? Of course not. I'm pleased all my problems are over.'

'Yer,' said Milly thoughtfully. 'Wish mine was.'

At the beginning Kate was apprehensive about herself and Olive working together. On Olive's first day she went about quietly doing what Kate asked of her. The next time she was in Kate suggested they had a cup of tea when the lunchtime rush finished.

They sat at the table.

'Olive, I know that you felt very strongly about what I did, but—'

'I'm sorry, Kate. I know I shouldn't have snubbed you like that after I lost my baby, but I couldn't help it. I was angry and wanted to hurt someone like I'd been hurt.' Her brown eyes misted over.

'I do understand, but I could never have been a good mother to Gerald's child.'

'I know.'

'It was bad enough leaving my son in Australia, and then to have to . . . I'm sorry.' Kate sniffed. 'I must be starting a cold.'

'It's all right. I understand.' She gently touched Kate's hand.

After that everything worked out just fine, and in a few weeks Olive and Kate were getting on very well. Olive was happy serving and talking to people, and didn't mind doing potatoes and any chores Kate asked her to.

'Dunno what you've done to our Olive, but she's brightened up a lot,' said Milly.

But one day when Olive came into work, Kate could see she had been crying.

'What's wrong?' she asked.

'It's that stupid husband of mine. He's joined up.' Olive wiped her eyes on the bottom of her overall. 'He's a married man with a child and he's exempt.'

'Why did he do that?'

'I dunno. Couldn't wait to get away from me, I s'pose.'

'I don't believe that for one moment.' But Milly had told Kate she thought her daughter and Ernie were going through a bad patch.

She had told her, 'When she ain't here she sits about moping all day, and that ain't no good. No man's gonner put up with that for too long.' Milly had been very worried about her daughter and Kate guessed it was she who had suggested Olive came to work here in the first place.

'He reckons he joined up now so he can get a cushy job before they called him up,' said Olive, interrupting Kate's thoughts. 'But I don't believe that. What am I gonner do without his money? What if he gets killed?'

'You mustn't think like that. Perhaps we can work something out with Milly. I'm sure she will have Dolly for you.'

'I've already talked to Mum, and I can do all day Sat'days if you'd like me to.'

Kate was overwhelmed. She could have cried out for joy. 'That's wonderful!'

When Olive had her first letter from Ernie and found out he

had a desk job in Wales it helped to cheer her up.

'Guess what? He's coming home for Christmas,' Olive told Kate eagerly some weeks later.

When Milly came in she said to Kate, 'Our Olive is a different girl these days. She's ever so happy.'

'I think it's the thought of Ernie coming home.'

Olive had changed in the past months. Gone was the dowdy way she dressed and did her hair. Somehow she appeared to have come alive.

'It's all your doing, Kate,' said Milly. 'Thanks. Ernie's gonner see a different wife when he gets home on leave next week. Might even find she's . . . you know' – Milly nudged Kate's elbow – 'when he goes back.'

Kate hoped not, as she selfishly thought that that could mean more staff worries.

Joe and Kate spent Christmas with Milly and the family. It was a very quiet affair.

Kate sat in the kitchen quietly talking to Tom while the others were in the front room playing with Dolly.

'Got to try and be cheerful for young Dolly's sake,' said Charlie, walking in. 'After all, Christmas is for kids. I only hope our Ted's getting a good dinner.' He went into the scullery. Kate didn't follow him – she knew he wanted to be alone with his thoughts.

'Bit different to the Christmases we had at the big house, Miss Katherine,' said Tom, pulling the shawl Kate had given him tighter round his hunched shoulders.

'That was a lifetime ago,' said Kate thoughtfully. 'And there wasn't a war on.'

'And my Dolly and Mr Edwin was here. I wonder how Mr Gerald's getting on?' He stopped when a fit of coughing racked his frail body.

'I expect he is managing,' said Kate, watching him anxiously.

Tom sat back exhausted and mopped his face with the edge of the shawl. When he recovered his breath he continued, 'I know I shouldn't speak out of turn but I'm glad you didn't stay with Mr Gerald.'

She smiled. 'I couldn't stay in that house after what happened.'

'I would think Mr Edwin would have turned in his grave if he knew what his brother did to you.'

'It's all in the past now.'

'Did you know Dolly looked for his will before Mr Gerald came to the house?'

Kate sat up. 'No, I didn't.'

'She didn't say anythink 'cos she didn't want you to think she was being nosy. She didn't find one.'

Kate slumped back in the chair. 'Well, that's one mystery that's always bothered me. I always thought Gerald had found it and destroyed it, though he said he hadn't.'

'No. Poor Mr Edwin. I expect as it all happened so quick, he didn't have time to make one.'

Kate patted Tom's hand. How different her life would probably have been if Edwin had. That had been the beginning of all her troubles.

As 1915 progressed everybody read the newspapers avidly. There was no end in sight to the war.

It seemed the whole world was being drawn into this conflict. Ships were being sunk and it was in May when the liner *Lusitania* was hit and that brought America into the trouble. Food was getting short, but most of the local traders kept Kate supplied at a price. Any shop that had a foreign name was a target for violence, even if the owners had been born in London. Kate was glad it was the name Trent above her shop; she would have been worried had it been something foreign. One of these days she would get it changed.

She often thought about Grace and Kurt, though she had never heard from them. Milly only had the odd card from Ted and she didn't know where he was.

In May too it was Joe's sixteenth birthday and Kate prayed the war would be over before he was old enough to join up.

'See they've got pictures of Lord Kitchener all over the place,' said Milly.

'Yes, I know. It worries me.'

'Mrs Duke was telling me that Mrs Bolton – don't think you know her – has lost two of her boys.'

'That's dreadful!' Kate looked at Milly. She knew she worried constantly about Ted and had aged considerably this past year. 'How is Mrs Duke?' she asked, to change the subject. 'Haven't seen her for I don't know how long.'

'She don't get out much these days. It's her feet.'

Kate smiled. 'Mrs Duke's feet have always been a topic of conversation for her.'

A week after Joe's birthday Milly didn't turn up for work. Kate was devastated and couldn't wait to shut the shop. As soon as the last customer left she closed the door.

After leaving a note for Joe she hurried round to Milly's and, pulling the key through the letter box, rushed in.

'Kate! I was just coming to see you,' said Charlie, looking up surprised.

'Why? What's happened?' She looked from one to the other. Milly looked a little distressed but not unduly worried. 'Is it—'

'It's Tom. He's had to go to hospital.'

Kate sank into a chair. 'What's wrong with him?'

'His chest, and he can't keep anything down,' said Milly, sitting next to her. 'Think he might have to go away to some sort of convalescent home for a special diet.'

'What, in wartime?'

'Yer. Daft, ain't it?' said Charlie.

Kate burst into tears. 'What's wrong?' asked Milly.

'I'm sorry. I thought it was Ted.'

'Oh Kate. I'm sorry I didn't let you know, but I went with him to the hospital and we had such a wait.'

She sniffed. 'It's all right.'

'Here, get this down yer,' said Charlie, handing her a glass.

'What is it?'

'Just a drop of whisky. Help steady your nerves.'

She smiled through her tears. 'To Tom and Ted, may they both come home safe and well soon.'

They both agreed with her.

A month later Tom died.

'The doctor said he was just worn out. Never got over losing Dolly, you know,' Milly said to Kate at the graveside.

'Well, he's with her now.' Kate put a small bunch of flowers on the mound of fresh brown earth.

A few days later Olive was helping Kate with the pies. 'Mum and Dad are looking old,' she suddenly said.

'I know.'

'That house is like a morgue now, with only the two of them rattling about in it.'

Kate smiled. 'It wasn't that long ago it was packed to overflowing. Have you thought about moving back in with them?'

'I did think about it, but Ernie don't think it's a good idea. I'm glad you got me and Mum to come and work for you. You've given us all a lift and a bit of spending money as well. I have to smarten meself up to come here.'

'No you don't,' said Kate quickly.

'I want to. 'Sides, you're a smart woman and I looked dowdy beside you.' She laughed. 'Then, when Mum has Dolly for a few hours that really pleases her, and on the other days she can come here and meet people. So she has the best of both worlds.'

'I'm more than pleased to have you both here with me. After all, you are my family.'

Olive smiled. She was a pretty girl, so much like her father.

It was a damp, dreary day on Monday 25 October 1915, a day that Kate would never forget. The gaslights in the shop hadn't been turned out all day and the windows were running with condensation. A few people came and went. Shoppers didn't stop very long – they were all eager to get home and into the dry. The men that came in at dinnertime sat at the tables waiting to be served.

'Who we got in helping today?' asked Bill, who came in from the market.

'Should be Olive.'

'Well, she's a bit late.'

'Yes, I know. I hope her baby's all right.'

'Reckon Milly would let you know if she was poorly.'

'I hope so.' Kate carried on dishing up the pies, mash and pease pudding.

'My missis wants to know where you gets your stuff from,' said Bill.

Kate smiled and wiped her damp forehead with the back of her hand. 'She shouldn't be going short, not with you and Bert in the know.'

He laughed. 'She thinks she misses out. Trouble is, there's so many things in short supply now.'

'I know. Tell her I've got some good connections, but it costs me, and sometimes I find I have to make do with something else.'

'Here, I hope we ain't gonner end up with horse meat in the pies.'

Kate laughed. 'Who knows what we'll finish up with.' She hurriedly put the dinners on the counter but kept looking at the door. She was beginning to get worried. Something must have happened to stop Olive coming in.

When Mrs Duke waddled in Kate felt the colour drain from her face.

'Kate love.' Her face looked full of grief. She came up and leant on the counter. 'I'm ever so sorry to tell you but—'

Kate dropped the plate she was filling and it fell with a crash to the floor.

'Bloody hell, Kate!' said Bill, looking up. 'Nearly choked meself. What yer trying to do, give us all a heart— Here, you all right?'

He hurried to the counter and helped Kate into a chair. 'Here, missis,' Bill said to Mrs Duke, 'what you bin saying to her?'

'I ain't said nothing yet. But you've guessed, ain't yer?'

Kate nodded. 'Is it Ted?'

Mrs Duke nodded. 'Can I have a sit-down, me bloody feet's killing me. I ain't walked this far fer years.'

Someone jumped up and gave Mrs Duke a chair.

'What's happened?' whispered Kate.

'He's bin killed.'

Kate could hear herself wailing but she couldn't stop. 'No, not Ted! Poor Milly! Poor Charlie! Who started this bloody war?' Tears were running down her face.

'Kate, Kate, calm down.' Bill was patting her hand. Someone was putting a mug of tea in her hands. 'Drink this,' said Bill. 'It's got a lot of sugar in.'

The usual babble that went on was suddenly silent. All eyes were on Kate. She took the mug with both hands.

'I'd like one of them,' said Mrs Duke.

'Coming up,' Kate heard someone say.

'When did Milly hear?'

'This morning.'

'Does Charlie know?'

'Don't think so, unless Olive's sorted that out.'

Kate sat back. 'I've got to go to her.' She looked about her. 'I must. Milly will need me.'

'Course she will,' said Mrs Duke. 'D'you want me to stay and finish giving all these men their dinners?'

A couple of them stood up. 'Don't worry about us, Kate. You go and see Milly,' said one of her regulars, who was wearing a black armband.

'This is a wicked world,' said Kate, staring into space. 'He was a young man with all his life in front of him.'

'There's a lot like that,' said Mrs Duke. 'There's a few now in Croft Street who've lost their boys.'

At this moment that was no consolation to Kate.

Gradually the shop emptied.

'You gonner be all right now, Kate?' Bill looked concerned.

'Yes, thank you. I'll walk back with Mrs Duke.'

'What about your boy?'

'Joseph? I'll leave him a note.'

'Will he guess?'

'I don't know. I hope not. Ted was Joseph's best friend.'

Kate locked the shop door and began the slow walk back with Mrs Duke. Although the old lady was talking, Kate wasn't listening; she was full of her own thoughts.

When they turned into Croft Street Kate felt her strength leave her. What could she say? Any words would sound inadequate. And no words would ever bring Ted back. She loved him like her own son.

'I won't come in, gel,' said Mrs Duke when they reached Milly's house. 'She don't want me in there fussing.'

Kate looked at Mrs Duke. Perhaps she wasn't such a bad old stick, and was more sensitive than she liked everybody to believe.

Chapter 35

Olive was in the kitchen holding Dolly on her hip when Kate walked in. 'Mum's upstairs,' she said in a hushed whisper.

Kate hugged them both. She swallowed hard. 'This is terrible news. Does your dad know yet?'

Olive shook her head. She put Dolly on the floor and wiped her tears away with the bottom of her pinny. 'It's always difficult to get someone out of the docks. Half the time the office don't know what ship they're working on. Mum thought it best we wait till he comes home.'

Kate went quietly up the stairs and pushed open Ted's bedroom door. Milly was sitting on her son's bed. She was chewing the corner of her handkerchief. Kate could see the screwed-up telegram in her lap. At her side were his drawings.

'Milly,' said Kate softly.

She looked up, her eyes red and swollen, her face tear-stained. She was suddenly an old woman.

'Milly. What can I say?' Tears ran freely down Kate's cheeks.

Milly stood up and holding each other close, they let their tears flow.

When they broke away they both sat on his bed. 'I was looking at these. That's Grace. It's a good likeness, ain't it?'

Kate nodded. 'It's very good. He was very talented.'

'She'll never know he's . . .' Milly couldn't say the word – it was too final. 'Wonder if she'd be upset?'

'I would think so. She was a sensitive young woman.'

'Oh Kate! What am I gonner do?' She gave a deep sob.

'I don't know.'

'I won't even have a grave to visit. It ain't fair. I want me boy back.' She gave a low moan.

Kate put her arm round Milly's shoulders. She didn't have an answer. 'Would you like me to go and meet Charlie and—'

Milly pulled away and shook her head, and after dabbing at her eyes, blew her nose. 'No, let him get home first. He wouldn't want to make a fool of himself in the street.'

'Would you like a cup of tea?'

'Yer, p'raps I would.'

'Do you want to come downstairs for it?'

'I'd better. Left poor Olive on her own all day.'

'She understands.'

They made their way downstairs.

'I've made some tea. I was just gonner bring it up,' said Olive.

'Where's Dolly?' asked Milly.

'In her pram in the front room. She's all right, she's dropped off.'

'She'll never remember her uncle.'

'Don't worry, Mum. I'll tell her all about him.' Olive sniffed as she poured out the tea.

Milly looked at the clock. 'You've finished early. How did you know?' she asked Kate. 'Who told you?'

'Mrs Duke came into the shop.'

'What, she walked all that way with her feet?'

Olive gave a faint smile. 'She couldn't walk without 'em. Sorry about that, Mum.'

Milly also let a slight smile lift her sad face. 'That's all right, love.'

They drank their tea in silence till Milly asked, 'Does Joe know?'

'No, not yet.'

For a while, the ticking of the clock on the mantelpiece was the only sound.

'I'm gonner stay the night,' said Olive, breaking into their thoughts.

'What about Dolly's things? Would you like me to go and get them?'

'No, thanks all the same. I'll pop round when Dad gets in.'

When they heard the key being pulled through the letter box they all tensed and sat up, waiting for Charlie to open the kitchen door.

''Allo, Kate, what you doing . . .?' His voice trailed off when he noted their faces.

Milly burst into tears and, rushing to him, hugged him tight.

He looked over her shoulder at Olive and Kate. Tears filled his eyes. 'Is it Ted?'

They both nodded.

'He's not . . .?'

They couldn't speak.

For a few moments the little group stood in silence as if in homage. The only sound was Milly's sobs.

It was Charlie who spoke. 'What did the telegram say?'

Milly fished in her overall pocket and gave him the screwed-up paper.

He straightened it out. 'Thought it might have been that he's been injured or taken prisoner. But this. This is so final.' He sat in the chair, and burying his head in his hands, he wept.

Kate picked up her hat, quietly said her goodbyes, and left. This was their grief, and it should be in private.

'I warmed up that pie,' said Joe when Kate walked in. 'Ma, what's wrong?'

Kate let the tears fall. 'Joseph, it's Ted.'

'Ted? Ted? What's happened to him?'

'He's been killed.'

Joe sat at the table. He stared at his mother, disbelief written all over his face. 'He can't be!'

'I'm afraid he has.'

Joe left the room and went upstairs. He didn't leave hi
bedroom all evening.

The following morning Kate gave him a black armband
'Would you like this?'

'Yes. When did you make this?'

'Last night. I couldn't sleep and I had to have something to
do. I've made one for Milly and Charlie as well.'

Joe kissed Kate's cheek. 'I'd better be off.' At the door he
turned. 'I loved Ted like a brother.'

'I know.'

When she went to make his bed she was shocked at the pictures
he must have spent the evening drawing. They were of faceless
Germans lying in a field. Some had bayonets through their hearts,
some were being hanged. They were violent pictures with barbed
wire and guns. Perhaps it was good for him to get some of his
anger down on paper.

Throughout the day many regulars came in and offered their
condolences. It amazed Kate that so many people knew about
Ted's death and cared.

'Thank you, Bill, for yesterday.'

''S all right. Bloody shame, though. Poor Milly and Olive. I
bet they're taking it hard.'

'Yes they are. We all are.'

Kate felt she was in limbo, and throughout the day only did
what was necessary.

Weeks later, things gradually returned to as normal as they would
ever be. Both Milly and Olive came back to work. But it was Joe
who was worrying Kate. He became morose and only spoke
when spoken to. He spent hours in his room, drawing. The
pictures were frightening, all about the war. Kate didn't show
them to anyone although Joe knew she had seen them but made

no comment. Somehow he had lost his sparkle.

At the end of November she found a note in his bedroom and her world crumbled. In it he said he had put up his age and had joined the army.

She sat silently in his bedroom. She couldn't cry, she was too much in shock.

There was someone banging on the door. They would go away soon. Someone was coming up the stairs. Perhaps it was Joe, he'd come back, they wouldn't take him. She eagerly pulled open the bedroom door.

'Milly! What are you doing here?'

'Kate! What's the matter? Why ain't the shop open?'

Kate handed her the note. 'How did you get in?'

'The back door was on the latch.' Milly read the note. 'Oh my God! What'd he do that for?'

'He loved Ted.'

'I know that, but this is— well, a bit extreme.'

'I think he felt he had to avenge Ted's death. Look at these pictures.' Kate showed Milly the drawings.

'They're frightening.'

'We don't realise what's going on in their minds.' Kate was shaking.

'Have you got any brandy in the house?'

'Why?'

'You're in shock, you need a drink.'

'No, I don't. I must get to work.' She stood up and threw the note to the ground.

Milly picked it up and, putting it in her pocket, followed her down the stairs.

'They might send him back when they find out his age,' said Bill.

'Dunno about that,' said someone else. 'Think they'll hang on to anyone daft enough to—'

'Shut it, mate!' said Bill.

'I was only saying.'

'Well, don't bother!'

All day Kate worked as if in a dream. All evening and half the night she kept herself busy preparing pounds of potatoes and making pies. When she looked at the many bowls of white potatoes, it struck her that Seamus would say, if he was here: 'You've got enough there to feed an army.'

She began to cry. Her baby had left her. All that they had been through together, and now she was alone. All she had was her shop. She felt so lonely and afraid. What if anything happened to him? Perhaps this was her retribution. 'Please, God, send him safely back to me,' she prayed.

She was overjoyed at her first postcard from Joe. It didn't say a lot, but at least she knew he was well and thinking of her.

Every day she read the papers, wondering where he was.

In December there was a lot of fighting in Turkey and a great many casualties.

Both Milly and Kate knew, like thousands of other women, that this was going to be a miserable Christmas.

There were no paper chains hanging from the shop's ceiling this year. There was no Christmas card from Joe.

'Come on, Kate, we've got to make the best of it for young Dolly's sake,' said Charlie as they sat down to dinner.

'Yes I know.'

With so many empty chairs at the table Christmas was a very half-hearted affair and everybody would be glad when it was all over and they could get back to work.

Would 1916 bring an end to this terrible conflict? Not many had any hope of that now. Kate's thoughts went to Joe. Where was he, and how was he spending Christmas? But what worried her most of all was whether she would ever see him again.

* * *

Joe sat in his trench clutching his rifle. He was cold and hungry. The order to fix bayonets had been given. The bombardment had been going on for days and he felt his head was going to burst. They had been told they were going over the top. It was Christmas and he knew he should be at home with his mother. He had never really thought of the shop as home till now. He remembered that warm place with the smell of her wonderful pies filling the air. Those memories brought a great longing to go home.

The only smells that permeated his nostrils here were mud, cordite and death.

A shell screamed over his head and he automatically ducked. The bloke next to him groaned.

'You all right, mate?' asked Joe, straightening up. He didn't answer. Joe asked again, but again the man was silent. Joe gently pushed him and watched him slowly slip face down in the mud. With his boot Joe turned him over, and in the half-light from the guns' flashes he saw half his head had been blown away.

Joe sat and stared. He shivered, then began to cry. He was scared. He didn't want to die. He wanted to be at home. Bile rose in his throat and he was sick over his mate, but he didn't know anything about it. He had gone to join Ted, like so many of them.

What am I doing here? Ted, why did you have to die? cried Joe silently.

At the beginning of March, Ron came in with a man Kate hadn't seen before. His overalls were covered with splashes of paint and he had a cloth cap pulled down over his eyes.

'This is the bloke I was telling you about, Katie love, and he said he can do your sign next week. That all right with you?'

'Yes, that's good. What do you want?' she asked the man.

He pulled on his homemade cigarette. 'Me money up front. Bin let down before.'

'Our Katie won't let you down. I can promise you that.'

'It'll have to be on Sunday. I work all week.'

'That's all right with me.'

'Don't let the Sally Army catch you working on Sundays,' said Ron.

'Some of us have ter work every day of the bloody week.'

Kate could see he wasn't a very happy man. 'How much?' she asked.

'A fiver.'

Kate swallowed. That seemed a lot, but she didn't argue and took the money from the box under the counter. 'I'll be out on Sunday, so will you be wanting anything?'

'Na, I'll provide everything. So, what'd you want it called?'

'Kate's Kitchen,' she said proudly.

'D'yer want a bit of fancy scroll work under the words?'

'That would be nice.'

'Right. I'll be 'ere about ten. Don't get up too early on Sundays, like to go to the pub Sat'day nights.'

'That's all right.'

On Sunday Kate could hear the man rubbing off Trent's name. She was quite excited – her name was going to be above the window and then it really would be her shop.

She gave him a mug of tea and left for Milly's.

'So, your name will be over the door?' said Charlie.

'Yes, I'm so thrilled about it. Only wish Joseph was here to see it.'

'Ain't heard any more then?' asked Charlie.

'No.'

'As I told Kate the other day,' said Milly, 'no news is good news. Right, dinner's ready.'

As far as Kate was concerned some news would have been welcome. 'I enjoy coming round here on Sundays, makes a change from eating alone all week.'

Much later, and before it got too dark, Kate hurried home. She wanted to see her name above the door. She walked up to the shop and looked up. Her face dropped. The words said 'Katie's Kitchen'.

'Oh, no!' she said out loud. 'That's not what I'm called! I'm a Kate, not a Katie. Only Ron sometimes calls me Katie. The man must have thought that was my name.' Well, she couldn't afford to have it changed so that's what it would have to be. She stood back to inspect it again. It did look rather nice though.

For days the new name was a talking point.

'I must say it does look rather grand,' said Milly as she stood back to admire it.

Some of the wags enjoyed singing, 'K-K-K-Katie, beautiful Katie . . .' But the novelty soon died down.

The letter that came at the end of April was completely out of the blue. It was Joe's handwriting and posted in England.

Kate frantically tore open the envelope and, after scanning the letter, sat and cried.

He was in hospital in Suffolk. He said he wasn't badly injured, and would be coming home shortly. He said he had so much to tell her.

'But he don't say when he'll be home then? Or how bad he's been injured?' asked Milly when Kate showed her the letter.

Kate shook her head. In many ways, she felt guilty that her son had been spared.

'And he don't say how long he's been there. I wonder what's wrong with him?'

'I wish I could go and see him.'

'He ain't given you his address. And what if he's on his way home? You might miss him.'

'You are right, but it's this waiting.'

'At least he's coming back,' said Milly sadly.

* * *

A week later Kate's prayers were answered when, just as she was closing, Joe walked into the shop. They both stopped and stared. For a few moments she stood looking at this young man whose army uniform hung on his lean frame. His face was pale and gaunt. He had lost his little-boy looks. In just these few months he had grown taller and older. There was even stubble on his chin.

She rushed to him and threw her arms round his neck. He flinched and she quickly stepped back.

'I like the name.' He nodded at the shop door and moved towards her.

'Sit down. Are you all right? Where were you injured?' She noticed he had a slight limp.

'I'm fine. Got a bit of shrapnel, that's all.'

'Shrapnel!' she cried out. 'Where?'

'In me leg, but it ain't that bad.' He began to cough.

'Joseph, that cough! Tell me, how bad are you?'

'Don't worry about that, that's left over from the pleurisy. But the leg – well, I was just bloody unlucky that's all. Only been out there a few days – we were in Turkey, and I got this, in me leg.' He fished in his trouser pocket and held out a small piece of metal.

Kate took it and turned it over. 'Where did it finish up?'

'Here.' He touched his thigh.

Kate quickly took a breath.

'It's all right.'

Kate didn't know whether or not to believe him. But she didn't care, she had her son back. 'So how long have you been in England?'

'Came back almost three months ago.'

'What? And you didn't bother to let me know!'

'Well, I know how you fuss so I thought I'd wait till I was on the mend.'

She turned away from him. 'All this worry I've had and you've been safe all the time. How could you?'

'I'm sorry, Ma. But I thought it was best this way. I didn't want you rushing all over the place. Besides, we never knew when we were going to be shifted.' He touched her hand. 'I could murder a cuppa. Been travelling nearly all day.'

'Let's go in the back room.' Kate couldn't resist giving him another cuddle when he stood up. Tears filled her eyes. 'I'm so lucky to get you back.'

'I've got a lot to tell you, and I've got to get some of the things I saw over there down on paper. Done some in hospital, but only outlines.'

'Those drawings you did before you went away were pretty horrific.'

'That's nothing to what I've seen.'

It was wrong that a young lad had been exposed to so much. 'Are you still in the army?' She held her breath waiting for an answer.

'No. They found out I was underage and now I've been injured I don't think I'll have to go back even when I'm old enough. Seems soldiers can't run fast with a gammy leg.' He sat at the table.

Kate let out a huge sigh. 'Thank God.'

'You'll never guess, but while I was in hospital I was with a lot of blokes from Australia.'

Kate almost dropped the cup she was holding. She sat down. 'The Australians are fighting?'

'There was a lot of 'em in the Dardanelles. Got quite friendly with one bloke, Pete. He lived near Darwin. Didn't you live there?'

She nodded. Fear gripped her again. Could her other son have been in this terrible conflict?

'I told him that. He couldn't believe you came back to England on your own. Reckons you must be quite a girl.'

She smiled half-heartedly, and put a mug of tea in front of her son.

'He's got my address and he reckons he's gonner look up your name when he gets back. It would be a right turnup for the books if he found out about my dad and Robert.'

Kate felt the blood draining from her face. She turned away from Joe and held on to the table. She felt her head swimming. She had so much to take in. First Joe was home and now she could one day have news of Robert, but did she want to know about her husband?

'This tastes good. Those Aussies all seem to be tall and good-looking. Must be all that fresh air. It sounds a great place to live. Would you like to go back there?'

Kate's heart froze. Surely he wasn't still thinking of going there? He hadn't said anything about that for years. 'It's got too many flies for me, and I couldn't stand the journey. Would you like something to eat?'

'I'm starving. The hospital food wasn't that good. The nurses were still going on about the Germans killing that nurse.'

'Edith Cavell.'

'That's right. Sad that.'

There was something different about him. He spoke with knowledge. He wasn't a young boy any more, he was a man.

'Milly and Charlie are going to be pleased to see you.'

'How they taking Ted's—'

'Pretty bad. Milly wants a memorial of some kind. Something to remind her.'

'Does she need something like that?'

'I think she's worried Olive's baby might not remember him and this way she'll have something to tell her children.'

Joe sat and played with the spoon in the sugar bowl. 'I'm gonner write about what I saw. I'm going to send my pictures to the papers. I'm going to make people see what I saw. Ma, it was awful!' Suddenly he began to cry.

Kate held him close. In so many ways he was now a man, but to her, he was still her baby.

Chapter 36

Everybody was pleased to see Joe back. There was laughter echoing round the shop again. Milly and Charlie were just as happy as Kate.

Kate heard Joe telling Charlie about some of the things he saw, and some nights his shouting would send her hurrying to his bedroom to comfort him.

His drawings were frightening, full of death and destruction: bodies lying in the mud; tortured faces on the dying; rats gnawing at bodies and flies buzzing all around them. There were bits of men strewn haphazardly over the pictures. Others showed men walking in lines with cloths over their eyes; they had been gassed. They were shuffling along holding the shoulder of the man in front, a pitiful sight.

Kate was deeply moved and upset at what she was seeing. It was beyond belief that men did this to their fellow men. And although he dismissed it, Kate knew Joe must have been near to the gas because of his cough.

One night Kate ran into his bedroom; he was shouting and flailing his arms about. 'You're not going to get me!'

'Joseph! Joseph.' Kate gently shook him. 'It's all right. You're home.'

He opened his eyes. He was bathed in sweat. He held her close for a while, burying his head in her shoulder. She could feel his tears through her nightgown.

'Let me get a cloth.' She gently eased him away and mopped his brow. She wanted to cry out. This was her son. She wanted to hold him and comfort him for ever. But he was a man now, and he had seen things that would have made older and stronger men crumple.

'Sorry about that,' he said, lying back exhausted.

'There's no need to be. Do you want to talk about it?'

He nodded and sat up. 'I don't think the smell of the dead will ever leave me.'

'Give it time.'

'You'd be talking to the bloke next to you only to find he was dead.'

Kate shuddered. Would he ever forget this?

She told Milly about his nightmares.

'It must be awful for these young lads. I wonder how my Ted went. Let's hope it was quick.'

Kate felt almost guilty at having Joe back and decided not to tell Milly too much after that. She had never shown her the pictures he'd drawn since coming home.

After a month, much to Kate's relief, the nightmares were getting less and Joe decided to go back to work. Mr Lacy was very pleased to see him. He had also started to send his pictures to the newspapers, but they were returned with letters saying they weren't what the public should see.

'One day they will get published, you wait and see,' said Kate, but deep down she had her doubts. People didn't want to see such carnage as it could be one of their own lying there.

August came round, and the war had been raging for two years. Two years since Seamus and Grace had left. Kate was still a little upset that they hadn't bothered to write to her. Ted had gone. Joe had been in the army and was considered a war veteran at the tender age of seventeen. Kate couldn't believe so much had happened in such a short time. She was intrigued as she picked up the letter addressed to Joe, with an Australian stamp, off the doormat.

'Who's it from?' she eagerly asked when he opened it.

'It's from Pete, Pete Higgs, the bloke I met in hospital,' he said excitedly. 'I told you about him, remember? Well, he's back home now. Fancy him bothering to write!' Joe read on. 'Guess what, Ma?' His voice was high with excitement. 'You are never going to believe this! His father said there was a man called Carter in the local government a while back – held quite a high office by all accounts. Pete says he's going to try and find out a bit more for me. That's great news! Wouldn't it be great if it was my father . . . ? Ma, you all right?'

'Yes.'

'And what about my big brother? I'd really like to know all about him. I wonder if he's been fighting in the war? You never know, I might even have been in the same trench as—' He stopped and folded the letter. 'Do we really want to know?'

'It would be nice to discover if Robert's married. I could even be a grandmother,' she said light-heartedly.

Joe laughed, which made him cough. 'You'd like that. Granny Carter sounds good.'

'It would be nice to hear from him.' But she wasn't so sure about her husband. Would he let Robert write to Joe? 'He was twenty-four last birthday,' she said reflectively.

'You still think about him?'

'Sometimes.' What if Joe wanted to go out there to find him? That night Joe wrote to Pete. Kate was worried. He appeared to be very eager to keep in touch.

It was later that month that Kate received a letter from Grace. In it was a photograph of Grace, Kurt and Seamus. Grace was holding a baby.

To Kate

Sorry I aint wrote before but we was travelling about a bit.

Anyway me and Kurt got married and weve got Kate. Hope you like the picture. Shes really lovely. We called her after you as you're such a nice lady and I would never have met Kurt if I hadn't been working for you. Seamus is well and loves it over here, so does Kurt. They both send there love. We are all very happy here and when this terrible wars over perhaps we can meet up again. Give Milly my love as well as Ted and Joe. There two lovely boys.

Lots of love, Grace xxx

Kate had trouble reading Grace's writing. She stared at the photograph. They all looked so happy.

'So she married him then?' Milly had been reading the letter Kate passed to her.

'Yes. She looks a lovely baby.'

'Wouldn't show this to them out there,' said Milly, looking at the photo when they were in the back room.

'Why not? Most of the men knew Grace.'

'Yer, but seeing her with a German ain't gonner please 'em.'

It surprised Kate that Milly said that with such hatred in her voice.

'You gonner write to her?'

'I can't. She didn't put her address on the letter.'

'That was clever. Reckon she was worried, if you ask me.'

'Worried?' repeated Kate. 'About what?'

'In case you tell the authorities.'

Kate laughed. 'Why would I do that?'

'He's a German without papers.'

'Yes, I know that.'

'Well, if you didn't, someone else might.' Milly looked angry. 'Makes me wonder if my Ted didn't know what they were up to and that's what made him go.'

'I wouldn't have thought so.' Kate knew she was telling a white lie, but did it matter now?

'D'you know, if I thought that was the reason my Ted got killed I'd go over there and throttle 'em both with me bare hands.'

Kate was taken aback at Milly's hatred, but how would she have reacted if Joe had been killed?

She looked at the letter and photograph she was still holding and smiled faintly. It was a good thing there wasn't an address. Grace was a lot wiser than everybody thought she was.

The war and carnage continued in Europe. Every day the customers commented on the news of the heavy casualties at the front. It saddened Kate to see her friends and men she knew come in haggard and angry. So many had lost sons and brothers, and every day Kate thanked God that Joe was home with her again.

Food prices were soaring and Kate was worried about putting up her prices, but she didn't have a lot of choice.

'I hope you ain't gonner water this tea down too much,' said Ron one day as he looked in the mug Kate had just given him.

'I'll just have to let it stew a bit longer like Josh used to,' she said, trying to make light of it.

'It's the pies I'm worried about,' said another punter. 'Reckon we could be eating horse meat soon.'

Kate laughed. 'You'd soon know if you were. I'm told it's very tough.'

A new threat was beginning to worry everybody. Zeppelins were seen in the skies and they were dropping bombs.

'It's bloody terrible, innocent women and children being killed,' said Charlie one Sunday when Kate and Joe went to dinner.

'They must be a wicked bunch,' said Milly.

'Good job that Kraut buggered off to Ireland,' said Charlie.

371

'Reckon he would have been hanged, drawn and quartered be now.'

Kate could understand the hatred people had for the Germans.

'What we gonner do if those Zeppelin things come over here?' asked Milly.

'Keep out of their bleeding way, that's what,' came Charlie's reply.

They laughed, but it was a nervous, worried laugh.

Months later, a letter arrived from Australia addressed to Kate. She felt her legs go weak. It wasn't Pete's handwriting. She was alone. Should she wait for Joe to come home before opening it? Had Pete found Robert? After all, Darwin wasn't that overpopulated and if her husband had been in government it would have been quite easy to trace him.

She sat looking at the unopened envelope on the counter. Was it from Robert or his father? She didn't remember what his writing was like. She was trying hard to find the courage to open it. Was she about to find the one thing she had been missing for most of her life? What if it was from her husband and it was bad news about Robert?

It was beautifully written. Her hands were trembling as she picked up the envelope and opened it.

To Mrs Carter.

I was given your address by a young man who met your son while serving in the Australian army. His name was Pete Higgs. He said the young man's name was Carter, the same as mine. Could he have been my brother? The reason I ask is because he said this young man's mother once lived in Darwin.

Many years ago my mother left Australia to return to England. I was wondering if you are the same lady, my mother, as it is such a strange coincidence. Not many ladies have left Darwin and returned to England on their own.

Kate had to stop as tears were stinging her eyes. This was from Robert, her Robert. After all these years. She held the letter to her breast for a moment or two, then wiped her eyes and continued.

I remember my mother. She was a lovely tall lady with reddy golden hair.

Kate touched her hair that was now sprinkled with grey.

I was sent away to school when I was eight and didn't see you leave, and you never wrote. I never knew I had a brother. I know my father had given you a bad time and I didn't blame you.

My father died five years ago. He had a heart attack. He never talked about you. I am married but no children yet. Amy and I work hard on our sheep farm.

Darwin has changed since you were here. If you are my mother, please write to me. There is so much we want to know about you and my brother, and, who knows, one of these days we may meet up again. I do hope this letter hasn't offended you, and though you may have a life you do not wish us to share, I would like to know.

Yours hopefully, Robert Carter

Kate stared at the paper and let the tears fall. He wanted her to write.

'Kate, you all right?' asked Milly, coming into the shop.

She quickly brushed her tears away.

'What's wrong?'

Kate handed her the letter.

'Your son?' said Milly, when she'd finished reading it.

Kate nodded.

'Well, I'm buggered! After all these years. He sounds a really nice lad and keen for you to get in touch. This is a lovely letter. You gonner write?'

'Yes. I can't wait for Joseph to come home.'

'I bet he'll be pleased! Why didn't you write to him all those years ago?'

'I did, but his father must have destroyed my letters – that's if they ever got there.'

'Well, you can tell your son all that now.'

Kate grinned. 'D'you know, I've waited seventeen years for this day? If it hadn't been for Joseph . . . ' She suddenly stopped.

'Just think,' said Milly. 'If my Ted hadn't been killed, Joe wouldn't have joined up and you would never have . . .' Milly's voice had a sob in it. She went to the far side of the shop.

She had been echoing Kate's thoughts. 'I'm so sorry,' Kate said, going over to her and putting her arm round her shoulder.

Milly sniffed and fished in her pocket for her handkerchief. 'Well, I suppose some good's come out of it.'

'Yes, but it was a heavy price to pay.'

'Honest, Kate, I'm really pleased for you. You've certainly got a lot to tell him about.'

'Yes I have.'

'You've done a lot in your life.'

Kate also knew she was very lucky. Now she had everything she could wish for. She had two sons, even if one was the other side of the world, was mistress in her own home with a very profitable business. She let her thoughts drift to Edwin, the lovely restaurant they'd had, but she didn't miss it – she had her own pie and mash shop. Rotherhithe was her home now. She thought about all those who had helped to shape her life here. She looked across at Milly. She loved her and Charlie and Dolly and Olive.

Then there was Ted. He was with Briony now. Kate held back her tears. Why did he have to die for her to find happiness?

She looked through the window at all the hustle and bustle outside. Rotherhithe was a long way from Darwin, but not even the war and the Zeppelins would make her move now.

Maggie's Market

Dee Williams

It's 1935 and Maggie Ross loves her life in Kelvin Market, where her husband Tony has a bric-a-brac stall and where she lives, with her young family, above Mr Goldman's bespoke tailors. But one fine spring day, her husband vanishes into thin air and her world collapses.

The last anyone saw of Tony is at Rotherhithe station, where Mr Goldman glimpsed him boarding a train, though Maggie can only guess at her husband's destination. And she has no way of telling what prompted him to leave so suddenly – especially when she's got a new baby on the way. What she can tell is who her real friends are as she struggles to bring up her children alone. There's outspoken, gold-hearted Winnie, whose cheerful chatter hides a sad past, and cheeky Eve, whom she's known since they were girls. And there's also Inspector Matthews, the policeman sent to investigate her husband's disappearance. A man who, to the Kelvin Market stallholders, is on the wrong side of the law, but a man to whom Maggie is increasingly drawn . . .

'A brilliant story, full of surprises' *Woman's Realm*

'A moving story, full of intrigue and suspense . . . a wam and appealing cast of characters . . . an excellent treat' *Bolton Evening News*

0 7472 5536 9

HEADLINE

When Tomorrow Dawns

Lyn Andrews

1945. The people of Liverpool, after six years of terror and grief and getting by, are making the best of the hard-won peace, none more so than the ebullient O'Sheas. They welcome widowed Mary O'Malley from Dublin, her young son Kevin, and Breda, her bold strap of a sister, with open arms and hearts.

Mary is determined to make a fresh start for her family, despite Breda, who is soon up to her old tricks. At first all goes well, and Mary begins to build up an understanding with their new neighbour Chris Kennedy – until events take a dramatic turn that puts Chris beyond her reach. Forced to leave the shelter of the O'Sheas' home, humiliated and bereft, Mary faces a future that is suddenly uncertain once more. But she knows that life has to go on . . .

'Lyn Andrews presents her readers with more than just another saga of romance and family strife. She has a realism that is almost tangible' *Liverpool Echo*

0 7472 5806 6

HEADLINE

Now you can buy any of these other bestselling books from your bookshop or *direct from the publisher*.

FREE P&P AND UK DELIVERY
(Overseas and Ireland £3.50 per book)

My Sister's Child	Lyn Andrews	£5.99
Liverpool Lies	Anne Baker	£5.99
The Whispering Years	Harry Bowling	£5.99
Ragamuffin Angel	Rita Bradshaw	£5.99
The Stationmaster's Daughter	Maggie Craig	£5.99
Our Kid	Billy Hopkins	£6.99
Dream a Little Dream	Joan Jonker	£5.99
For Love and Glory	Janet MacLeod Trotter	£5.99
In for a Penny	Lynda Page	£5.99
Goodnight Amy	Victor Pemberton	£5.99
My Dark-Eyed Girl	Wendy Robertson	£5.99
For the Love of a Soldier	June Tate	£5.99
Sorrows and Smiles	Dee Williams	£5.99

TO ORDER SIMPLY CALL THIS NUMBER

01235 400 414

e-mail <u>orders@bookpoint.co.uk</u>

availability subject to change without notice.